EXPOSURE

A Thriller

JANE HARVEY-BERRICK

HARVEY
BERRICK
PUBLISHING

CONTENTS

PROLOGUE

THE COMPUTING POWER INSIDE THE SLEEK, CONCRETE AND glass building, locally known as the Doughnut could probably send several manned space craft to Mars. Instead it watched and waited, processing billions of phone calls, mobile signals and satellite images on a daily basis.

There were literally hundreds of thousands of watchwords on the list, and hundreds of thousands of people that were watched: each word or person could trigger a green flag. Two watchwords together and you got an amber flag; three, and the red flag sent an automatic alert to a member of staff for immediate processing.

When the message came through to Agent Jeffries, she'd just cleared her desk as a preliminary to going home.

She raised her eyebrows: the watchwords – and the caller – had done more than trigger a red flag, it was as if the balloon had gone up. But Agent Jeffries couldn't quite work out why: it all seemed fairly mild, hardly red flag material. But this alert was Priority One so she had no decision to make: she knew what to do.

She pressed the buttons on her office speed dial, with a memorised number that nobody was allowed to write down.

A voice at the other end answered quickly.

"Good afternoon," she said. "This Agent Jeffries, GCHQ

1

173982. We have a red flag alert for you. The information is coming through the secure channel now."

There was a slight pause.

"Thank you, Agent Jeffries. We'll pass that along to the Chief of Staff."

The line went dead.

Agent Jeffries picked up her ready-packed bag and headed home. She didn't think about the call she'd made or the information she'd passed on. That's how it was supposed to work.

CHAPTER ONE

"SOMETIMES YOU'VE JUST GOT TO JUST BAT ONE DOWN THE line," growled Frank.

She felt like slamming the phone down which wasn't as satisfying as it sounded since she was talking on a mobile. Instead she gritted her teeth, her jaw clenched fiercely.

The silence, nevertheless, was interpreted correctly.

"Come on, Helene, you're a great reporter – I know that. We all know that."

Too right, she thought: One Pulitzer, two Orwells and counting.

But of course she didn't need to remind him. She just took it on the chin – and seethed in stony silence, her contempt palpable.

"I need something commercial from you," he said in a tone close to pleading. "Something I can sell. Can't you do a celebrity story? That's big in England, right? That's where the money is. Nobody wants to read another misery memoir, Blood Diamonds or orphans in Angola or wherever the hell you get orphans these days. You've gotta give me something juicy."

Oh, bugger that! she thought. Anyone can write that rubbish. Any blogger or twitterer or mediocre media hack can churn that out. Some jejune, joyless voyeur. That wasn't her style.

The silence lengthened. Someone had to speak and Frank had nothing left to say.

"I'll get onto it," she muttered.

She flicked the phone shut feeling like she'd just had cut-price root canal surgery by a Lithuanian blacksmith. Frank had that affect on quite a few people. It was one of the reasons he made such a good agent.

She felt exhausted by resisting the inevitable. Who wanted hard-hitting journalism these days? Who wanted honest reality not some cheap piece of manipulative TV sadism. Celebrity sells. The painful truth was her stuff didn't. Not anymore. Newspapers couldn't afford to keep real journalists. They paid writers for 800 word columns, or 1500 word opinion pieces by 'personalities'. News, real news, was wired from Reuters, one of the few agencies still making a living for journalists and the rest was culled ruthlessly from a handful of gaunt-eyed freelancers who could, would and did turn their hand to anything. Corporate brochures were a profitable sideline for many. Fleet Street had no more fat left to trim. The poor beast was emaciated.

She leaned back in her seat, willing the tension away, letting the wash of voices flow around her soothingly. The train was busy and in these days of enforced economy she'd had to travel second class.

She stared moodily at her reflection in the dirty window. Short, dark hair, thin face, large brown eyes and a permanent frown mark between her narrow eyebrows.

She closed her eyes, the face older than she wanted to see.

What next? She rubbed her aching back thoughtfully. She could compound the joy by checking her bank balance but a few hours' difference since she last looked wasn't going to add any zeros to a balance of nil. That had been the case pretty much since being a Lloyds Name had made her virtually bankrupt back in the nineties. Plus, she didn't like to dwell on failure.

She began a slow massage of her temples trying to fend off the incipient migraine. It was a pity Frank's name began with 'f'; the temptation to call him back and use a lazy, but favourite alliteration was growing. Logic and commonsense felt like threadbare friends.

There's nothing like a good wallow, she decided and so the waves of self-pity and lack of appreciation settled over her unchecked.

It was some minutes before her consciousness tuned into one voice in the crowd. Some journalistic antenna had twitched.

"Yah. The police guy said, 'You're not just SAS, are you? You're high up.' *Pause.* What? No. I didn't shoot anyone. I didn't need to. Well, all the police were standing around with their thumbs up their arses and they were scared; they didn't know what to do. The station was a real situation. *Another pause.* Yes, I was scared but I react to adrenaline, I'm not frozen by it. It's the training. Yah, so I nicked a gun and took over. I gave the gun back later when it was all calm again and you know what? They tried to say that my train ticket had gone over. I mean, I just gave them back their station and they say the ticket isn't valid! A ninety-five pound ticket. What's that about?"

She glanced over her left shoulder and casually let her eyes wander over the man sitting on the other side of the train one row behind. His voice said mid thirties but he looked younger. Tall, very tall. Lanky. Tanned wrists and face. Suit. No tie. Curly blond hair. Longish. Blue-grey eyes.

An ex-SAS officer? It seemed unlikely. Besides, when did the SAS ever advertise themselves in public? Even ex-SAS. Especially ex-SAS. The few military types she'd known would keep something like that quiet. This guy was no low profile Andy McNabb. Curiouser and curiouser.

"Yah. So what's the sit-rep with you? *Pause* Ha ha! It means 'situation report'. Sorry. Force of habit. Yah, okay. Later."

Phone call suspended, the man stood up and stretched awkwardly. His suit was unremarkable, certainly not custom made but his shoes in all probability were expensive. Highly polished. Brown.

Never wear brown in town. She was reminded of her ex-brother-in-law. He was the only person – well, the only man –

she'd ever met who still cared about being seen to wear the right clothes in the old style: tweed ties for a country weekend, plus eights on the golf course. Strictly speaking the train wasn't in town any more. Even so: brown with a grey suit? She raised her eyebrows. Maybe he just didn't want to look like a banker.

A large suitcase that she assumed was his was still in the rack above his head. So when he threaded his way up the crowded aisle she guessed he wasn't getting off immediately. And yet... he was carrying a tan briefcase. It reminded her of a type her father had carried on his daily commute. Gieves and Hawkes? This one was worn and battered. It looked cheap – a bit like the man, now she could see him close up.

She closed her eyes then opened them again, a thought occurring to her. How many men took their briefcase to have a pee? None that she could think of. None she'd ever known. What was he carrying that was so important he couldn't leave it behind for three minutes? His passport? More than one passport? His sandwiches? A gun? Or maybe he just wanted people to wonder what he carried in his case.

Once he disappeared down the carriage her attention started to wander, interest evaporating. She had more immediate, personal concerns.

But when he came back to his seat she couldn't help glancing up: years of being a professional busy-body was habit-forming. He brushed past her and caught her eye as she looked up. She looked away quickly, embarrassed.

The man's hair was damp as if he'd run wet hands through it. Okay, so maybe the train was out of paper towels.

She was amused and, she had to face it, with nothing better to do with her time, intrigued.

He folded his spidery frame back into the seat and leaned his head against the window, eyes closed. The briefcase was wedged firmly between his knees. It looked uncomfortable.

God, these seats were so badly designed. She was too short to make any real use of the headrest. Instead it forced her head forward at an awkward angle that had made her neck ache within ten minutes of sitting down. Only by wadding her coat into a makeshift cushion and pushing it into the small of her back was she able to get any rest. Thank God it wasn't high summer or the aroma of warm armpits would have made the journey more unbearable. What was the superlative? Unbearabler. Hells bells and buckets of blood as mum would have said. Her brain had fried.

"I'm a bloody awful journalist and a lousy wordsmith and I deserve to go back to being a junior on the Wilmslow Advertiser," she said, almost aloud.

If it still existed. Local papers were closing like old curtains these days.

Helene sighed and shifted wearily on her hard-packed seat. This journey never got any shorter.

She sighed again, the headache worsening with each rattle of the sleepers. Passing for 45 but on the slippery road past fifty, she was scarily close to retirement, with a dwindling pension pot, decimated by a falling pound and anxious stock market: it was terrifying. Bad luck and thirteen years of a bollocks Labour government had seen to that. Only work kept the dragons at bay. And now the work didn't want her.

The train pulled into another rural station and there was a muted shuffling as people rearranged and re-seated themselves. A mother with two attractive teenage daughters got in at the rear of the carriage. They were loud in the way of people who had been talking outside and suddenly come inside. West Country accents. Rather charmless.

But the man behind didn't think so. Or maybe now his phone conversation had finished he was looking for another audience.

"Where are you from?" he asked the mother conversationally. "You sound like you're from around here – or maybe Somerset?"

"Zommerzet!" laughed the older girl. "No, we're proper Cornish!"

"Ah," he said. "I knew there was an accent. So you're really local?"

"Yes," said the mother. "Not from here though. From near here."

Wherever 'here' was it was clearly, in her mind, inferior to where she came from. Camborne, perhaps?

"Where are you from?" said the older girl, in a mildly polite but honestly uninterested voice.

Well, at least Helene still knew the difference between 'uninterested' and 'disinterested'. The thought was reassuring.

"I've come from Nottingham," he said. "I've got a place there. Well, an apartment in London, too. But, I was born on the Equator. In Zambia."

"Cool!" said the girl, her interest piqued very slightly.

Helene wondered if the girl had ever heard of Zambia before.

"Are you down here on holiday?" said the mother who apparently didn't care for Zambia or any country beginning with the letter Z.

"Yah, sort of," he said. "Actually I'm helping out my girlfriend. Her parents have got a cottage here. Somewhere near Newquay..."

Helene strained to hear the next bit: it sounded like 'Tianamen Bay' which was unlikely but you never knew with the Cornish.

"How long are you staying?" asked the mother.

"Er... six or seven weeks. I've been ill, so I'm down here for a break. Meningitis. It's more dangerous than people know."

There was a deep silence.

"Oh, I *do* know," said the mother. "My son had it... Streptococcus, pneumococcus, everything, he..."

"Yah," said the man. "I flat-lined six times. I was here but not here, you know?"

Helene was impressed. No matter what the topic of conversation he was able to turn it around to himself... She'd known others like him – men mostly, but not exclusively – and had been bored at many a dinner party until freed from restraint by wine or a change of topic.

The man chatted amiably about his remarkable recovery until the train drew into Bodmin Parkway.

"This is my stop," he said. "It's been great to meet you... you're lovely!"

"Luvverly!" echoed the girls and giggled.

He tugged the suitcase from the overhead rack and hefted it easily. He joined the queue to exit the train and disappeared into the crowd.

Helene put on her distance glasses, hoping to see more, curious to catch a glimpse of the girlfriend he was on his way to meet. She spotted her instantly: dyed blonde hair, cherry red pea-coat. Older than she'd have guessed. From money. The woman stood out from the ranks of holidaymakers dressed in their Bank Holiday kagoules and dog-walking clothes.

Pushing her face against the glass, and shading her eyes from the sun, Helene watched them from a distance. She saw him scoop the woman into a long and passionate kiss. When the woman came up for air her face was pink with pleasure and embarrassment. Then she leaned her head against his chest coquettishly as they walked out of the station together. It was like watching a scene from a film. Pure Hollywood. The happy ending we all want. Pure schmaltz.

That was it. He was an actor starring in the film of his own life. Fascinating. An A-grade lesson in self-actualisation.

The train pulled gently out of the station and Helene lost sight of them. Pity. She'd have liked to have seen the car the woman drove. She imagined something flashy but not too expensive: a BMW Z4 perhaps.

Attention to detail had made her a good journalist. She checked her laptop had a signal and googled Zambia. She was right. It wasn't on the Equator. Not quite. Had he done a little rounding up to add to the drama, or was it a mistake? A not very clever give-away? Perhaps he had just been spicing the moment for the benefit of the teenage girls. And their mother.

Unwanted, the idea squirmed into her brain, insinuating, tantalising – reckless. It was dangerous – having nothing to lose.

She called up Frank's number before she had time to think or to talk herself out of it and listened for the single dial tone of his NY office.

"Helene?"

He sounded surprised. "Didn't think I'd hear from you so soon."

"Look, I've got something you might be interested in," she said briskly. "It's something I've been working on for a while. I wasn't going to say anything until I'd got clarification on a few points, but... in the light of our last conversation... I've been working on this article about mercenaries and the double lives they lead with their friends and families. Drama, tears, love and death, borderline psychos in the public... Unstable security for celebrities. What do you think?"

"Tell me more," he said.

She played for time.

"I can't say too much; this line isn't secure so I'll have to keep it general, you understand. There's a guy I've been talking to – ex-SAS. Into some heavy scenes in Somalia and Sierra Leone..."

"Goddam, Helene! Not blood diamonds again, I told you..."

"No, no, no! Listen Frank. This guy's into something here in Britain, too, and there's something going on with Langley. He hasn't given it all up yet. He needs... persuasion. I've got to show him he can trust me... that takes time, it takes..."

"Aw come on! He'll never go for that! You're a reporter for crissakes, remember?"

"Yes, but Frank, this guy is growing a conscience. I'm telling you, he's going to spill the beans and it's going to be big. But you've got to give me time. And I'm going to need some good will from you; you know what I'm saying?"

"Huh. How much is this 'good will' gonna cost me? You ain't given me nuthin' yet. You could be blowin' smoke out your ass for all I know."

Charming.

She lowered her voice theatrically.

"I'm talking DC, Frank. High up. I *can't* say more."

Which was true.

Frank was silent. That was unusual. He must be thinking. He was one of those men that couldn't think and do any other activity at the same time – except maybe scratch his...

"How much you want, Helene?"

"This is going to be big, Frank. I'm talking *Spycatcher* big. I'm talking... White House."

She heard him take a breath and imagined him sitting in his office – a small, hairy Jabba the Hut.

"How come you didn't mention any of this before? You'd better not be yanking my chain, cos if you are..."

"Frank! Come on! How long have you known me? I won a Pulitzer for pete's sake! Look, if you don't want it, that's fine: I'll take it to Hawkins."

"Oh don't get your panties in a bunch: you know you can't work for that jerk. Not since..."

She didn't want to be reminded.

"Yes, whatever. But I'm serious, Frank. Make the right choice and you won't regret it: this is a once in a lifetime opportunity."

"Aw shit, you're making me nervous."

That was both of them then.

"If it was anyone else but you, Helene, I'd tell them to go screw themselves."

Such a delightful chap, charm school notwithstanding.

"Okay, I'll take it to Mac," he said at last, "but you gotta give me a bit more. Who is this guy? You gotta name names."

"You think I'm going to feed you that?! What am I, some cub reporter still wet behind the ears?"

"Okay, okay. Pedal off the metal, Ms High-and-mighty. I'll talk to Mac. I'll see if I can get you five now and another five when you turn in the piece. I'll need at least twenty thousand words. And photos. Good stuff."

"Frank, please don't insult me. I want sixty up front and another forty when you get the story. Sterling. Plus I want serial rights, syndication, expenses and the usual per diem. Non-negotiable."

"Oh, come on! Nobody gets a deal like that – not even Syd Harris."

"True, but that's because he's dead. Once in a lifetime, Frankie."

"You're busting my balls, Helene!"

"Yes, well, you'll grow another pair eventually. S'long, Frank."

"Wait, wait! Look, I gotta okay it with Mac. Just gimme an hour, okay?"

"You've got 30 minutes, Frank, or I'll take it to Hawkins."

"You're a bitch, Helene."

"You can sweet talk me all you like, Frank. Thirty minutes."

She snapped the phone shut, her heart hammering a deranged Ginger Baker solo. One hundred thousand pounds plus serial and syndication. This was going to make a nice bit of padding for her frail pension pot.

Of course, she had bugger-all to go on, having just made the whole thing up.

CHAPTER TWO

THE COTTAGE WAS COOL AND SHADY, EVEN IN THE HEAT OF summer. It was really two fisherman's cottages knocked into one. The lime wash rendering was smooth on one half and attractively textured on the other where it had been combed over granite. Wisteria grew around the deep windows, unusual in this part of the world where the salt-laden south westerlys regularly decimated the softer variety of plants that occasionally recklessly mistook themselves to grow in the mild climate.

Before she had turned her key in the door, her phone beeped. A text. From Frank. Just three words: 'You got it'.

Helene stood staring at the text for a second longer than necessary then closed the phone slowly.

When she pushed open the heavy front door, divided stable-wise into two sections, a depressingly small pile of post lay on the doormat

The inevitable statements because all her utilities and credit cards were on standing order, a flyer for a new Chinese restaurant in Penzance and a handbill about an afternoon tea party at the local church hall, now long since passed. The oldest mail had been stacked neatly onto the kitchen table.

More mailers. Nothing personal. She missed letters, proper

hand written letters, full of news and the personality of the writer. Emails had obvious advantages, but still...

Helene stared around her tiredly. Familiar yet unfamiliar. It always took her a while to get used to being home again.

Home. A word that resonated with so many suppressed feelings. Home ought to be the answer to the question people of a certain age – her age – too often asked: Is this all it is?

In her teens home had been somewhere she longed to leave: the neat ex-authority terrace with the tidy garden and suffocating cul-de-sac. In her twenties it was a pit-stop of unwashed clothes and half eaten meals, dozens of messages and dates scrawled on notes and stuffed in a diary; half-remembered names sketched on paper napkins, useful contacts, full of possibility. In her thirties, home had been a smart, salary-sapping future nest, with a husband and dinner parties, long days at work, air travel, foreign hotels, smart, clever people, political discussions in a dozen accents, half a dozen languages. But somehow the nest had never been feathered and the husband had disappeared along with the detritus of a faintly happy marriage. And so, in her late forties, she had landed at last in this remote corner, a place that was not England and not quite foreign either. Her neighbours were kind: welcoming but not effusive, thoughtful but not intrusive and at last Helene felt she could breathe again. And yet when she looked in the mirror, the face looking back was barely her, barely recognisable, the beauty of youth had long since faded, the spirit squashed, the soul dented and bruised.

Helene kicked her bag into a corner, unzipped her city boots and tossed them into a basket of discarded footwear, swapping them for a pair of salt-encrusted trainers.

Stuffing her door key in her back pocket she headed back out.

The breeze was sharp and cool, whipping her hair into her eyes with sudden flurries as she left the protection of her miniature front garden. She stretched, her aching back appreciating the gesture. Then she walked briskly up the steep lane that led to the church, a slim, dark figure against the bright, summer flowers.

Many of these Cornish churches were built on rising ground, the churchyards oval, an echo of a much older, pre-Christian site of prayer. The spirit of thousands of years' worship hung blanket-like, a cocoon of peace, of sanctuary. It was soothing.

Helene followed a familiar route through the graveyard, softly crushing the long grass full of daisies, buttercups and cow parsley. The steep hedges were engulfed with a tide of sea thrift growing through the piled granite. She imagined maidens of an earlier time weaving flowers in their hair as they danced through the...

"Oh, for crissakes!"

She snapped out loud. Even her daydreams had become tired stereotypes. What the hell had happened to her? How had the glittering It-girl of Fleet Street become this burnt-out, prosaic, provincial shell? It wasn't even the usual story of booze and drugs. One of the reasons that Helene had been so successful was that she'd stayed clean, kept sharp, not been distracted by the crude rewards of eighties decadence. It was time that had caught her, that was all.

From a distance she was what you'd call 'a fine looking woman'. Certainly men and women of a similar age admired her wiry body, thick, spiky hair, carefully dyed, and casually certain wardrobe. Even younger women recognised that she still had power, and instinctively steered their men folk away from her. The men, regretfully steered, silently agreed that they'd still do her, given the chance. Which they wouldn't be given: not by Helene and not by their watchful women.

At the end of the churchyard, an unmade road fell away below her, leading down to the coast path. Instead of turning left and heading towards the inviting stretch of sandy tourist beach, she turned right and picked her way across a stony trail, heading for the tiny cove of Trenow, where she was less likely to have to speak to anyone. It was harder here to walk in London silence and keep your eyes on the path or fixed to a spot directly above someone's head. Down here people still said 'Good morning' and 'Good evening' with a smile, expecting, demanding a friendly response. It was one of the things she liked about the place, unwilling to despise it as her younger self might once have done.

She needed to think and the deep peace that the horizon gave her was renewing.

A low, smooth boulder offered her an acceptable perch. She sat carefully, hugging her knees to her thin chest, burying her face in bony kneecaps, only her eyes peering out. Thinking, thinking. Choosing. Deciding.

When she finally stood up she was cold and stiff and age had definitely caught up with her. There was just the faintest nudge of arthritic pain in her left hip.

Her stomach rumbled uncomfortably, reminding her that unless she wanted to dine on dry pasta and soy sauce, she'd better put some effort into hunter-gathering at the local supermarket.

She yomped back to the cottage and retrieved her car keys from the hook inside the larder.

The garage door was stiff but operable. It was one of the reasons that she'd bought this cottage. Careful foresight had ensured that she invested in a cottage with space to garage a car and not the one with a better view.

The car was a small but newish Renault. It started first time and Helene made a mental note to thank the loyal Mr Jenkin who mowed her minute lawn and turned over the engine once a week.

She wondered what *he* was doing now. Not Mr Jenkin but the nameless man. The train man.

She put the car into gear and reversed carefully between the granite gate posts.

A tap on the windscreen made her jump.

"You're back then?"

The white haired woman smiled and waved a dog lead at her. The dog on the other end looked deeply unimpressed at being yanked by the throat.

Helene wound down the window.

"Hello, Mrs Jenkin. How nice to see you."

"And you, dear. Staying long, are you?"

"I really couldn't say."

"Oh, I don't know! Always coming and going – you career girls! You don't want to leave it too late, you know."

Helene smiled thinly. She was quite aware of the 'it' the older woman was referring to and she was of an age when being called a 'girl', even by an octogenarian was an irritant.

"Do thank your husband for me, Mrs Jenkin. He's been most attentive to my poor, neglected garden – and to my car."

"Oh, I wouldn't let him hear you say your garden is neglected, dear," said Mrs Jenkin. "He fair dotes on those roses of yours – to the detriment of our own, I might add. Bless him."

Helene wondered if Mr Jenkin felt blessed. It seemed unlikely.

"Well, do thank him for me. You're both so kind, looking after the place while I'm away. I'm so lucky to have such good neighbours."

It was said with such an air of sweetness and sincerity that Helene almost believed herself.

Mrs Jenkin smiled again, the very picture of a lovely old biddy, instead of the steely old battleaxe she really was.

Despite herself Helene rather admired her. Nothing got past Mrs J.

Helene threaded the car through the tangle of narrow lanes and enjoyed the sensation of being behind the wheel of a car and the illusion it gave of being in control of one's destiny.

Out on the main road she accelerated briskly and the little car seemed keen to shake some village dust from its tyres.

The supermarket car park was depressingly full. Helene had forgotten that it was changeover day and that tens of thousands of visitors were, like her, stocking up for their self-catering apartments.

The deli had been picked clean and the fruit and vegetable selection was similarly barren. Helene chose the best from the runt of the litter left-overs. Milk, butter and cheese were thankfully in plentiful supply. It wouldn't do her bone density any harm to up the calcium intake.

At the check-out she spied a rack of OS maps and helped herself to a selection of 1:25,000 Explorer maps from Lands End to Padstow.

"Planning on doing some walking, are you?" said the cashier.

"Mmm," said Helene, "possibly."

"Got a dog, have you?"

"No, no dog."

"By yourself, are you?"

"Apparently," said Helene, ending the conversation.

Back home she stowed the shopping briskly and spread out the map that covered the Newquay area.

Was there any cove, bay or village that sounded like 'Tianamen'?

After searching for some time she came across the name Trevarrian. It was a small bay located midway between Watergate and Mawgan Porth. And it had a pub. A good place to start. Keen-eyed locals, chatty staff, used to tourists: perfect.

She squinted at the map. Damn. There was also Tregurrian, just a mile up the coastal path. She imagined a centuries old antipathy between two feuding hamlets that would be utterly incomprehensible to any 21st century visitors.

Half-heartedly she prepared some food. Some people loved to cook but she had always found cooking for one to be a disturbing and ultimately pointless task. She couldn't imagine how people found pleasure in exploring recipes, hunting down rare and peculiar ingredients, then spending hours cutting, chopping, mincing, filleting, or macerating raw ingredients until they resembled soup. Rebelliously, she layered a piece of salmon steak in rock salt and shoved it unceremoniously under the grill until.

There had still been some Cornish earlies in the supermarket and these she boiled, smothering them with butter, black pepper and more salt. Half a dozen broccoli florets were her sole concession to healthy eating.

After she had washed up, leaving the dishes draining, she wandered around the cottage, reacquainting herself with its nooks and crannies. She stroked the lovely cedar dining table that had been a wedding present from her parents and had survived one divorce and several moves. A studded sea chest on the bedroom landing was a memento of a long forgotten ancestor. It added a jauntily battered air to the otherwise modern fittings. And it seemed appropriate in a cottage where the rhythm of waves rolling onto the beach carried up the lane.

Her bed was luxurious, dominating the room and slightly at odds with smallness of the deep-set windows. It was the largest bed she had been able to get into the cottage. It had caused the delivery men some furious head scratching and a few tense moments until someone suggested they hoist it up through the coffin hatch: an opening at the top of the cottage that Mr Jenkin had told her about. It was where, in a previous century, they removed a body when the occupant died, instead of trying to carry it down the narrow stairs... abracadaver... or, more likely, dropping it down the stairs. She wasn't sure if she believed him, but the Cornish were an oxymoron of practicality and romanticism. On the other hand, the church was just up the road, so it really was a case of hatch, match and dispatch – with equal rapidity.

She'd left the bed made up. It bothered her to leave it uncovered; it had seemed too naked as well as sterile and unwelcoming. A made up bed promised occupation or at least regular visits: a statement of unwarranted intent. But now the sheets had the slight mustiness of disuse. She tore them off, feeling satisfaction in replacing them with fresh linen from her seaman's chest. The small room was soon suffused with the smell of lavender from the sea chest, a pomander having been an amusingly anachronistic but useful gift from her aunt.

As she wafted the duvet over the bed the house breathed softly, settling around her like snow. She longed to fall into the bed and cocoon herself forever, listening to the wind in the eaves and the seagulls' cry echoing down the chimney stack. They could find her shrivelled body and, leaving her wrapped in her duvet, post her out through the coffin hole.

Instead she continued to prowl around the cottage, taking stock of her possessions until the midsummer sky had turned a purple-blue and stars began to appear in the east.

It was confounding how one never really got used to living alone, she mused. The cottage rested easily on its aged beams and granite walls. Although she had never shared this place, this sanctuary, with anyone, she still found herself straining for the sound of footsteps, of occupation, or life. Maybe she should get a cat. In a few years she could be the mad old biddy with a cottage that smelt of cat wee and used teabags. Yes, it would be good to come home to a living creature, to have that small, furry body winding itself around her ankles in greeting. Of course it would have to be a latchkey cat.

She padded barefoot through the galley kitchen, wrapped in an oversized Arran sweater, hugging a mug of hot chocolate. The door was bolted, the downstairs windows closed. She didn't bother to pull the curtains, not in high summer. It was far more pleasant to come down in the morning to find the curtains open and light streaming in.

Tired at last, she climbed the stairs to bed, making a nest of the duvet and a defensive wall of the pillows.

She stretched out, relaxing her body bone by bone and allowed her breathing to deepen. Breath by slow breath she drifted into sleep.

The ringing phone was sudden and demanding.

Swearing, her eyes already used to the dark, Helene flung herself upright and reached for her phone. But it wasn't her mobile that awoken her, it was the landline. Furious but alarmed at the same time, she rushed headlong downstairs and tackled the phone like a full-back.

"Yes? Who's this?"

A man's voice spoke.

"Hi. Could I speak to Claude, please?"

"What? No. There's no Claude here."

"Are you sure?"

"Yes! I'm quite sure? Who is this?"

"Sorry to bother you. I must have misdialled."

The man rang off.

Helene was left with the dial tone buzzing in her ear.

She replaced the receiver thoughtfully. That voice had sounded very familiar. But how could it be?

She shook her head. Her frazzled brain was playing tricks on her. It couldn't possibly be...

She went back to bed, her body tingling and her mind alert and restless. She forced herself to lie in bed, her eyes staring drily at the ceiling until dawn filtered through the curtains. Then, beaten, she slept.

CHAPTER THREE

WHEN HER MOBILE CHIRRUPED GENTLY AT 7.30AM, THE short sleep had been enough to leave her feeling tolerably refreshed. Years of training, she reasoned. Or possibly just years of years.

Having no cat to let out, she poured some muesli and dried fruit into a bowl. But before she could soak the mixture in milk she changed her mind, put the unappealing rabbit food back in the cardboard packet and rebelliously grilled some streaky bacon.

When the meat was comfortably wedged between two pieces of toast and drenched with ketchup, Helene dragged one of her precious dining room chairs outside and enjoyed the warmth of the morning sun that streamed into her tiny courtyard garden. The scent of dog roses, so carefully tended by Mr Jenkin, began to have a somnolent effect.

She tried to imagine what it would be like to do this every day. What would it be like to feel the infinite peace that the cottage brought to her? Why had she spent so many years running away from it, chasing the next big story, driven, ambitious? What was so appealing about a life lived on aeroplanes and in second-rate hotels, when she could have this? She sensed that that the cottage could give her contentment without obligation, pleasure without complacency.

Her phone trilled softly: You have messages.

It was from Frank: "Contract on your email. Sign by return. Exclusive, Mac's orders. F."

Her shoulders hunched irritably.

Ok, so one last blast. Better make it a good one.

She dressed carefully: good jeans, walking shoes (not boots), checked-shirt over a white Tee, day pack with raincoat, water, and Chanel sunglasses. In an overnight bag, she put spare clothes, a dress with heels and her phone charger. Be prepared.

The Explorer map, still spread over the dining table, was last.

Almost last.

She was just about to leave the cottage when she remembered the contract. She hesitated for a second, hand hovering over the door latch. Then she went back inside, fired up the computer, grateful her village had at last been blessed with broadband, and printed out the contract. She signed it, stuffed it in an envelope and took it with her. There was no pointing hunting for stamps: the maid hadn't been around lately.

Although it was still early, the dog walkers and old folks were already up and about. Probably church-goers, too. Helene was glad she'd got away early: the locals were so used to her cottage being unused that they felt no compunction in parking across her drive, blocking her in. Then with smiles and apologies they'd release her after the service, on the rare occasions their paths crossed.

She left the small, dusty village with mixed feelings. Nevertheless, it was pleasant driving along the main road and letting the little car rattle up the dual carriageway: she was in no particular hurry. The pub she was heading for wouldn't open much before 11.30am and she had only a small amount of walking to do beforehand. She decided to check out Tregurrian first then freewheel into the slightly less small hamlet of Trevarrian.

It was a warm day but with a cooling breeziness typical of coastal areas – and one of the things that she cherished after too many searing summers reporting on desert despots, living with salt tablets and sunstroke.

After an hour's driving, she stopped the car at the top of a dirt track, and parked on a dry, yellowing verge. She climbed out of the car and simply stood. The view was breathtaking. She gazed at the horizon, half hypnotised, soaking it up, drinking it in thirstily. Why would anyone want to live anywhere else? The pale, sandy beach wrapped around an arc of velvety blue granite cliffs, punctuating and enclosing the scene.

Locking her car, she walked loosely down the hill, swinging her arms, towards the uneven collection of buildings. There were a few pretty cottages, some 60s developments and a tidy caravan park, already lively with children playing and families packing for a day at the beach below. There didn't appear to be any smart holiday homes; nothing that she imagined the man would be staying in with his expensive girlfriend. She knew it was dangerous to make assumptions but it was all she had to go on. That and instinct born of years of listening to her gut.

There was no footpath to Trevarrian which confirmed her prejudice of there being no love lost between the two hamlets. Instead she walked along the coast side road, standing with her back pressed to the granite hedges to let the occasional car pass. The small fields were turning golden with wheat, promising an early harvest, and the air was soft. She felt a sense of well-being that was at odds with her current assignment – if it could be called that. She felt an uneasy, remembering the contract stuffed into her day pack.

Trevarrian was larger and clearly more successful than its near neighbour. As well as the usual mix of cottages and newer houses, it boasted a corner shop, rather extravagantly entitled a 'country larder', as well as the pub and yet another caravan park. There were also some promising-looking, larger cottages. There was bound to be someone in this village who worked as a cleaner. They always knew everything about the places that they cleaned. One displayed one's peccadilloes to the cleaner at one's peril.

It didn't take long to stroll around the village but all the same Helene was glad to find that the pub was open for business. Instead of taking a table outside, jaunty with a sun umbrella advertising Pimms, she headed into the dimly lit nether regions. Although she would have preferred an outside table for herself, the people who could tell her what she needed to know would be inside.

Hunched over the bar was the usual selection of regulars: old men and unemployed builders sipping their stout or Betty Stoggs, a local brew that smelt of hay and summer fruit, with just a hint of treacle... or so the advertisements declared.

She smiled politely, waiting to be noticed. No point coming over like an impatient, time-is-money DFL (down from London) tourist today.

The barmaid was efficient, pouring her a frothy shandy and explaining the specials on the lunch menu: risotto for the vegetarians, sausage and mash with onion gravy for the more discerning.

She could see the men were taken aback and slightly alarmed when she leaned against the bar, apparently disposed to chat.

The boldest of them turned his back pointedly but Helene was able to muster more than sufficient charm to have him reluctantly turn back towards her and even to chuckle throatily at some of her gentle jokes about in-comers, in which she included herself.

"I suppose you must get a lot of tourists here," she said, finally herding the conversation in a more fruitful direction. "Or maybe it's mostly second-home owners around here?"

The oldest man screwed up his face and grunted. Helene suspected he had been going to spit but then restrained himself in view of the company he was currently keeping.

"Argh. Useless lot," he said. "Taking homes from locals, houses empty three-quarters of the year. It's no good for anyone. It's killing the place. But they don't think of that. Them bankers' bonuses are a scandal."

There was a lot of head-nodding at this.

"What do you call a hundred bankers chained to the bottom of the sea?" said the ginger one, pausing for an attempt at comic timing. "A good start!"

Helene laughed appreciatively.

"It's such a shame," she said, drawing the conversation back towards a useful line of enquiry. "I'd love to live somewhere like this... if I could afford to. I've always wanted to live in a small village and become part of the community. I think that's so important, don't you, to take part and do something?"

Yes, yes. They all nodded in agreement although Helene suspected the three of them had done nothing more useful for the local community than keep the pub in business since the no-smoking ban had come in. Which was heroic of them, really. Times were tough for beaten up pubs with dated decor, although she had to admit the shandy was better than she'd expected. At least, the lemonade wasn't flat, and the wine menu looked promising. Perhaps that was the presence of the caravan park. Perhaps not.

"Do you have many second homes here?"

"Argh. More than our fair share and that's the truth."

"Are they all new people? I remember meeting someone once who told me that they'd been going to the same cottage for thirty years. I always thought that sounded so lovely."

"Don't really know any of 'em," said the older man.

The others shook their heads.

Helene was disappointed and sipped her shandy wondering how to frame her next question.

"Except for the Colonel, o' course," said the third one dreamily.

The others nodded.

"The Colonel?" said Helene, in an encouraging tone.

"Yas, his family 'as been coming y'ere since I was a lad," said the older man, whom Helene judged to be about 70, although you couldn't always tell with these seadog types.

"Does he still come?" said Helene.

"Naw. Dead these ten years. The wife comes now and again. She's alright, Mrs Colonel. Never speaks down to us.

Not like her daughter. Flighty piece. Time she got married. She pretends she's still 30 but I've known her since she was a *chile vean* an' I'm telling you there's no change from 40 there."

The men smirked and Helene smiled politely, not allowing the irritation to show.

"So she owns the cottage now, does she?" she said, still conversationally.

"Argh. With that brother of hers. He's not so bad, tho' we don't be seeing him that often. Not like missy. Her and her fancy man. Now *there*'s a story."

"Oh?"

"Yas. Summat funny about that fella."

"Oo's that then, Alf?"

"You know," said the older man, "that long drink o' water what she's been mucking about with. You must 'a seen him: talks a lot 'bout hisself. Been in y'ere a couple o' times. Was in last night coming the big I Am."

Helene was pretty sure she'd hit the jackpot and discovered what she wanted to know. Even better, the barmaid had timed it perfectly and arrived with her sausage and mash so Helene was obliged to leave her new friends and take a table in the corner.

The sausages were meaty, locally shot, and just seasoned enough. The mash was creamy and the gravy excellent. This place was full of surprises. Helene gave her plate the attention it deserved, keeping an ear open for anything else concerning the Colonel's daughter and her unlikely boyfriend.

She learned that their house was called 'Balaclava' and was one of the older cottages in the village. Not only that, the cleaner, someone named as 'Avril' had reported that the Colonel's daughter never rose before 11am and that a scandalously large number of champagne bottles had been seen in the recycling bin. Oh, and that missy never did any cooking but her male guest, the 'toy boy', had been seen with an apron on in the kitchen.

There was then a lengthy discussion about whether or not it was manly – or 'nancy' as the three so delicately phrased it – to cook. After some disagreement they concluded that it was alright if you were a) as rich as Gordon Ramsay, or b) nearly Cornish like Rick Stein.

"He's not a bad bloke, just a bit fond o' his own voice," said the older man in conclusion.

At least you've got something in common then, thought Helene darkly.

"Talk 'o the devil," muttered Ginger.

Helene's heart skipped a beat and she looked up as casually as possible.

It was him. There was no mistake.

The same lanky frame that she remembered from the train but today he was wearing fawn chinos with a pale blue shirt that matched his eyes. He looked like an older version of Prince William but with more hair.

"Top of the morning, Clive. Another day in paradise!"

His voice was the same light tenor.

"Argh. Mornin'."

"I've got another one for you: What's the difference between a dead cat on the motorway and a dead banker on the motorway? [*Pause*] There are skid marks around the cat!"

Helene looked at Ginger who had just enough grace to blush slightly.

The man leaned easily against the bar, adopting the air of one who belonged, a hail fellow well met.

He caught Helene's eye and smiled.

"Ah! Ladies present: we'd better keep it clean, chaps."

Then he spoke directly to Helene.

"I hope that little joke didn't offend you."

"Not at all," said Helene smiling back. "I don't have a cat."

For just a second the man was caught out but he rallied quickly and Helene recognised the spark of challenge in his eyes.

The barmaid poured him a glass of red wine and he raised his glass to her: one, nil.

Helene raised her nearly empty shandy glass in reply.

He walked boldly towards her: the challenge had been accepted.

"Ah, I see you've been enjoying the bangers and mash.

Susan really knows how to spoil us." He nodded towards the beaming barmaid. "And I see your glass is empty: may I buy you another?"

"Thank you," said Helene, "but I generally buy my own drinks until I know someone."

He bowed slightly.

"Then let this time be one of the exceptions. Another shandy?"

Helene smiled: "I'd love a mineral water. I'm driving later. Sparkling, please."

Ginger sat with his mouth hanging open: he'd obviously never seen such smooth moves from his bar seat before. Helene had to agree the man was good. She'd have to be careful.

He returned with her drink and his own large glass of Merlot, then sat down, assuming his purchase of her drink had also purchased her company for the time it would take her to finish the fizzy water.

A small part of Helene was tempted to use the water to cool his assumptions. Her younger self might have acted on the temptation but she had other fish to fry and more bait to lay.

"Do you live around here?"

Helene opened the bowling.

"It'll be home for a few weeks," he batted back easily. "You're visiting, I take it."

"Yes, I'm walking the coast path. It's a gorgeous part of the world."

"It's odd," he said, looking directly into her eyes, "but I have the most peculiar feeling that we've met before."

He batted straight to the boundary.

Helene felt her heart beat a little faster, but she raised an ironic eyebrow.

"No-one has ever said that to me before!"

He smiled.

"No really. But you're right: I can imagine how that sounds – I mean, you hardly know me. In fact, let me introduce myself: Charles Paget, at your service."

"Helene La Borde."

They shook hands. His grip was firm, the skin warm and dry.

"Well, Helene La Borde, have we met before?"

Helene shook her head and kept smiling even though the expression had just frozen on her face.

He kept looking at her. She kept talking.

"I suppose it's possible but I doubt it: I have a pretty good memory for faces."

He smiled back. "What a coincidence, so do I. And your face does seem familiar."

Helene began to feel uncomfortable. He was keeping her on the hook – letting her wriggle.

"Well, I spend most of my time in London..." she said hesitantly.

"Another coincidence, so do I."

He beamed at her.

Helene was annoyed that she'd let him take charge of the conversation. She tried to claw it back.

"I think one of the gentlemen at the bar said you owned a cottage in the village."

He nodded, not bothering to correct her.

"Yah, 'Balacalva'. It's up at the top of the hill."

"That's an interesting name for a house, especially down here."

"Hmm. I think it used to be called 'Waterloo' but it was changed 150 years ago. A modernising feature."

Helene acknowledged the witticism.

"Well, I'm so glad it hasn't been updated further or you could be living in a house called 'Helmand'."

He smiled enigmatically.

Helene wasn't sure if he'd understood her joke and not found it funny, or simply missed the reference. Either way she was on the back foot – again. This guy was good.

The silence held as Helene sipped her water, gazing out of the window, her colour rising slowly.

"I'm going to guess that you're a writer," he said at length, leaning back, a slight smile twisting his lips.

Helene was startled.

"What makes you say that?"

He shrugged his shoulders and stretched his arms across the back of the window seat.

"You have a way with words and you look – creative."

Helene decided to try for the boundary.

"My turn: you don't look like a banker. And you're definitely not a farmer. I'd say you were ...a soldier. No, wait, an ex-soldier. Am I right?"

He leaned forward and looked her in the eyes, speaking softly.

"And I'm going to guess you're a journalist. Am *I* right?"

She held his gaze, then nodded.

"Some say so."

He leaned back again.

"But I'm on holiday," said Helene, trying to look relaxed.

He smiled seductively.

"Me, too. Another coincidence. People will talk."

"I've noticed that. And when they do talk, what do people usually say about you?"

"Are you interviewing me, Ms La Borde? Or is this strictly off the record?"

Helene laughed lightly.

"Off the record. Like I said, I'm on holiday."

"Well, off the record then, I'd say it depends on who you ask."

He paused. "What would *you* say about me?"

"Me? I've only just met you."

"Sure, but using those journalistic instincts of yours... what would you say?"

Helene crossed her arms and tilted her head to one side.

"I'd say you can be very charming – when you want to be."

He raised his glass to her.

The match was interrupted abruptly.

"Charles? Charles! I thought you were getting a bottle of wine. You didn't say you were having a drink here. I've been waiting! Who's this?"

"Suse, darling. Meet Helene, a very charming journalist. Helene, this is Susan Hunterdown."

"How do you do?" said Helene and held out her hand.

The other woman looked her up and down coldly, sensing potential competition.

"Hi."

She ignored Helene's outstretched hand. "Charlie! I've been waiting ages!"

Helene's handshake withered. The man seemed to enjoy Susan's ill manners and Helene's annoyance.

Normally Helene didn't like to cause un-marital discord but the gremlin of mischief was whispering in her ear and she was prepared to make another exception. She withdrew her business card from a silver card case and held it out towards him between two fingers.

"I'd be very interested to hear how an ex-military man copes with civvy life. For an article I'm writing. Call me."

Susan was red with barely suppressed temper but the man took the card smoothly and placed it in his wallet. He was clearly enjoying the encounter between the two women.

Without rushing, he stood up and drained his glass.

"Well, delightful meeting you. Bon chance," he said.

"Ciao," said Helene.

The whole pub could hear Susan's strident complaints all the way up the lane. The men at the bar were thrilled – this was better than telly.

Helene was pleased, too: Phase One accomplished. She'd laid enough bait: she was certain he'd phone.

CHAPTER FOUR

HELENE TOOK THE LONG WAY HOME, DRIVING THROUGH delightful narrow lanes, shielded by high stone hedges. She stopped just once to buy stamps – and to post her contract.

Her hand hesitated as she held the thick envelope at the mouth of the post box. Closing her eyes and saying a brief prayer, she posted it and didn't look back.

By the time she arrived at the cottage her spine was aching again and she was feeling hot and uncomfortably moist. Finances hadn't run to aircon when she'd bought the Renault.

As she turned into the track that led to her village, she was trying to decide whether she felt hardy enough to dig out a shortie wetsuit and head for the beach, or to open a bottle of wine and sink into a hot bath. At the moment it was forty/sixty.

But as she pulled into her drive Mrs Jenkin leapt in front of her, straddled the car's bonnet and Helene had to do an emergency stop on her own gravel.

"Oh, Miss La Borde! What a to-do we've had. The police have been here. But Ron has been at the allotment and no-one was here – I mean *I* didn't have your number. Alfie's been barking and fashed hisself into a lather. Oh, it's terrible! Terrible!"

"What on earth has happened? Are you alright?"

Helene got out of the car, genuinely worried that the old woman was going to have a stroke, she was so purple in the face.

"Come and sit down. Let me get you a glass of water."

Helene went to use her key then noticed that her front door was hanging open.

"What the... What's been going on?"

"That's what I've been trying to tell you! Someone broke into the cottage while you were out. I saw these two shifty-looking characters – in suits – if you don't mind! And they did something funny with your front door and I saw it open. I think they jimmied the lock. And I knew they were up to no good because you don't have any friends. So I called the police and they asked me if you were in the house and I said 'No', I'd seen you drive away and then they didn't seem to think it was an emergency and they took so long to get here and Ron was at the allotment and Alfie was howling. So I stood outside and I shouted at them to get out! Yes, I did! And one of them looked out at me and he had this evil look on his face and I knew he was a wrong 'un. So I told him that God was watching and knew his sins and that the police were on their way and my husband would be back any moment. And I kept shouting and Alfie kept barking and then they left. They ran up the lane towards the church and by the time the police got here there was neither hide nor hair of them. So the police went away again. They gave me this piece of paper to give to you. You're to phone them when you get in. Oh, oh! What a carry on."

Helene took the piece of paper. It had a crime scene reference number on it and instruction to call the police should she found that anything was missing.

Mrs Jenkin was still a dull shade of magenta so Helene put her arm around the older woman's beefy shoulder and drew her gently into the cottage. She saw at once that the place had been subjected to a thorough search: drawers had been emptied out and every book had been torn from the shelves, shaken and dropped. Mrs Jenkin collapsed onto a kitchen chair that groaned ominously. Helene gave her a glass of water and looked around anxiously. When Mrs Jenkin's colour seemed more natural, Helene ran upstairs to see what damage had been done there: her sea chest was open but the bedroom was still closed. Flinging it open she saw that the room was undisturbed; it was probably only because of Mrs Jenkin's lifelong nosiness that the intruders hadn't had time to search it. Not that they would have found anything: nothing interesting had happened in the bedroom for years.

Helene felt shaky but hearing Mrs Jenkin wheezing downstairs helped to steady her. She hurried back into the kitchen.

"I think we could both do with a cup of tea, Mrs Jenkin."

"Yes, dear," said the doughty lady in an unusually quavering voice. "With four sugars, I feel that fashed!"

To her surprise and dismay Helene found that her hands were shaking as she made the tea. She reminded herself that it was just the adrenaline: her body was telling her to react to the shock, to run – the primitive fight or flight that we're all born with.

Knowing that couldn't stop her body reacting and a knock on the door made her jump, scattering sugar over the worktop.

Angry that she felt so vulnerable in her own home, Helene squared her shoulders and marched towards the door. A young PC was standing there, notebook in hand.

"I'm PC Wearne. Are you Miss La Borde?"

"Ms."

"Sorry?"

"It's Ms La Borde: M, S. Ms."

"You are Helene La Borde?"

She sighed.

"Yes. Come in."

The young officer hesitated then introduced himself as Police Constable Michael Penrose. He took off his cap and had to bow his head so he could enter without braining himself.

"La Borde? Is that a French name?"

Helene pointed him to a seat and the man sat down. "No, Breton. Tea, Officer?"

"Oh, no thanks. I've just had a... er,.. Can you tell me what time you left home this morning, Miss La Borde?"

"About 8.30am."

"It was 8.35am, Officer," said Mrs Jenkin. "I happened to notice because I was baking some shortbreads and I didn't want them to burn because they do so easily if you don't watch them and it was biscuit Sunday at church: we have coffee or tea after the service and I make the biscuits. Well, I saw Miss La Borde get her car out of the garage and I said to Ron, that's my husband, I said, 'She's off before church'. And he said, 'I expect she doesn't want to get blocked in,' and I said, 'she's early for a Sunday,' and then he said..."

The PC was nonplussed at the tsunami of words pouring from Mrs Jenkin's hard worked mouth. Helene decided to help him out.

"I left about 8.30am and, as you see, I've just got back," she said.

"And where were you today?"

"Walking the coast path," said Helene smoothly.

He nodded and wrote a few words in his notebook. "Has anything been taken?"

"I don't think so but I haven't really had a chance to look around."

"Well, let us know if you find anything. My colleague left a crime scene number with your neighbour."

He rose to go.

"Is that it?" squawked Mrs Jenkin. "Aren't you going to ask me any questions? Aren't you going to interrogate me? I saw the whole thing you know. It was 2pm this afternoon that I saw them. Strangers! I know the correct time because I was wanting to watch 'Waterloo Bridge' with Vivien Leigh and I thought I'd miss the start and I do like Robert Taylor. I happened to look out of the window and I saw them at once. I do think you ought to ask me some questions: I can describe what they looked like. One was ordinary and the other was a darkie. They were both wearing suits. Well, you don't see that much around here, not unless there's a funeral on, like we had for Bertie Shaw last week. And even then, the way some young people dress... and the white one had cold, dark eyes like a fish. It made me feel quite faint just to look at him. They jimmied the lock – I saw them do it. Opened this door in a few seconds. Chilling, it was, what with Ron up at the allotment and me here by myself."

"Who's Ron?"

"My husband, of course, I already told you. He looks after the place when Miss La Borde's away, which is most of the time..."

"So your husband has a key to Miss La Borde's house?"

"Of course he does. I... what are you suggesting, young man? My husband is as honest as the day is long. It's for a favour that he prunes her roses and makes sure her post is put on the table..."

"I'm sure PC Penrose wasn't suggesting anything untoward," said Helene, bravely cutting across the current. "Yes, Mr Jenkin has a key to my cottage and I leave a spare with my solicitor in London. And that's it. Besides, as Mrs Jenkin told you, the men, whoever they were, picked the lock. They didn't have a key."

And although she didn't want to admit it to herself, the intruders must have had a considerable level of expertise to have opened the door so quickly. Besides, workaday burglars didn't usually wear dark suits. So who were they – and what did they want?

Her thoughts were interrupted by a pounding at the door. An out of breath Mr Jenkin was standing, trembling in her doorway.

"Are you alright, Miss La Borde?" he stuttered. "I just heard about this awful business from Brenda."

"She's fine," yelped Mrs Jenkin from the kitchen table. "I was the one that saw it all and this police officer is accusing us of aiding and abetting the criminals!"

Mr Jenkin looked from one to the other in utter confusion. The young PC was bleating denials and Mrs Jenkin was building up a head of steam. Helene felt like laughing but instead half collapsed into an armchair and let the wall of sound tumble over her, tremors running through her like short bursts of electricity.

In the end it was Mr Jenkin who took charge. He marched

the young PC all around the cottage and insisted that Helene look to see if anything had been stolen or damaged. He checked and re-checked all the window fastenings and even gave the coffin hole a good kick to make sure it was secure, and only then did he dismiss the young PC Penrose with dire warnings about dereliction of duty.

"Thank you, Mr Jenkin," said Helene weakly. "I really feel... well, just... thank you. Thank you both." And she squeezed Mrs Jenkin's hammy paw. "If it hadn't been for you – and Alfie, who knows what they... thank you."

Mrs Jenkin was nearly speechless with pleasure.

"Not at all, my dear. It would be a pity indeed if neighbours can't look out for each other. And a woman on her own is always a target. As I've said to Ron a hundred times, haven't I, Ron?"

"You were very brave," said Helene sincerely. "But please don't ever put yourself in danger again. It's just a house and you're worth a lot more than mere things."

Mrs Jenkin swelled to ever greater dimensions at the new idea she'd been brave and it was with many declarations of long-held affection ringing in Helene's ears that Mr Jenkin was finally able to manhandle his wife out of the cottage whilst she renewed offers to help tidy up; all of which Helene refused.

"They'll not risk coming back after this palaver," said Mr Jenkin over his shoulder, "but don't forget to bolt the door afore you go to bed, Miss La Borde."

Helene promised faithfully to do so and was finally left in peace.

The rush of adrenaline had passed and Helene felt weak and shaky. She was surprised to recognise that Mrs Jenkin's almost sympathetic bulk had been reassuring whilst sitting in her kitchen. Now she was alone without even a cat for company.

She finished her cold tea with an expression of distaste then began to return order to the cottage. She hesitated: PC Penrose hadn't suggested dusting for fingerprints. She had his number punched into her mobile and was about to dial when it occurred to her that the men who had so efficiently broken into her cottage would have been unlikely to make the rudimentary mistake of not wearing gloves. Still... she stared down at the phone and imagine the dirt and chaos if she insisted on a forensic team. Who knew when she'd get the cottage back?

She sighed and pushed the phone back in her pocket. Shivering slightly, she drew all her curtains, despite the fact the daylight had not yet faded. Flimsy as they were, the privacy made her feel safer.

How flimsy indeed are the things that lull us into a false sense of security.

It was then that she noticed that her computer was on. She frowned trying to remember whether or not she had turned it off before she'd left that morning. She remembered printing out the contract, but had she shut it down? Or had the intruders turned it on to gain access to her files? Either way, it would have been a matter of moments for anyone to download her entire hard-drive to a memory stick and, if you knew what you were doing, with or without a password. She tried to work out if the machine had been tampered with. It looked the same: a box with a screen, keyboard and mouse. Even if someone had tampered with it, even if they'd deleted the hard-drive, she carried a complete back up at all times.

Helene knew that there was nothing of interest in her files; most of her contacts were easily traceable: one or two wouldn't want to be found by the police but the men who'd searched her cottage definitely weren't police. So who were they?

The thought revolved in her head as a chilly feeling of dread crept over her. Then she recalled her conversation with Frank.

"Oh God!"

It was a moment of madness but she had been overheard, she was sure of it. She'd been a journalist long enough to know that any phone conversation could be listened in to at any time. Say the word 'bomb' and 'Buckingham Palace' and an automatic red flag would alert the authorities. She suspected that 'White House', 'Langley' and 'Spycatcher' would have had the same effect. Damn it, she more than suspected.

Unthinkingly, stupidly, naively, she'd got herself put on some spook watch list. And she had no idea how to get herself off it. What was she supposed to do: look up GCHQ in the Yellow Pages and phone them up to admit it was all a mistake? Yeah, that was going to work.

Her mobile chirruped softly interrupting her thoughts: 'I'll be there in 10 minutes. Pack your grab bag.'

There was no name and the caller ID was 'unidentified'.

Helene's knees gave way and she fell hard against the corner of the kitchen table, bruising her hip.

The pain helped her focus. Someone was trying to scare her – and they were doing a helluva job. It was a bizarre message, too.

As a young woman she'd reported from many war zones and for years had slept with a grab bag next to the bed. They all had. Your grab bag contained everything you needed for an emergency evacuation: passport, phone with charger, contact numbers, Swiss Army knife, dollar bills (the currency of choice in many anti-western countries), credit cards, a bottle of water and water purification tablets, torch, First Aid kit including tampons (ideal for staunching blood loss in trauma wounds), cereal bars or dried fruit, a packet of baby wipes, a pair of latex gloves and a cigarette lighter: Survival 101.

She'd also slept in her underwear and baggy shirt on a regular basis, no matter how hot and steamy the country; it would be dumb to have to evacuate in the nude and staying to get dressed could be a bad mistake: death was fatal.

Two years ago she'd added a solar-powered phone charger to her grab bag, along with a notebook laptop. But war reportage was a young person's game and she was no John Simpson either. Not anymore. The phone and laptop had never been used.

She thought the grab bag was still in the under-stairs cupboard. Hopefully without the requisite bottle of water otherwise it would be a bottle of algae by now and probably classed as a chemical weapon.

Her reverie was broken by a light tapping on the kitchen window and she realised she was still pinned painfully against the kitchen table. She struggled to her feet, confusedly wondering if it were Mr Jenkin come to check on her... except Mr Jenkin unfailingly tapped on the front door. Who tapped on a window at night? She was no Juliet so it certainly wasn't Romeo.

Her heart began beating so quickly she thought she was having a heart attack and she gasped for breath. *It's just a panic attack*, she told herself. *Take deep breaths: think calm thoughts.*

She looked around for a weapon, grabbing a heavy frying pan.

The tapping continued.

"Who is it?" she cried, half choking, half crying.

"Charlie. Turn off the lights and let me in through the window."

"What? Who?"

"Charlie! Charles Paget. Let me in, damn it! I'm a sitting duck out here."

Thinking back on it, Helene could never say for sure why she opened the kitchen window for him that evening, but she did.

Silhouetted against the light of a waxing moon, the lanky figure poured himself silently through the window, jumping from the worktop like some giant, exotic cat.

He closed the window behind him and pulled the curtains shut.

Helene's eyes were still adjusting to the dim light.

It was him. No doubt. She could smell his aftershave.

"What are you doing here?" she whispered, outraged. "How do you know where I live? This address isn't on my business card!"

He ignored her. "Did you get my message?"

"What message?"

"Have you got your grab bag?"

"Yes, but..."

"Then there's no time to waste. Let's go."

He put his hand on her arm but she twisted free, lurching backwards away from him. His touch had electrified her into action.

"No. No! You tell me what the hell is going on! I come back here to find burglars in my house and my elderly neighbour traumatised. Now you're here acting like the Milk Tray Man. I want answers."

"I can give you answers, but not here. We have to go."

"No. Tell me *now*."

"This isn't a bloody game," he said almost calmly. "Get your bag now or I can guarantee neither of us will be going anywhere for a very long time. Do you understand?"

He paused.

"I'm going right now, Helene. With or without you. Your choice."

"Wait," she said.

She fumbled in the darkness and felt her way to the under-stairs cupboard where she retrieved her old grab bag. Then she shoved in the backpack from her daytrip and stood up.

"I'm ready."

"Leave your mobile," he said, "or they'll use it to trace us."

Silently she handed him her phone.

"Leave it."

She turned it off and left it on the kitchen table.

"I must leave a note for the Jenkins or they'll worry," she said.

"Be quick. Tell them you've gone to stay with a friend."

She scrawled a note and left it in plain view.

Sound travels long distances at night, and they both heard the noise of a powerful car engine at the same time.

"Damn it! We're too late," he growled. "We're trapped: they'll see us if we leave by the front door."

"The kitchen window?" she ventured.

"Too visible."

He looked around desperately.

"The coffin hatch!" gasped Helene.

"What?"

"This way."

She ran up the stairs, her bag thumping clumsily against her leg.

She tugged at the stud plasterboard that covered the large, square hole in her bedroom wall.

"Help me!"

A shower of old paint dusted their feet and debris was strewn across the expensive carpet. Beneath the layers of age, a curious doorway was revealed.

The man forced open the unwilling door cautiously. Helene prayed its gentle squeaks wouldn't give them away.

He peered out. The coffin hatch faced out into the Jenkins' garden. Leaving this way, they would be unseen by anyone watching the front door, the courtyard garden or the kitchen wall.

The man slid his thin body through the opening and dropped gently to the ground.

"Throw me your bag," he hissed.

Helene pushed the bag out and watched as he caught it easily.

"Come on!" he whispered, trying to sound encouraging.

Good God! she thought. I'm 47 years old. That's at least twenty years too old to be jumping out of second-storey buildings.

"I'll catch you! Come on!"

His voice was tense, urgent.

Helene thought it would be a good time to start praying to St Christopher, or possibly even St Jude, the patron saint of lost causes. Instead she closed her eyes briefly, awkwardly fumbled her way through the peculiar door, then dropped to the ground like a sack. He caught her clumsily, or perhaps more truthfully, he broke her fall.

Scooping up her bag he grabbed her arm with his free hand. Then he hauled her behind him like an elderly sheep that was not willing to follow the leader.

He flung her bag over the Jenkins' chest high garden wall, then placed two large hands under the cheeks of her backside. Helene felt herself flying over the wall, her left hip complaining sharply.

He cleared the wall easily and vastly more elegantly, then dragged her after him as they headed for the church.

What are we supposed to do now? she wondered fleetingly. Seek sanctuary?

Instead they ran past the church, through the churchyard, Helene tripping over some collapsed headstones as they tore towards the coast path. Her breathing was soon thundering so loudly she was sure that anyone could easily have heard her laboured breaths from some distance and followed them. But there were no sounds of pursuit. Evidently the watchers didn't know about coffin holes. At least not the kind people had in old Cornish cottages. Thank God.

Helene could smell the iodine of salt and seaweed; she realised that they'd arrived at the lonesome Boat Cove. The tide was well out and she stumbled over the pebbles and sand as the man continued to heave her behind him. A small RIB was bobbing on the slight, summer swell.

He tossed her bag into the boat and Helene wondered if he was going to do the same with her. Instead he splashed through the water and leapt in. Helene followed with far less grace feeling the cool night water flow through her trainers, soaking her trousers up to the thigh. She flopped over the side of the dinghy like an indignant sea bass and tried to catch her breath.

He gunned the engine and they slid into Mount's Bay. From an ungainly position on her back, Helene could see the orange-yellow glow of Penzance street lights and the dramatic illumination of the Mount itself.

She had no idea where they were going and she didn't ask.

CHAPTER FIVE

Lying on her back, Helene felt every jarring jolt through her throbbing hip as the boat leapt across the water. And she felt stunned with everything that had happened – and the speed at which it had happened.

She stared glassy-eyed at his profile in the half moonlight, questions churning around in her head. Slowly her breathing returned to something like normal and she sat up, propping herself against the broad rubber side of the boat.

Instantly she felt the sting of salty spray on her skin and the wind sliced through her thin jacket. The man ignored her.

Adrenaline rush over, Helene's scattered wits began to coalesce and she started to feel annoyed again.

She waited for him to speak but his eyes were fixed ahead of him, a slight frown creasing his otherwise untroubled face.

"What did you tell Suse?" she ventured at last. "I mean Susan."

There was a brief pause before he answered, a slight smile curling the corners of his mouth. He shrugged.

"Nothing. I expect she's updating the status on her Facebook page by now."

Helene didn't know what to say. 'Sorry' seemed deeply inappropriate.

"Is Charlie Paget really your name?"

He glanced at her, eyebrows raised. "Yes. Unfortunately."

"Okay."

Helene was desperate to stop the tremor in her voice. She breathed deeply.

"Well, are you going to tell me what all this is about, Charlie Paget? You promised me answers back at the cottage."

"I told you what you needed to know to get you out of there in one piece."

Helene looked at him sceptically. She waited for further information and the silence stretched uncomfortably. She tried again.

"Are you saying those men were going to... what... question me, arrest me... 'do me in'?"

Her voice began to rise in disbelief.

He turned on her angrily.

"I've told you already, don't you listen? This isn't a bloody game. Who do you think you are messing up people's lives like this?"

She blinked in astonishment.

"*You* accuse *me* of messing up people's lives? You're the one who came to my home in the middle of the night like some cut-price James Bond. I've been thrown out of a two-storey building then tossed over a disturbing number of Cornish hedges by some... by you! And you say *I'm* messing up *your* life! I'm a middle-aged has-been reporter! Just let me off at the next harbour and we'll pretend this little fantasy of yours never happened."

He looked at her calmly.

"Are you really so monumentally stupid?" he said coolly. "Listen, Ms Journalist: when you start bandying about words like 'Langley' and 'White House' people will hear you, no matter where you are. And then you turn up in *my* girlfriend's village and start asking questions about me. You think people are so dumb that they won't put two and two together? You've put yourself in danger, you've put me in danger and you've put Susan in danger."

Helene was stung to reply.

"You left her behind fast enough: you can't be that bothered about her."

His shoulders gave an impatient twitch.

"It was safer to leave her behind because she doesn't know anything."

"Nor do I!" bellowed Helene.

He looked at her steadily.

"You've made a damn good job of making people think you do."

Helene was silenced.

She turned to stare at the silky black water passing beneath them, trying to force her numbed brain to make some sense of what was happening.

By the time he finally slowed the engine, Helene was shivering uncontrollably. She couldn't imagine ever being warm again. Her summer walking wear offered little protection against the sea at night. Her hands were numb and her face frozen: at least it was cheaper than botox. She couldn't have moved quickly if her life had depended on it.

The man seemed unaffected. He steered the RIB towards a dark opening in the cliffs. The beach shelved gently and he rode the dinghy straight up onto the sand.

He threw Helene's grab bag onto the beach and jumped out. Then he held out his left hand towards her and she took it gratefully.

They didn't speak.

He reached into his jacket and Helene took a step backwards, dropping his hand. She expected to see a gun but she was wrong. Instead a long-bladed knife glinted in the starlight. He walked towards her and Helene gasped.

He could kill her here, gut her like a fish and no-one would ever know. Months from now her bloated, sea-worn body would be discovered and they'd call it an accidental drowning.

Lurid images fled through her mind and she tried to force her body to move. She succeeded only in stumbling, catching her balance awkwardly with one hand on the wet sand. He loomed over her.

But instead of slicing her open, he plunged the knife into

the RIB. The escaping air hissed softly and ten thousand pounds worth of boat deflated like a tired party balloon.

He caught her frightened gaze.

"We won't be needing it," he said, a hint of humour softening his features.

Then he pointed at the cliff face, leering some ninety feet above them.

Helene shook her head dumbly. No way. Not even in daylight.

"It doesn't matter," he said casually. "I'll pull you up. Have you ever abseiled?"

"Once," she said, her voice hoarse with tension.

She couldn't admit that it had been in the controlled environment of an indoor climbing school, the distance similar but considerably less terrifying.

At the same time she guessed he'd summed up the terror in her eyes.

"Okay. I'll go first. I'll tie your bag to the end. When you see the line drop down, loop it around your waist and put your arms through like this."

He demonstrated briefly.

"Brace your feet against the rock as if you were abseiling. Yank three times – hard – and I'll bring you up."

He didn't wait to see if she'd understood his instructions.

Paralysed, she watched him tie the rope through the handles of her grab bag and begin to scale the cliff. He climbed effortlessly, his hands and feet finding invisible holds, muscles working easily. He was soon out of sight, merging into the rocks. All she could hear was the sudden cascade of grit as his fingers dislodged pebbles.

She felt utterly alone.

Helene's senses, frozen with cold, gradually began to unthaw and she looked around her. She knew they'd headed west because she'd seen the flare of lights from Penzance on her right. In the distance she could see a lighthouse blinking. She guessed it was the Longships Lighthouse which meant they must be near Land's End. In which case this was probably one of several smugglers' coves on this stretch of coast: easy to access from the sea, with a sandy, softly shelving beach and any number of caves in which loot could be stored. The only access from land was by rope. And now the RIB was history, her only escape was above.

At length she heard the nylon line snaking softly down the cliff and felt hugely relieved despite her fear of the climb ahead. With trembling, uncooperative fingers, she passed the knots around her waist as he'd shown her and tugged hard three times. Leaning backwards she tried to breathe deeply, quelling the terror that welled up.

She felt the rope tighten suddenly and slowly she began to rise up the cliff, her dead weight hanging in his hands. The rock was greasy with spume and moss beneath her feet and her wet trainers slipped repeatedly. A sharp piece of granite jabbed her shoulder and she grazed her hands trying to steady herself. She tasted blood as she bit the inside of her lip.

He continued to pull steadily. The rope bit through the thin cotton of her jacket, rubbing raw a patch of skin behind each arm. Soon it was agony and perspiration began to run down her face. She didn't dare take a hand off the rope again, so the sweat stung her eyes.

When she saw the lip of the cliff silhouetted against the lighter night sky, she hooked a leg up as high as she could and clawed her way onto a smooth, grassy bank. She lay gasping like a landed fish. Seconds passed before she could squeeze open an eye: he was looking down at her, smiling slightly.

Every muscle ached: her hip and back were protesting at the rough usage and Helene felt every one of her fifty-plus years – more, if the truth be told. She knew from bitter experience that she'd be stiff as a post by morning.

She didn't allow for the fact that most people, when faced with a midnight race, sea race and cliff climb, would be equally if not more fatigued. Helene had never been able to help but whip herself with a caustic sense of her own inferiority.

"Are you okay to move?"

What a stupid question. She doubted she'd ever be able to move again.

"Time to go."

He loped off with her grab bag and she had no choice but to force herself to her knees and crawl after him.

Dear God, she thought, as she clawed her way across the tussocky grass; if I ever get through this alive I shall never bitch about my Pilates class ever again.

She raised herself painfully to a standing position and stumbled clumsily, trying to avoid any rabbit holes. If she broke an ankle now he'd probably toss her back over the cliff anyway.

He stopped abruptly and she nearly walked into him.

"We're here."

She looked up, cuffing the hair from her eyes.

A small, fixed-wing aeroplane was parked on the cliff top.

"You've got to be joking."

She couldn't help speaking the words out loud. He seemed entertained, as if he'd known she'd react like this.

"Have you ever done a parachute jump?" he said calmly.

The blood drained from her face.

He smiled, his teeth very white in the moonlight.

"Hopefully you won't have to."

He didn't offer her a parachute.

The plane had four, tiny seats. He crammed her bag into the back and pointed at the front, right hand cockpit seat.

He didn't seem to have any intention of helping her in, so Helene dragged herself up and collapsed gratefully into the bucket-like seat. He pulled free the chocks and slid in next to her.

The engine started with a roar, horribly loud in the night air. He indicated that she should wear some earphones hanging behind her. She put them on, wishing irrelevantly that she could reach the baby wipes in her grab bag for hygiene's sake. She'd travelled by too many grotty airlines to want to chance an unpleasant ear infection, but this time she had no choice. They looked fairly clean in the dark.

His voice, electronically amplified, crackled in her ear.

"Buckle up."

But before she'd clipped herself in, he'd begun to taxi across the uneven grass. When he reached the end of the field, he turned the plane in a half circle and opened the throttle. Pointing towards the cliff edge, the plane began to speed up.

With mounting horror Helene realised that he was going to launch them hang-glider like from the cliff. But the field was very small and the grassy runway too short, far too short!

The plane seemed to freefall off the cliff edge and Helene's stomach was sucked upwards. A strangled squawk forced its way out of her throat as she squeezed her eyes shut. Her hands gripped her seat, waiting for a crash to splinter them onto the water.

Except it didn't.

The plane's engines struggled throatily and the man managed to pull the nose up so they appeared to skim across the surface of the water.

"You can open your eyes now." His voice sounded amused.

"You... you bastard! Why didn't you tell me you were going to do that?"

He raised an eyebrow and gave the same irritating half smile.

"Would it have made a difference?"

Yes, it bloody well would, thought Helene. I'd have climbed back down that bloody cliff and swum home.

"Where are we going?" she managed to ask in a stilted voice.

"North."

"Could you be a little more specific?"

Her sarcasm didn't seem to have any effect on him.

He hesitated briefly.

"Scotland," he finally said with some reluctance.

"Okay." She pursed her lips. "Scotland's a big place."

After an even longer pause, he relented.

"I've got a base there. I need to go somewhere I can think, somewhere we'll be safe – for a while, at least."

His lips pressed together in a thin line. He obviously wasn't prepared to give her any more detail; she had no choice but to accept it.

He reached behind and passed her an old tartan blanket.

"Try to get some sleep," he said roughly. "We'll be flying through the night."

Helene didn't think there was much chance of that but the throb of the engines was oddly soothing and with the blanket draped around her, her eyes began to close as tiredness washed over her.

She was nearly asleep when she heard his voice drifting through the headphones:

"By the way," he said. "You look pretty damn good for an almost-fifty year-old."

CHAPTER SIX

IT MUST HAVE BEEN SEVERAL HOURS AFTER DAWN WHEN Helene's battered body struggled into consciousness. She felt as if every joint had been welded together by the work experience lad. Her neck creaked ominously as she moved her head.

She opened one eye, squinting into the bright sunshine. She really hoped she hadn't dribbled.

"Good morning!"

Charlie's blue eyes, amused and unsympathetic were turned towards her.

"Are we there yet?" she croaked.

She regretted the words as soon as they tumbled from her mouth: she sounded like a petulant child.

"Just beginning to make the descent," he replied.

Helene didn't think it would be much of a descent. They were already so low they were practically mowing the grass.

"Just making sure I keep us out of radar sight," he said, answering the unspoken question.

"Oh."

He lifted the nose of the plane slightly and they rose up over a low range of hills, plunging down the other side into a wide U-shaped valley sculpted by ancient glaciers.

Helene felt as if she'd slipped out of time. It wouldn't have surprised her to see giant, Jurassic ferns, or a herd of brontosaurus drinking from the lake.

But the valley was lifeless: there wasn't a single building, stone wall or even a lost sheep: just miles of short grass, fringed by pink heather.

The lake glimmered in the morning light, a natural reservoir, banked in by a terminal moraine that also hid the valley and made it inaccessible by road. Which, she reasoned, was probably why he'd chosen it.

The plane sank lower until the wheels were skimming over the ground and they landed with a soft thump. They bumped along the rough turf and Charlie throttled back. At last the plane came to a rest and he turned off the engine.

The sudden silence was overwhelming.

Helene pulled off her headphones and drank in the deep peace. She peered out of the Perspex screen, gazing around at the scenery until her eyes came to rest on his.

"It's beautiful," she said.

"Thank you."

She felt the colour begin to rise in her cheeks again so she was grateful when he opened his door and jumped out.

Stiff-legged, Helene followed him half falling out of the plane. Even so, her body was grateful for the change of position. She stretched awkwardly, trying to ignore the myriad aches and pains.

Not bad, she told herself.

He threw her grab bag at her feet and pulled his own backpack out of the plane. Then he went to the storage panel in the side of the craft and fished out a heavy piece of camouflage netting.

Without being told, Helene helped him spread it over the fuselage and wings, so it would appear hidden should anyone be searching for them by air.

How paranoid does that sound? she wondered.

No matter how bizarre the situation might seem to her, he clearly wasn't taking any chances.

Disconsolately, she heaved up her grab bag and looked around for any sort of shelter. Charlie had headed off down the valley so Helene stumbled after him, keeping one eye of his retreating back, and one on the uneven carpet of heather beneath her feet. Just when she felt miserable enough to ask him where they were going, an old crofter's cottage separated itself from the piles of rocks that littered the valley floor. It looked derelict and any hopes she'd begun to hold of a hot shower seemed dashed. On the other hand, she'd settle for a bed of bracken and a tin of beans on a camp fire right now. The only food she'd had in the last 24 hours had been the sausage and mash at the Trevarrian pub.

My God! Was that really only 20 hours ago?

But the croft was merely the set dressing for something extraordinary.

Charlie moved a piece of old sacking in the gloom of the croft's interior, and from behind it Helene could see the soft blue light of an electronic keypad.

He tapped in some numbers and a thick steel door slid open, then he disappeared downwards as if into a well, footsteps producing a hollow ringing from the metal ladder.

She followed him, a sense of wonder overwhelming her. He flicked on a light switch and a compact, modern, well-fitted suite was revealed inside something that looked and felt like a submarine.

"Good grief! I didn't think places like this really existed. Did you build it?"

He shook his head, pleased by her reaction.

"No. It was built by some millennium end-timer; you know, one of those nuts who thought the world was going to fall apart on New Year's Eve 1999."

"How did you end up with it?"

His reply was brief.

"Luck."

She decided to stick to more neutral territory.

"What do you do for water? How do you heat it? Can you heat it?"

He smiled at her mournful expression.

"There's a ground source heat pump, plus it's pretty well insulated. And there's a grey water tank that's got a filtration system. It's got its own generator, too, so pretty much all you need to bring in here is fresh food."

Helene nodded slowly.

"What about the outside world?"

He frowned.

"I mean: how do you keep in touch with people: I didn't notice an Internet cafe around here?"

"There's a satcomms if I need it," he said evenly. "I can hook up to the internet with a laptop but it's totally secure. Anyone trying to find me would be routed through Singapore, Istanbul and a dozen other places."

"I wouldn't have thought anyone would ever even know this place existed."

He looked at her steadily. "Someone always knows."

Silence.

Helene stood awkwardly in the middle of the space, her grab bag still in her hands. Without further words, he sat down at the kitchen bar-top and for a moment rested his head on his hands. When he looked up she could see the tiredness in his eyes.

"Look," she said, suddenly feeling some small concern for him, "why don't you get some sleep? You look exhausted."

"I didn't know you cared."

"Don't flatter yourself," she said firmly. "But we need to figure out what's going on – you're no use like this. Get some sleep."

He nodded slowly.

"What are you going to do?"

"Type up my notes. I still have a story to write. At least, I think I do. Do I?"

He shrugged.

"Just make me look good."

"I'm a journalist not a novelist," she said testily.

He laughed out loud and she couldn't help smiling with him.

"You're right," he said, rubbing his eyes wearily. "I'm not going to win any verbal fencing with you right now, Ms Journalist."

"Sleep won't change that," she said, raising one eyebrow.

He smiled again, saluted smartly and headed toward a small cubbyhole that stood in for a bedroom.

"By the way..." he said turning towards her.

"I'm not tucking you in," she said quickly.

He smiled again.

"Nice idea, but I was going to say that there's some coffee in the fridge and sugar and tinned milk in the cupboard – if you want it."

She shook her head.

"I like mine black."

"What a surprise," he muttered under his breath as he closed the bedroom door.

Helene made herself some strong coffee and unearthed a couple of cereal bars that weren't too far past their sell-by date.

She surveyed the rest of the den. It was clean, almost comfortable, but above all safe. Surely it was safe?

Unable to order her thoughts, she unpacked her grab bag and dug out the unused laptop. She plugged it in, watching the screen flicker into life. Her fingers hovered over the keys for several seconds before she began to type.

Starting with a timetable of everything that had happened, she then brainstormed some possible theories as to who the men in her cottage had been: theories that became weirder and wilder as she wrote. Then she re-read them several times, deleted a few lines, before concluding with a list of questions to ask Charlie when he woke up. It helped her dazed equilibrium to find a routine she understood in this bizarre and disturbing situation.

When she was reasonably satisfied with what she'd written, she dragged out a wrinkled Tee and some clean underwear from her bag. Her jeans were covered in green moss stains but unless she was going to wear her evening dress, dirty jeans would have to do for now. Even if there had been a washing machine in the den, which there wasn't, she would have felt too vulnerable, too exposed, to sit around in her underwear. It was just too intimate.

The tiny shower cubicle was functional and very clean. She

had no idea if there was any hot water but decided a cold shower would do the job almost as well. She'd undertaken ablutions in far seamier surroundings.

But the water was deliciously hot and Helene basked in the steady, massaging, stream, luxuriating as the water poured down her face and sore, stiff back. After many minutes, she turned off the shower reluctantly and dressed slowly; she was relieved her grab bag had supplied a small pot of face cream as well. Without its daily dose of moisturiser, she rather suspected her face would succumb to gravity rather more than it already did.

She was reminded of the day when she'd bought the travel-sized moisturiser with its trumpeted anti-wrinkle properties.

"Have you used this product before?" the sales woman had asked.

"Yes," Helene had replied, rather sourly.

The memory depressed her.

She left the shower cubicle in a cloud of steam. It took her a couple of seconds to realise that Charlie was sitting at the table reading the file on her laptop. He was looking considerably more alert, a thoughtful expression on his face.

She was annoyed.

"Interesting reading?" she said waspishly.

He wasn't the least abashed at having been caught reading her files. She even suspected that it was deliberate.

"You've got some pretty far out theories," he said, looking up at her. "That doesn't mean they're wrong, of course."

"Perhaps you'll share your ideas then," she said thinly.

"Yah. It's possible."

She couldn't tell if he meant that his ideas were possible or sharing them. His cryptic replies were aggravating.

"I hope you didn't use all the hot water," he said at last.

"Probably," she said, spitefully.

He shrugged his shoulders. "I'll risk it."

His equanimity seemed designed to rub her up the wrong way, too.

He was gone for some time and Helene was so absorbed in her work and the steady stream of her thoughts, that she was barely aware of him until she felt him peering over her shoulder.

He was wearing just a towel and she could smell his warm, damp skin and the spicy scent of the same shower gel that she'd used earlier.

She shifted her chair away from him so he could read what she'd written more easily. She couldn't help noticing that his chest was taut and well muscled with a pale scar across his left shoulder. She couldn't tell if it was from injury or operation but it added rather than detracted to the overall picture.

He looked up and Helene held his gaze, forcing her thoughts in a more profitable direction.

"We need to talk, Charlie."

He smiled suddenly. Helene was forcibly reminded of the cocksure arrogance she'd witnessed on the train, so very long ago.

"Usually when women say that to me they mean, 'where is this relationship going'?"

"That's exactly what I was going to ask," replied Helene, also relaxing into a smile. "But as I'm nearly old enough to be your mother, I think it's going to be a quite different sort of conversation."

"You don't look anything like my mother," he said.

Helene turned back to her computer, irritated.

"I'll make some lunch – or possibly breakfast – while you get dressed," she muttered.

"Okay, Helene," he said easily.

She was relieved when he left the room again, a handful of clothes in his arms.

"Get a grip," she told herself severely.

She rummaged through the freezer and found a couple of microwaveable ready-meals. Suddenly she felt very hungry; cereal bars were a poor substitute for real food. Or as real as a microwave meal could be.

A set of plain, white plates were stacked neatly in another cupboard and some handsome cutlery was located in a drawer underneath the hob.

Everything in the den was carefully designed to maximise

the minute space. It reminded her of a yacht, but happily without the unpleasant rolling sensation of being below deck.

She laid the table and then decided it looked too prim. Instead, she pushed the cutlery into a pile and when the microwave pinged, gratefully heaped the steaming food onto the plates.

He reappeared fully dressed in a long-sleeved grey T-shirt and jeans.

They ate quickly and in silence, their hunger taking them by surprise. When they'd finished, he leaned back comfortably and she carried the plates to the sink, dunking them in a bowl of soapy water.

She turned round and looked at him. He stared back, gaze even, if slightly guarded.

"Cards on the table, Charlie," she said. "What's going on? Why are we here?"

He gazed at her thoughtfully, blue eyes unblinking.

"Cards on the table: I don't know."

Helene was taken aback.

"What do you mean, you don't know? You must know!"

She sounded far more shrill than she would have liked.

He shook his head.

"I've been trying to work it out, but it doesn't make much sense."

Helene refused to believe him. Because if he didn't know...

"There must be a reason why men have been to my house – twice," she stuttered. "And there must be a reason why we're here – why you came to get me."

She rubbed her temples, hoping to push some order into her thoughts. "So, let's start at the beginning."

"Shoot," he said, leaning back in the chair. "I was living pretty much trouble-free until I met you."

He looked aggravated enough to mean it. If that were true...

It was against every impulse that Helene had to speak first, to explain to him what had brought her to his door. As a journalist she was far more comfortable being the one who asked the questions: the one who was in control. But this situation was far from usual. And she did owe him an explanation.

She took a deep breath.

"You were right about me being a journalist. I used to be a pretty good one. For over 20 years I covered every major conflict from Kosovo to the First Gulf War. I've broken stories on five continents... but... I just stopped getting that buzz from it. Or rather... I was getting too much buzz from it, from the adrenaline, rushing from one conflict to another. Nothing else felt real but I'd got... I don't know, complacent, bored even and I started taking risks. They say when you stop caring, it's time to get out. So I did: I worked on the dailies for a while then went freelance: did some work in Angola and a few other places but I couldn't go on like that. It was becoming... harder. I haven't worked for a while and then..."

She paused, embarrassed by the admission she was about to make.

"And then I overheard you talking on the train. I was sitting a couple of seats in front of you when you got the Paddington service two days ago. Do you remember? You were talking on your mobile about an incident somewhere – police and guns were involved – and it gave me an idea for a story. One last story, I suppose."

She looked up, feeling like she'd been in a confessional. He was watching her closely. Then he smiled.

"I knew I recognised you when I saw you in the pub yesterday. I wasn't sure if it was coincidence or if you'd been following me. I decided to find out. But later that afternoon I spotted a couple of spooks checking out Susan's place. I knew it had to be connected to you; I just wasn't sure how."

"Why did you assume it was to do with me?"

"Because I don't believe in two coincidences in one day," he said, leaning towards her.

She automatically leaned away from him.

Fair enough: his logic was inarguable.

"And how did you find me?" she asked, frowning. "The business card I gave you only had my mobile and email on it: I'm ex-directory."

He rolled his eyes.

"That's pretty straightforward, actually. Most people are clueless about how vulnerable they are: we're watched, heard, listed, catalogued, checked on a thousand times a day."

He shrugged.

"But before I even got near you, I heard the report about your break-in on the police frequency. I knew then we didn't have much time. I was almost too late."

Helene felt a strangled scream building up in her throat at the emphasis he put on 'too late'.

"But I still don't get it: who were those people?" she managed to choke out.

He shook his head slowly.

"NSA, CIA, MI6, some other spook squad, who knows."

He locked his eyes on hers.

"Helene, I'm pretty certain they were there because of something you said: someone you spoke to. So, you tell me. What did you do?"

She swallowed.

God! she thought. I feel such a fool.

"I... I told my agent, my booking agent, that I had something big. I may have mentioned 'Langley' and... um... the White House."

She looked down, cringing away from the derision in his gaze. She knew she deserved it – and much worse.

"And... what?" he said angrily. "You were just making that up? You thought you'd lead them to me? Unbelievable."

His look was scathing.

"But you knew that already," she said shakily. "I can't begin to imagine how you knew either. Look, I don't know what came over me... I wasn't thinking clearly."

He raised his eyebrows at this. But he had another question for her.

"How much are you getting paid for this story?"

She was startled, unwilling to admit the unpleasant truth.

"Well, I don't...." she began.

"Helene," he said softly, his voice barely louder than a

whisper, "whether you meant to or not, you've sold me down the river. How much?"

"Enough to retire on," she said defiantly.

He nodded slowly. She couldn't meet his gaze.

"How are you involved?" said Helene, hopelessly trying to keep a grip. "Obviously you must be on a watch list somewhere. Are you ex-military? Ex-SAS?"

He didn't answer. She began to feel desperate.

"Charlie, I've told you everything. Clearly these people are afraid that we know something and we've just established that I know sod-all; so it must be you – something you know. The only way we're going to get out of this mess is if we're open with each other."

He stared at her.

"So how much are you being paid?"

"Oh, for goodness sake!" she snapped. "One hundred thousand pounds. Okay? Plus serial rights. Plus my per diem of £150 a day. That's it. Do you want a cut of it, is that it?"

He smiled maddeningly.

"No. I just want you to be open with me: like you said."

He was infuriating!

"Okay, so now you know."

She was embarrassed and irritated in equal amounts.

He smiled again. "Thank you, Helene."

The smile faded slowly and he shook his head wearily.

"I still can't figure out why I've been targeted and why now." He looked up, his blue eyes appealing. "I'm being honest here. I haven't worked for a couple of years either. I was pretty ragged after my last op and I needed some down time. So whatever it is, whatever's going on, it's a slow burn."

Helene tried to put all this together.

"When I made that stupid phone call," she said cautiously, "I only mentioned places in America because my agent is in New York and I thought that would be of more interest to him. So I said: DC, Langley, the White House."

She looked up. "Well, you know that bit already. Have you ever worked in any of those places? I know it's a long shot, but if you have, that could be the connection."

"Yeah," he said slowly. "I have. Just once."

"Go on," she said gently, trying to hide the sudden interest in her voice.

His gaze drifted away, remembering something in his past.

"Mostly I've worked in Africa or South America but there was one op stateside about three years ago. It was kind of a weird one, too. Top, top secret stuff."

Helene's antennae twitched.

"Weird how?"

"Well, for one thing, I was booked as a solo, which is unusual. Normally it'll be a group booking: a team I often work with, guys I know – the usual suspects, you could say." He smiled at some private joke. "But this was different: all the operatives were solo and all from different backgrounds. I think the idea was that none of us knew each other so we wouldn't be able to have too many pieces of the puzzle. All I had to do was get my bird in and out. The other two picked up the package."

"So you did what... the flying?"

He nodded. "Yep. That's my speciality, you could say."

"Hmm. I'd noticed!" said Helene shortly.

She paused. "So, what was in the package?"

He grimaced.

"Not what..."

Helene swallowed.

"The package was a person? You were involved in a kidnapping? Who was it?"

He shrugged.

"I don't know and I didn't ask. I never even saw his face. But it was a man. Oldish guy, I'd guess by the way he moved. The other three picked him up, like I said, and they'd already bagged him by the time they got him on the chopper. We finished the op and I flew him up to Nevada. We were met my some local muscle and then we went our separate ways. I never saw any of them again."

Helene processed the information.

"So the only thing we've got to go on is when and where this happened. Does that give us anything?" she said hopefully.

"Maybe," he said, wrinkling his face in concentration. "But the thing is I *did* know one of the other guys on the op: Bill Bailey. We'd met on a bi-lateral training mission some years back. Of course, we didn't let on because it was obvious that would have been a major no-no: no name, no pack-drill. But, yah, I know one of the guys."

Helene sat back.

"Good. The fact that he's a friend is a definite bonus.

Charlie shook his head impatiently.

"I didn't say he was a friend," he corrected her. "I said he was someone I'd met through training."

Helene frowned.

"Will he help us? Can you trust him?"

"No," he said shortly. "Actually, Bill's what the old man would have called a chiselling little weasel."

He examined her worried expression.

"But don't worry about it: I can handle him – if I have to."

Helene breathed out slowly. "Then that's where we start," she said. "Do you know where he is?"

"Not exactly, but I think I know how to find him."

Helene waited impatiently.

"And? Are you going to let me in on the secret?"

"Well, I might just do that, Helene," he said smugly. "But first answer me one question..."

She rolled her eyes.

"Fine. Go on."

"Did you pack a bikini in that grab bag of yours?"

CHAPTER SEVEN

THE SUN WAS HOT AND HELENE WAS GRATEFUL FOR THE protection of her sunglasses. She was still squinting in the bright light of day, having spent too many hours cooped up on a plane. Although really she had no grounds for complaint, having just travelled first class.

She caught sight of herself in the plate glass window of the arrivals lounge and had to smile. With the sleek, blonde French plait and designer leisure wear, her own mother wouldn't have recognised her. She'd travelled under the name Eliza van Cartier and somehow Charlie had arranged a fake passport, and first class ticket worth several thousand pounds.

'Miss van Cartier' had enjoyed the free champagne and smoked salmon and had slept comfortably for most of the journey from LAX, where they'd changed planes.

Charlie had travelled separately under the name Oliver Parrick, a businessman from Perth. They hadn't spoken since Heathrow the day before. It was better to minimise the number of opportunities for them being seen together, he'd said.

Helene hadn't minded that bit: it was easier for her to concentrate when his clear, blue eyes weren't boring into hers.

After two days of preparation, they'd hiked out of the valley and caught the bus to the nearest town and from there, travelled on to Glasgow. Charlie had left her to go shopping – with a fake credit card – and had also left specific instructions on what to buy: a good bag, expensive clothes and a wig that changed her appearance.

It had been more fun than she'd expected. And if it hadn't been for the squirming anxiety she felt constantly in the pit of her stomach, the whole experience would have been a gas.

Charlie hadn't said what his plans were but when they'd met up again, he was carrying the fake passports and had dyed his own hair dark brown. In fact with the charcoal grey suit he wore, she'd nearly walked past him in the street. Just something about the smile on the stranger's face had made her look twice. He was also wearing brown contact lenses.

Helene hadn't wanted to know how he'd got the fake passports, although she could have made a shrewd guess but she'd insisted on paying for her ticket – when Frank had paid her, of course. And when it was safe for her to access her bank account.

But he'd refused.

"The tickets are on me: my pleasure."

Helene was insistent.

"No, I must pay you. I mean: I want to keep a reckoning of everything so I can pay you back when I can."

She didn't want to be in his debt.

He'd smiled, rather patronisingly.

"It's not a problem, Helene, because I didn't pay for the tickets."

He'd sounded like he was explaining to a child.

"Oh. Then how?" said Helene, feeling rather dim.

He sighed theatrically.

"I hacked into the air miles accounts of a couple of people who spend way too much time travelling by plane. They won't even notice. Satisfied?"

Helene rather wished she hadn't insisted on knowing, but she couldn't stop herself from demanding the truth. It was an ingrained habit, after all.

"And the clothes? The money?" she pressed.

His lips twitched as if he were trying to suppress a smile.

"Trust me when I say you don't owe me a penny."

Helene wasn't happy but further probing had got her nowhere.

"I can't be involved in anything illegal," she had said loftily.

He'd laughed outright at this.

"Fraud isn't illegal? Obtaining money from Frank under false representations – that's not wrong? Helene, you're probably on the FBI's 'Most Wanted' list by now."

In the end she'd just had to give in, with rather poor grace.

Once in the airport arrivals lounge, Helene had slipped into the women's bathroom and changed out of the expensive clothes. She pushed them into a supermarket carrier bag and stuffed them in a bin. Pity. It was much harder to leave behind the very desirable It-bag that she'd so enjoyed carrying. Her grab bag was shabby by comparison, which was exactly the look she was now going for.

She'd arrived first class as Eliza van Cartier and now she was leaving cattle class with her new identity as April Summers, an aging hippy chick with cut off denim shorts, long, untidy hair that made her look like Goldie Hawn and tie-dyed shirt.

Nobody gave her a second glance as she lounged in the sunshine at Honolulu's international airport.

Released from the confines of the aeroplane, she enjoyed the feeling of freedom that the softly scented air and sun's warmth gave her.

Whilst she waited for Charlie she was fascinated to see the parade of humanity that passed before her: the young and hopeful, the wealthy elderly visiting from all over the world to enjoy the gentle climate, the astonishing beauty of the native Hawaiians, the corpulence of some of the older ones, and a stream of tanned young men, casual in shorts and T-shirts.

Charlie was one of them: he was now dressed as a surfer dude in baggies and flip-flops and sported a fresh buzz cut. It suited him. She was glad to see that his eyes were back to his natural blue. But she had no idea from where he'd managed to acquire the seven foot surfboard in a battered carry bag. She knew better now than to ask.

"Hi there, April," he said, casting his eyes up and down her new identity, approval in his voice.

She shifted uncomfortably.

"So where next?" she said.

He shrugged as if the answer was obvious.

"We find Bill."

"I guessed that bit," said Helene, thinly. "But where do we start? I mean, he might not even be using the same name by now."

Charlie looked unconcerned.

"Bill wasn't the sharpest pencil in the box; that's one of the reasons he was chosen for the grunt work, I think. He was always mouthing off about spending his fee on 'fast cars, fast waves and fast babes' – his words, not mine. He was a bit of a tosser," he said thoughtfully. "I got the impression he reckoned he was a Big Wave rider; it was probably just hot air. But he did talk about coming to live on the Islands when the job was over."

Helene felt depressed despite the beauty of the day. It was a needle in a haystack, but... and it was a big but... she had lasted this long as a journalist for a reason: she was good at finding people who didn't want to be found. It was just a case of asking the right people the right questions. And a question of time. She didn't know how much they had of that.

"Then I guess we should start with the mother lode: Waimea Bay," she said.

He looked at her with surprise.

"Yeah, that was my guess, too."

I wasn't born yesterday, kiddo, she smiled to herself.

The fact was that she'd spent enough time at her cottage in Cornwall to have met any number of surf dudes: men who never grew up, never shouldered any responsibility that took them away from the sea. Their lives were ruled instead by the tide times and weather charts: when a low pressure rose over the Atlantic and a powerful swell arrived on the shore, jobs, homes, girlfriends and children were left behind for the call of the waves. Many capable young men – and not so young – spent their summers in the West Country and their winters in warmer climes, chasing the waves, the restless waves.

Helene understood the impulse all too well, although it wasn't surf that called her.

She wondered what happened to them as they grew older. What was attractive about a beach bum at 20 or 30, maybe even 40, was sad at 50. What did an old surfer do – paddle away?

But even the surf rats, the grommets who'd never yet left Cornwall dreamed of the big one: Waimea Bay, pumping a winter swell of 30 plus feet. Only a few were brave enough, or foolhardy enough to surf that monster.

She knew that, unlike Britain, Hawaii had no continental shelf, which meant as the swell got near to the Islands the weight of water was rapidly forced upwards, creating a massive, hollow wave that broke onto a razor-sharp reef. If you missed your footing or get munched by the blow out, the coral was waiting to tear holes out of your frail carcass of soft skin. It was the Holy Grail of surfing.

That was in the winter. In the summer, the islands were a tourist haven for travellers from mainland States, Japan and Australia. Right now that included April Summers and her toy boy Wes Oaks.

They hopped on the dusty bus with a load of other surfers and beach Bettys to get to Oahu's surf Mecca: Waimea.

The journey took over two hours but by listening, chatting, blending in, they worked out that the all the serious surfers hung out at either Sunset and Turtle Bay or Haleiwa. From there the surf wannabes could chill out, listen to the weather reports and hang out with the old guys who'd surfed Waimea in the sixties and some who even remembered Duke Kahanamoku, although as he'd died in 1968, Helene reckoned it was a bit like saying you'd seen the Beatles playing the Cavern before they got famous.

Parts of Oahu fitted Helene's idea of a perfect Hawaiian island. Other parts were built up and touristy: tower block hotels blotting the perfect sunset. It must have been paradise once.

Surfers didn't like to think about this: they liked to think they were free spirits, bucking the trend of nine to five, but they were actually part of a huge, multinational industry powered by petro-chemicals and the worldwide thirst for oil. All those super light weight thrusters and easy-to-carry longboards: they were made from fibre glass, polyurethane and epoxy resin — by-products from the oil wells that pumped across the Middle East, 9,000 miles away. And although neoprene wetsuits weren't much used in Hawaii where the ambient water temperature was a constant 23°C, neoprene was the material that allows European and US surfers to take to the waves all winter where the water is just 7°C or 8°C. You could even buy neoprene balaclavas or helmets to help cope with ice cream headaches or ward off surfer's ear — so long as you didn't mind looking like the Gimp.

As the bus rattle down the Kamehameha Highway Helene felt a sense of well-being that was at odds with the unfeasible task that lay ahead. She couldn't help it: the warm air, the light hearted people, the beauty of the island: I'd have to be a miserable old bag not to feel its charm, she thought.

Charlie lounged at the back of the bus, the very picture of the surfer dude who had little luggage and no worries.

Even so, by the time they stepped off the bus at the small town of Haleiwa, they had a rough plan.

The driver told them that ads for spare rooms would be pasted on the central lettings board.

"Don't take a room at Madam Jo's," the driver yelled out of the window as he drove away, "not unless you want to be kept awake all night by the banging!"

Helene wondered if he meant it was near a building site: except that builders didn't work at night, not even in Hawaii. She soon learned that Madam Jo's was the local knocking shop.

"It could be a good place to gather intel," Charlie whispered in her ear. "You know, research."

She threw him a supercilious look but he just grinned at her, unabashed. He turned back to the board, still smiling, and made a show of studying it carefully.

Several of the ads were house shares which would have

given them good access to info, but not the privacy that they were going to need – especially as Helene was keen that no-one discovered she was wearing a wig. She wanted to hide the laptop, too. Although lots of younger surfers had a cheap laptop so they could Skype their parents and face-time their friends on networking sites, it didn't fit in with Helene's image – and more privacy just meant fewer questions.

Eventually, Charlie pointed out something that could be suitable: double room for rent in quiet home. $185 a week, in advance.

They got directions and found they could walk to the location. The house was in one of the quieter streets, just behind a shaper's shop, and minutes from the harbour.

The woman renting the room was an elderly Hawaiian momma, with thighs like a couple of redwood canoes and vast swathes of flesh engulfing her stern face. Helene thought she saw a likeness to the Easter Island carvings.

She looked coolly at Helene in her skimpy shorts but seemed to take to Charlie who charmed her by noticing pictures of her grandchildren on the mantelpiece.

"I have to tell you," said the woman when they'd finished talking about her youngest grandson who'd be starting a course in business studies at the University of Hawaii at Manoa in the fall, "I mind my own business..." sniffing in Helene's general direction, "but I won't tolerate drugs in my home. You want to smoke a spliff, go to the beach or to the harbour front but don't do it here."

"That's fine, ma'am," said Helene. "My drug of choice is chocolate."

The woman's face was stony.

"I don't mind what time you come in at night," the matriarch continued, "just be quiet about it."

"We'll be good, I promise," said Charlie, smiling broadly. "You'll hardly know we're here."

He handed her the week's rental in advance.

The woman patted him on the hand, told him that his mother must miss him. Then she led them upstairs with heavy, even steps.

She showed them the bathroom, opened the door of their bedroom and left them alone.

Their room was light and airy, if simply furnished. Too simply: there was just one double bed. Helene looked at Charlie in some alarm. He shrugged, smiling broadly.

"We're supposed to be a couple. It would look weird if we had separate rooms. Don't worry: I'll be on my best behaviour – Scout's Honour."

Helene felt irritated but tried very hard not to let it show too much.

"I very much doubt that you were ever a Boy Scout," she said appraisingly.

Charlie sat on the bed and leaned back on his elbows. He grinned back at her.

"You'd be surprised: there's a lot you don't know about me."

Helene had no doubt of that. She stood awkwardly before walking to the window to look out.

"Well," he said, stretching, "time to check out the waves, I think." He put on a Californian surfer voice: "Hang ten with some of the dudes."

"I'll come with you," she said.

"Don't you trust me?" he asked, pretending to look hurt.

Helene laughed.

"Not particularly, seeing as you've asked, but actually I thought I'd just chat to some of the girlies watching their boyfriends display some testosterone."

She turned her back modestly, gazing out the window, while he put on some surf shorts and a ratty old Tee. She caught herself wondering what that long, golden body would like if she turned to watch, then gave herself a severe talking to for having such improper thoughts. To say that life was complicated enough was rather an understatement. She didn't need to fuel the look she sometimes caught in his eyes.

Even so, she felt a wave of sadness surge through her; she was filled with something like regret, doubt, desire. And she knew if she let herself go, she'd be lost.

They didn't go to Waimea straightaway but hitched a ride to Jocko's in the back of a beaten up old Chevy truck. Charlie helped her climb into the back and then passed up his battered board bag.

"Why don't we go straight to Waimea?" asked Helene when he had asked for a ride to Jocko's.

He sighed, as if she was missing something obvious, but a smile tugged at the corner of his mouth.

"I know *you* think I'm almost perfect," he said, "but I'm only a reasonably competent surfer. I caught some action at Suse's," he paused and smirked, "but those were only summer waves and nothing over five foot. So I'm just being a bit cautious because the heavy swell of Pipeline or Off-the-Wall can get up to 15 feet even at this time of the year. And even though *you* think I'm indestructible, it could do some serious damage." He shrugged. "Jocko's is a slower, mellower wave: at least that's what the guys on the bus told me.

It turned out that he was both wrong and right: Jocko's could give Newquay's Fistral a run for its money any day of the week and twice on Sundays. The wave was pumping nine foot of frothing ferocity, a cross-wind making it unpredictable. Thankfully, this wave broke mostly onto sand (at least Helene couldn't see a reef): if Charlie wiped out, all he'd damage would be his pride. She hoped.

Helene watched him paddle out through the channel: the water glinting around him as he cut through the waves, the muscles in his arms and back rippling silkily under his skin like a beautiful machine.

Suddenly the swell broke unexpectedly in front of him and a tower of white foam roared forwards. Helene felt her stomach tense but he duck-dived through it expertly; in fact, with the calmness and easy grace with which he did everything.

Helene saw him bob to the surface on the far side of the wave and allowed herself to breathe again. She shaded her eyes against the sun to watch him as he continued to paddle steadily towards the line up, just behind the break.

He sat astride the board like a cavalryman about to go into battle, looking over his shoulder every now and again, waiting for a bigger swell to rise up and carry him upwards.

Slowly, a green monster began to raise its head behind the line up. It was the signal. Every surfer was suddenly alert. Charlie lay face down on his board, his back arched, and started to paddle hard, his feet raised out of the water to limit the drag.

The wave rose higher and higher, lifting him upwards. Then just as the wave threatened to break over him, he pointed the nose of the board downwards, sprang to his feet and tore across the face of the wave, the white curl chasing him like an angry sea creature.

He turned the board on its fin, carving brutally through the wave, slashing up the face and hurtling down again. He carved a couple more turns before the wave began to lose its power. Then he pointed the board up the wave for one final time before sailing over the top, catching air, then diving down the other side and disappearing out of sight.

Helene held her breath until she saw him break the water again and paddle back towards the line up to repeat the brilliant, pointless exercise.

After he'd surfed a half dozen or more waves, Helene got bored. She was tired of squinting into the sun, trying to pick him out of the small group of surfers sitting at the line up. She went to get a drink from a pretty shack further up the beach.

She loitered, sipping a freshly-squeezed pineapple juice and listening to the gossip: who was doing what to whom, where and how often; which waves were totally awesome; and where the best parties were to be found. If it weren't for the fact that she was on the hunt for information, she would have found it tiresome, trivial and depressingly immature. At their age she'd been working for a living and had already visited her first war zone and seen her first dead body. Were these kids just going to waste their entire lives? Was being a happy no-mark slacker so appealing?

When she felt her blood pressure rising uncomfortably, she sat down with her juice and let the scenery sooth her. She was surprised to be joined by several girls and wondered if it were her enigmatic charm; but it turned out it was just the best place to catch some rays and eye up the surfers at the same time.

She let the conversation drift over her as her eyes started to close. She pulled her hat over her face and felt her body relax.

Suddenly she felt drops of water on her stomach and arms. That's odd, she thought to herself, it's raining. She pulled the hat off her face and stared upwards. But the sky was perfectly clear and blue. Charlie was standing over her, letting the seawater run off his body and drip onto her.

"Eww! That's cold!" she said.

Then her eyes opened wide. One side of his face was covered in blood.

"Oh my God! What happened?" she said.

"Don't freak out," he said, smiling down at her. "I just wiped out and caught some coral. It looks worse than it is. Head wounds always do."

"Oh for goodness sake!" said Helene, gasping as her heart restarted. "Are you trying to give me a stroke! Come here – let me look."

She pulled him down beside her and inspected the wound. Up close she could see it wasn't too bad – just a small cut – but with blood mixing with seawater, it bled profusely.

"You'll live," she said at last.

"Like I said," he replied, smiling.

Helene pulled an antiseptic wipe out of her shoulder bag and carefully cleaned the wound and wiped off as much of the blood as she could. The bleeding was already stopping.

As she finished, he grabbed her hand and kissed the palm.

"Thank you," he said, looking up at her from under his eyelashes.

The look was seductive, which was really annoying.

"No seriously!" giggled one of the girls sitting nearby. "I thought you were his *mom*."

Helene scowled.

"Ignore them," muttered Charlie, pulling her to her feet. "By the way," he said smiling, "did I mention that you look gorgeous when you're angry?"

"Oh for crying out loud!" she snapped. "Grow up, will you?"

She stalked off up the beach and he watched her, a broad smile stretched across his face.

Helene had walked nearly half a mile before she felt herself calming down. She found a small coffee shop and ordered herself a double espresso. She found caffeine soothing: it didn't seem to get her wired like it did some people.

It turned out that the coffee bar was a hang out place. People came and went exchanging gossip. Helene tuned into the conversations and realised that all the kids were excited about some big party that was going to be held that night. That could be a good place to try and find out about Bill – if he was into that sort of scene. Whatever: getting to know the locals would be useful.

Helene studied the young people around her: she'd long learned how to read a crowd to work out who would be the most useful to her. As a journalist reading faces was essential: it helped you to work out which were the important questions, and which answers were only partial – or downright lies.

She honed in on a pale skinned girl who seemed younger and shyer than the rest. The girl looked as if she wanted to join in the conversation, but wasn't sure how. She was anxiously biting her lip when Helene went up to sit at the table next to her.

"Excuse me. Do you have any sugar on your table?" said Helene.

"Oh... s...sure – here," she stuttered, seemingly surprised that anyone had noticed her enough to ask a question.

"Thanks," said Helene. "I'm April."

"Oh! I'm Jenny. From Cleveland."

The girl smiled shyly.

"So, Jenny-from-Cleveland, are you here on holiday?" said Helene in a friendly manner, as she stirred a spoonful of sugar into her coffee. Having asked for sugar she could hardly not use it, even though she hated sweet drinks.

Jenny had never seen the ocean before, any ocean and was feeling rather overwhelmed by the experience.

She'd been persuaded to come out to the islands for the summer by her boyfriend, Dylan. The plan was to get a job bussing tables and enjoy the laidback lifestyle, sun, sea and surf.

"That's him over there – isn't he hot!" said the girl dreamily.

Helene craned her neck to look at the boy pointed out to her as he slouched into the coffee shop.

He was good looking in a traditional way: square jaw, even features, good body. But his eyes were small and rather mean. And he was already checking out every woman in a halter neck and sarong.

Poor little Jenny Wren: just 18 years old and so in love.

Helene felt a sisterly interest in protecting the little fledgling and was inclined to try and open those pretty eyes but she just couldn't bring herself to burn the hope that shone within them. Instead she talked to Jenny about her plans for the summer.

Jenny was delighted to have someone seem so interested.

"We're staying with Dylan's uncle for a couple a weeks but then we're going to get a shack on the beach," she said. "Dylan says they have the showers outside which sounds really cool, don't you think?"

Helene agreed she could think of nothing cooler.

"We're gonna find one with a coconut tree outside and we can have fresh coconuts for breakfast. Maybe we can find a banana tree, too. We won't need to buy any food. Dylan's gonna go fishing and we're gonna eat fish stuffed with bananas. I don't know: do you think that sounds kinda funky?"

Helene agreed that although baked bananas were pretty good, stuffing them in a guppy might be taking it a step too far.

They laughed in a comradely way.

"I'm really glad I met you," said Jenny shyly. "I was feeling kinda lonesome. I don't know anyone here – except Dylan – and... and I've never been good at making friends. It's been great talking to you: it's kinda like talking to my mom. Hey! Maybe you can be like my Hawaiian mom!"

Helene could think of nothing that thrilled her more. Poor Jenny Wren.

"Hey!" she said, her puppy-like enthusiasm boundless, "I

could introduce you to Dylan's Uncle Bill. He's got this awesome place right on the beach. Maybe he could help you get a place, too. Dylan says he helps loads of his army buddies when they come out here."

Helen's instincts and her kindness to the little waif had been rewarded with information that actually interested her. An ex-army man called Bill: it sounded promising.

"That would be great, honey," said Helene, "but we're fixed up okay for a place to stay. But, yeah, I'd love to come and see you and meet Dylan's Uncle Bill. What's his address?"

After chatting for a while and learning a bit more about Uncle Bill, Helene led her new friend back to Dylan and left her wrapped around him. Jenny gave Helene a hug, begging her to come visit soon. Dylan put a proprietary arm around the girl and steered her away without a backwards glance.

Helene chewed over Jenny's news. She daren't feel too hopeful, no matter how well the information dovetailed with what she'd learned about the man they were looking for. But it sounded promising.

She walked back down the beach to find Charlie.

By this time 'Wes' had surfed back in and was presently entertaining a pair of nubile bikini-clad twins who had just flown out from New Jersey for a holiday and were hoping to meet some surfer guys; and they just *loved* his British accent.

Helene felt the gremlin of mischief tugging at her.

She pulled her sunglasses over her eyes and sashayed over to the picturesque trio.

"Sorry, girls, he's taken," said Helene, laying her hand on Charlie's chest with an air of ownership.

The twins pouted prettily and might have tried a bit harder but they got no further encouragement from Charlie now his watchdog had started to growl, so they left for better hunting. Helene smiled to herself as he watched their departing backs with an expression of disappointment.

"Down boy," she said quietly, dropping her hand from his chest. "We're working. Remember? And I think I've got a lead: apparently 'Uncle Bill' is an ex-army guy who entertains other ex-army buddies at his place on the beach: it's at Sunset on the Turtle Bay side; near Backyards."

Charlie was impressed.

"That sounds promising. How did you find him so quickly?"

"By keeping my mind on the job," she said tartly.

They agreed to check out Uncle Bill's beach house as soon as possible. Jenny had given a pretty good description of what they'd find: an impressive, modern condo overlooking the beach. That was the easy part. Helene had no idea if it was the right man, and if it were, how they were going to get him to tell them what they wanted to know: if, indeed, he knew anything. There were no guarantees. But it was their best and only lead.

They hitched a lift into Haleiwa and walked back to the boarding house in silence, each wrapped up in their own thoughts.

Helene felt tired. Her encounter with Jenny had unaccountably depressed her and she felt overwhelmed by the task ahead. She was glad when Charlie said he was going to scope out Uncle Bill's place; she would have some precious moments alone.

Since her husband had faded out of her life a decade since, there had been no-one permanent in her life. For a few years she'd hooked up with a Reuter's correspondent that she'd met on various assignments. In the end they realised that the only thing they had in common was work and the thrill of the chase. When that was gone, well... Helene had become used to spending a lot of time by herself and now she enjoyed it. She'd always been self sufficient so it had been rather irksome to have Charlie's constant presence – even if they were partners, of a sort.

After Charlie had left, she pulled out her laptop and got her notes up to date. She added a few more questions to her growing list of queries. There still wasn't much to go on but she felt that if she kept chipping away, a shape might emerge from the morass, the list of could-be's and maybe's that grew longer with each new morsel of information. She kept coming back to the reason why the stranger had been kidnapped and not killed. It nagged at her. Surely, you kill someone to shut them up: so either the stranger had something that the mysterious customers wanted, or something he knew – something that made him too valuable to kill. A further possibility was that he'd been taken to keep someone else quiet. And if the 'customer' were US Secret Service, NSA or CIA as Charlie seemed to suggest, then the secret must have national significance.

She tried to think of reasons that would be of national significance to the US: terrorism had to come top of the list, followed by some sort of industrial espionage. Perhaps. Maybe. Maybe not.

She tried to narrow it down. It depended on who their enemy was – assuming it was just the one, of course. She started to type out a list of possibilities.

- CIA: homeland security through obtaining information on foreign governments and political powers.
- Secret Service: protecting the President, VP, their families, former leaders, presidential candidates and foreign embassies.
- NSA: primarily Treasury roles, such as counterfeiting of currency and US treasury bonds and investigation of major fraud.

She ruled out FBI as they were mostly involved with internal criminal investigations and intelligence gathering.

Then she changed her mind: she couldn't rule out anyone yet. Not even the UK National Crime Agency. After all, if they thought something was happening on their turf, they'd want to know about it; it was always worth their while to keep in with the CIA. NCA looked into cyber crime, drug and people trafficking.

- MI5 and MI6: intel and surveillance at home and abroad – anything involving British security.

Oh, and she mustn't forget the Serious Fraud Office. In fact...

She swore forcefully and slammed her laptop shut.

Exhausted by the near endless possibilities, the faceless, nameless enemies that were arrayed against them, she felt helpless. She lay fully dressed on the bed and stared at the ceiling, willing sleep to take her. It seemed impossible that she would ever get her life back: how could she? How could this crazy rollercoaster ride end well? Or end at all. Maybe she'd condemned herself to a lifetime of running, of cheap hotels and an uncertain future. She descended further into the blackness until finally the tears ran down her face and she was wracked with sobs.

It had been a long time since she'd cried herself to sleep.

She woke up, her eyes hot and puffy, to find Charlie standing over her, his face concerned.

"Helene? Are you okay? Has something happened?"

She tried to speak but the tears and misery were too fresh in her memory and she choked on the words of denial that sprang automatically.

He sat on the bed next to her and scooped her into his arms. Her body resisted for a fraction of a second, her back stiffening and then her defences gave way. She collapsed into him, clinging on as if he were the only thing in the world that could save her from drowning.

God! She so needed to be held.

He stroked her hair gently, quietly, until her tears had lessened.

Embarrassed she pulled away.

"Sorry about that," she muttered avoiding his hesitant eyes. "I'm just a bit strung out. Any luck with Uncle Bill's place?"

He let her change the conversation and didn't mention what had passed between them. She was grateful.

"The good news is it's definitely him," he said, watching her as shed paced up and down the room.

"And the bad news?"

"The guy's still a tosser."

Helene smiled weakly.

"More joy. This is your call, Charlie. How do we approach Uncle Bill? Is this where I turn into Mata Hari and seduce him?"

"That could work," he said, smiling slightly, "Or..."

"Or?"

"I scare the crap out of the bastard until I get him pissing down his own leg."

She was surprised by his vehemence.

"I think I prefer your way," she said evenly, controlling the tremor in her voice.

"Funny," he said, "I was going to say the same thing to you."

Their eyes met.

"Well," she said at last looking away, "we're invited by Jenny – maybe we should pay a call."

He smiled.

"It would be rude not to."

CHAPTER EIGHT

Even if Charlie hadn't already scoped out Uncle Bill's place it would have been easy to find it. Loud, insistent music pumped into the soft night air. Party Central.

Dozens of beautiful young things wafted around, adorned with leis and followed by a pack of surf rats with goatees and the ubiquitous flip-flops. This was a luau with attitude.

Uncle Bill, it seemed, was spending his blood money as fast as he had earned it: every night was party night at his place.

Which made things both easier and harder.

Easier, because no-one was exactly checking ID at the door; and harder, because getting him by himself wasn't going to be easy.

Helene felt self-conscious. She was easily the oldest woman there although lusting over the party girls were several men who must surely be drawing their pensions, or near to it. They had the look of hard cases, maybe the ex-army buddies Jenny had mentioned. Helene gave them a wide berth.

Of course the self-consciousness might have been to do with the fact that she was wearing a halter-neck velour jumpsuit in a lurid purple, slashed to the waist at the back and not much higher at the front.

Charlie had chosen it for her from a cheap, beachfront store. He'd enjoyed her astonishment and appalled expression but pointed out that she needed a party outfit if their plan was to work. The jumpsuit fitted her like a glove, or possibly a bit more snugly. He obviously had a good eye when it came to sizing up women's clothes. Perhaps practise made perfect.

He was wearing the same baggy shorts matched with a loud Hawaiian shirt. Although to be fair, she hadn't seen any quiet ones.

It had made her nervous to leave the laptop as well as the back up in the hotel room but she couldn't risk being caught with the memory stick on her in Bill's house. Instead Charlie found a loose tile behind the toilet that was just about big enough for a makeshift safe. That was the best they could do. Helene chewed on a fingernail as she watched him stash it away.

When they arrived there were people, cars and surfboards everywhere. Helene couldn't tell if the party was in full swing or just getting warmed up: it had been a fair few years since she'd been to something like this. Helene suspected that if she did any deep breathing she could get high without trying. Either Uncle Bill had the local police in his pocket or smoking hash was so commonplace that no-one gave it a second thought. Probably the latter if their landlady's comment earlier was anything to go by.

"You look great," said Charlie encouragingly, pulling her hand away as she tried to hitch up the front of the jumpsuit in a vain attempt to cover a bit more chest area.

"I look ridiculous!" she huffed.

He smiled.

"No: hot, definitely hot. Come on, dance with me."

He pulled her into an embrace.

"I can't dance to this music!" she said faintly.

"I'll show you."

He moulded his body into hers and they swayed to the music. She could feel the strength in his arms and the heat of his body was making her feel dizzy.

Despite the crowds, Jenny spotted them instantly. Helene guessed she must have been looking out for her. She wasn't sure if she was sorry or not that Jenny's presence had brought the dance to an end.

"Oh, April! I'm so glad you – and Wes – came. It's... it's pretty wild, isn't it?"

She hugged Helene tightly and Helene couldn't help but respond with real warmth. Poor little bird.

"So, where's Dylan?"

Helene looked around her.

"Oh... somewhere. He went to get me a drink. I don't really know."

She'd been dumped already.

"Uncle Bill is over here: you wanna come meet him?"

"I'd love to."

Charlie signalled with his head and wandered away. Jenny didn't comment on his disappearance: she was too used to the men folk disappearing suddenly.

'Uncle Bill' was a man of about fifty: a dissolute fifty with avarice and alcoholism etched into his thin, mean-looking face. Helene could imagine that Dylan would look a lot like him in twenty years or so. Possibly sooner. She was also reminded of Charlie's description of Bill as a 'chiselling little weasel'. It looked pretty near the mark.

When Jenny introduced her as 'My friend, April', Bill looked her up and down like a prize heifer. She wouldn't have been entirely surprised if he'd pulled her lip out to check her teeth. Although to be truthful his gaze hadn't lifted far above Helene's small but shapely embonpoint.

Helene tossed her long, blonde hair over her shoulder and thrust out one hip. She felt a complete fraud, but Uncle Bill probably wasn't a man of great subtlety.

"Great party," she said, trying to sound even more brazen than her outfit. "I like a good party."

"Do you?" he said, taking the bait.

"The trouble is," said Helene, lowering her eyelashes, "it's so rarely worth the effort. Do you know what I mean? Most men seem to just want the entrée but I prefer three courses."

He raised his eyebrows. Poor Jenny looked from one to the

other. This was not how she'd imagined it would go, introducing her friend to Uncle Bill.

"Do you have anywhere I can freshen up?" said Helene.

"Sure," said Bill, an unpleasant leer spreading across his face. "If you go up those stairs, take the second door on the left."

"Perhaps you can show me," said Helene.

"I'll show you, April," said Jenny eagerly.

"Oh, I don't want to spoil the party for you," said Helene, glancing at Bill. "I'm sure Dylan must be looking for you."

"Do you think so?" said Jenny hopefully.

"Sure! Why wouldn't he?"

Helene felt a stab of guilt at the look on the younger woman's face. In fact Helene could think of a dozen reasons why not, and all of them were wearing short skirts. He was a chip off the old block by the look of things.

"I'll show you the way," said Bill. "I don't want you getting lost. That would be a great shame."

"What a gentleman," said Helene.

"Yeah, that's me," said Bill.

He showed her to the door and she sashayed up the stairs. Following her, his eyes were magnetically attached to her backside. She could feel them burning into her at every step.

When they got to the top of the stairs he pointed to a door on the left that she suspected led to the master suite. She opened it and walked in. It was a large room dominated by an enormous bed. Bill followed her in, locking the door significantly behind him.

The sound made her sweat.

He took her by surprise when he pushed her roughly onto the bed.

"Hey!" she said. "There's no need for that."

Without warning he slapped her twice, hard.

"Who are you?" he said. "What do you want?"

Shock and pain made her eyes water. The tremor in her voice was real.

"I'm just here for the p...p...party."

"Bullshit!" he sneered. "Who are you? Who sent you?"

Obviously Uncle Bill wasn't quite as stupid as he looked. An ugly, native cunning burned behind his watery eyes.

He raised his hand again but the soft click of a gun being cocked froze him.

"On your knees," whispered Charlie. "Hands on your head."

Through blurry eyes, Helene saw Charlie appear from behind a curtain. He moved with the controlled precision of a predator but his face was taut with barely suppressed fury.

Bill lowered himself to the floor and raised his hands.

"I've been waiting for you – or someone like you," he said hoarsely. "I always knew this day would come: I just didn't know when."

He bowed his head, his body trembling.

"Here's the thing, Bill," said Charlie softly, "you might make it till morning if you tell me what I want to know."

"I'm not in it anymore, man," said Bill in a rush. "I've been out for a year now. I don't know nothing."

"That's alright, Bill," said Charlie almost conversationally, "because I want to know about something that went down three years ago. I'll refresh your memory: you picked up a package from Carmel, California and it was delivered to Nevada. You remember that job?"

"I don't know what you're talking about, buddy," said Bill, his eyes rolling, as if he'd be able to make them see the danger behind him.

Charlie looked at Helene.

"Throw me a pillow."

"What?"

Helene was still frozen on the bed. She struggled to understand what was being said.

"Throw me a pillow," said Charlie quietly, "so I can shoot this bastard in the leg without upsetting all those nice boys and girls downstairs."

Helene was pale, except for the livid spot on her cheek where Bill had hit her. Awkwardly, she reached across the bed and threw a pillow covered in a black, silk pillowcase. At least it wouldn't show the blood: it was so hard to get blood out of silk, she thought inconsequently.

"Can you dance with one leg?" said Charlie, taunting now. "Shall we find out what happens if I shoot off your kneecap?"

Helene could see the sheen of oily sweat break out on Bill's face. Suddenly she was glad: those slaps had hurt. In some separate compartment of her brain the violence of her thoughts shocked her.

"Okay, okay," said Bill, licking his dry lips. "Maybe I do remember something but I don't know anything. You dig?"

Charlie processed his answer for a second. "Let's go through it again," he said. "Who contacted you about the job?"

"It was through the employment listings page in the newspaper: The Los Angeles Times," Bill stuttered quickly.

"Don't yank my chain, Bill," said Charlie, an edge to his voice.

"I'm not!" jabbered Bill. "That's... that's how I'd get recruited for a job: I'd look in the classified section and there'd be a coded message. I'd turn up at the location, get the brief, do the job and watch the money go into my bank account. That's all! I swear. I never knew who booked me, it was safer that way: safer for them, safer for me. I didn't *want* to know."

It was clear that Charlie believed him because he went on to a new question.

"Did you see the target that night?"

Bill's shoulders relaxed a fraction.

"No. I never saw his face. I was look-out; the number two guy did the snatch."

"Where did you take him from? Describe the place."

Bill shook his head worriedly.

"Some clapboard place on the coast." Then a thought occurred to him, a memory. "It didn't look much from the outside but it had a whole bunch of security. The number three guy was some sort of computer geek cos he got us inside pdq. Whoever ordered the job must have expected that."

"Pen and paper," said Charlie to Helene. "Bill is going to draw us a map."

Helene pulled a small notebook and pen out of her shoulder bag. With a shaking hand, Bill drew a rough sketch of the shack's location and handed it to Helene. His eyes darted back and forwards restlessly.

"And you never knew who he was?"

"No, I swear," Bill choked.

"And you never saw the other men again?"

"No. No, never. There was a fourth guy who flew the chopper but I never spoke to him. That's all I know."

Helene saw Charlie give a small smile. But his next words didn't match his expression.

"You're disappointing me, Bill. You haven't given me anything useful and you haven't given me a reason not to shoot you."

Bill started babbling. He hadn't heard any hesitation or mercy in the cold voice behind him. A shudder ran through Helene as she watched the scene play out.

"I... I think one of the guys, the number two guy, was some sort of religious nut," Bill babbled. "I thought he was a Buddhist, maybe, cuz... cuz he kept chanting the whole time but it turned out it was some other Asian thing – 'sin' or 'shin' or some whacko thing. I don't know! He kept chanting these words over and over again. I remember it because it was driving me crazy, and me and the number three guy gave him kind of a hard time over it. Really, I don't know anything else, I swear it!"

"I believe you, Bill," said Charlie. "But I think I'll shoot you anyway."

He stood back and took aim.

Helene gasped.

"No!" she whispered. "Don't kill him."

"We don't want any loose ends," he said, frowning but without taking his eyes off the back of Bill's head.

"Please, don't," she said again, a wave of revulsion running through her.

By this time Bill was begging and crying, snot and tears streaming down his face.

Charlie finally looked at Helene then back at Bill. He raised the gun and brought the butt down hard on Bill's head, felling him instantly.

"Thank you," said Helene, her voice shaky.

But Charlie wasn't finished. He stepped forward and casually kicked Bill between the legs hard enough to rupture a testicle.

"I don't like men who hit women," he said.

Their eyes locked.

"Then thank you twice," she replied, huskily.

He held out his hand and she took it gratefully. Together they walked down the stairs, his long arms wrapped around her waist, supporting her weight, and slowly made their way through the crowds of dancers, drinkers and smokers. From the corner of her eye Helene spotted Jenny, still alone, still looking lost and very young.

Helene and Charlie made their way back to the boarding house by taxi. The driver kept looking at Helene in the rear view mirror as if he wanted to say something, but in the end he just shrugged his shoulders and dropped them off at the harbour without comment.

They slipped into their room without attracting the landlady's attention. Then he got some ice from a fridge in the kitchen, made it into a pack and held it gently against Helene's cheek.

"It'll help with the swelling," he said.

"Thanks."

She took the icepack from his hand and went to stand by the window, feeling the ocean breeze cooling the air.

"Where do we go from here, Charlie?" she said. She turned to search for his eyes in the darkness. "I don't really see how we can use what he told us."

She felt helpless, the weight of hopelessness pressing down on her.

He looked thoughtful.

"Maybe not... but I've been thinking about what Bill said; about the fact that the guy was chanting during the job."

His voice seemed to come from a long way away.

"It seems to me that when a merc starts getting religion, it's time for him to get out of the game. You can't have that sort of conflict going on in your head because then you'll start to doubt yourself and if you do that, the game's up and you're dead, or wishing you were."

The words came out in a rush, then he paused and sighed softly.

"If the guy was doing a Buddhist chant," he said at length, "we'd head for Nepal, I suppose."

Helene followed his train of thought. She was trying very hard not to think about Bill and the scene in the bedroom – it made her palms sweat and her heart begin to gallop. She pulled her mind back to Charlie's summing up. It made sense. Sort of.

"I need to get online to check something," he said suddenly. "Can I use your laptop?"

Helene was taken aback by the eagerness in his voice.

"Of course," she said. "But is it safe? Won't they be able to use it to find us?"

He shook his head. "I added a programme to it that will make it untraceable. Didn't I mention that?"

There was the hint of a smile in his voice.

"No. You didn't mention it... I'd have remembered," she said, amused and slightly annoyed. "What are you going to look up?"

"I'm not sure but there's something about the chant that Bill mentioned: he said he didn't think it was Buddhist, right? I need to check something..."

Helene scrabbled behind the toilet to locate the loose tile. Wrinkling her nose slightly she felt behind the U-bend and pulled out the laptop and handed it to him.

He leaned back on the bed, the laptop balanced on his crossed legs.

Helene returned to the window, gazing out, while he checked a number of websites. She thought of Jenny back at the party: you don't have to be 18 to feel lost and alone.

"Bingo!" he said, excitement evident in his tone. "Here it is: I knew there was something at the back of my mind. It wasn't a Buddhist chant; I think it was Shinto – the Japanese religion. Listen to this:

'Shinto teaches that certain deeds create a kind of ritual impurity that one should want cleansed for one's own peace of mind and good

fortune. Those killed without being shown gratitude for their sacrifice will hold a grudge and become a powerful and evil that seeks revenge.'

Helene listened intently, her eyes on him.

He continued thoughtfully.

"Maybe the Number Two felt he needed rather a lot of purification."

He paused.

"So... what does that tell us?" said Helene. "It could mean he went to a Shinto temple..."

Charlie shook his head.

"They have shrines: I think the temples are Buddhist, although it's not too clear. They seem to share a lot."

He frowned in confusion.

"So he went to a shrine," Helene continued, "and got purified. That doesn't help us much unless we go to every shrine and find out if any westerners have prayed there lately. How many Shinto shrines are there in Japan?"

He scanned the website.

"Eighty thousand. Or more."

They were both silent, both thinking the same thing: We're fucked.

Helene pulled off her wig and pushed damp hair out of her eyes.

"Okay, let's think. We've got to narrow this down. Let's assume that if this person, this mercenary," she glanced at Charlie, "if he feels he's got to 'purify' himself, is praying at a shrine going to be enough? What is an Anglo-Saxon mercenary, who's grown a Japanese conscience, going to do? What if he feels so bad that he decides to do it properly: renounce his lifestyle, renounce the world? I mean, it seems to me that if you start praying in the middle of a... er... job, then, like you say, he's got big issues. He's going to try to pay his penance not just by praying but by becoming the holiest priest ever, right? So my question is: how does a westerner become a Shinto priest? It can't be that easy..."

She took over the seat in front of the computer and flipped through a couple of search engines.

"Look," she said, "there's a place here that helps people train to be Shinto priests. God, I love the internet!"

She read the words carefully:

'You would already need to have a long established relationship with the Jinja in question — that's the place where priests worship — before being allowed to take their training programme. So while the programme itself may be short, it may take a few years of being associated with the Jinja to be allowed into the training programme. The programme through the Kompira Jinja in Shikoku is comprised of a minimum of two five-day long sessions held a year apart. The interim year is intended to be used by the student to go back to their home Jinja and practice what was taught. The programme is held annually in May.'

"Damn, we've just missed it."

Charlie shrugged. "It's still a place to start. If he is training to be a priest, he's not going to exactly blend in so we should be able to find out pretty quickly. Where did you say this Jinja is?"

"Shikoku: it's an island in the south west of Japan, Kagawa Prefecture. It says here that about a thousand years ago it was a holy place."

She sighed.

"So, another one of our long shots."

"Hmm," he said, "it's pretty thin."

"Bordering on anorexic," she agreed, "but what else do we have?"

"There is one other lead," he said. "We could look for this shack in Carmel. I'd should be able to find the place where we landed and we can use Bill's map after that — try to work out who the mark was. Knowing that could help a lot."

Helene looked hopeful but Charlie's face was puckered with distaste.

"Trouble is, we'd be in the NSA's backyard and that could make things a lot harder. But either way, it's information that's three years old."

Helene's diaphragm felt like it was being squeezed, the breath leaving her lungs in a sharp rush. She definitely didn't like the sound of pitching up on the NSA's or CIA's doorstep:

that was like tempting fate... or tempting fate even more than they already had. It felt like a lose-lose situation.

Charlie was watching her eyes carefully. Then he reached into his baggies and pulled out a quarter.

"Heads we go to Carmel, tails we go to Japan."

He threw the coin up in the air and caught it. He looked down then grinned at Helene.

"Looks like we're going to Japan."

"Darn," she said. "I didn't pack my *kimono*."

CHAPTER NINE

HELENE LAY AWAKE AS THE SOFT DAWN LIGHT GREW stronger. Her eyes burned with tiredness but her mind whirled, leaping from thought to memory to idea to confusion once again. Her mind constantly returned to Bill no matter how hard she tried to push the memory away. She could picture the malice in his eyes when he'd hit her; the perverted enjoyment he'd felt in watching her pain and the fear that had blossomed in her eyes. And then she saw him writhing on the floor with Charlie standing over him, his expression that of one who was barely in control of his desire for blood. A shudder ran through her. She turned her head to look at him.

He lay close by her side breathing softly and evenly, his chest rising and falling rhythmically, his lips slightly parted.

Carefully she propped herself on one elbow and looked down at him. His skin glowed golden in the early light, his face younger and more innocent than she'd ever seen it. She studied the planes of his cheeks, the curve of his mouth, the gentle puckering of his forehead as his dreams raced behind his fluttering eyelids.

She let her eyes rove over the pale scar on his shoulder and the satisfying muscles of his chest and arms. But when she looked back to his face, the wide, blue eyes were open, watching her thoughtfully.

"Hello," he said quietly.

Helene was embarrassed that he'd caught her gawking like this. But there was nothing triumphant about his face, just a puzzled question in his eyes. She felt herself flush, her cheeks and neck becoming hot.

She swung herself out of bed abruptly, heading for the bathroom next door, feeling exposed by the briefness of the T-shirt she'd slept in.

"Helene," he said.

She stopped and turned round.

He was still lying in the bed, but leaning up now, staring at her, his left hand stretched out towards her in invitation.

Helene's stomach lurched and she felt a delicious warmth begin to spread through her. But her trained, rational mind protested.

"No, Charlie," she said in a low voice.

She heard him sigh softly and lie back. She clenched her teeth as she left the room.

∼

Before they left Hawaii Helene insisted that there was one more thing they had to do. She bought an envelope and put in $1,000 and a first class open return ticket to Cleveland in Jenny's name.

Then they stopped at Bill's place and a sleepy looking girl promised faithfully to give it to her.

Later that morning, Jenny opened the envelope, her eyes wide with wonder as she read the brief message:

From your Hawaiian fairy (god)mother

There was no signature.

She shoved the envelope into the pocket of her jeans and didn't show it to Dylan.

∼

This time Helene and Charlie travelled steerage. There was no point trying not to stand out when there was 6'3" of newly blond hair and blue eyes at your side among a cargo of five foot five Japanese with dark eyes and black hair.

So they sat together: two Australians travelling tourist class – David Hunter and Stella Liddle.

"Couldn't you have chosen a name for me that Japanese people are going to actually be able to pronounce?" complained Helene.

"Well, I did think of calling you 'Stella Rimington'," he said, smiling wolfishly.

"Very funny," she snorted. "We are trying to avoid detection by the authorities, so naming me after the former head of MI5 seems like attracting attention. You do remember the bit where men with dark intents came to my house?"

"You can't blame them for that," he said, his teeth very white in his tanned face. "I've had some thoughts about dark intents when it comes to you... But I did gallop in on my white horse to save you, didn't I?"

"You're in a very good mood for a man on a wild goose chase," she said.

"And there was me thinking you'd win the Little Miss Sunshine Award," he shot back.

"Yes, you bring out the best in me," she said rather sarcastically.

He smiled broadly. "I've always suspected it: I have that effect on women."

She didn't bother to reply.

He kissed her suddenly on the cheek.

"What's that for?" she said in surprise.

"Just so," he replied, the corner of his mouth twitching as if he was trying to hold back a smile.

Landing at Narita International, Tokyo was a shock. After the laidback Hawaiian Islands the noise and flood of people was bewildering. Plus, the gentle warmth of Hawaii had been replaced by a humid fug of heavy, damp air. Tokyo in the summer was going to be unpleasantly moist outside of any air-conditioned building.

Helene had spent years in the Middle East so she could just about read Arabic but the spider's web of Hiragana, Katakana and Kanji was beyond her. She bought a phrase book and traveller's guide for an exorbitant price at the airport shop. Charlie had found a map in English and *Romaji* at the tourist office and worked out that they could get the *shinkansen* bullet train to Osaka and then local trains to Kotohira, the nearest town to the Kompira Shrine. Neither of them felt confident enough to try driving: especially as there was little chance of them being able to read the road signs the further they were from Tokyo − it would be more hit and miss than either of them liked. Besides, the train was more democratic and less likely to draw attention to them.

Helene purchased some *ongiri* rice balls wrapped in seaweed from a smiling *mise no hito* who spoke a type of English that was almost incomprehensible: although still better than Helene's non-existent Japanese. She gathered that one set of rice balls was stuffed with tuna and the other pickled apricot but she had no idea which was which. Lunch was going to be a lucky dip.

Charlie came back with the train tickets and a new baseball cap. His face had a pinched look about it and Helene recognised that he was on edge.

"What's the matter, has something happened?"

He gave an irritated twitch of his shoulders.

"Too many CCTV cameras. Too exposed. Too easy to get picked up."

Hence the baseball cap.

It might hide his hair and cast a shadow over his face but there was no way he could disguise 6'3". Helene was finding it easier to blend in, having bought a dark brown wig that was cut into a sharp bob. From behind she would be unremarkable on any CCTV images. A pair of heavy sunglasses helped to mask her face. She was slight enough to blend in with the majority of Japanese.

Helene was worried: she'd never seen him so strained − not even when he'd been holding a gun to Bill's head.

"Come on," she said. "There's something else − tell me what's up?"

"It's nothing, I'm fine," he snapped.

"You're not fine: you're as fine as a man with two broken legs. Just tell me, will you, or I'll go bonkers trying to guess?"

He turned to look at her.

"I think we're being followed – I think..."

Her stomach lurched and her hand flew to her mouth.

"Are you sure?"

"No. I just thought I saw someone tailing us when I went to get the train tickets: an Asian, Japanese, I guess."

He rubbed his eyes tiredly. "I paid cash so they won't be able to trace us through credit cards and I didn't see the guy again but..."

Helene didn't know what else to say. If they were being followed it made their job a lot harder – and more dangerous – but there was nothing they could do but go on.

"Maybe it was just coincidence."

"Maybe."

"Okay," she said, trying to use words to quell the rising panic. "We'd better get out of here then. Tokyo's a big place: we ought to be able to disappear."

He nodded, his eyes flickering, checking out faces in the crowd, looking for warning signs.

Helene wanted to take his hand, but was worried the gesture would be unwelcome.

"I booked the first train I could," he said, "but it's not till tomorrow morning: everything was booked up – some festival or something."

Helene felt panicky.

"What do we do?" she said, trying to sound calm.

He looked down at her briefly.

"We'll head for the city: keep your head down and don't look up or the cameras will see your face. They've got facial recognition software that could find us in minutes. Keep the sunglasses on, too."

Helene tried to remember if she'd looked up at all without her sunglasses on in the last 40 minutes since they'd landed but he didn't give her time to think: instead he hustled her away from the arrivals area.

Luckily there was a sign in English for the train into the

city: the Narita Express. Helene kept her head down and tried to avoid walking into the person in front of her.

The train was busy but not overwhelmingly so: it wasn't like the pictures Helene had seen where uniformed train officials shoved people onto overcrowded carriages using hands clad in immaculate white gloves. Maybe that was just in rush hour.

This was altogether more relaxing although Charlie was on edge on the whole time.

He waved away her offer of a rice ball but Helene was feeling hungry. An orange juice and cereal bar on the plane several hours since was no substitute for a proper breakfast.

She chewed thoughtfully on her rice ball while the Express rocked rhythmically from side to side. The *ongiri*'s seaweed wrapper acted as a convenient way of holding the soft, sticky rice together – a bit like the folded crust of a Cornish pasty, now she thought about it.

It was tasty and not too stodgy, despite the starch. She'd got the tuna.

She opened a box of fruit juice that she'd bought at the same time. It was a dark purple like red grapes, but according to the colourful translation, it was made from 'devil's root'. Helene wondered if that meant it was mandrake, but who knew.

It tasted okay: not too sweet.

She offered him the juice but he shook his head and continued to stare out of the window. If he wanted to sulk, best leave him to it.

Helene began to wish they were back in Hawaii: everything had seemed so much more possible then.

"So," she said as a conversational opener.

He didn't reply.

"So," she said again, feeling a little desperate. "Our train isn't for 24 hours: any idea how we're going to spend them?"

Still no reply.

"There are some reasonably priced hotels listed in this guidebook?" The words sound like a question.

He shook his head.

"No hotels: too easy to find us in a hotel."

She opened her eyes wide.

"Do you really think so?"

"I know so. We have to stay on the move."

Helene sighed. That sounded tiring. She'd have given anything for a comfortable hotel room and a hot shower. Well, not anything perhaps; certainly not life and liberty.

"Okay," she said, carefully, "how about we do some sight-seeing – we are supposed to be tourists after all."

As he didn't contradict her, Helene took it that he approved of this plan. She turned to her guidebook and tried to find some inspiration. She was appalled to see that her hands were shaking ever so slightly.

They changed from the Express onto another over-ground train that circumnavigated Tokyo's key tourist areas. The JR Yamanote line was thronged with people who, as Helene's mother might have said, were in their Sunday best. They were certainly dressed for a Saturday night out, and instead of the neatly coiffed salarymen and women, there were Teddy Boys with enormous quiffs, Elvis look-alikes, and gangs of Lolita Goths playing to the crowds with their brightly-dyed hair, bizarre costumes and outlandish make-up. They were certainly more colourful than the whey-faced, misery merchants and emos familiar in British cities.

Just watching the other passengers was truly an education in the dichotomy of the Japanese personality, Helene thought.

They got off at Shinjuku. Helene had worked out that this was the key shopping and entertainment area. Certainly the Japanese people seemed in a frantic hurry to have a good time. Huge, street-side video screens blared out a bewildering cacophony of ads for food, beer, films and a range of teenage J-pops bands that were so similar Helene wouldn't have been the least bit surprised to learn that they were manufactured in the same efficient way as the latest Honda. There were three vans driving around broadcasting competing adverts at an ear-splitting level. And then there was a group of people in matching T-shirts protesting at the vans broadcasting at top volume: the protestors were using megaphones. How very Japanese.

To her relief, there were enough gaijin for them to blend in a little. Most of them seemed to be young Australians or Americans. Helene saw only one black person, unsurprisingly in a group of Americans, and he was attracting a number of stares. The Japanese were very open about it: they stared at anything they found unusual. Helene was glad that her wig and sunglasses gave her a degree of anonymity.

One of the plazas was full of free entertainment: buskers, dancers, DJs with outdoor decks, musicians of varying ability, bongo drummers, tap dancers, and dogs: lots and lots of dogs. In fact there were two parks dedicated to man's best friend: one where big dogs could exercise; and one for the more bijou beasts. Helene was reminded of Mrs Jenkin's dog, Alfie. He'd have liked the corral for smaller canines.

She wondered briefly what the Jenkins had made of her sudden absence.

They meandered through the heaving streets, flowing with the crowds, stopping to look in shop windows, watch the street vendors selling red bean snapper cake, large pancakes stuffed with a variety of confectionary, *takoyaki* laced with spring onions and bright pink ginger, and generally act like a couple of tourists without a care in the world.

In fact, stopping to look in shop windows gave him a chance to check their back trail and see if anyone was following them. Helene figured it was an almost impossible task to pick out a face in the hordes, but then again, his instincts had kept them safe this long.

Without a particular plan in mind, Helene led them away from the shops and strange entertainments of the main streets. She was surprised and rather relieved when her aimless rambling led them through one of the narrower streets only to find a beautiful park opening up before them.

"Shall we go in?" she said. "It's only ¥200 each?"

Which was about £1.20.

He shrugged. "It's as good a place as any to waste some time."

Helene carefully counted out the money and they were admitted.

"Oh, this is lovely!"

She couldn't help feeling the pleasure of such a delightful place. Her shoulders relaxed and she felt she could breathe again.

"This must be amazing when the cherry blossom is out," she said enthusiastically. "Can't you imagine it? Rows and rows of cherry trees filled with pink blossom. It would make the most wonderful snow-fall of petals."

She glanced at Charlie: he was smiling at her.

"What?" she said.

"Nothing. It's just... you're not like anyone I've ever met before."

Helene was taken aback. "You think?"

He grinned at her.

"For sure! We're on the ride of a lifetime, probably being hunted by any number of international agencies, and you can still... you can still enjoy this park. That's pretty amazing. *You're* pretty amazing."

His blue eyes were suddenly serious.

"Oh. Thanks," she said, looking away.

Helene was embarrassed. She must be a real simpleton to have been able to forget that they weren't really tourists. She wouldn't make that stupid, naïve mistake again.

The park was enormous. It looked as if it might have had western influences once as the layout had a European feel about it. They strolled past a greenhouse full of strange and showy tropical plants and watched while some children threw left over bits of rice ball into a pond of giant coy carp.

Further in, the neat shrubs gave way to soaring Cedars, tulip trees and the elegant cypresses so beloved by Japanese artists. Even Charlie seemed to relax slightly, some of the wariness leaving his face.

After an hour of pleasantly aimless wandering, they sat down at a lakeside tea shop, the still water framed by graceful water lilies, sumptuous in their over-grown beauty. Helene rested her aching feet gratefully and together they sipped the bitter green tea that was served everywhere.

Charlie leaned back, massaging his temples. Was there a grey hair amongst the blond? Maybe it was just a trick of the light.

He saw that Helene was watching him.

"You don't think we're going to make it, do you?" she said.

His blue eyes closed briefly as if he were very tired. Then he looked directly at her and again she was dazzled by the depth of colour in his eyes.

"The odds aren't good, Helene," he said softly. "Unless we can work out why we're a target, we're not safe anywhere. Finding guy Number Two is more than a long shot."

Helene decided to try out a crazy idea that had been swirling around her brain. He could only tell her she was a fool: that would be nothing new – and nothing she didn't know already.

"What about if we draw them out?" she said.

He raised his eyebrows in question.

"Well," she continued in a rush. "What if we contact the people who are after us and... and try to work out what they want?"

"I'm listening."

"You know you said that the programme you'd put on the laptop makes it untraceable... are you willing to risk your life on that?" she asked.

"I have before now," he replied carefully.

Helene took a deep breath.

"Okay. So what about if we set up a website that's going to attract their attention? The people you've been talking about would have programmed spiders to trawl the internet all day and everyday for anything weird, dangerous, or totally out-there... all those conspiracy theorists – they watch them all the time, right?"

"And what would you put on this website?" he said thoughtfully. "How would you attract their attention?"

"I've been thinking about that," she said in a neutral voice. "How about we just put up a skeleton website and when you click on it, it comes up with the words, 'Langley', 'White House' and 'Spycatcher'?"

A slow smile spread across his face.

"That's brilliant!"

"Thank you!" Helene laughed, relieved. "Then we leave them a place where they can post us a message. Hopefully they won't be able to resist. Depending on what they say, we might be able to start to work out what it is they think we – or rather you – know, if we can start a dialogue with them: whoever 'they' are."

He nodded slowly.

"Okay," he said. "Let's do it. We'll need to go somewhere private so I can set this up. It won't take long but I'd rather not be watched – but no hotels."

Helene was delighted that he'd thought her silly idea worthy of acting upon.

"I think I saw something in the guidebook that might help us," she said.

She flicked through a few pages, frowning.

"Yes, here it is. All-night coffee shops. They're called *Manga Kissa* – cyber cafés. If you've missed your train home it's where the kids go to watch DVDs and anime, play computer games, things like that. Yes, look here: you check in at the reception desk and get your own cubicle – it costs about ¥2500 for eight hours."

She turned another page.

"There's one not too far from here. Oh, and you'll like this bit, you can also play darts and get a massage at some of them."

"Fantastic," he said, looking at her archly. "I like a game of darts."

"You're on," she said. "I never miss a bulls-eye, by the way."

"What's the wager?" he said.

"I haven't decided yet," said Helene, smiling back.

The *Manga Kissa* was deliberately hard to find. Despite the fact it was in a guidebook, it was clearly supposed to be the kind of trendy in-place that was found by word-of-mouth, the location passed around like a secret code. The entrance was on a back street that surprised Helene with its shabbiness; everything else she had seen in Tokyo was notable by its cleanliness and newness. A couple of earthquakes and World War Two strikes by US warplanes had helped to update the architecture.

In contrast to the sparkling high rises and shops surrounding it, 'Genji-yo!' was discreetly dull and artfully worn. It reminded Helene of those brand new mirrors that interior designers used to swear by, with deliberately distressed gold frames and carefully warped glass.

Charlie pushed open the heavy, prison-like door and they walked into a warm fug of beer and cigarette smoke. It came as a bit of a surprise after the nicotine-free pubs and coffee houses of Britain Inc.

The soft hubbub of conversation died as they entered. Obviously not many gaijin followed the guidebook's advice to search out the seedy back street.

"Not exactly what I'd call a stealthy entrance," he muttered. "God! This place makes me feel old."

Helene had to smile: even Charlie was nearly a decade older than most of the clientele; she must look as old as the kraken to these teeny boppers.

A nervous looking young man stood up to welcome them – or show them the door if it turned out that they'd come in by mistake.

"*Rashai!*" said the young man politely, making little attempt to mask his anxiety at their unexpected arrival.

It amused Helene to see his elegant bow offset by a T-shirt that was printed with a spatter pattern of blood straight off some CSI crime scene. His hair was also thoughtfully tousled, gelled into astonishment with erratic spikes projecting out at odd angles. It must have taken a long time to achieve that casual, just-got-out-of-bed look.

Shooting worried looks at them, the host escorted them to a table that was in the main room and exposed to too many pairs of curious eyes. Helene shook her head and the young man looked puzzled.

She pulled out her dictionary and looked up the words for

'private' and 'cubicle' which the guidebook had promised was a Genji-yo! speciality.

"*Koshitsu?*" she said hopefully.

The host looked even more worried.

"I think that's the right word," said Helene to Charlie, frowning.

It certainly didn't seem to be having the effect she'd hoped for. Suddenly a young woman near the bar started laughing.

"Ku-ga!" she giggled. "Ku-ga!" pointing at Helene.

Several of the other clients started laughing, too. Helene had no idea at what. The host looked embarrassed.

"Ku-ga! Ku-ga!" shrieked the young woman, her hand over her mouth, in fits of giggles.

"I've no idea what she's saying," said Helene rather desperately, flicking through the pages of the guidebook's dictionary. "It says here that '*Kugatsu*' is 'September' and '*kugun*' means 'air force'. That doesn't make any sense."

But it seemed to make sense to their young host because he bowed deeply and led them, at last, to a private cubicle.

It had everything they wanted: wi-fi, a table, chairs, a comfortable looking futon couch and privacy.

Helene ordered a coffee and Charlie ordered a beer. She hoped that the place served food but without her having to turn to the guidebook for help, the host returned with a handwritten menu in the Latin script the Japanese called *Romaji*. Even with the English translations, they were little wiser about some of the dishes: 'bee larvae with vegetable' was particularly memorable. In the end Helene had no choice but to resort to the page of helpful phrases: the guidebook was turning out to be good value for money after all.

She practised the sentence she'd picked out a few times and when the host returned she was ready with:

"*O-makase shimasu.*"

Please decide for me.

The host nodded his understanding: he looked as relieved as Helene at the simplicity with which they had managed the ordering of food. He returned shortly with two hot towels scented with lemon which were deliciously refreshing after a hot, sweaty day, tramping through the city. Soon after that the food started arriving: the ubiquitous miso soup with tiny pieces of tofu floating on the top; bowls of rice, without which no meal seemed complete; some steamed fish and vegetables in mouth-watering colours; spicy wasabi dip; a thick, brown sauce that may or may not have been some sort of soy; and a dish of tempura – the type at present obscured by deliciously light cornflour batter: vegetables unknown and unnamed.

"Fucku?" said the host smiling and bowing.

"Pardon?" said Helene.

"You want fucku?" said the man, still smiling, still bowing.

"No, I do not!" she said with warmth.

The host looked perplexed, his eyes flicking worriedly between them, unsure how he had offended her.

"I think," whispered Charlie, "he was asking you if you wanted a fork."

"Oh," said Helene.

The host backed away nervously, leaving them to their meal. He didn't come back with a fork.

The impromptu meal was delicious and Helene was ravenous. Charlie watched wonderingly as she packed away vast amounts of food. She'd always had a rather camel-like ability to feast after a famine.

When at last she placed her chopsticks by the side of her bowl and leaned back replete, Charlie had been busy at the computer for some time.

"How's it going?" she said.

"Okay. I'm just hacking into a server account. With a bit of luck it could be several weeks – even longer – before they realise they're hosting a rogue site."

"You're pretty good at all this," she said.

"All what?" he said, still concentrating on the small screen.

"This cyber-crime stuff. How come you've never done it full time?"

"What are you talking about?" he said abruptly, looking up at her. "I'm not a criminal."

Helene frowned. "Sorry. I didn't mean it like that. It's just... all these things you know, hacking and that."

She paused. He waited.

Eventually he said, "Apology accepted. I suppose you could call it... counter intelligence."

There was more silence.

Charlie re-focused on the computer and Helene was blaming the contentment of a full stomach on her uncanny habit of opening her mouth only to change feet. She tried to remember what her father had said about speaking only to prove that you were a fool.

There was a gently tap at the side of their cubicle. Helene was glad of the interruption. The host was peering nervously at them.

"Okay?" he said anxiously.

"Delicious," said Helene. "Hang on... *oishikatta!*"

"Ahh!" the host smiled happily and chattered away in Japanese as he cleared the table and retreated bowing gracefully.

"You've made his day," said Charlie.

"I have that effect on people," said Helene, hoping to keep the tone light.

"By the way," he said innocently, "I think I've worked out what that girl meant when she said 'ku-ga'."

"And?"

He smiled.

"She was calling you a cougar."

Helene scowled. The young girl had thought she was one of those older women who frequented clubs to prey on, and seduce, younger men.

How humiliating.

CHAPTER TEN

Helene spent the next few hours dozing on the futon couch. It was rather hard but surprisingly comfortable and supported her aching back beautifully.

Charlie, who seemed to need no sleep, tapped away at the computer and drank more coffee than was good for any normal human being.

"Okay," he said, at last. "I've done as much as we need. Come and have a look, Ms Journalist."

Helene stretched carefully, feeling every vertebra in her back creak. She missed the comfort and quiet luxury of her own bed. When you get to a certain age, she had decided, sleeping in your own bed was one of life's great pleasures.

She pulled up a chair and sat next to him to look at the computer. The screen was plain black with the words written in white:

> **Langley?**
> **White House?**
> **Spycatcher?'**

There was a button saying 'Comments' in the bottom right hand corner.

"Nice design," she said sarcastically. "Minimalist."

His face was impassive. "I thought you'd like it."

Helene looked at his face. What aren't you telling me, she thought. Then she looked at the web address: **www. HeleneofTroy.com**

"Oh, very funny!"

"I thought you'd like that." Now he was smiling.

She sat back.

"So what do we do now? Just wait, I suppose?"

He nodded. "Yah, they'll be in touch."

"Are you sure? How do you know?"

He shrugged. "It was your idea... but it's a good one, trust me. I know."

She looked at him thoughtfully.

"Interesting use of words, Charlie: 'trust'. I don't really know anything about you and yet I've trusted you with my life."

He pretended to look hurt. "Have I let you down?"

She paused.

"No-o. But I don't *know* you. I don't know how you're going to react in any given situation and that makes me nervous."

He shrugged. "No-one really knows how they'll react – or what they're capable of – until they're put in a situation."

"Point taken. But Bill, for example: you were really going to kill him, weren't you?"

He nodded, watching her, examining her, testing her perhaps.

"Why?" said Helene. "Because he hit me?"

"No," said Charlie, meeting her gaze, "because he's a loose end. I still think I made the wrong decision there: I used your judgement and not my own. That's a dangerous thing to do – I mean dangerous for someone like me."

Helene nodded slowly.

"I think I see what you're getting at. You mean like the Number Two man we want to find: he didn't trust his own judgement anymore because he was putting his faith in a higher power, so to speak."

"Exactly," he said. "If you lose your focus, the way you do things, you're finished."

"So you never have any doubts?"

"Not in the way you mean: not about a job, no."

Helene shook her head.

"I don't get that. You kicked Bill in the balls because he hit me, but you were prepared to kill him because he was a loose end? And what about the man that you helped to kidnap? Didn't you ever think about him? Did it never occur to you that it was wrong? ...that by any standards of humanity you shouldn't have been involved in something like that?"

Her voice had begun to rise, the questions rushing out of her.

He shook his head and shrugged.

"Maybe he needed kidnapping."

"Oh come on, Charlie!" she snapped. "How can you be so blasé about it?"

"Look," he said fiercely, his voice hard and low, "don't come so bloody high-minded with me. I do what I do because I'm *good* at it. Maybe you can't compute that, Ms Journalist, but I didn't choose this life: it chose me *because* I'm good at it – one of the best. I work when I want to work for people I choose to work with. I make judgements every day about what I'm prepared to do and what I won't do. That doesn't make me any different from most people who work in an office and count paperclips. So don't come all holier-than-thou with me. You know nothing about me. *Nothing!*"

He was really angry. But Helene felt that she was finally getting somewhere.

"Then tell me," she said, leaning forward. "Tell me about your life. I *want* to know about you, the real you, not the one you wear like a mask the rest of the time."

He was silent, studying her.

Helene sighed.

"This doesn't get reported," he said.

"Of course not!" she said sharply, looking up again. "I'm just trying to understand you."

He looked sceptical.

"Oh well," she said, "it's up to you. If you can't trust me by now..."

She went back to lie on the futon.

"Do you believe in God, Helene?"

His question was so out of left-field, she was almost speechless. He'd just performed one of those mental cartwheels that made her dizzy.

"What? Er, I think so, yes. I mean I don't think God is a man with a long, white beard sitting on a fluffy cloud, but, yes, I believe that there's a higher order at work. I know that when I've been in the foxhole I've prayed."

"Were your prayers answered?"

"I'm still alive." She paused. "Do you believe in God?"

He smiled at her suddenly: it was like the sun coming out on a day full of rain.

"My dad was a vicar."

"You're kidding!"

"No, it's true. I was brought up in a vicarage on Hayling Island."

Helene opened her mouth to say the word 'Zambia' but then she closed it again. That was a conversation for another time: she hoped there'd be another time.

"I can't imagine you in a vicarage," she said at last.

"Why not?" he smiled impishly.

"Because you're the archetypal bad boy," she said, smiling again. "You'd have ended up flirting with half the members of the Women's Institute and the Mothers' Union: probably at the same time."

He laughed. "Well, it's true I did get sent away to school..."

Helene smiled back. "And I bet you were the leader of the high jinks that must have surely ensued."

He suddenly looked young and mischievous.

"Well, there was that time that I led a break out: we were pretending it was Colditz and I was Jock Hamilton and my friend Ben was Bill Goldfinch. We'd built a glider, more of a kite really, and we got caught about to launch ourselves from the roof. Probably just as well because it would have flown like a brick."

Helene laughed out loud.

"Yes, that's about what I'd have guessed your school days were like. And then what?"

His smile withered and his gaze hardened.

"Life," he said shortly.

Helene was disappointed: just when he'd started talking about himself. But she recognised a full stop when she was shown one.

"I think I'll try and get some sleep," she said, stretching out on the futon again and yawning.

"Mmm," he said.

His gaze had returned to the computer.

She watched him for a while, then her eyes began to close and soon she was asleep. Confused dreams ran through her like small, brightly-coloured fish making it impossible for her to hold on to them. Every now and then she awoke and looked up to find him still seated at the computer, still working – on what, she couldn't say.

At six in the morning, the host tapped on the cubicle and showed them, by pointing at his watch, that Genji-yo! was closing.

Helene rubbed her scratchy eyes and Charlie packed away the laptop. He looked surprisingly fresh for someone who had just spent the night staring at a computer screen, fortified by enough caffeine to speed an entire football squad.

Helene, by comparison felt like the bottom of a parrot's cage and was far less coiffed than she would have liked. She pulled her wig straight and popped a mint in her mouth. That was the morning ablutions done. If they had time she hoped to find a shower at the train station.

When she stumbled out onto the pavement the brightness of the morning sun made Helene squint. She pulled her sunglasses out of her bag, although it might be considerably better if she put the whole bag over her head, she decided on reflection.

Several other Genji-yo! stalwarts were leaving at the same time. One of them was the young woman who had called her a cougar. She girl's mouth was an 'O' of recognition. She bowed deeply in the feminine style and said, "*Ku-ga sama,*" in a reverent voice.

Helene was nonplussed. She went from wanting to punch the girl to blowing her a kiss. The girl giggled and tottered off into the morning, high heels clip-clopping along the street.

Helene smiled to herself.

It was still unbearably early, but the streets were already beginning to fill up. The food vendors were opening along with several *shokudo* eateries that were raising their shutters. Even the plastic display food in the windows looked good to Helene. Never mind, she could pick up something at the station: more rice balls, if necessary.

They made their way to the nearest local station and waited with a gaggle of other early risers for the circle line. Half an hour later they were at the mainline Tokyo station.

The entrance looked like Helene's old Victorian-built grammar school: red brick with white stone window trims. Inside it was the usual Japanese sleek emporium to Mammon, with low, silvery ceilings and one corner of the enormous concourse opened up into a substantial department store.

It took them a while to find the correct platform for the *Hikari* train to Shin-Osaka.

But there were no showers: the nearest were 30 miles away at Narita Airport. Helene sighed. Another day without washing: it wouldn't kill her but might make her an unpopular travelling companion. Thank goodness the train would be air conditioned. She sniffed surreptitiously at her armpits. Bearable: just.

Her stomach rumbled uncomfortably and embarrassingly loudly.

"You can't still be hungry!" he said. "Not after last night."

"Of course I am," said Helene. "Last night was last night. I need to keep up my sugar levels or I'll get grumpy."

She perused the possible food outlets.

"In that case," he said, "there's a shop selling about twenty different types of KitKat over there."

Helene glanced over her shoulder: he was right.

Helene had never seen a KitKat covered in pink icing

before. Or was it pink chocolate? It was hard to tell from the picture. Either way, Helene was pretty sure she wanted to try one. Life was a journey full of experiences after all.

She bought one packet of the pink KitKats and one packet of the regular type just in case. Then she went to one of the plastic food shops and pointed at several interesting looking examples. She had no idea what she'd ordered but none of it looked like squid brain or bee larvae so she thought she'd probably be all right.

"Okay," she said. "This should do it: let's head for the train. Hopefully there'll be some tourists we can mix in with."

Their train arrived with military precision and after some hesitation they managed to find their seats. Blending in was out of the question. Every step they took, they were watched openly: they were the only gaijin in the carriage.

"I guess it's not the tourist season," said Helene, sadly.

Charlie didn't reply.

She sighed. Maybe he'd be less grumpy if he ate something. She was a great believer in the healing properties of chocolate. Not that she'd call herself an addict.

She opened the packet of pink KitKat as Charlie watched her disapprovingly. Something to do with a Protestant upbringing, she decided. Helene, on the other hand, had long ago decided that one of the benefits of being a grown up was eating chocolate for breakfast if you wanted to. One of the downsides was that on reaching adulthood, one rarely wished to.

The chocolate, if you could call it that, was nauseatingly sweet albeit slightly cherry-flavoured. If he hadn't been watching, Helene would never have finished the bar. But she wasn't going to allow him to dictate what she did or didn't eat either.

It was a relief to swallow the last piece of KitKat and wash it down with some bottled water: thank goodness she hadn't bought fruit juice − the sugar rush might have pushed her over the edge.

Charlie was clearly in no mood for talking. He was staring out of the window and Helene couldn't tell if his eyes were closed. Something about the rise of his cheek made him think they were. Perhaps he was tired after all. She gave him the benefit of the doubt and let him be.

She pulled out the laptop and amused herself by writing descriptions of the passing scenery. One of the old names for Japan was 'the land of a thousand autumns', and was therefore at its most beautiful as the leaves turned, but also when the cherry blossom bloomed. Even in the heat of summer Helene found much to admire. For one of the most populated countries in the world, there were still pools of untouched beauty and as the train sped westwards, Mount Fuji held the valleys in thrall.

The velocity of the bullet train made it seem as if the mountain was gliding towards them. Its symmetry was perfect and, just as in every tourist postcard Helene had seen, snow-capped, even in July. She could understand why it was so revered by the Japanese who seemed to worship the ever-changing perfection of nature. The mountain had even been given an honorific: Fuji-*san*.

But as the train charged onwards, Helene was appalled to see the foothills blighted by a squatter camp of concrete buildings and factories puffing out thin, grey smoke. She had seen suburban sprawl threaten to overrun the pyramids in Cairo but she had not expected such a lack of respect for the environment here. When she read in the guidebook that 50% of Japan's coastline had been substantially altered by the addition of concrete, she shut the book in disappointment.

Eventually, Charlie seemed to shake off his bad mood and accepted some of Helene's table picnic. The strange-looking skewer things were surprisingly tasty. Once he started eating, he managed to hoover his way through just about everything, although he declined the cherry KitKat. Helene couldn't blame him.

"Sorry," he said, looking up.

"For what?" said Helene, genuinely puzzled.

"For zoning out back there."

She shrugged. "It happens. Don't worry about it."

He went back to staring out of the window and Helene,

feeling more relaxed, went back to tapping out scenic descriptions (where she could faithfully omit any mention of concrete). She was glad the tension had been broken.

Every now and then she looked up from the screen to watch the world sail past. Despite her disappointment with the Japanese' attitude to their land, she couldn't help comparing the sleek bullet train with the tortuously slow Paddington West Coast service. The distance from Tokyo to Osaka was about the same, but it took twice as long to go from London to Penzance.

A couple of hours later they had arrived.

Shin-Osaka station was hideous. An architectural abomination of grey, utilitarian 1960s concrete. Helene was still surprised that the Japanese could build something so ugly. It looked like a giant multi-storey car park. Maybe they had used British architects.

Changing onto a local train line, they were carried at a far more stately pace than the *shinkansen*.

The slower speed suited her mood. The *shinkansen* has been so energetic: it was peaceful dawdling along, sitting without responsibility, being carried towards their destination, or, if Helene were feeling fanciful, towards their destiny.

They changed for the last time at Takamatsu. Everyone chose their seats quickly as the train left promptly. Still no *gaijin* – in fact they seemed to be the only tourists of any nationality.

"Have you seen anyone following us?" said Helene.

He shook his head.

"No, I think we're clean," he said calmly.

Helene was filled with relief.

That, of course, should have made her nervous.

CHAPTER ELEVEN

IN A SEAT ACROSS THE TRAIN'S GANGWAY A BEAUTIFUL DOLL-like girl-woman, with bright brown eyes, rosebud lips and porcelain skin was taking her seat. Charlie was all but staring and Helene could practically hear his gears revving up a couple of notches.

It was understandable, she thought, fairly; the girl was exquisite.

As if she could hear their thoughts, the girl looked up, her eyes wide and innocent. She was probably used to the adoration of strangers. Her smile could have melted glaciers. She could even have thawed Mrs Jenkin, which was a tougher job.

The girl-woman rose gracefully and shuffled towards them with tiny, shy steps.

"So sorry, please," said the girl, bowing slightly. "May I speak English with you to practise me?"

Charlie grinned. "Yes, I'd love to practise you."

The girl's expression was puzzled and Helene realised he'd spoken too fast and too colloquially. She gave Charlie a stern look.

"Yes, please do practise with us," she said gently, looking at the girl and indicating the seat opposite. "Your English is very good."

"Ah, thank you!" said the girl.

She sat down carefully perched on the edge of the seat like some rare, exotic bird of Paradise, her hands folded politely on her lap, her back straight, not touching the plastic behind her.

"You are from English?" she said, her porcelain brow furrowing in concentration.

"No, we're from Australia," replied Helene, slowly and clearly. "It's nice to meet you."

"Ah, forgive, please. Osaturaria. You speak English?"

"Yes, we do," said Charlie, softly.

But his tone had changed completely. There was something about the girl's freshness and naive way of speaking that had bewitched him. The flirtatious, innuendo-ridden Flashman had gone, to be replaced by something altogether surprising – an almost paternal softness.

Helene shook her head: would she never cease being astonished by his quicksilver changes of mood?

"I am very happy to meet you," said the girl formally. "My name is Matsumoto Mayumi."

"Pleased to meet you, Mayumi," said Helene. "I'm Stella and this is David."

As Helene had predicted, Mayumi had some trouble getting her tongue around 'Stella' but after a few tries, she seemed to have got the hang of it.

"David-*san*, Sterra-*san*: you holiday?"

"Yes," said Charlie. "We're travelling around. We spent some time in Tokyo but we wanted to see a bit more of the country so we're going to Kotohira. We've heard the Kompira Shrine is worth seeing."

Helene was surprised that he'd given her so much information. It seemed unnecessarily reckless.

"Ah so!" said Mayumi smiling happily. "Kotohira is my living place. You meet my family, please? My uncle is *ryokan*."

She giggled, embarrassed. "My uncle has *ryokan*. You stay, please?"

There was some delay while Helene looked up a translation for *ryokan*. It turned out to be a small, family run, traditional Japanese hotel. Perfect. They'd be harder to find in a place like that. Plus, Helene was keen to try out a traditional Japanese bath house. She felt very grubby next to this delicate, fragrant girl-woman.

Mayumi chatted cheerfully about her family: she had one older sister who was married and living in far away Hokkaido; a younger sister who was at school; and her mother who did the cooking at the ryokan. She didn't mention a father.

They learned that Mayumi herself was about to start studying at the *daigakku* – university – which would have made her about 19, and she wanted to become a *senshu*. Helene's dictionary translated this as 'player' but even with all their ingenuity neither of them could quite work out what this meant.

Then Mayumi told them all about the shrine they were about to visit.

"Kompira-*san* is special shrine for sea-people and Emperor Sutoku-Tennō. Is 1,368 stair to top. Is very happy view. You like much."

"And they teach people to be priests there?" said Helene.

"Ah, yes. Is famous school there. When *sakura* flowers. In fifth month. In May month."

She seemed less interested in the priests than in the cherry blossom. In her broken English she waxed lyrical about the importance of the petals to the Japanese: the metaphor that demonstrated the transitory nature of beauty.

In fact Mayumi seemed much keener to tell them about the local *kabuki* theatre, Kanamaru-za, which, she said, was the oldest in Japan. Helene had read enough in the guide book to work out that this didn't necessarily mean very much. There were very few truly ancient buildings in Japan, war and earthquakes had seen to that, but at the same time the Japanese seemed to have a curious habit of rebuilding. Even some important shrines, which Helene would have thought were too holy to be touched, were rebuilt every 20 years in a traditional design. It was, it seemed, a way of making the buildings forever new, forever ancient, forever original. It was one of the many contradictions that Helene was learning about this most unknowable people.

The train moved sluggishly into Kotohira.

Helene's guidebook said, 'A place where you can enjoy a cultural historical atmosphere in a gateway town'.

Either the guidebook was out of date or the person who'd written it had never been to Kotohira, in Helene's opinion. It looked like a one-horse town, where the horse had died. They disembarked from the train, Charlie shouldering a heavy rucksack, Helene carrying the small carry-on bag with the laptop.

Mayumi led them down through the town, pointing out the pertinent features. The town hall seemed as if might have once housed a sixties washeteria and the police station was a block of concrete. The place reminded Helene of Slough.

And yet, and yet, there was beauty, too. A large pagoda-type wooden structure was, Mayumi proudly told them, the largest lantern in Japan and the new marine museum was a pretty sugar cube of crisp, white render backlit by a pure blue sky.

They strolled along the river before stopping in front of a collection of low, wooden buildings surrounded by a lovely, informal garden. The river ran right through the grounds, willow trees leaning down to the water and a miniature avenue of maples.

"My uncle *ryokan*," Mayumi announced, almost proudly.

"It's beautiful," said Helene. "And so peaceful."

"Yes, I'm sure we'll enjoy staying here," said Charlie.

Helene wasn't certain Mayumi had understood them but the girl bowed deeply.

"*Arigato gozaimasu*, Sterra-*san*. *Arigato gozaimasu*, David-*san*. Please to come in."

Following her example, they removed their shoes, leaving them at the entrance and stepped up into the reception hall. The wooden floor was covered with a number of *tatami* mats and several couches were carefully placed around the room. A large bouquet of pink and white flowers was tastefully arranged in a vase as a centrepiece. Helene admired the skill: her own flower arranging consisted of trying to place a bunch in water whilst keeping the same organisation of stems as the florist.

Mayumi invited them to sit down and went off to find her uncle.

Charlie shrugged off the rucksack and flung his elongated body onto one of the low couches. He seemed too large in this careful, delicate place.

"I wonder if they have hot springs here," said Helene hopefully. "I would just kill to have a good soak."

"Would you?" he asked, raising his eyebrows.

"Well, no," said Helene. "But I'd love to be able to soak in a natural hot spring and look and this beautiful scenery."

"You know you don't wear clothes in a Japanese *onsen*," he said, his voice neutral.

"How do you know that?" said Helene.

"I know what's important," he replied. "Besides, I read your guidebook." Then looking at her, "I wonder if they have mixed bathing here, because..."

Helene was relieved when Mayumi returned.

She smiled and indicated that they should leave their luggage.

"My uncle very happy to meet you. Follow, please."

They shuffled after her, Helene embarrassed by the parlous state of her socks. She hoped Mayumi's uncle wouldn't notice. He probably would: people always notice things when you don't want them to.

Mayumi ushered them into a room that looked like a modern office with a bank of computers and austere filing cabinets. It wasn't at all what Helene had expected: it was so modern, so business like. It was in stark contrast to the rest of the *ryokan*.

Behind a large, rosewood desk sat a man approaching his twilight years but there was no avuncular sparkle in his eyes; in fact they were the coldest, deadest eyes Helene had ever seen. And unlike the rest of the Japanese people that she had met so far, he didn't stand up and bow when he saw her. Her smile wilted, her footsteps faltered, and she looked at Charlie to see his reaction. His face was set and expressionless. A shiver ran through her.

Still puzzled, Helene turned round to look for Mayumi in

case there was some mistake, some way in which they had already offended their host, but Mayumi had slipped away closing the sliding door behind her silently.

But the room wasn't empty. Far from it. There were two men, heavies, one of whom looked he'd just walked off the set of a samurai film; the other an ex-sumo wrestler, his vast flesh severely encased in a dark suit. And, wearing a triumphant expression, was Bill Bailey.

Helene gasped in shock and took a step away from him. Charlie put a protective arm around her and drew her towards him.

Bill smiled. It was a chilling sight.

Silence.

"Hello, April or is it Stella now?" Bill rasped. "Betcha didn't expect to see me again, didja?"

There was no doubt. It was Bill from Hawaii: the uncle of Jenny's boyfriend. The man Charlie had wanted to shoot. The man she hadn't let him shoot – the loose end he had said was a mistake to leave loose.

Oh, this was bad.

Bill walked towards her and Helene couldn't help but notice that he had a distinct limp, probably originating from an inability to comfortably wear trousers at present.

She cowered as he raised his hand towards her but the man behind the desk barked an order and the sumo-heavy placed himself between her and Bill.

"This bitch deserves it!" Bill snarled, turning to complain to the man behind the desk.

Helene felt momentarily relieved when Bill didn't try to come any closer. But then she felt sick and dizzy and stupid, so stupid. Why had she insisted that Bill be saved? Why? She knew why: because she hadn't wanted to see Charlie damage his own soul further with Bill's execution. And she hadn't wanted blood on her own hands.

Weak! she said to herself. *You're weak, that's why!*

Charlie had told her that once a merc loses focus it's over for him. And now the compassion that Helene had insisted on was just about to cost them their lives. No good deed goes unpunished.

She thought she was going to be sick or pass out. Her knees gave way but Charlie supported her.

The man behind the desk barked another order and the samurai-heavy brought two chairs. Helene collapsed gratefully, sitting slumped against Charlie. She could hear his heart beating as she leaned against him: it was strong and steady, as always, and, like a child, she was soothed by it.

Bill stood and fumed in impotent anger but the man behind the desk ignored him: a buzzing fly to be waved away. It gave Helene a flutter of hope.

Instead the man behind the desk stood up and offered the civilities that had been lacking so far. Helene felt an insane desire to giggle. Hysteria wasn't far behind.

"Please accept his apologies," the older man said in perfect English, indicating to Bill. "I regret the manners of this man: it is so hard to get good staff these days."

Helene glanced at Charlie but his face was unreadable. Bill, by contrast was practically frothing at the mouth but wise enough not to go against the desk man who was clearly in charge.

"My name is Matsumoto Hiro. Welcome to my *ryokan*."

"Er, thank you," said Helene, weakly, struggling to sit up. "My name is Stella..."

Mr Matsumoto interrupted her with a wave of his hand.

"Please do not insult the intelligence of either of us with this fiction. I have given you my name: you should now return the civility."

The tone of his voice made Helene sat up straighter. A glance at Charlie told her that this was no time to play games. It was dawning on her that they might be in a lot more trouble than she'd thought, even from when she'd first spotted Bill. It was confusing: either things had got a lot worse or maybe, possibly, hopefully, they were just a shade better.

Helene was many things but she was not a fool. She now had a very strong suspicion that Mr Matsumoto was *Yakuza* and somehow Bill was tied up with him – an employee of uncertain job description. She remembered thinking at the time that the Hawaiian police had been unusually unobservant when it came to the large quantities of recreational drugs that had been available at Bill's party.

She realised the man behind the desk was still waiting for an answer. She sat up straighter and gave herself a mental shake, trying to corral her scattered wits.

"My name is Helene La Borde and this is my... friend, Charles Paget."

"Thank you, Miss La Borde, Mr Paget. This is a much better beginning."

Helene was silent, wondering what was going to come next.

Mr Matsumoto stood up and went to stand by the window, gazing up at the mountain that loomed over the ryokan. His suit was of an immaculate cut in a luxurious light weight silk. His fingernails had been manicured and his steel-grey hair was smooth and sleek. Helene felt frayed and dirty: it suddenly crossed her mind that she might be about to die rather unpleasantly.

"This mountain," said Mr Matsumoto, "is a very holy place. The shrine here has been under the protection of my family for a thousand years. I make sure that I know of everyone who comes here: worshippers, tourists... and others."

He turned to look at them.

"You, I think, Miss La Borde, Mr Paget, come into the category of 'others'."

"I told ya what they did to me!" roared Bill, unable to hold himself in check any longer. "I deserve to get even. I want to kill that bastard and as for that bitch..." he licked his lips lasciviously and Helene tried to swallow the bile that rose in her throat.

Mr Matsumoto turned slowly to stare at Bill, the silence stretching uncomfortably until Bill dropped his gaze. Helene didn't think it was wise to interrupt a man like Mr Matsumoto. And Bill had done that twice in two minutes.

"As I was saying," said Mr Matsumoto, "you are not tourists."

"No," said Helene, "we're not."

"Then why are you here?"

She took a deep breath.

"We're looking for someone," she said.

"Who?" Mr Matsumoto asked politely.

"I don't know," said Helene. "I know that sounds ridiculous," she spoke hurriedly, "but... but we're looking for a man who did a... er... job with Bill and Charlie three years ago."

"And what sort of job was this?" said Mr Matsumoto flicking a glance at Bill who looked, if possible, even more shifty.

The question was clearly directed at Charlie, who up until this point had remained stoically silent.

He spoke calmly, his voice showing that he was in control of himself – unlike Bill, who looked like he was about to have a stroke.

"I was hired to fly a helicopter to and from a specific location in Carmel, California. Bill, here, and two other men were hired to find and transport someone I assumed to be a US citizen and take him to a secure location. It was supposed to be an anonymous job and it was just coincidence that I recognised Bill. And that was it. I never heard anything about the job again – until now. For some reason, after all this time, this job has become... of concern. Helene and I have been followed since we left Britain..."

Helene looked up when she heard this – it was certainly news to her.

"We need to find out why," Charlie continued. "And Bill, rather reluctantly, gave us a clue as to how we might find one of the other members of the team: someone who might have information we can use. We believe him to be in Kotohira. That's why we're here. That's the whole story."

Mr Matsumoto nodded.

"Not quite the whole story, I think. What is your involvement, Miss La Borde?"

"I'm a reporter," she said. "I got mixed up in this through a foolish and idle boast and now Mr Paget and I are working together to our mutual advantage."

"She's a goddam reporter!" shouted Bill. "How much more do you need to hear? She could blow everything!"

Bill really must be as dense as he looked to keep on interrupting Mr Matsumoto, trying to give him orders. Even though she felt herself to be neck deep in trouble, Helene couldn't help thinking that Bill was skating on very thin ice.

Mr Matsumoto ignored the outburst, his bodyguards maintaining their flanking position.

"You wish me to believe, Miss La Borde, that you have no interest in my business?"

"No! I'm sorry but I've never even heard of you before. Bill... he never mentioned your name, I swear it. I don't even know what it is you do – except that you have this beautiful *ryokan*. But," she said, raising her eyes to meet his flat, black stare, "I believe I can now begin to guess who and what you are – if not what you do, exactly. But my primary concern – my only concern – is to solve this mystery... so I can go home again."

Her answer seemed to please Mr Matsumoto because he smiled suddenly. It was like seeing a hungry wolf lick your hand instead of tearing out your throat.

"May I offer you some tea?" he said politely. "*O-cha? Matcha?* Or you prefer European black tea, perhaps?"

"Thank you," said Helene, "but I have would like some *O-cha*, please: I find it very refreshing."

Out of the corner of her eye Helene saw Charlie give her a tiny smile.

"And Mr Paget? Coffee, perhaps? I understand it is your beverage of choice."

"Thank you, but *O-cha* is fine. Helene's instincts are usually right on these things," said Charlie.

Helene wasn't quite sure what he meant by this but was in no position to ask him. It seemed like a vote of confidence.

Mr Matsumoto clapped his hands and shot out an order. Helene thought Bill was going to have a heart attack: this was not what he'd expected at all.

"I hope you have been enjoying my country," said Mr

Matsumoto conversationally while they waited for the tea to arrive.

"Oh, yes!" said Helene with real warmth.

The words tumbled out of her mouth uncontrollably, a verbal torrent. She tended to talk when she was nervous. Now was definitely one of those times.

"We visited the most beautiful park yesterday: it must look magnificent when the cherry blossom is out. But I think the maple trees were my favourite part. It must be wonderful to see them in the autumn."

She stopped, remembering that this was very far from a normal conversation. Perhaps some atavistic part of her recognised that engaging with Mr Matsumoto might help save her. Might.

"Do you have a garden at home, perhaps?" said Mr Matsumoto. "The English are great gardeners, I believe, although I have not been fortunate enough to visit your country."

Helene sighed.

"Sadly, I have no skill as a gardener although I do have a small garden. But my neighbour, an elderly man, seems to do magic with my dog roses."

Strange, she thought. She felt utterly detached. The part of her body that recognised danger was screaming at her to run, but another part felt calm and matter-of-fact. It was surreal to be discussing horticulture with a man that she still thought was going to kill her. It was almost an out-of-body experience, watching herself chat to Mr Matsumoto.

Mayumi entered carrying a large tray whilst Mr Matsumoto expressed his delight with Helene's description of the scent of her dog roses on a summer evening.

"Ah!" he said, as the tea was served from a delicate blue tea-pot. "You have met my daughter Mayumi."

Mayumi smiled and bowed.

"Yeah, dad. Just like you asked me to."

Helene stared. It was Mayumi, but the sweet, hesitant school girl seemed to have been replaced by an older, harder woman, although still very beautiful. Now they were together,

Helene could see the family resemblance – something about the eyes. But now Mayumi had no trace of an accent.

"Please forgive our little subterfuge," said Mr Matsumoto, clearly following the direction of Helene's thoughts. "I thought it would make things simpler; and Mayumi is so good at greeting people."

Helene tried to smile.

"She had us fooled; she's a credit to you, Mr Matsumoto."

He beamed and indicated that Helene should drink her tea. There were three cups: one for Mr Matsumoto, one for Helene and one for Charlie. Neither Bill nor the heavies were offered refreshment, and Mayumi left after kissing her father on the cheek and bowing respectfully. She left without looking at Helene again, although she cast an appraising glance at Charlie.

Helene sipped the tea with trembling hands. She felt herself reviving slightly as the hot liquid eased its way down her parched throat. But increased awareness also made everything seem more terrifying.

The cup rattled as she tried to place it back on the tiny saucer.

"Now," said Mr Matsumoto, his voice changing tempo again, "to business. I find myself with a dilemma. My employee," he nodded towards Bill, "would like me to dispose of you. He has indicated that a number of painful methods might be used. In his own way he is quite inventive."

Helene sloshed some tea over her hand although it was some seconds before she realised it had scalded her.

"He seems to have some deep resentment to you, Miss La Borde. I wonder why that might be?"

Bill leered at her.

"I... I don't know," stuttered Helene, her eyes drawn to Bill like a rabbit in the headlights.

"Mr Paget, you are a professional, are you not?" said Mr Matsumoto, turning to Charlie. "It is most surprising to me that you left William unharmed during your... encounter in Hawaii."

Bill unthinkingly rubbed himself where Charlie's boot had done the most damage.

"Please tell me why this is," continued Mr Matsumoto.

"Helene asked me not to."

"Ah, so?" said Mr Matsumoto raising his eyebrows in polite disbelief.

Charlie saw that he needed to expand on his answer.

"Helene is a good person: she is not a murderer. She is not... like us."

"I ain't no murderer!" yelled Bill, leaning threateningly towards Charlie. "That's a goddam lie! I never killed no-one that didn't need killing."

A hidden signal sent the two bodyguards lunging towards Bill. At that point he completely lost control: he was spitting and swearing, his eyes rolling in his head like a jellied pinball machine.

Mr Matsumoto stared at him in some distaste as the bodyguards forced him to his knees.

"The issue is one of loyalty," said Mr Matsumoto calmly, pulling his eyes from Bill as if the sight contaminated his vision. "Bill has confirmed in his own words that he took part in this 'job' you have described – at a time when he was employed by me. I am not happy that he, as you might say, was moonlighting. And now he has brought his shame to my door. He has brought both of you to my door – and I must decide what to do with you."

He turned to Helene.

"I would like you to wait outside, Miss La Borde. Mr Paget, please remain where you are."

"Oh, but..." Helene looked in panic at Charlie.

"Yes, go," he said, gently. "It'll be okay."

Helene's legs didn't feel up to the job of getting her out of the room but she managed to stagger to the door and half fall through it. She stumbled to one of the *futon* couches and sat shaking, tears running down her face.

She heard a single shot and her heart jolted painfully.

CHAPTER TWELVE

SECONDS STRETCHED INTOLERABLY AS HELENE WAITED. SHE was barely aware that her nails were leaving half-moon gouges in the palms of her hands, violent tremors making her body shudder.

The door slid open. Helene could hardly bear to look up.

The first bodyguard walked out backwards and the second followed. Between them swung a carcass, wrapped in the rather good rug that had decorated Mr Matsumoto's office floor. Helene's eyes were drawn hypnotically to the swinging body.

After a short absence, the thinner of the bodyguards returned and jerked his head authoritatively at Helene. She was to go back in.

Her knees felt oddly liquid and she held onto the wall for support, her heart pounding.

The room was much as she had left it. Mr Matsumoto was seated behind the desk, the lone heavy took his place, guarding the door... and Charlie was finishing his tea. Of Bill there was no sign.

Helene tried to take in what she was seeing but her body was having trouble processing the scene. Charlie stood up swiftly and gently led her back to the chair.

Mr Matsumoto waited until she was seated again and then spoke.

"My family has built up our business interests over several generations. Loyalty is rewarded: employees who go into business for themselves are... discouraged. Those who bring the business into disrepute are dealt with."

It was clearly an explanation for Bill's absence. Helene's eyes fluttered to a spot on the floor where a few spots of a dark liquid had been hastily wiped away.

"A pity," said Mr Matsumoto, following her eyes. "The rug was commissioned by my father."

Helene didn't know if this was some attempt at humour but questions unborn died in her throat. This man, sitting here so calmly, had just taken – or ordered to be taken – a human life. Helene had seen death in the hot fire of battle, in sudden and terrifying conflagrations of metal and flesh: she had never before witnessed murder. Except, of course, Mr Matsumoto had been careful in that respect. She had witnessed nothing and thus had nothing to report – or regret.

"You look unwell, Miss La Borde," he said, solicitously. "Perhaps you would like some more tea?"

Mr Matsumoto indicated towards the teapot and Helene realised that she was still gripping the sides of her chair, her knuckles white, her face frozen with shock.

Charlie leaned forward and poured some of the fragrant green tea into Helene's eggshell thin cup, earning a small frown from Mr Matsumoto.

"I have been having a most interesting conversation with Mr Paget," said Mr Matsumoto, looking away from Helene's shaking hands. "I believe I can help you... both of you."

"Why?"

Helene stuttered out the word before she realised she had spoken.

"Why, Miss La Borde?" he replied, raising his eyebrows. "Because you are a guest in my home and in my country. And because I can. And, if I am truthful, because your search does not impinge on my business interests."

He paused, cocking his head to one side like a small bird, the black eyes watching her thoughtfully.

"Do you not wish for my help?"

Helene wanted to scream out, No! You're a murderer! A crime lord! I want nothing to do with you or your kind.

Instead she mumbled numbly, "Thank you. That is very... kind."

Her brain felt anaesthetised, but it was enough for Mr Matsumoto. He nodded.

"I am a businessman, Miss La Borde. That is all. The sooner your business is concluded, the sooner I can again concentrate on mine."

Charlie made her jump when he reached over to squeeze her hand softly.

"Mr Matsumoto is going to help us, Helene. Tomorrow we'll visit the shrine. If the priests know anything, Mr Matsumoto says they will tell us. Okay?"

Helene nodded dumbly.

Mr Matsumoto clapped his hands. Business was over.

"And now," he said, "I understand that you would like to try our delightful tradition of *onsen* bathing. We have some of the best hot springs on the island. I would be happy for you to be my guest this evening. You will find everything you need in your rooms."

He stood up and held out his hand in the western style.

"It has been a pleasure to meet you, Miss La Borde, Mr Paget. I trust you will spend a pleasant night in my ryokan."

They shook hands and were escorted from the room.

Helene was having trouble remembering to breathe. Her skin felt unpleasantly moist and sheen of sweat glistened on her face.

"What... what happened in there, Charlie?"

He looked at her carefully.

"A loose end was tied up. That's all."

She stared at him.

"How can you be so calm? A man was murdered in front of your eyes and... and..."

"And what, Helene?" he said, in a sharp whisper. "Would you rather it had been me... or you?"

Helene looked appalled at the thought.

"No! Of course not, but..."

"But nothing. Bill was a murderer, a rapist and a bad businessman. There was nothing either of us could do for him. Jesus, Helene, you gave him one big, fat chance when we left him alone in Hawaii but he didn't take it. You just can't help some people. No, forget about Bill and just be grateful that we're standing here having this conversation instead of you waving me a fond farewell as you sail towards St Peter's Gate – and I don't."

Helene wasn't sure how serious he was being but she could see he was trying to help her.

"I'll put in a good word for you with St Peter," she said, trying to match his easy tone – and failing miserably.

Even to her own ears her voice sounded shaky and strained.

Charlie shrugged, smiling slightly.

"Doesn't matter: I have friends and family in both directions."

~

Mr Matsumoto had given them a pair of rooms that were next door to each other, windows looking out towards Kompira-*san*.

Helene found a pretty, cotton yukata dressing gown and pair of wooden clogs in her room. Her grab bag had been laid carefully on a low table. In a corner of the room was a small, recessed shrine. If there was an earthquake the shrine would most likely survive, even if the occupying guest didn't. How very Japanese.

She couldn't see a bed so Helene's best guess was that a *futon* was stored in one of the cupboards. She hoped it would be laid out for her when she returned from bathing; she felt too tired and weak to wrestle with a heavy mattress. If wasn't laid out for her, she decided she'd simply sleep on the floor.

There was a knock on the wall. It meant Charlie was ready and would be waiting outside for her.

Helene flung off her dirty clothes and slipped on the yukata which felt cool against her hot skin. She grabbed her wash bag and plodded across the room, her clogs making her sound like a lame horse. She was looking forward to being clean but her mind was in such a ferment she hardly knew who she was, let alone what she felt. At the last minute she remembered to pull off her wig. She didn't bother to look in the mirror.

Charlie was leaning against the wall, looking cool and elegant in his brightly coloured gown.

"Ready?"

Helene nodded, unable to trust her voice.

A smiling woman directed them to the bathrooms with many smiles and gesticulations. There were separate changing rooms for men and women as well as segregated bathing areas. With a grin and a wave Charlie disappeared and Helene watched as the door swung closed between them.

She felt old and tired and burdened with an intolerable weight. She pushed open the door to the women's changing room and inside saw a small cabinet of six lockers with baskets for the yukata and clogs. There was a pile of fresh towels – none of them much larger than a face cloth. Instead of feeling a flush of embarrassment she mechanically removed her gown, placing in the locker with the clogs, and slowly washed herself using the wooden bucket and western style shower. To preserve some modesty, she hung the small towel over her arm and let it hang in front of her, then she opened the only other door in the cubicle, assuming it must lead to the *onsen*.

A slight smell of sulphur hung on the air and steam drifted across the surface of the hot spa.

Only one other woman was present, an elderly lady who myopically greeted her, "Konbanwa!"

Helene replied awkwardly before draping her towel over a rock and sliding into the hot, spring water. The air was warm and almost spicy; she closed her eyes as the heat relaxed her aching joints.

The old woman frowned and, when she realised she was sharing her bath with a gaijin, promptly rose up like an aging Venus and clip-clopped from the *onsen* muttering to herself.

Helene had no idea if she'd committed some unforgiveable breach of *onsen* etiquette or whether the old woman detested the idea of sharing with a dirty foreigner. Too bad: the water was marvellously soothing.

The men's *onsen* was on the other side of the ryokan. Helene felt relief that Charlie was some distance away from her. Her brain was whirling with unwanted images, ideas, thoughts. The refrain of a hymn kept circling round and around:

> *I danced on a Friday when the sky turned black;*
> *It's hard to dance with the devil on your back.*

Is that what I'm doing? she asked herself. *Am I dancing with the devil?*

Helene sat for so long that she was almost asleep; she sat up with a jolt when she realised that stars were beginning to appear and she could no longer pick out the image of the heron mosaic on the tiles. She felt emotionally drained but her mind had been eased and she had made a decision: she had to go on. Whatever Charlie was, whoever he was, this game had to be played out.

She didn't doubt that larger powers were at work: the pond was very large and she was a very, very small fish.

Helene pulled herself out of the *onsen* feeling slightly shrivelled. She had barely noticed the arrival and departure of two younger women. Was it *onsen* etiquette to acknowledge leavers and new arrivals? She didn't know. Nor care much.

Back in the changing rooms she pulled on her yukata. It felt good to be clean again. She was pleased that Charlie hadn't waited for her, although she did think she felt ready to face him. But as soon as she returned to her room, he knocked on her door.

She shuffled to the door.

"Howdy, pardner," he said, smiling although she noted his eyes were careful. "You were gone for hours: I was beginning to wonder if you'd done a bunk."

"And miss out on all this fun?" said Helene, raising an eyebrow.

He smiled broadly, clearly relieved at the return of a degree of her equanimity.

"I've ordered some food," he announced. "I asked them to send up one of everything on the menu to my room – I thought you'd be hungry... and I don't want you getting grumpy."

"Marvellous," said Helene. "Just give me a minute to get dressed and I'll be right over."

In truth she didn't feel very hungry but his thoughtfulness was touching.

She dressed quickly, pulling on a T-shirt and pair of wrinkled harem trousers. Then she plodded to his room in her wooden clogs. She really wished she'd packed the flip-flops that she'd worn in Hawaii.

He opened the door before she'd even knocked on his door.

"No chance of a stealthy approach in those," he said.

Helene smiled wryly.

"Maybe that's why they give them out: not very ninja-like, are they?"

Charlie stood back so she could enter. Spread out on the low table was a mouth-watering buffet. He'd been true to his word and ordered one of everything: prawn tempura rolls; salmon skin rolls; fried tofu; salmon teriyaki; dishes of rice; a plate of sashimi; yakiniku grilled meat; some lightly seared fish; thick, white *udon* noodles; rice crackers; something that looked a bit like chicken curry; miso soup; and two flasks of the green O-cha.

Helene sank onto the cushions arranged around the table and sat cross-legged, more or less comfortably.

Silently he filled a small bowl and handed it to her.

She held one of the tempura rolls between her chopsticks and chewed thoughtfully.

"You're very quiet tonight," he said.

She looked up, meeting his gaze.

"I was thinking about Bill."

Charlie sighed. "I was afraid you'd say that."

"We have knowledge of a murder," said Helene, "and if we don't report it we're complicit in it."

"So? What do you want to do?" he frowned. "Report it to the local police, hope they're not connected to the ryokan – and hope that we wake up alive in the morning?"

Helene shook her head.

"No, of course not, but that doesn't mean that I'll ignore it. Do you understand what I mean?"

He stared at her.

"I suppose you mean you'll write about him in the story for your agent. No holds barred – even about me."

Helene stared back.

"I'll protect your name, Charlie, but that's all I can promise."

He hesitated then nodded.

"I suppose that's about what I'd imagined you'd say." He shrugged. "You've got to do what you think is right, Helene, I know that. But I'll do what I have to do to protect myself, too."

Helene wasn't sure what that meant but she had no choice but to agree. Even so, she felt relieved that things were in the open between them. After a fashion.

Back in her own room, her stomach uncomfortably full, Helene discovered that the futon had been laid out for her with two hard pillows and a thick quilt. Another flask of hot water had also been left together with a pot of the powdered *matcha* tea that she found too bitter.

Relieved that she wasn't going to be sleeping on a hard *tatami* mat, she flopped down onto the futon and pulled the quilt over her. Curled up, she listened to the boards creaking in the room next door as Charlie paced up and down. It seemed to go on for hours and Helene started to feel tense again. When the pacing finally stopped, Helene fell into an uneasy sleep.

The sun was some way advanced when she woke suddenly and precisely. For the first time in several days she felt refreshed and alert. The feeling was surprising.

She glanced at the dirty clothes still in a pile on the floor where she had dropped them. Hopefully the ryokan would have a laundry somewhere: her meagre stock of clean clothes had just run out. She bundled up the washing and left it in a plastic bag by her door. If she could bear it, she'd ask Mayumi what to do.

Charlie's room was already empty, so she made her way along the narrow corridor to find that breakfast was held in another large room in the ryokan. The morning meal didn't differ substantially from the evening meal except for some fermented soya beans, rice porridge, plus more grilled fish.

Charlie had acquired a map of the shrine and he was just pointing out the route to her when Mayumi arrived. Today she was wearing jeans and carrying a pair of well-used hiking boots.

"Dad's asked me to take you up to the shrine," she said, cheerfully. "He's arranged for you to speak to someone who can help you – tell you what you need to know."

"Thanks," said Charlie. "Give us five minutes and we'll be with you."

Helene nodded coldly and Mayumi left. She didn't mention the washing.

"She's helping us," he said leaning towards her. "It wouldn't kill you to be polite to the boss's daughter."

Helene nodded irritably.

"I know: it just makes me uncomfortable knowing that she's *Yakuza*."

Charlie looked equally annoyed.

"They don't call themselves that," he said standing up. "They're known here as *ninkyō dantai*. I thought you'd like to know: you don't want to go getting your facts wrong in your article."

He stood up in one fluid motion and stalked off.

Helene followed him with her eyes, thoughtful.

When they met up outside, he was working hard to seem like his old self but Helene thought she detected a new wariness about him.

Mayumi led the way through a shopping arcade filled with

souvenir shops and udon eateries, chatting easily to Charlie and all but ignoring Helene.

As they left the small town behind them, the path began to climb the side of the mountain, twisting through a dense forest. It gave them shade from the heat promised by the early morning sun and Helene was grateful for that. After 15 minutes of hiking uphill Helene's calves started to protest but Mayumi and Charlie continued to climb steadily, talking with animation about the scenery and the history of the shrine.

"Yes," said Mayumi, "this shrine is said to guard against evil and is dedicated to seafarers: I guess that's why your guy picked it, being an ex-marine and all."

Helene's ears pricked up.

"So you know who we're looking for?" she said.

"Of course!" said Mayumi, smiling condescendingly. "You don't think a gaijin could come here to learn to be a Shinto priest and nobody would notice, do you?"

Helene was silenced. She decided to save her breath for the hike.

Halfway up the mountain, they came to the main entrance. A massive, wooden structure was decorated with the traditional curved roof, but instead of dragons guarding the tiles, a pair of strange sea-creatures stared at each other across the expanse. A pilgrim dressed in the white uniform of the *henro* watched their progress without comment.

It felt like entering another world – or another time.

A little further up stood the usual treasure hall and beyond that a temple complex with a large square to the front, a cluster of wooden buildings around it.

Helene realised that the beliefs of Shintoism and Buddhism had been integrated in one, handy ecumenical site of worship. Japan was a very confusing country. Perhaps pragmatism was the defining characteristic.

Turning to look behind her, Helene was rewarded with views down into the valley. Kotohira was spread out like a quilt, a patchwork of white buildings, red rooves and green fields. It was bigger than she'd realised. It reminded her a bit of Canterbury.

"Now comes the hard bit," said Mayumi, glancing conspiratorially at Charlie. "Five hundred and eighty-three steps up to the main shrine."

She looked at Helene who was still catching her breath.

"If you're not up to it I can call a palanquin to carry you," she said, not bothering to hide the bitchy amusement in her voice.

"I'm fine," said Helene, wiping the sweat from her eyes.

Inside she was thinking: Damn you! I'm half your age but I'm still here, lady!

The path got steeper and the stone steps deeper. Helene was red in the face but pleased to see that even Mayumi was a little short of breath and her animated conversation with Charlie had been curtailed.

They passed a series of stone markers carved with flowing Kanji. They looked like gravestones but for all Helene knew they could have been displaying sacred texts. They were followed by huge cliff carvings of some curious beast.

"Those are *tengu*," said Mayumi, in answer to Charlie's question; "mountain demons."

"Why do you have demons near a shrine?" asked Helene.

Mayumi shrugged. "Why do you have gargoyles on a church?"

Helene's palm was itching to give the younger woman a good slap. On the other hand, it was probably not the best spirit in which to enter a shrine and talk to a priest, she reasoned.

After another stiff hike, they finally they reached the inner shrine.

It was smaller than the other buildings, painted in red, enclosed by a cliff on one side and a dense thicket of trees on the other.

Few of the pilgrims and none of the tourists had bothered to come this far. It seemed they were alone. Helene was beginning to feel conspicuous and paranoid when Mayumi motioned for them to enter the shrine.

It was cool inside, the stone floor smooth under their boots. When Helene's eyes had adjusted to the gloom of the shadowy interior she saw a man wearing a pale blue gown, not unlike a kimono, kneeling with his feet hidden, facing towards an altar. His hair was light brown instead of black; she knew instinctively that this was the man they had come so far to see. He rose in a single, graceful movement and bowed to the shrine. Then he turned to greet them.

"Hello, Charlie," he said.

CHAPTER THIRTEEN

So the man knew Charlie's name. Was that because Mr Matsumoto had told him, or because Charlie had lied about there being 'no name-no pack drill'? Helene couldn't decide – which meant that deep down she still didn't trust him.

The priest motioned to them to step outside: either because he wanted to talk in daylight or perhaps because he was afraid they'd sully the shrine.

"I didn't think I'd see you again," he said.

"No," said Charlie. "None of us did."

After a brief pause, the priest held his hand out and the two men shook hands. Charlie introduced Helene but it seemed that the priest and Mayumi were old friends. Interesting.

"I'll leave you to it," she said. "I've got some business for dad. I'll see you later."

Helene wondered what sort of 'business' the daughter of *Yakuza* might have at a Shinto shrine and Buddhist temple. But she wasn't going to argue; she was too glad to see her go – that beautiful face was unsettling now Helene knew who and what it belonged to.

She turned her attention to the priest.

He was a man of middle height between thirty and forty, stocky build with hazel eyes that slanted upwards ever so slightly, lending his face a subtle, cat-like quality. It was the same when he moved: silkily, but assured. She could imagine him being an effective soldier but the expression on his face was peaceful: a man at ease with himself.

"What shall I call you?" said Helene.

"I go by the name Kazuma now," he said. "It means 'harmony'."

"Is that what you have achieved here?" asked Helene, not sure how to proceed with this potentially bizarre conversation.

The man's lips made a slight moué of amusement.

"Life is a journey: mine is not yet complete – even the wishes of an ant reach to heaven."

Helene smiled back. Instead of being irritated by his opacity, she found his company soothing.

"I'm afraid," she said, "that Charlie and I have come a long way to interrupt your harmony. Will you talk to us about California three years ago? We've already spoken to Bill..." she hesitated... "and we wanted to speak to you – and the Third Man – if we can find him."

The priest stared into the distance, his gaze taking in the trees, the valley and the clouds hovering behind the distant mountains.

"I don't like to talk about things that happened then," the priest said at last. "I was a different person; coming here has allowed me this second chance."

He paused and Helene sensed that she wasn't the only one holding her breath.

The priest went on slowly, "My faith teaches me: 'Our eyes might see un-cleanliness, but let not our minds see un-cleanliness. Our ears might hear un-cleanliness, but let not our minds hear un-cleanliness.' I have done many unclean things in my former life and now I must atone for them."

He looked directly at Charlie.

"I believe," said the priest, "that to commit evil is to be impure: those killed without being shown gratitude for their sacrifice will hold a grudge and become a powerful and evil kami. This unquiet spirit will seek revenge. To do good is to be pure. I have a lot of good left to do."

Helene tried to untangle the meaning behind his words.

"So... you'll help us?" said Helene. "We just want to get our lives back."

"Is that right?" said the priest.

He cast a long glance at Charlie whose expression was veiled. Then the priest looked at Helene, his own gaze direct and open.

"What do you want to know?" he said.

Helene breathed a sigh of relief.

"Can you tell us who the man was that you kidnapped three years ago?" she said.

"No," he said. "I didn't know then and I don't know now. But..."

Helene allowed herself a glimmer of hope.

"But you're not the first person to ask me this. As Charlie can tell you, when a job is done the mercs don't talk about it afterwards: it's safer for their clients and safer for them. Someone with loose lips doesn't last long in that business. I haven't spoken about California to... anyone but a month ago the person you call the Third Man came to see me. He thought he'd recognised the target – the man we took, but he wasn't sure. He showed me a photograph but I couldn't be certain."

"Do you have the photo that he showed you?" said Helene.

The priest shook his head.

"No, he wouldn't let me keep it: said it was too dangerous. But sincerity is a witness to truth."

Then the priest smiled.

"But I drew a picture of the photo he showed me and what I remembered about the man: I somehow thought I might need it one day. It seems that the day has now come."

From his robes, he pulled out a scrap of paper that had been folded many times. He passed it to Helene, throwing a glance at Charlie that Helene couldn't interpret.

She unfolded the sheet with clumsy hands but it wasn't the revelation she'd hoped for. The lively pencil sketch was of a middle aged man with thinning hair and a goatee beard, the face thin with haunted eyes. She didn't recognise him.

She showed the picture to Charlie.

"Do you know him?"

Charlie shook his head.

"No, I never saw him before; I mean, I don't recognise his face."

It was a crushing disappointment: Helene had been so sure that seeing the kidnap victim's face would answer the questions that were piling up.

Helene stared at the priest thoughtfully.

"But the Third Man: he thought he knew this guy. Who did he think it was? Did he give you any clue?"

The priest shook his head slowly.

"No-o. Once he saw that I didn't know anything more, he clammed up. But I'm pretty certain this guy must have had something to do with IT because that's Hassan's field."

"Hassan?"

Helene looked at him, hope flowering again.

"The Third Man," said the priest. "His name is Hassan Ali. These days he has a legit computer security firm that operates out of offices in Riyadh and Dubai. Does that help?"

"Oh, I could kiss you!" said Helene, then realised what she'd said.

"Er, sorry, priests probably aren't supposed to be kissed," she stuttered.

He smiled broadly.

"Not at all! We're allowed to marry – and I rather like being kissed now you mention it."

Helene laughed but leaned forward to plant a demure kiss on the priest's cheek. Then she carefully re-folded the sketch and stuffed it into her back pocket.

"Even in one single leaf on a tree, or in one blade of grass, the awesome Deity presents itself," said the priest in response.

Charlie stood up, too.

"I have no idea what you're talking about, but thanks for everything, mate."

They shook hands again and turned to leave.

"There's one more thing you should know," said the priest. "I've known Hassan for a long time: it's one of the reasons he came to see me. The people who hired us didn't know we knew each other and we preferred to keep it that way. We didn't know you, Charlie, and the other guy seemed like a weak link, so we kept schtum. But when Hassan was here he was on edge and he thought he was being watched. It takes a lot to rattle that guy. And I'll tell you something else that didn't make sense to me – maybe it'll make sense to you. He said: 'I can't believe he worked for them'. It sounded so weird, it stuck in my mind. Does it mean anything to you?"

Helene and Charlie shook their heads. The priest shrugged.

"Well, sorry I couldn't help more. Good luck, you guys. Remember: sincerity is the mother of knowledge."

He re-entered the shrine and sank to his knees, a sculpture once more in prayer.

Helene was excited, a fluttering of hope making the blood run more swiftly through her veins.

"We have to find Hassan Ali. We're getting closer to the truth: I can feel it."

Charlie looked worried.

"What's the matter?" said Helene. "We're getting closer to solving this. This is good news! Isn't it?"

"Yah, I guess. But what worries me is that Hassan visited Kazuma a month ago – three weeks before we got involved."

Helene was stopped in her tracks.

"Oh God! You're right."

The realisation was more than disconcerting. Helene sat down again, the air knocked from her lungs.

She pressed her fingers to her temple.

"Let me think: let's go over what the chain of events," she said. "A month ago Hassan either sees the man he kidnapped – the man he *thinks* he kidnapped – or a photo of him. For some reason this encounter – or photo – worries him. But he's not sure it's the same man because it was three years ago so he brings it to Kazuma to check. So either Hassan saw this man or saw his photo – in a newspaper, perhaps. Well, he can hardly admit that he's a kidnapper so he watches and waits to see if there are going to be any repercussions. Then he starts to think he's being watched. He comes here to see his old buddy but Kazuma can't help him so he leaves again. And then we parachute into the middle of whatever it is. Which makes me think… that you were being watched *before* I got involved."

She paused to look at Charlie but he avoided her gaze.

"And there's one more thing we know…" she continued, "we know that Hassan saw a picture our Mystery Man somewhere unexpected because he said: 'I can't believe he worked for them'."

Charlie was following her thoughts.

"Yes," he agreed, "that implies that Mystery Man was working for someone that Hassan would never expect him to. That would make sense if…"

"If," said Helene, "the Mystery Man was working for the US government or one of their representatives. Now what sort of a person ends up working for the people who kidnapped him in the first place?"

Charlie shrugged. "Stockholm Syndrome?"

"Unlikely," said Helene shaking her head. "There wasn't enough time for that to happen."

"Maybe the kidnapping was just a warning," said Charlie. "You know, a kind of we-can-get-to-you-anywhere warning to make him toe the line."

"Maybe," said Helene. "But in that case why go to the trouble of getting together four out-of-towners to do the job? Why not just hire some local talent to give him a scare? Or somebody on the payroll already? That would only make sense if it was because local people – I mean Americans – would recognise this man. So he must be somebody high profile. Or he was."

"But he wasn't rich," said Charlie, "because Bill said he was living in a shack – that was the word he used, a 'shack'."

"Yes," said Helene, "but a shack with a lot of high tech security. So who does that sound like?"

Charlie nodded thoughtfully.

"Someone out of the mainstream?" he suggested. "Maybe an independent who got too dangerous… maybe because of something he knew?"

Helene sighed. "It's a possibility but it's a lot of 'maybes', too. We need to find Hassan and somehow we need to get him to talk to us."

Charlie nodded. "Okay. We'd better head back to the ryokan. I need to get us tickets and ID. It'll take about 24 hours but Matsumoto can help us."

Helene balked at the idea.

"We don't need his help, do we?" she said. "I feel really uncomfortable with the idea of owing a man like that any favours... I mean, any more favours. Surely the less he knows about what we do next the better?"

Charlie shook his head.

"We don't have a choice, Helene. And Matsumoto is not someone to cross. I would have thought even you would have realised that by now. Besides, he's the one with the contacts in this town. If we want to move fast we're going to need his help."

Helene knew he was right, no matter how much she disliked the thought.

"Damn," she said. "We should have asked Kazuma-*san* to send a few prayers in our direction: I think we're going to need them."

At that moment Mayumi reappeared.

"Speak of the devil," muttered Helene and Charlie threw her an irritated look.

"Did you guys get what you wanted?" said Mayumi.

Charlie scratched his ear thoughtfully.

"Not sure: another piece of the puzzle, perhaps. But we'll be pulling out as soon as we can make the arrangements."

"Pity," said Mayumi, eyeing him up and down as if he were a prize stud. "But there's still plenty of time for me to show you around. Both of you, of course," she added, looking reluctantly in Helene's direction.

"Another time I'd be delighted, Mayumi," said Charlie, turning the full wattage of his smile on her, "but we really need to get back and make plans. And I need to tell your father where we're at."

Helene threw Charlie a sharp look but it bounced off him

regardless. He just seemed to be a bit too cosy with his new *Yakuza* friend.

"Do you have wi-fi?" Helene asked Mayumi. "I'd like to get online if I can."

"Of course," said Mayumi, over her shoulder. "This is Japan."

Helene walked back to the town in silence, leaving a distance of some yards between her and Mayumi and Charlie, who chatted away like old friends. Helene's hip was hurting like blazes but she was damned if she'd let either of them know.

Her thoughts and feelings had done another revolution since Kazuma had revealed the date of Hassan's visit. The great weight of guilt had fallen away on learning that it wasn't her involvement that had interrupted Charlie's sabbatical. It might have speeded things up though...

Back at the *onsen* Mayumi and Charlie went their separate ways. Even at a distance Helene could sense the frisson of regret. Charlie jogged to catch her up.

"You're very quiet," he said.

"True," said Helene. "I've got a lot to think about."

He cast a sideways glance at her. "Any conclusions?"

Helene shook her head.

"Not really. Other than that we have to find Hassan and persuade him to speak to us. The fact that Kazuma has helped us is in our favour but other than that we can't guarantee Hassan will tell us anything... well, we'll just have to cross that bridge when we come to it."

He followed her into her room. Helene felt was irked by his too casual assumption of invitation. She lowered herself carefully to one of the floor cushions and eased her aching hip into a cross-legged position then opened the laptop. It hadn't occurred to her to try to hide it – not in a *Yakuza*-owned guesthouse. Besides there wasn't anything about their business that Matsumoto didn't seem to know.

Charlie stared out of the window, unspeaking, his mind clearly somewhere else.

Helene tried to ignore his silent presence and instead surfed to the website that he'd created.

'You have 1 comment.'

Her pulse fluttered.

She opened the comment box with some difficulty, her hand trembling over the laptop mousepad.

Helene read it quickly:

NO ONE WILL BELIEVE YOU

She read it again and then it read it out loud as if it could possible make more sense that way.

"We've had a hit on our website," she said. "It says: 'No one will believe you.' What does that mean? Who won't believe what? I don't get it?" She looked at Charlie. "What do you think?"

"It means," he said slowly, "That they think we know more than we do. It's a warning to you not to publish."

He slumped down next to her and they sat staring at the screen. He was so near that she could feel the damp heat of his body.

After a short pause, Helene typed in a reply. Before she pressed the 'send' button, she showed it to him. A smile tugged at his mouth.

"Yeah, that's good," he said.

Helene pressed 'send' and the message spiralled away: 'Someone always believes'.

"The thing is," said Helene, closing down the laptop, "maybe we really do know more than we realise – we just haven't put the pieces together yet. Charlie, can you access facial recognition software from here, from this laptop?"

He nodded, "Yah, I can do that."

"What would happen," said Helene, "if you put in Kazuma's sketch of the Mystery Man?"

Charlie shook his head slowly.

"I'm not sure: facial recognition software works by comparing digital images. A computer program uses algorithms – a maths program, right? It compares landmark features against a database of faces: the relative size, position and shape of the nose, eyes, cheekbones and jaw. Then the computer searches for matches. I think there are too many variables with a sketch because it's not an exact rendering."

He looked up, registering the disappointment on her face.

"Could we at least try it?" she said.

He sighed.

"Honestly, we'd be wasting our time. We'd need to get the original photo from Hassan. Or at least get the name of the person he thinks it is and find an online photo. Sorry, Helene."

"Oh, well. It was worth a punt. I don't suppose there's any point in emailing the drawing to Hassan, is there?"

"I doubt it. I mean, what would you do if you got an email like that? I know what I'd do: I'd run like hell and bury myself so deep no-one would ever find me."

"I guess so," agreed Helene sadly. "Well, unless you've got a better idea it looks like we're going to Dubai."

He opened his mouth to speak.

"Before you ask," interrupted Helene, "no, I haven't packed a burkini."

He laughed.

"Pity. But I was going to say we should check that he's definitely going to be in Dubai. Kazuma said he had offices in Riyadh, too."

"Fair point. Although I can't imagine he's going to advertise his movements at this precise moment – not now he knows he's being watched."

"I disagree," he said. "He's better off staying in plain sight and looking like the poster boy for clean living. That way the Feds, or whoever, have nothing to report."

"Oh okay," said Helene, pleasantly surprised by his optimism. "Let's assume Hassan has an assistant who manages his diary. If I can find out who his customers are I can probably blag the info by pretending to be a secretary from another company."

"Good thinking, Bat Woman."

Helene raised an eyebrow.

"Don't sound so surprised," she said crisply. "This is my area of expertise now."

He mimed locking his lips and Helene frowned in irritation. Turning her back to him she opened the laptop again. It didn't take long to find out that one of Hassan's key customers was a private security firm operating out of west London.

"I'll need to use the phone," said Helene. "Do you think Matsumoto has a secure line that he'd let us use?"

"I'd be surprised if he didn't," replied Charlie. "You feel okay owing him another favour?"

"No," said Helene. "Frankly I think this is going to come back and bite us in the backside, but what other choice do we have?"

He shrugged and stood up. He slid the door closed behind him and Helene was left alone with her thoughts.

Twenty minutes later she was starting to feel annoyed when he finally returned.

"Okay, we can use his office: Mayumi has fixed it for us."

Helene forced herself to restrain a comment. Arguing with Charlie about the boss's steely-eyed daughter would get them precisely nowhere. She hated biting her tongue all the time: it didn't come naturally and it was starting to give her ulcers.

Charlie led her back to the boss's office. Helene tried to force herself to keep her eyes from the floor even though they seemed magnetically drawn to the spot where she had seen Bill's blood. At least the rug hadn't been replaced yet.

Helene gave herself a mental shake and prepared her script for getting the information she wanted.

She dialled the number she'd found on the security company's website and listened to the ring tone. The call was answered quickly.

"Good afternoon, Shippos Security. How may I direct your call?"

"Oh, good afternoon. This is Julie Fielding calling from the International Herald Tribune. I'd like to speak with Mr Fenner, please."

There was a hesitation whilst the receptionist decided how to answer.

"I'm sorry, Miss Fielding, but Mr Fenner isn't available. All press enquiries have to go through our publicity department: if you'll just hold the line, please…"

"No, I really need to speak to Mr Fenner. I'm going to be in London soon and I'd really like to schedule a meeting. Could you put me through to his assistant, please?"

The receptionist was clearly an old hand at dealing with the Press.

"I'm sorry but Miss Williams isn't available at the moment. I can put you through to publicity straight away."

"If you could just give me Sadie Williams' email, I'll contact her like that," said Helene.

"You mean Paula Williams: I'm sorry, Miss Fielding but it's company policy not to give out personal email addresses. You can contact our publicity department on…"

"You know what," said Helene, "I think I'll just drop in next time I'm in town but thanks for your time."

She replaced the receiver with a grin on her face.

"Got it," she said. "Paula Williams."

He saluted her, smiling.

"Oh, Queen of Blaggers, I am in awe!"

"Thank you, kind sir," replied Helene acidly. "I do this for a living, you know."

"What, lying? Pretending to be someone you're not? And there was I thinking that was just me."

He smiled broadly and Helene resisted the urge to throw something heavy at him. He had a knack of tapping into her more aggressive side.

She took a deep breath and dialled again.

"*Masa alkhair*, Cube IT Solutions," said the disembodied voice.

"*Masa alnur*," replied Helene. "This is Paula Williams from Shippos Security. I have a call from Mr Fenner for Mr Ali: may I put it through."

"I apologise Miss Williams, but Mr Ali is in our Riyadh office until the conference and then back on Tuesday. Can I…?"

"Oh, of course," said Helene. "I'll call him there. Thank you very much. *Ma'assalama*."

Charlie looked at her.

"Why did you cut her off? We don't know where the conference is."

"Because," said Helene, "if I'd have said anymore she'd have guessed that I wasn't Paula Williams. Besides, there can't be that many international IT conferences in the next couple of days that feature Shippos Security and Cube Solutions."

He was trying very hard not to look impressed.

"You speak Arabic," he said.

It wasn't a question.

Helene shrugged.

"Sure. I lived in Kuwait for several years. I'd have been a pretty poor journalist if I hadn't."

His look was enigmatic. Helene shrugged. Whatever.

She was also right about finding the IT conference: it took her less than two minutes. She smiled, pleased with herself.

"So?" he asked, frowning enquiringly.

"Pack your bucket and spade," said Helene. "We're going to the seaside."

"Bognor Regis?" he asked, raising his eyebrows in theatrical disbelief.

"Close... Bahrain."

"Bugger Bognor!"

CHAPTER FOURTEEN

TWENTY-FOUR HOURS LATER THEY LANDED AT BAHRAIN International Airport, a strip of land in the north-east of the archipelago.

Helene could feel the heat burning through the thin soles of her shoes and her clothes sticking to her on the short walk to the sleek line of waiting taxis. It felt familiar: she'd missed being in this part of the world.

She had decided to stick with 'Julie Fielding' of the International Herald Tribune. There was no point attempting to get a better alias: if Hassan Ali was any good at his job – and she suspected he was – he'd have her banged to rights within minutes, whatever name she used. She figured it was better to make her alias obvious to him in the hope that it would signal her good intentions. She hoped. Or maybe he'd just think she was dangerously inept...

Charlie called himself Jason Hector, which seemed to fit in with their 'Helene of Troy' theme. As he'd said: what better place to hide than in plain view?

Thankfully the taxi was air-conditioned, although Helene could see that the external temperature gauge was topping 39°C. Mind you, it could get almost that hot in London in a bad year – but usually without the air-con. Cornwall, beautiful Cornwall, was always cooler.

A dust storm was brewing and the visibility was reducing rapidly. On the short ride from the airport to Manama, Helene stared through the window, gaining hazy impressions of a yellow landscape with palm trees, a thin strip of blue ocean in the distance, all set against a backdrop of high-rises as the city sped towards them.

She was glad she didn't have to breathe the dusty air outside. The air inside the taxi was cool and smelled of spice.

"So which hotel did you book us in to?" said Helene, breaking the silence.

Charlie smiled. "It's a surprise."

"Somewhere low key, I hope," said Helene, not very hopefully.

He didn't reply but he looked very pleased with himself.

The Manama Ritz exceeded every expectation of an elite number of top-class hotels. It had its own 22-berth marina with a private island attached. A clutch of small villas faced the sea and the main hotel was the last word in splendour but with less opulence and more true elegance than Helene had expected.

The taxi swept them to the entrance and a uniformed flunkey glided towards the car, opening the door with a practised flourish.

"Nice choice," she whispered. "Subtle."

"Nothing but the best for the Herald Tribune," he replied.

"On expenses, is it?" enquired Helene.

Charlie didn't reply, merely continuing to smile at her.

At least they'd wouldn't have to travel far to the conference: it was being held on site.

The reception clerk was equally well trained, summoning a guide to show them to their twin-room villa; Helene assumed their minimal luggage was having its own guided tour as it was expertly whisked away out of their sight. The only thing they carried between them was Helene's shoulder bag and the laptop case.

Mr Matsumoto had been most helpful in supplying them with fake passports, visas, credit cards and appropriate clothing. It worried Helene but Charlie had brushed aside her concerns. And with bigger problems to face, Helene had no choice but to let it go. For now, at least.

Their villa was exquisite. Each of the twin bedrooms was beautifully furnished with rattan doors opening out onto a shaded terrace overlooking the sea. The living room was more comfortable and less corporate than was usually found in such hotels, although they'd possibly overdone the display of vases and anodyne photos in frames. But at least it was equipped with every possible electronic entertainment device and technology to ease one's visit.

A conference programme had been thoughtfully laid out on the coffee table. It said that Hassan Ali from Cube IT was speaking at 10.30am. Very thoughtful of the hotel staff. Useful to know.

Helene continued her tour, wandering through the villa. Her bath, almost big enough to do laps in, overlooked a small, private garden. At present the tub was filled with cold water and scattered with rose petals. She felt for the poor maid who would have to scoop those out on a regular basis. The villa also had its own private infinity pool, just a squeak from the real life ocean; the blues of each body of water not quite matching: a lapse in attention to detail, Helene thought smugly. It was the only imperfection she could find, in truth.

Perhaps their guide had taken the scenic route because Helene discovered that her case had already been delivered to her bedroom. It had also been emptied, the clothes hung in the wardrobe and her wash bag filleted into the bathroom. It made her feel uncomfortable, but that was what people expected in expensive, high-end hotels. Other people.

Charlie tapped on her bedroom door, his lanky torso leaning against the frame.

"Is madam happy with her room?"

Helene couldn't help smiling. "Not bad," she admitted. "Not bad at all."

It had been some years since that her job had paid for such luxury.

"One aims to please," he smirked. "By the way, have you seen the security they've got here?"

Helene nodded thoughtfully. She'd have had to be amazingly unobservant not to spot the armed guards at the entrance and exit points.

"Do you think they're here all the time or just for the conference?" she wondered.

"I'm guessing for the conference: but it could be someone heavy who's staying here."

"Do you know any of the... er... security staff?" said Helene.

Charlie shook his head.

"Not so far but I think they're mostly just regular army – not specialists. I'll let you know."

"Yes, keep me up to date with the sit-rep," said Helene.

He looked momentarily surprised, then replied: "Ten-four."

"Okay, see you later," she said.

He frowned.

"Where are you going?"

"You're on *my* home turf now," she said. "Trust me. I'm going to go and find out how to contact Hassan Ali at the conference tomorrow."

He watched as she stuffed a thick wad of Dinars into an envelope.

"If you get into trouble, speed dial 1," he said, tossing her a sleek, black phone.

She gave him a withering look but pocked the phone all the same.

They arranged to meet up in a couple of hours and Charlie phoned to order a light meal to be eaten on their private terrace. Helene intended to have a swim in the pool after and maybe book a massage – as it was on expenses. But first she had to find Hassan Ali – otherwise she was going to look damned stupid.

She wandered back through the delightful grounds, casually observing the other guests. More conference attendees were arriving, if the array of men in a variety of inelegant leisure wear were anything to go by. Helene took a detour when she heard a pack of British businessmen braying loudly by the bar. She didn't want to be noticed. There appeared to be far fewer women attending, and those who were seemed to be taking the opportunity to relax under the sunshades, I-pods plugged in and sunglasses discouraging casual solicitation.

At reception Helene asked to see the conference organiser.

"Is there a problem, madam?" said the concierge, sounding alarmed.

"Nothing that I'm sure can't be sorted out in a moment," said Helene.

She was escorted to a small office and greeted by a young but suave man in a business suit with flashing dark eyes, Arabian profile and an American accent.

"Good afternoon, Miss Fielding. My name is Aamil al-Rahhbi and I'm the conference organiser. I believe you have a small concern?"

"Thank you, Mr al-Rahhbi. I'm sure it is a very small concern. You see, I am very keen to meet a certain person attending the conference. It would help me enormously if I and my colleague Mr Hector could be seated next to the person at lunch, for example," said Helene.

"Ah, I see. My regrets, Miss Fielding, but the luncheon seating has already been arranged," said the young man.

"Naturally," said Helene. "I would expect such perfectionism towards organisation from an establishment of this kind. I realise that my request would incur some difficulties and I would, of course, wish to compensate your team for their additional work."

The young man nodded to show that he understood.

"Well, it might be possible," he said softly. "And who is the gentleman you wish to meet?"

"Mr Hassan Ali of Cube IT," said Helene.

"Ah, that is a particularly difficult case," said the young man.

Which didn't surprise Helene at all. She was used to the subtle bartering that was required.

"Of course," she said, standing as if to leave, "I understand. Thank you for your time."

The young man looked slightly panicked.

"Oh, but I'm sure an accommodation can be made for you, Miss Fielding," he said quickly.

Helene turned.

"Thank you so much, Mr al-Rahhbi. I am very grateful. Please assure your whole team of my gratitude and if a small gratuity could assuage their extra efforts, I would be delighted."

He looked relieved that she had understood.

Helene passed him the well-stuffed envelope. The young man slipped it into his pocket without a second glance. Very smooth.

Satisfied, Helene allowed him to usher her from the office.

Mission accomplished.

When she got back to the villa, Charlie was nowhere to be seen. Slightly relieved, Helene decided against a massage, instead changing into a newly acquired swimming costume and plunging into the private pool. The water was warmer than she would have normally liked, but it was refreshing all the same. For a moment she had a pang for the chilly seawater of the Jubilee Pool in Penzance's outdoor lido. Another lifetime.

After swimming some twenty or so lengths, she eased herself from the pool and flopped onto a lounger under a sun umbrella and was soon fast asleep.

The sun had shifted several degrees before the sensation of being watched woke her abruptly. Charlie cast a shadow over her.

"Hello, sleeping beauty," he said. "I thought I was going to have to wake you with a kiss."

"Knowing my luck you'd have turned into a frog," she said.

"Not necessarily," he said, sitting close to her on the sun lounger. "Would you like to risk it?"

Helene could see that his hair was damp from the shower and she smelled the soap on his cleanly shaven skin; his blue eyes were teasing, inviting.

"I've booked us a place at lunch with Hassan Ali tomorrow," she said, avoiding a direct reply. "We'll have to find a way to make our move then."

Charlie smiled and stood up.

"Dinner has arrived – I'm ready when you are."

Under his steady gaze she wrapped her towel primly around

her and tried to walk naturally. She could feel his eyes burning between her shoulder blades.

She wished she'd kept the yukata but as it was several thousand miles away she changed into a long-sleeved blouse, the useful harem pants and a new pair of flip-flops.

The humidity of the day increased as evening approached, the air heavy and moist. Helene felt overdressed but Charlie looked comfortable in chinos and an open-necked shirt. Conversation felt too awkward so she gave her attention to the food – a delicious array of delicate, portion-sized dishes: *machboos*, fish with rice; sweet rice with dates; falafel; spicy chicken wrapped in pita bread; a glutinous looking fish sauce; several delicate pastries; and a *dalla* pot of thick, black coffee.

Helene used the silence to tease out an idea that had begun to squirm around in her mind.

Replete at last, Helene leaned back. Charlie was sipping from a tiny coffee cup. He watched her look up, a smile twitching at the corner of his mouth.

"How do we get him to talk?" said Helene, steering the conversation towards business.

There was no need to explain whom she meant.

Even so, Charlie sighed and rolled his eyes.

"Luck: work on his conscience – I don't know," he said. "We'll have to wing it."

Helene nodded slowly.

"Okay. I've made a photocopy of Kazuma's sketch. I thought I'd let him catch a glimpse of it at lunchtime then invite him to meet us here at the villa. At least then we can talk to him in private. But will he come?"

"I wouldn't take bets on it," he replied. "Not if he wouldn't talk to Kazuma – someone he knew and trusted."

Helene felt a shiver run through her.

"What would scare a man like Hassan?" she said. "An ex-mercenary, a rich and successful businessman. What would scare him this much?"

"I've been trying to work that out," he said. "Someone more powerful: that's all I can come up with."

"Yes, that's what I thought, too," she agreed. "And who is

powerful enough to follow us across three continents – and to have the technology to find our website – someone who might be bothered by the words: White House, Langley and Spycatcher?"

Helene looked directly at Charlie. "You see what I'm saying?"

"Jesus!"

He sat up straighter.

"So my theory is," continued Helene, her voice barely louder than a whisper, "that whatever we've stumbled into, it goes all the way to the White House – maybe even to the President himself. That's why we're being hunted and that's why Hassan is so scared. I've been going over and over it: it's the only thing that makes any sense."

Charlie stared back at her.

"I think we'd better check the website," he said at last.

"We should do it out here," she said. "We'll have to assume that we're under surveillance. The rooms could be bugged."

"It wouldn't make any difference," he said. "If they were watching us they could hear everything we're saying right now using a boom microphone. The beach is our best bet: we'd know if there was anyone with a quarter of a mile of us."

"We'll if they're listening now," said Helene, "they know we're getting closer. We have to get to Hassan straightaway... the website can wait."

"Agreed," he said. "I found out which room he's staying in." He raised his eyebrows at her irritated expression. "I had to do something while you were out," he said, looking smug. Then his expression changed and became hard. "I think we should invite Mr Ali for a walk on the beach."

Hurrying now, Helene made one adjustment to her wardrobe: she changed her flip-flops for a pair of trainers. She hoped she wasn't going to have to run after such a filling meal, but better safe than sorry.

But by the time she'd made her way through the hotel's grounds and lobby she was feeling sweaty and distinctly underdressed. Several women guests, draped with designer evening dresses and festooned with jewels had swept their gazes up and down and found her wanting; even some of the hotel staff looked mildly shocked at her lack of adornment.

Typical: she'd have been less obtrusive if she'd looked like a high-class hooker.

"Pay no attention," he said, hiding a smile.

Helene wasn't surprised that he'd noticed the negative attention she was getting: he seemed to notice everything. It was comforting to have his support – if that's what it was.

The irony was that to the men of the hotel, those robed and those in suits, she may as well have been invisible. Helene tried to remember when it was that men had first stopped looking at her. From her fortieth birthday? Between forty and forty-five? Post fifty? She couldn't remember, nor did she care. Much. It would have been a liberating thought... if weren't so damned depressing.

At Hassan's door they encountered their first serious problem: two serious problems weighing at least 200 pounds each.

"*Masa alkhair*," said Helene, nervously.

The two bodyguards exchanged a glance. Helene immediately caught their mood. She realised she'd made a mistake: it had been too long since she'd been in the Middle East.

"You should do the talking," she whispered to Charlie. "I'll stand back."

Silently she passed him the photocopy in a sealed envelope.

"Evening, gents," said Charlie. "We'd like to see Mr Ali, please."

"He is not to be disturbed," said the human portcullis on the left.

"He'll want to see us," said Charlie.

"No exceptions," repeated the giant in good English.

"It's important that he gets our message," said Charlie, the slightest hint of granite in his voice.

It made the guards look directly at him for the first time. This man commands, their body language seemed to acknowledge.

"Please give him this envelope and we'll leave," said Charlie.

He didn't offer to bribe them: there was no point insulting the men who were going to help.

Portcullis accepted the envelope with a nod of his head: Helene and Charlie had no choice but to leave.

"What now?" she hissed.

"There are only two ways to leave the building from here," he said. "Down the fire exit and along the main corridor. Take your pick. Have you still got your phone?"

She nodded.

"Good. Phone me if you see him first: speed-dial 1."

"And do what while I'm waiting for you?" said Helene impatiently. "Am I supposed to wrestle him to the ground, knocking out the two goons first, of course?"

"I wouldn't be at all surprised," said Charlie coolly, "but I was rather hoping you'd use your charm. I'm told you have some."

"Great plan," snarled Helene, and stalked off.

God, but he could put her back up.

She waited, spending two frustrating minutes thinking of things she should have said to Charlie to cut him down to size.

But then she heard someone leaving Hassan Ali's hotel room and walking towards her. He was alone. He was about the same age as Charlie, she noted, but shorter and more wiry-looking. His mouth seemed to be permanently pouting. It made Helene think of botox.

He saw her at once and his face hardened.

"Miss La Borde? Is this a subtle threat?"

He surprised her: his voice had a Black Country accent that he seemed to wish to suppress. Hassan Ali held up the photocopied sheet of paper. Helene realised he hadn't used her alias.

"No!" said Helene startled. "We just needed to get your attention so you'd talk to us."

"We? Who's with you?" he said, his eyes narrowing.

"You must know," she said softly. "You know who I am and you know why I'm here. You must know *who* I'm with."

She paused but he didn't reply: "The man who flew the helicopter," she said, "We must talk to you. Please. Will you come with me now?"

"If you're lying to me, Miss La Borde," he said slowly, "I'll choke the breath from your throat and leave your corpse in the desert for the cormorants to feast on your dead eyes. I hope I'm being clear."

"Crystal," said Helene, trying to swallow with a throat as dry as bones. "I'd like to phone my partner to join us, if you don't mind."

"No tricks!" he snapped.

"None, I promise," she said, her voice crackling with sincere fear.

She pressed speed-dial 1 and heard Charlie's curt, "Yes?"

"He'll meet with us," said Helene, "where we agreed. Five minutes."

"Are you wearing a wire, Miss La Borde?" Hassan asked silkily.

Helene shook her head dumbly as Hassan Ali swept a small, black device up and down her body, pushed her round and repeated the exercise across her back.

"So far, so good," he said.

They walked down the main staircase. Helene was glad he had decided against the lift: she didn't think she could have faced being alone with him in a confined space. Walking helped to disguise the trembling in her legs.

A spectacular sunset cast a bloody glow over the beach. Charlie was silhouetted at the water's edge.

"Thanks for coming," said Charlie.

"I do recognise you," said Hassan.

Then he swept the device over Charlie who stood, arms stretched out as if preparing for crucifixion.

"What do you want?" said Hassan.

"Who is the man in the picture?" said Helene.

"Why do you want to know?"

Helene spoke quickly, spitting the words out.

"Because if we don't find out soon, the agents who are undoubtedly following us will catch us and lock us up for a hundred years – or kill us. I don't want that to happen without knowing why," she said. "We know it's to do with the man of three years ago that you, Bill Bailey, Charlie and Kazuma kidnapped. We suspect he knew something that the US government wants kept quiet. All *we* want to do is find out enough to make them leave us alone."

"Just talking to you is dangerous," said Hassan.

"You agreed to meet with us, mate," said Charlie. "And you know they're probably watching us. Passing on what you know is the only thing that's going to keep you alive now. Which is why you're here."

"Maybe I'm here to kill you," said Hassan calmly.

Charlie shook his head. Helene shook her knees.

"No," said Charlie. "If you wanted to kill us you'd have had it done as soon as you heard we were here."

Hassan smiled.

"True." He seemed to be weighing his decision. Then he spoke.

"The man we took was a US citizen: his name Wally Manfred," he paused as if expecting a reaction from them. "He is – or was – part of an underground team of computer hackers, dedicated to finding out all the dirty little secrets that the US government would rather were kept hidden. The hackers call themselves the Gene Genies. They developed the program that was used by Wikileaks to reveal top secret information on Guantanamo Bay detainees. That's how powerful they've become. Three years ago the Gene Genies were just getting going but they were pretty vocal and the media were starting to take them seriously: Wally Manfred was their founder. My guess is that the spooks thought stopping him would stop the Gene Genies... or he came across something so sensitive that we were hired to remove him."

Helene was floundering in the excess of information after such a long drought. But something came to her from the morass.

"When you talked to Kazuma you said to him, 'I can't believe he worked for them'. What did you mean by that?"

Hassan looked at her, a calculating expression on his face.

"I don't know why Kazuma trusts you," he said after a short pause, "but he's never led me wrong before so I'm going to tell you what I know. A month ago I came across an old article on a website. I was surfing hacker sites for a client. That's when I saw his photo: Wally Manfred. I recognised him straightaway. The article said that he was working for the US government, specifically the NSA. It seemed so unlikely that it caused a lot of noise in the hacker community at the time. Some people didn't believe it and thought it was some kind of set up to discredit the Gene Genies. Which is ironic when you think about it. But the point is the photo was taken *after* we did the job. The US government must have had some serious leverage on him to turn a guy like Wally Manfred."

Helene shivered.

"What do you think he found out?" she said.

"I've been trying to work that out. All I can tell you is that before he disappeared – before we disappeared him – he'd been researching the Wall Street Crash of 1929 and the US debt at the end of the First World War."

Helene looked at Charlie blankly. He shook his head, bewildered.

"Since then I've looked everywhere I can think of," said Hassan, "but I couldn't find anything else. All other traces of what he'd researched have been pretty comprehensively wiped: I couldn't say by whom. The trail I could find – Wally Manfred's one weak spot was that he had – has – a daughter living in San Bernadino. She's still there. I've checked and re-checked her bank balance and there's been no change in her status in the last three years: no excess money either going into or out of her account and she doesn't have a new car. So if Wally Manfred has been bought off, the money hasn't gone to his daughter."

"But they wouldn't need to buy him off," reasoned Helene. "By kidnapping him they'd already shown that they could get him any time they wanted to and, by extension, her. They wouldn't even need to threaten her."

"Maybe," said Hassan, "but there's something else. Shortly after that photo was taken, Wally Manfred was diagnosed with advanced Alzheimer's. I tracked him down and ever since he's been living in a home for dementia sufferers in a retirement village near his daughter. Here's the weird bit: I've checked his medical records and there is nothing, I mean *nothing* that shows he's had any medical tests whatsoever in the last seven years."

"Which means what?" said Helene, struggling to take in all the new information.

"It means," said Hassan impatiently, "that up until the day he was institutionalised, Wally Manfred was as healthy as you or me."

"Oh my God!" said Helene quietly as the realisation sank in. "We have to find that poor man!"

Charlie nodded. "Yes, whatever he knows, that's the key to this."

Hassan shrugged. "Yes, I think so. Whatever it is – it's big. NSA big."

"Will you help us?" said Helene.

Hassan looked at her levelly, the failing sun lengthening his shadow into an alien spindle.

"I already have. I'm done. I'm just a businessman these days. I have a good life: I'd like to keep it that way. They'll leave me alone now."

"You seem pretty sure of that," said Helene, bitingly.

Hassan smiled. "I am. I've passed the baton: they'll follow you now. I'm past history."

Helene nearly choked.

"You... you've set us up!"

"I wouldn't say that," said Hassan, curling his plump lip. "You got what you wanted. I got what I wanted: that's a fair trade."

Helene was breathless with indignation.

"He's right," said Charlie, breaking his silence. "We've got what we need: it's time for us to go."

But Helene wasn't finished yet.

"Don't you care about Wally Manfred?" half choking as she spat out the words.

Hassan almost laughed out loud.

"No! Why should I? All I care is that I never hear his name again."

"But why did you tell us and not Kazuma?" said Helene, her voice becoming shrill.

"Who says I didn't?"

Helene's mouth dropped open in shock.

Hassan walked away leaving her and Charlie to the night.

CHAPTER FIFTEEN

THE AEROPLANE BEGAN ITS FINAL DESCENT. HELENE PEERED out of the dirty window and was rewarded by the sight of a wide, flat valley, ringed by yellowing hills and a summer blue sky.

Passengers had been cheerfully informed by the captain that the temperature in San Bernardino was currently a pleasant 88°F which Helene worked out was about 31°C: still considerably cooler than Bahrain and with a welcome lack of humidity. She felt as if she'd been damp ever since she'd left Hawaii.

Charlie woke up as the wheels touched the tarmac and the small jet bumped and shuddered to a standstill. He looked relatively refreshed considering they had just travelled for 24 hours, leaving their Manama villa in the early hours, travelling east and re-crossing the dateline in the process. Technically it was two days later. Or was it? Helene's tired brain refused to cooperate.

She'd spent most of the journey typing up her notes, trying to create a narrative thread, honing her questions, refining her theories. She hadn't been able to go online during the nightmarish tangle of flights, so whether or not the NSA were still communicating via the website was unknown to her. Truthfully, Helene had been appalled by what Hassan had told her. She and Charlie had discussed the ramifications at length – with few conclusions. Neither could work out why Wally Manfred was still alive when it would have been so much easier – and cheaper – to have killed him. It wasn't as if the efforts had subdued the Gene Genies: if anything the reverse was true.

"Looks like we're here," she said, rather pointlessly.

Charlie nodded but didn't speak.

Helene eased her stiff body out of the economy bucket seat and stretched slowly, an orchestra of creaks joining her in sympathy. He moved with his customary felid grace. He reached into the overhead locker and pulled out a smart, canvas shoulder bag and a jacket: his entire complement of luggage. Everything else had been jettisoned at Manama. Helene was similarly unencumbered, reverting to her grab bag and a change of underwear. She was wearing a new wig, cut into a blonde bob and feature sunglasses; Charlie made do with an LA Galaxy baseball cap that he'd picked up when they'd changed planes in Los Angeles.

Helene hadn't been happy when he'd shown her the new passport. She was now travelling as 'Mona Samovar'. She couldn't say whether she was most annoyed at being named after a teapot or the implications attached to the first name. He didn't say and she didn't ask: which was beginning to sum up their present relations. He was travelling as 'Jack Duncan', a carefully neutral name.

First they had to find a car. Easy enough, the airport boasted a choice of six rental companies. The shuttle bus took them direct to a massive parking lot. A line of chesty saloons covered in a fine film of dust were paraded in front of them.

Yes, the clerk had told them, they were all latest models and yes, they all had SatNav and air-con as standard: automatic, naturally. Charlie paid a week's rental in advance, although 'paid' was rather a loose term these days. Helene slumped gratefully into the armchair-size seats and Charlie blasted the fetid air with super-cooled air-con.

He punched in the address for Arrowhead Springs and they cruised out of town past a MacDonalds museum and small shopping mall. A sign proclaimed: San Bernardino – 99th largest city in the US. Helene wondered irrelevantly who had made 100th.

The road rose up into the hills, snaking past arid foothills, scrubby vegetation, and very little else. Occasionally a huge truck passed them carrying livestock, if the air holes in the sides were anything to go by. Helene felt a brief pity for the animals inside that were soon to be carcasses. She knew how they felt.

As they climbed higher, she was immediately struck by the bizarre appearance of an enormous rock formation. It looked primitive, almost manmade.

"I can see why this place got its name," he said.

Helene nodded silently.

On the side of the mountain a natural formation of eroded soil and rock marked out a gigantic arrowhead, pointing directly at the unusual combination of hot springs and cool mountain water at the foot of the hill: the eponymous Arrowhead Springs.

The road whisked them past the outcrop and Helene wondered what it must have looked like to the Native Americans who had lived there centuries before the palefaces arrived. Well, like an arrowhead, obviously, but she wondered if they'd been aware of the healing properties of the sulphurous hot springs. Probably: she reckoned that hippies in the seventies thought they'd invented homeopathy and holistic thinking, but really they were only picking up the threads of centuries of knowledge, most people having been blind-sided by the immediate and obvious benefits of medicine and scientific study. Helene could certainly vouch for the improving soak in Kotohira's *onsen*, although the soothing water didn't seem to have done much to improve Matsumoto's milk of human kindness. Better not think about that: better not think about the blood on the floor...

Helene shook her head and tried to concentrate on what she was going to say to Wally Manfred's daughter. It was hard to think past, "Hello", let alone plan a subtle strategy that would encourage the daughter of a kidnapped computer hacker to talk. What had Charlie said about Hassan? We'll have to wing it.

Eventually the SatNav informed them that they had reached the end of their journey: they were still less than forty minutes from the airport.

Charlie pulled into a long, snaking estate, fringed by a parched ring of mature trees. The houses were older than Helene had expected, 1930s one-storey buildings, large units but with surprisingly small gardens, the wooden frames shoulder to shoulder as if preparing to circle the wagons and ward off some surprise attack.

One of the smaller houses caught Helene's eye.

"This is it," she said, "3744 Elder View."

The house had an air of sadness if not outright neglect. The lawn had been mown but not recently; the shutters had been painted, but a couple of years back; the windows had been washed once but were now covered with the omnipresent dust.

Charlie parked across the street and half a block up. They were watched by a small group of bored children, playing in the street, their ragtaggle of bicycles abandoned on the brown verge.

One of the bolder ones yelled out, "Who you come to see?"

Helene turned round and smiled.

A small, tanned face with grubby nose looked up at her owlishly. She suspected that this child should have been wearing his spectacles but refused to do so. He fancied himself as the leader so Helene decided to humour him. The boy wiped his hand across his face, spreading the snot in a glistening snail trail. Helene was revolted and amused at the same time.

"Do you know Barbara Manfred?" she said.

"She won't speak to you," said the snotty child.

"Why's that?"

The child looked up and up as the man's height cast him in shadow.

"She don't like people, mister, specially not strangers. My

mom said she's got blues, but I ain't never seen her wear nothing blue."

"Does she have any friends?" asked Charlie carefully. "Maybe people who come and visit her sometimes?"

The boy shook his head and Helene noticed that the other children were silently agreeing from a safe distance.

"Naw. She don't want no friends. Just them men who come sometimes, but I don't think she likes 'em much, cuz they never stay long, no never mind."

"Who do you think they are then?" said Helene softly.

"My pa says they're the Feds and that Miz Manfred is a retired bank robber. I don't think girls can be bank robbers, can they?"

The rest of the dusty children shook their heads in unison. Equal opportunities wasn't a term they were likely to learn around here.

"And what does your mum, er, mom say about Ms Manfred?" prompted Helene.

The child shrugged.

"She says that they're just IRS and Miz Manfred ain't done paid her taxis. But I don't think that's right neither cuz I ain't never seen her take no taxi."

Helene and Charlie exchanged glances.

"Thank you," said Helene. "You've been very helpful."

And in lieu of anything better, she gave the child a half-opened packet of chewing gum. He seemed disproportionately pleased with his trophy and went off to show it to his gang, with no intention of sharing it.

Helene followed Charlie up the driveway past an elderly pick-up truck that, at some point in the past, had been reversed into something solid. He knocked on the door frame and waited.

There was no answer.

"Maybe she's not in," said Helene.

"She's in," said the man. "Her pick-up is here and the kids would have said if she'd gone out."

He knocked again and motioned for Helene to do the

speaking. She spoke softly but clearly, unwilling for her voice to reach the goggling children.

"Miss Manfred: we're not Federal agents. We're here to help you – you and your father. Will you come and talk to us, please?"

There was some scuffling behind the door.

"Go away! I can't talk to you!" said a light, girlish voice.

"Please, Miss Manfred," persisted Helene. "Barbara, we know what happened to your father three years ago. We know that you're scared but if you talk to us, we can help you."

"You can't help me," came the reply, in a voice that was near to tears. "No-one can help me. You have to go now or they'll know! Go away. Please!"

The shuffling retreated.

Helene tried again but it seemed Barbara Manfred had said as much as she was going to: as much as she could.

"We could come back tonight," said Charlie quietly. "So no-one knows we've been here. She might talk to us if she thinks no-one will know."

"I suppose so," said Helene wearily.

Charlie frowned.

"If we leave the car a mile or so back on the highway and hike in, we can get to her without anyone seeing us. It's worth a punt."

"Okay," said Helene, half-heartedly. "Let's do that. In the mean time I think we should go and find Manfred senior."

"You're the boss," said Charlie easily.

Helene nearly swallowed her gum.

Warm Creek Nursing Home was less than a half an hour's drive from Arrowhead Springs. Helene took her turn at the wheel and the SatNav guided her easily. It must make being a spy so much easier, she reckoned. Not that this was how she thought of herself: she was still a journalist and she had one hell of a story to tell. Nearly.

The nursing home was set amid the low foothills some

miles out of San Bernadino. The modern, low-rise building was painted a soothingly pale terracotta. Neat lawns and young trees were framed by a secure looking fence: either to keep the patients in or, possibly, visitors out.

But it seemed security wasn't the main concern as Helene and Charlie were buzzed in through a pair of electric gates, no questions asked. Helene could see that the inmates were making the most of the pleasant weather, or rather their carers were, as they were pushed or escorted around the grounds. Some just sat, slumped in a haze of memories, lost to the present world. All seemed to be in either early or more developed stages of dementia.

Helene could hardly bear to watch. Her mother had died confused and scared, surrounded by strangers, while Helene had been working abroad; home just one day too late to say goodbye. She was haunted by the last image she held of her mother: a thin, frail, wild-haired woman who knew no-one and nothing – except that she wasn't at home and she desperately wanted to go there. "Won't you let me go home?" she'd wailed. She'd called for Helene, begged for her, but could not recognise the daughter who stood before her, crying, unable to comfort or help.

It was the only thing about being single that really terrified Helene: the thought that one day, she, too, might wake up and not be able to remember who she was or where she belonged; not to be able to recognise familiar faces; to be lost and fearful. It was a terrible to thing to lose control of one's body, but to lose your mind was to lose yourself.

"Are you ready?" said Charlie.

"Not really," said Helene. "I hate places like this."

He shrugged. "Most people do, I would have thought," he said, a serious expression on his face. "Although hopefully not the people who work here. At least it seems pretty calm here."

"I can't imagine why that might be, can you?" said Helene sharply.

He didn't reply but compressed his lips into a thin, bitter line.

"Let's find out," he said at last.

They followed the signs to reception and a well appointed blonde woman, on the slippery slope from sixty and dressed as a nurse, fielded their enquiry.

"Mr Manfred? Why, yes, he's one of our guests. But he doesn't see anyone. Who did you say you are, honey?"

"Mona Samovar," said Helene, mentally wincing at the ridiculous name. "I live in London and this is the first chance I've had to come out here to see Wally. We used to work together."

"Well, gee, I hate to disappoint you when you've come all this way and all," said the nurse, who didn't sound in the least bit disappointed.

"Barbara asked us to drop by," said Helene, clutching at straws. "Barbara Manfred, his daughter."

At that the woman's face tightened still further.

"His daughter you say! Harrumph! All I'll say is that young lady is no better than she ought to be. Well, I suppose as you've come all this way... why don't you and your son wait in the garden, honey, and I'll go get Wally. Maybe you'd like a glass of iced tea, too?"

"Thank you," said Helene, gratefully on both counts. "That would be marvellous."

Once the nurse had gone Charlie raised an eyebrow.

"Your son?"

Helene tried a wry smile. "Technically, I am nearly old enough to be your mother."

"Hmm. Would that count as an Oedipus complex?" he said.

Helene couldn't be bothered to reply.

She led them to a bench under a tree that the nurse had pointed out, and an Hispanic orderly dressed in a white uniform brought them their drinks. The iced tea was sweet enough to set Helene's teeth on edge. And, despite the heat of the day, Charlie pulled a face and tipped his drink under the bench. Helene half expected to see the grass wither instantly.

After a short wait, Helene saw a dumpy black woman approach with a wizened man strapped into a wheelchair, a panoply of St Vitus Dance making his limbs jerk in unison. He seemed unaware of his surroundings, a thin line of drool hanging from his lower lip.

The nurse frowned and used a clean tissue to dab at the man's mouth. Unwonted tears came to Helene's eyes: she felt ridiculously grateful to see that small act of kindness towards one so helpless. She hoped that when her time came... then she shook the thought away.

A new feeling of horror overcame her when she realised that the man in the wheelchair was undoubtedly the one from the photograph that Hassan had shown them. But the last three years had taken a terrible toll on the once vital face and strong, stocky body.

"Hello Wally," said Helene in a strangled voice.

And despite her best efforts she couldn't keep the tears from welling, threatening to brim over at any second.

"Is this the first time you've seen him in a while, ma'am?" said the nurse carefully.

Helene nodded wordlessly.

"It's probably a bit of shock for you. You sit back down, miss. Don't you be frettin' yourself. It gets Wally all upset: he likes people to be calm."

"S-sorry," said Helene.

"That's okay, ma'am, I understand. We get a lot of that here. But really the patients are just like children: you gotta keep 'em comfortable and busy and they're good as gold. See Jimmy over there?"

She pointed to an elderly man with white hair sitting serenely holding a cup of tea.

"Jimmy used to be in removals: you know, movin' folks from place to place, shiftin' their furniture. Well, he kept on movin' all the furniture in his room and one day he moved half the living room down the hall and no-one knew how to stop him. But then I figured even removal men gotta have a rest during their work so I said to him, 'Now, Jimmy, you shouldn' be doin' that: you's on your tea break'. An' he stopped: jus' like that. You gotta know how to talk to 'em is all. They's still people, ma'am."

Helene took a deep breath, reached forward and gently took Wally's hand between hers.

"Hello, Wally," she said. "It's Mona. Genie sent us. You remember Genie?"

There was no reaction in the man's face, not so much as a flicker of recognition. Helene tried again.

"We stopped by to see Barbara – she said to say 'hi'. You know, Barbara, your daughter?"

Nothing. But Helene was intrigued to see the expression of disgust on the nurse's face.

"Have you met his daughter Barbara?" said Helene, looking up.

"I met her," said the nurse, with pursed lips.

"We saw her today," said Helene. "I didn't think she seemed very well."

"I wouldn't know," said the nurse. "She don't come here."

"What, never?" said Helene surprised. "She's only half-an-hour away."

"Half-an-hour, half-a-day, half a lifetime to some folks," said the nurse enigmatically. "Some kids push their parents in here and never see 'em again. Say it's too hard. Well, I'll tell you what's too hard: havin' children what is so ungrateful that they don't have the time of day for you – that's hard."

Clearly the nurse felt strongly on this point.

"So Barbara has never been here to visit Wally?" pursued Helene.

"Mm-mm. She come just the once, not long after Wally come here," said the nurse.

"So, Barbara didn't bring him here herself?"

"No, ma'am," replied the nurse curiously. "He come by ambulance. Most of 'em come by ambulance."

Of course. That made sense. But Helene couldn't understand why Barbara wouldn't visit her father?

"Did you say you used to work with Wally?" said the nurse.

A perceptive woman, Helene could tell.

"That's right," she replied. "Er, has Wally ever said anything about his work? Does he talk about it?"

"Are you really friends of his?" said the nurse. "You're not from SAMHSA, are you?"

She saw the blank look on Helene's face.

"So you're not from the Substance Abuse and Mental Health Services Administration?"

"No, why would you think that?" said Helene, honestly confused.

"All them questions you's asking," said the nurse.

Helene wondered why the nurse would be bothered about the authorities checking up on Warm Creek Nursing Home.

"Is there something you can tell me about Wally?" said Helene cautiously. "Something about his treatment here?"

The nurse looked intently at Helene, studying her face and then repeated the process with an examination of Charlie.

"I'll tell you cos you say you friends of Wally here," said the nurse. "I could get into a lot of trouble for talkin', see, but I gotta say somethin' to someone or I'll just about bust a gut."

Helene gave her a small smile of encouragement and reassurance. A thought came to her – something Hassan had said...

"Has Wally really got Alzheimer's?"

The nurse glanced around her then lowered her voice to a whisper.

"I've worked in nursing homes all my life," she said. "I've seen good ones and I've seen bad ones. This is one of the good ones: staff here make sure the patients are as good as they can be – all 'cepting Wally."

Helene felt her body tense. The nurse paused before plunging in to what she really wanted to say.

"Wally's meds are never done off the drug cart: no, he's treated special by the doc. *Real special.* No-one else is allowed to touch his meds. I don't know what they're giving him, but I'll tell you this: he ain't like no Alzheimer's patients I've ever seen. If you ask me, they doin' it to keep him quiet. It's a scandal – that's what it is. It's evil!"

Although it was the second time she'd been told this, the nurse's words confirming Hassan's original theory, Helene still felt the shock of the revelation.

"That's awful!" said Helene, weakly. "Does his daughter know? Is that why she doesn't come?"

The nurse gave Helene a long, appraising look.

"I reckon she knows. But that's not the reason she don't come here."

"Then why?" said Helene.

"I saw her the day she came to see him," recalled the nurse. "She was screaming and yelling about how he'd been kidnapped and he shouldn't be in a place like this and how she was gonna call the po-lice on us and all sorts. But then she calmed down a bit when they said she could see him. I was finishing up Wally's breakfast at the time so I done saw and heard the whole thing – and I tell you... when she walked into that room, she didn't know him."

"You mean she didn't recognise him – because of the dementia, because of the drugs?" said Helene.

"No, ma'am," said the nurse emphatically. "I mean she didn't *know* him. She took one look at him and said, 'That's not my pa'. Well, at the time I thought she meant he just was so different because that's how folks feel when they see a family member as has got the dementia, but after I'd thought about it a while I knew that was wrong: she didn't know him cos this ain't her pa. I don't know who this poor soul is, but he ain't no Wally Manfred."

Helene stared at Charlie. She couldn't believe what she was hearing. He shook his head, his blue eyes stormy with anger and disgust.

Helene stood up slowly and held out her hand to the nurse.

"Thank you for telling us," she said.

"Just promise me one thing," said the nurse, ignoring the held out hand. "Promise me you'll find a way to help this poor soul cos I have surely done all I can. People round here who talk about Wally Manfred, they don't last long in this job. But maybe I done a good thing tellin' you. I guess I'll just have to see about that."

Helene reached down to stroke Wally's hand, hoping to see something in his face: but it was the same empty mask of almost-humanity. She watched, sickened, as the nurse wheeled him away.

She turned to Charlie, her face crumpling. Wordlessly, he scooped her into his arms as tears washed down her face.

"We're going to get those bastards, Helene," he whispered into her ear. "I promise you, we're going to get them."

CHAPTER SIXTEEN

HALF WAY BACK UP THE DRIVE CHARLIE HAD TO PULL OVER so Helene could vomit over the well cut lawn.

She staggered back towards the car and rinsed her mouth out with a bottle of water, made tepid by the hot sun.

"I feel so dirty, don't you?" she said, squeezing her eyes shut, trying to force away the dreadful images inside.

Charlie nodded, his eyes tight.

"I've seen some bad things in my time, Helene, things I wouldn't tell anyone, not even you, but this... this is some sick shit."

Helene rubbed her temples, wishing she could rub away the pounding headache that sunshine, sickness and heartfelt disgust had brought on.

"We have to get Barbara Manfred to tell us what she knows," said Helene, trying to think clearly through the miasma of shocked that clouded her brain. "She knows this poor man isn't her father, so that must mean she knows that her dad is alive somewhere, in all likelihood being held against his will. Her silence is proof of that."

"Yah, maybe, or else she's scared they'll do the same thing to her."

"No, it must be more than that," said Helene. "Otherwise they'd have brought the real Wally Manfred here and treated him to the chemical cosh. They just couldn't risk that this man would speak."

"So who is he?" said Charlie.

Helene shook her head.

"I don't know. Probably some poor sod who just happens to look like Wally Manfred, is my guess. I reckon they keep him there as a reminder to the Gene Genies about what could happen. But it would also discredit any work that Wally Manfred did while he was still playing with the full complement of marbles. Anything that he wrote or said in the year before the kidnapping would be discredited because anyone looking now would think it was just the onset of dementia. They – the US government – wanted to make sure that no-one listened. Remember what the message on the website said: 'No-one will believe you'. Maybe they said the same thing to Wally Manfred. Maybe he didn't listen."

The thought made her shiver.

"No," she said, "we need to go back to the research that Hassan started: well, the research Wally started. America's debt at the end of World War One and the 1929 Wall Street Crash. Somehow, that's the key – I know it is."

"Okay," he said, not looking convinced. "Let's find a motel and take a break. You can spend some time online and I'll get some kit for our sortie tonight."

"Oh?" said Helene. "What sort of kit did you have in mind?"

"Hiking boots, torches, warm jackets. It gets cold in the mountains at night and it's pretty rough terrain out there from what I could see." He smiled. "I was a Boy Scout, remember?"

Helene still didn't know if that was true. She sort of hoped it was.

Ten minutes further up the highway they found what they were looking for. Charlie pulled up in the parking lot of a small, but tidy roadside motel.

"You've got to be kidding me!" said Helene, staring about her in amazement.

"Well, it's a bit of a come-down from the Manama Ritz,"

agreed Charlie, "but it has a certain bijou charm, don't you think?"

Helene gazed at the bizarre collection of buildings in front of her.

The Wigwam Motel was certainly unusual. Helene had never seen anything quite like it. Nineteen 30 foot high teepees were arranged around a kidney-shaped swimming pool and barbecue area. On closer inspection Helene could see that instead of wood and skin, the teepees were made from a frame, clad in concrete and rendered with stucco.

"Pity though," said Charlie, "the Ritz suited you."

"Yeah, maybe," said Helene, "although I'm strictly champagne aspirations on beer money."

"But this is rather colourful, don't you think?" he said. "It could even catch on in Milton Keynes."

It was certainly novel, Helene had to agree. She sat staring at the parody of Native American culture while Charlie went to book them a teepee.

"Small, but perfectly formed," he smiled after checking them in. "May I escort you to your twin-room wigwam, madam? Pow-wows after dinner."

"Geronimo," said Helene.

It was good to have something to smile about after the shocking encounter with 'Wally Manfred'.

Once they'd settled in, which took about 30 seconds as they were down to the bare minimum of luggage, Charlie went to explore the town and get the supplies he said they would need.

The teepee was homely but clean. Helene made herself comfortable, wagon-wheel headboard notwithstanding, sitting cross-legged on one of the beds, and pulled out the laptop.

The first thing she did was to log onto the Helene of Troy website. There was one message. It was amazing how nervous she felt opening it up – it was sinister to think that external forces were arrayed against them. And right now the only people could help her were a mercenary on a need-to-know basis and the terrified daughter of a kidnapped man.

She opened the message:

" YOU CAN'T TRUST HIM

Her heart missed a beat, an unpleasant thrill fluttering through her body. The message could refer to Kazuma, Hassan or even Wally Manfred, but she couldn't help thinking that they had someone else in mind; the message was to her and she was pretty certain they were referring to Charlie.

She tried to ignore it. *Of course they want to rattle me*, she told herself. *That's how they operate: divide and rule.*

But... a voice whispered, the devil at her elbow, *what if it's true: what if they're right? You don't really trust him, do you?*

She exited the site and closed her eyes.

Think, she told her tired brain. Think. What had Wally Manfred found out that had put him and his daughter in such danger? What was the connection between the way the US financed the First World War, the 1929 Wall Street Crash and Wally's disappearance? Well, money, obviously, but what else? And what had something that happened nearly a hundred years ago have to do with – well, everything else?

Helene was still staring at the laptop screen when Charlie returned. She may have had the screen in front of her but in her mind's eye she was seeing the poor creature kept insensible at the Warm Creek Nursing Home.

"We need a plan," she said, without looking up.

"Yah, we really do," he agreed. "We need to go back to see Barbara Manfred and find out what she knows; and we need to find out what Wally knew."

Helene looked up at him curiously. "And we have to find a way to help that poor man at the nursing home, don't we?"

Charlie shrugged his shoulders impatiently. "He's not the priority."

Helene felt the heat of sudden anger surge through her.

"Not the priority? How can you say that?" she gasped, her voice shrill. "You saw what they'd done to him!"

"He's collateral damage," said Charlie coolly.

"Damn you, Charlie!" she shouted, nerves frayed, senses bludgeoned. "Don't you have a soul?"

"Listen!" he said, lowering his voice to a furious whisper.

"Number one priority is to get out of this damn mess alive. Do you understand? We're not bloody crusaders. We're not here to save the world: we're here to save our own damned hides – got it?"

"No!" Helene flashed back. "No! You're wrong! We're here to do the right thing!"

He glared at her, contempt in those blue eyes.

"Oh, get off your high horse for one fucking moment, will you?" he sneered. "You're the one who's getting paid £100,000 for this 'story' or had your forgotten that? Maybe you should donate it to the welfare of puppies and kittens, if you're so damned holier-than-thou. You know, you're so bloody self-righteous but you're making money out of this. You're just a journalist who has stumbled on the story of a lifetime but you're too damned pathetic to see it through. Who the hell are you to judge me?"

Helene felt the blood drain from her face. She couldn't believe he was attacking her like this.

His gaze softened as he stared down at her.

"Helene, I'm sorry. I didn't mean it like that..."

But she brushed away his outstretched arm and stumbled outside.

She leaned against the side of the tepee forcing herself to take deep breaths. Slowly, the wind knocked out of her, she sank to the ground and rested her head on her knees. She felt very old and very tired.

Charlie followed her outside and crouched down next to her. He was close but he didn't try to touch her.

"I'm sorry," he whispered. "I really am. But sometimes you're so naïve: you don't seem to understand the level of danger that we're in. This is no game and we're not going to wake up and find it's all a terrible dream. We're deep in the NSA's back yard, finding out things they've kept secret for a hundred years, perhaps, and I'm just trying to keep us alive – if that means I put you – and me – before that poor bastard in the nursing home, then I make no apologies for that. I care about you, Helene."

Helene shook her head wearily.

"I know, I know. I'm sorry, too. I know you're right. And you're right about me, too – about my motives, I mean. It's just when I saw him there – I keep seeing him – when I saw what was being done to him, I promised myself that I'd do everything I could to stop it. But you're right: I can't save the world, even if I want to sometimes."

She smiled sadly.

"Come on," he said. "Come back inside and I'll make you a nice cup of tea. It's my mother's remedy for all ills. Who am I to gainsay a lady?"

"Who indeed?" whispered Helene.

Charlie helped her up and, holding her hand in his, led her back inside the tepee. She lay limply on the sofa whilst he boiled the kettle.

"Look," he said, "holding up a small package. Proper English breakfast tea. Don't say I never give you anything."

"My knight in rusty armour," she said softly.

He poured the boiling water over the tea and let it brew for two minutes before he brought it to her.

"Proper English tea," he said, "made with boiling water, not boiled water. Two sugars and no milk."

"Thanks," she said.

They sat in silence, sipping the hot, sweet tea. Helene began to feel revived. No wonder it was recommended to people who'd had a shock.

Her brain was still churning away but she felt she was on an even keel again.

"I know you're right," she said again. "I am earning money out of all of this."

He smiled. "I'm glad one of us is."

Helene frowned.

"Well, at least let me share it with you."

He brushed a strand of hair from her eyes.

"Don't worry about it," he said. "It's cool."

Helene felt unable to continue that line of conversation so she sat up, moving slightly away from him and simply said, "What's the plan for tonight?"

"I bought a map of the terrain," he replied, dropping his

hand, "and I've found a way in but it means climbing up the escarpment behind the house. It's not an easy climb in daytime, but it'll be even harder at night."

He paused.

"And you're wondering," said Helene, "if the old girl is up to it."

He looked at her wryly.

"Well, I *was* wondering but then I decided that if you had to tunnel your way through with your bare hands reinforced steel girders wouldn't stop you. Not that I'm saying you're stubborn or anything, of course. One wouldn't wish to be ungentlemanly."

Helene laughed out loud.

"You're good for me, Charlie," she said. "God help me for saying so, but you make me laugh."

He grinned. "It's my magical way with women – or something."

"Definitely 'or something'," agreed Helene.

His smile faded.

"Once we've climbed the escarpment, we have to get down the other side. It's loose scree so it could be tricky. I'll have you roped up and we'll take it easy: it should be okay. Besides, it's a waxing moon so that's in our favour."

Helene nodded.

"I'll be fine. I'm more worried about how we're going to convince Barbara Manfred to talk to us. Any ideas – other than terrifying her even more than she already is?"

Charlie shook his head. "The only plan I can come up with is some way of... I don't know... showing her that we've got a real chance of getting her out of this... some way of..."

"Giving her hope?" Helene finished his sentence.

"Yah," he agreed. "Bit of a long shot?"

"I guess that's what we're used to," said Helene. "What other kind of shots have we ever had?"

She pushed herself off the bed and inspected the rest of the supplies Charlie had bought: some basic climbing equipment, a pair of soft hiking boots in her size, a warm fleece, head torches and two pairs of thin, leather climbing gloves: one large, one small.

There was also a grocery bag with pasta, sauce, bacon, some bread and cheese, a couple of cartons of fruit juice and a large bar of dark chocolate – Swiss.

"Good hunter-gathering," she said.

"Just call me the Galloping Gourmet," he replied.

"Nah, you're too young to remember that!"

"My mum used to like that programme," he said. "Not that it ever improved her cooking. Moi, on the other hand, I can cook up a storm."

"Talented and modest, too," said Helene dryly.

"Absolutely," he said, rattling the dried pasta into a tiny saucepan and covering it with water. "Modesty is an over-rated virtue, don't you think?"

"Hmm, over-something," she replied.

"By the way," he said, "have we had any more contact on the website?"

Helene couldn't say why, but for the first time she lied to him.

"No," she said. "No messages."

CHAPTER SEVENTEEN

AFTER A COUPLE OF HOURS SPENT EATING AND RESTING, they left the concrete teepee and headed out of town once again, passing several families who showed little expertise at the barbecue, if the clouds of carcinogenic black smoke were anything to go by.

Helene wriggled her toes in the walking boots. They were wonderfully comfortable despite their newness. Charlie had also bought her two thin pairs of walking socks which he insisted she wear together to cut down on any potential blistering. He also made her rub Vaseline over her feet. An old army trick, he'd said. It felt rather peculiar; faintly insalubrious, definitely unpleasant.

In the falling dusk, time seemed to drift away. It wasn't hard to peel back the layers of years and see the land as it once had been and, after the eventual and inevitable demise of mankind, how it would be again. It was beautiful in a harsh, uncompromising way.

Helene rolled down the window and felt the last heat of the day lose its savage intensity. By the time they reached Arrowhead Springs, night had fallen. Charlie cut the engine and in the vacuum of silence, Helene heard a sobbing, wailing howl.

"Good God! What was that?" she said, eyes trying to

penetrate the gloom. "It sounds like the Hound of the Baskervilles."

He must have been smiling because she could see his teeth, very white in the darkness.

"Just a coyote. Nothing to worry about. Although I think they might have mountain lions in this area."

Helene couldn't tell whether or not he was joking. She hoped he was; it certainly suited his style of humour. And then she wondered if he'd got a gun. He clearly had the knack of acquiring one wherever he went, not that it would be that hard in America: home of gun-lovin' culture. On the other hand, handguns were definitely harder to buy than rifles – and she was sure he wasn't carrying a rifle. She hoped he did have a gun; and then she hoped he didn't. She never again wanted to see that icy expression on his face when he was preparing to shoot Bill: she never wanted to see it again.

Climbing the scree above Elder View was harder work than even Helene had imagined. For every step she made upwards, she seemed to slide down two. No matter how hard she tried to dig in her toes like Charlie showed her, she made little progress. Even scrabbling with her hands and lurching upwards like some fatally wounded goat didn't help progress much.

In the end she sank to the ground, her breath coming in harsh gasps, all attempt at a silent, stealthy ascent fallen to the dust.

"This is hopeless," she said, hacking noisily. "I'm never going to make it up there. We'll still be at it come dawn. You'd better go on without me."

"I never leave a man behind," said Charlie calmly. "You're doing fine." He wasn't even out of breath, damn him. "Even so, I think it would be faster if we roped ourselves together and I help you out a bit."

"Thank God for that!" said Helene, who had no pride left.

In the end, Charlie had to practically drag her to the top of the escarpment like a bag of old laundry, or just an old bag. If he found her hard going, if he found her slowness an unbearable irritation, he didn't show it. She was a journalist on the slippery slope to fifty: not an ex-marine of thirty. Some things you just can't fix.

Once at the top, when she was able to breathe without gasping, Helene was able to look down the valley to the small community of Arrowhead Springs below. The famous spa hotel was lit up like Christmas and she could see cars moving along the road in the distance, their red tail lights glowing like tiny devils. She was reminded of the mountain demons on Kompira-*san*, the gargoyle faces leering out at her.

"Are you okay to move?"

"Yup. Fit as a flea," she wheezed.

"Just imagine you're walking through thick snow when we make the descent," he said. "Keep your toes up, bend your knees and try not to lean back. I'll be holding on to you so you won't be able to pick up too much speed. Ready to try?"

Helene nodded but before she launched herself down the escarpment, Charlie reached up towards her. For a second she thought he was going to stroke her hair, and a tremor ran through her, but instead he turned off the lamp on her head torch.

"No need to announce our arrival," he said.

Helene tried to follow his advice and keep her centre of gravity as low as possible. It was hard work on the knees and thigh muscles and soon the lactic acid was burning; she was afraid she'd get a cramp if she didn't rest soon.

When the slope seemed to ease off at last, at the moment when she couldn't have gone on, Helene allowed herself to slither into a sitting position and catch her breath. She could feel perspiration all over her body, rapidly cooling her in the night air. She was grateful once again for Charlie's forethought in providing her with the fleece. He was a useful guy to have around, however she looked at it. She shook away the poisonous memory of the website's message. Of course she could trust him: she wouldn't have got this far without him – she'd probably be languishing in some rendition centre, dressed in an unflattering orange jump suit, vainly trying to prove that she knew less than nothing.

A small river of shale dribbled past her and Charlie

gracefully slid to a halt at her side. His eyes glittered in the moonlight and Helene couldn't help thinking that he was enjoying himself. This was what he was good at: he'd said so himself.

They descended the last 200 yards in complete silence and then crept along the alley that serviced the back yards of Elder View. When they got to Barbara Manfred's house, Charlie stopped so suddenly that Helene nearly blundered into him.

"Problem?" she whispered.

He nodded.

"Yah. See that blue light blinking under the bush?"

Helene nodded dumbly.

"It's a laser trip wire," he said, "badly hidden. Pretty amateurish but even so..."

"Can you get round it?" whispered Helene.

He smiled, his voice condescending.

"Of course! Just give me five minutes."

He slid into the darkness and Helene was left alone.

Five minutes when you're waiting for an exam or for your driving test passes in a flash; five minutes when you're waiting for a bus is an irritation; five minutes waiting to hear if your loved one has survived surgery is a lifetime.

Helene didn't know how long she crouched alone in the darkness but it felt like forever.

Suddenly she noticed the blue light disappear and then just as suddenly reappear. Maybe he hadn't managed to disable it after all. Maybe they'd have to climb back up the escarpment empty handed and then what?

When Charlie reappeared by her side, looming out of the night, Helene nearly yelped.

"What are we going to do now?" she said, gulping away her fear.

He grinned.

"Go straight in. I've looped the alarm around a by-pass rather than disable it. If I turn it off they'll know there's a problem. It's okay, you can go ahead: knock on her door. I'll be right behind you."

Helene swallowed then stood up. She felt very vulnerable,

utterly exposed in the moonlight, walking towards Brenda Manfred's back door: at every second she expected sirens and alarms to wake the living dead.

But nothing happened, unless she wanted to count tripping over a loose paving stone and nearly going arse over tit.

Pushing herself to her knees, she wiped her filthy hands on her equally filthy jeans, then tapped timidly on the backdoor.

There was no reply. She knocked a little louder, painfully aware of how easily sound travels at night.

"Barbara," she whispered hoarsely, "it's Helene La Borde. I came by this afternoon. No-one knows we're here: we just need to talk to you. Five minutes of your time, please."

She heard the familiar shuffling sound that told her Barbara Manfred was behind the door listening.

"Look," said Helene, "we know that your dad stumbled onto some important information: information that was sensitive enough to get him kidnapped. We're trying to work out what's been going on – and we've been out to Warm Creek Nursing Home: we know that poor soul isn't your father. But we can't go any further unless you help us."

The shuffling sounded nearer.

"Go away," said a scared voice. "I can't talk to you: they'll know if I talk to you. The house is probably bugged."

Charlie crept up behind Helene and whispered in her ear.

"Tell her the garden's clean: tell her we've disabled the alarm system and she can come out and talk to us and no-one will know."

Helene relayed the information and waited, holding her breath.

"How... how do I know I can trust you?" said the voice with a quaver.

"I can't prove anything to you," said Helene, "but we could be your only chance to help both you and your father... and that poor man at Warm Creek Nursing Home. I can't make you trust me – but I hope you will. I'm a journalist and I'm going to do my best to get this known to the widest possible audience because, I admit, that's the safest thing for me to do now, I'm in so deep. I promise that I'll do my best to help you: that's all I can promise."

They waited, the silence stretching painfully.

At last they heard the sound of the door being unbolted and a scared face peered around the door.

"Hello, Barbara," said Helene. "This is my friend Charlie who has been helping me – and I'm Helene."

The woman took another step towards them, twisting her hands nervously in her hair, eyes darting from side to side. She was in her late twenties, unhealthily pale as if her skin never saw the sun, bitter lines cut in grooves around her mouth, and a greasy complexion that showed poor attention to basic nutrition. A wreck of a young life. Fear seemed to leak from every pore.

"I can't come outside," whispered the girl. "They make me wear a tag." She pulled up the leg of her tracksuit trousers to show a thick bracelet of dark plastic – an electronic tag. "They know if I go out: they watch me all the time."

Helene's pity for the young woman intensified.

"You'll be okay here on the doorstep," said Helene kindly.

"W-what do you want?" Barbara whispered, looking around her nervously, as if expecting NSA agents to leap out at her.

What did they want? That was the six-million dollar question.

"Did your father tell you," said Helene, "what he'd found out about the link between the Wall Street Crash in 1929 and the US debt at the end of the First World War?"

Barbara's slight frame trembled, whether from fear or cold, Helene couldn't tell. Probably both. She shook her head wordlessly.

Helene tried to reboot her brain and think of another approach.

"Did he tell you anything about the Gene Genies? Did you ever meet them?"

Barbara shook her head again.

"No, he said it was safer for me if I didn't know anything. He got that wrong, didn't he?" she said, the bitterness plain in her voice.

Helene felt desperately sorry for her, to have her young life stolen like this.

"I'm sure your dad thought he was doing the best he could to protect you," said Helene, knowing it made no difference at all.

Barbara shrugged.

"Is there anything you can tell us about the Gene Genies?" continued Helene gently.

"Mmm, not really," muttered the girl. "But I met one of them once. He called himself 'Hank Howlin' Wolf'. It used to make dad laugh because he said the guy couldn't play the guitar for nuts."

At last they were making progress. The girl was beginning to trust them. Either that or she hadn't talked to anyone in a very long time.

"Did you ever know Hank's real name?"

Barbara looked at him for the first time. Her defensive posture seemed to soften slightly.

"Dad said he was called Hank Wolford but it could have been a made up name: it sounds like a made up name, don't you think?"

She almost smiled.

"There's a man in Britain called Bamber Gascoigne," said Charlie, smiling back, "and that's his real name!"

Barbara giggled.

"Fancy that!"

"Do you know where we could find Howling Hank?" said Helene.

"Um, I don't know where he lives," said Barbara, still directing her answer to Charlie, "but dad said he used to like to play at the Hog's Breath Inn on one of their open mike nights. That's over by Carmel," she added helpfully.

A memory was triggered and Helene felt a flicker of hope.

"Your dad's house was in Carmel, wasn't it? Do you know what happened to it?" she said.

Barbara's face turned to misery again.

"I dunno," she said. "I think they pulled it apart when they searched it. They took everything that was inside anyway."

"Can you give us the address?" said Helene.

"Sure," said Barbara, "but you won't find anything there. It's a bit north of Del Cievro Road, in the woods near Macomber Drive. It's kinda hard to find if you don't have a map. I could draw you one," she offered shyly.

"That would be great, Barbara, thanks," said Helene. It would be useful to check it against Bill's sketch.

Barbara disappeared back inside and returned a minute later with a hastily drawn map on a piece of paper torn from a notebook. The girl's handwriting was poignantly childish. She handed it to Charlie who pocketed it with a smile.

"One last thing," said Helene. "Did your dad ever give you a secret codeword – something the Gene Genies used amongst themselves? Something so that Hank would know to trust us?"

Barbara looked from Helene to Charlie.

"Is she serious?"

"Well, yes," said Helene, feeling rather foolish. She decided to persist, however odd it sounded. "I mean, if we manage to track Hank down, how will he know that we are who we say we are? How will we get him to talk to us?"

"I dunno, maybe..." said Barbara. "There is one thing though: I didn't think about it at the time but it struck me as kinda strange after..."

"Yes?" said Helene, aware she was grasping at straws.

"Well, the last time I saw dad before he... before he disappeared... he drove down from Carmel. He didn't seem any different so I wasn't worried. He stayed at the Wigwam Motel – you know it? Uh huh? Well, he didn't like staying here with me cuz he said it reminded him of when mom was alive. Anyway, we went out for dinner and he started talking about how mom always liked history. And after Adolf Hitler she thought the most evil man in history was Matthew Hopkins."

Helene had no idea where this conversation was going and from the look on Charlie's face, neither did he.

"I thought you'd know," said Barbara, sounding disappointed, as she searched their faces and finding no recognition, "you being British and all. Matthew Hopkins was the Witchfinder General: he was responsible for the deaths of hundreds and hundreds of women. He used this old book called 'Hammer of the Witches', *'Malleus Maleficarum'* in Latin, to justify himself. I wondered after if dad told me that as a sort of secret code between us. I mean, why bring it up then? Why did he come over like that: we usually just skyped each other. But the NSA or whoever would never ask about my mom's hobbies. I mean, she's been dead these fifteen years, right?"

"I suppose not, no," said Helene. It seemed like a rather slender reliability report to offer to Hank, even if Wally had ever thought to mention it to him – which seemed extremely unlikely. But beggars can't be choosers. Especially not desperate beggars who were being hounded across three continents at the last count.

Helene couldn't think of another question and Charlie had remained largely silent. So that was it; Barbara had given them as much as she could. Which wasn't much at all.

"Will you... will you come back and see me?" whispered Barbara.

"We'll try," said Charlie, his smile fading. "We'll try."

Barbara nodded her head slowly, her sad mouth twisting further downwards. She'd probably heard a lot of people say they would try to help her. She stepped backwards into the house and was about to lock the door when she turned and said,

"You know: I've got used to living like this. It's only been three years but sometimes it seems like it's always been this way. Sometimes I think I could live like this for a hundred years – but it's the hope that kills me."

Without another word or a backward glance, Barbara locked the door and Helene heard the deadbolts shooting back into place.

Helene felt very, very angry. People's lives were being ruined by a government that was supposed to care about them. It was sick. And she was going to do her damndest to stop it. The tiny patch of garden felt contaminated and Helene wanted to get the hell out of there. But first Charlie had to spend several precious minutes resetting the laser alarm before they could move on.

They made the exhausting climb up the escarpment in silence and Helene didn't even bother to swear when it started to rain, making the ascent even more hazardous. Her nails were torn and bleeding from slipping on the loose scree time and time again, and even Charlie was beginning to tire as he pulled her up yet again as she fell to her hands and knees yet again. The rest of the climb was a nightmare of burning muscles and grazed palms and Helene was too tired to speak.

Forty minutes later she collapsed gratefully into the car, dozing, headlights in the road a mere memory as Charlie drove her back to the Wigwam Motel.

At least they had one more sliver of information: they knew how to find one of the Gene Genies.

CHAPTER EIGHTEEN

HELENE HAD WANTED TO CHECK OUT OF THE WIGWAM Motel straight away but Charlie vetoed the suggestion.

"We don't want to go off half-cocked," he said. "Besides, I need to sleep and you've looked better. It'll take us five or six hours to drive over to Carmel. If we leave after breakfast we'll arrive mid afternoon. That'll give us time to scope out the place and find out a bit more about Hank Wolford."

Helene was exhausted but wired. She tried to relax by filling the bath with the hottest water she could stand and soaking in it, but instead of it making her feel sleepy, she felt like she'd had a shot of pure adrenaline and was wide awake. She tiptoed round the living room, listening to the soft, throaty breathing of Charlie in sleep. She would have liked to peep through the door of his room that he'd left ajar and watch the rhythmic rise and fall of his chest but she was afraid he'd wake up to find her standing over him like some creepy voyeur.

Instead she typed up the most recent events into the notes on the computer and spent a couple of hours searching for information on Howlin' Hank Wolford and possible variations on the spelling. It turned out that Barbara was right in one important respect: Hank was a regular at the Hog's Breath open mike night – and there was a session due in two days' time. If they couldn't find him before then, at least they had a shot of tracking him down.

She used all the techniques Charlie had shown her for tracking down a person: taxes, bank accounts, parking fines, welfare cheques – anything and everything she could think of to find a person online. But Howlin' Hank was a ghost. If it weren't for his love of the guitar, he'd have been impossible to find. She supposed it wasn't so surprising – he was one of the Gene Genies after all, and he'd know how to hide a trail.

There was, however, a Dolly Wolford living in Carmel. A sister, maybe? A wife? Maybe a mother or a daughter. Helene trawled birth certificates and marriage certificates but came up with zero. She tried under Dorothy, too, but still nothing. If the woman was related to Howlin' Hank, it was impossible to prove online. Even so, Helene made a note of the address. Being a journalist was a lot like being a detective: you never knew what was going to be a clue and what was going to be a red herring. Information was kept until you knew which category it fell into.

Eventually with no more useful jobs to do she lay on her bed, willing herself to sleep. But the bastard mistress Sleep was playing away: instead Helene spent the night wrestling with the covers and lying in a knot of sheets, eyeballs as dry as Injun country.

Light was creeping through the thin curtains when Helene gave it up as a bad job and left the wreck of her bed. A quick, chilly shower revitalised her more than hours of thrashing about failing to rest.

She toasted half the loaf bought as supplies and started frying bacon. After a short time she heard the sounds of life from Charlie's room and soon he stumbled into the kitchen, hair on end and eyes sleepy. Who needed an alarm clock when frying bacon did the job so much more congenially?

Helene couldn't help smiling: Charlie looked so young and vulnerable, even though she knew both were an illusion.

"Blimey," he said, happily. "Bacon sandwiches! I could get used to waking up to those every morning."

"Nah," said Helene. "Think of your cholesterol levels in ten years' time."

"I'd rather not," he said. Then he looked at her speculatively. "Perhaps I need a good woman to look after me."

"I rather suspect," said Helene archly, "that you'd prefer a bad one."

He smiled enigmatically and contented himself with chewing his way through an obscenely large plateful of food.

"Haute cuisine," he said at last, leaning back in his chair and stretching has hands behind his head.

"I'm not just a pretty face," she replied.

"I never doubted that," said Charlie, almost seriously.

Helene turned away, the dirty dishes providing her with an excuse to lean over the sink. When she felt in control of her voice again, she told him what she'd learned during her night of wakefulness.

"I can't help thinking that Dolly Wolford must be connected to Hank Wolford," said Helene. "It's such an unusual surname."

"It's certainly worth a try," agreed Charlie. "Let's give Ms Wolford a call, after we've visited the Hog's Breath Inn."

They had a plan. Sort of.

~

It took only minutes to pack up and sign out of the Wigwam Motel. Helene felt almost sorry to be saying goodbye to the jaunty lodges. It had been rather fun waiting for John Wayne to wander in, pretend to speak Sioux or Cheyenne. Helene had always suspected that the real life Native Americans must have played a few practical jokes in those films from the fifties and sixties: instead of saying something serious like, 'Whiteman speak with forked tongue,' they were probably saying, 'Whiteman is an asshole with hot air shooting out of his exhaust'. She'd have to take the trouble to find out some day.

They drove west, the sun already well overhead, skirted Los Angeles, a smudge of dirt on the horizon, and drove north up

Interstate Five, a road running parallel to the Pacific Ocean from Mexico to Canada.

They stopped at a roadside Taco Bell half way into their journey and Helene watched in amusement as Charlie loaded up with more calories: a thick tortilla called a *chalupa*, chilli beef and a smattering of salad. She made do with a limeade sparkler: lemon and lime soda poured over ice.

Finally they turned west again and made their way into downtown Carmel. It was the most un-American town Helene had ever seen: it was more like a sort of Hispanic Poundbury-on-Sea. There was even a thatched cottage selling sweets. Helene wondered if they'd wandered onto some giant movie set by mistake.

But the SatNav showed they were bang on target and directed them to the Hog's Breath Inn. They managed to find a parking space not too far away; Charlie insisted that transportation shouldn't be too far away should a quick getaway be required.

The Hog's Breath Inn was built partly of red brick and partly of whitewashed adobe construction, with several buildings arranged around a pretty courtyard, a huge *chimenea* at the centre.

They took a seat at the bar and Helene picked up the menu. It was vaguely Tex Mex with an emphasis on meat. Charlie browsed the menu over her shoulder but suddenly his hand shot out and grabbed it from her.

"Wow!" he said. "Look at this: You can have a Dirty Harry Burger and a Dirty Harry Dinner... this is Clint Eastwood's place – I've read about it!"

"Yes, I know," said Helene calmly. "Can I have the menu back now, please?"

"But this is immense!" said Charlie. "I mean, Clint really comes here... the man's a legend. We could see him any moment!"

"I doubt it," said Helene, amused by Charlie's puppy-like enthusiasm. "He probably hires people so he doesn't have to come in."

"Let me dream, Helene," he said crossly frowning at her.

"Clint was my hero when I was a kid: he was just the coolest – 'I know what you're thinking: Did he fire six shots or only five? Well, to tell you the truth, in all this excitement I kinda lost track myself. But being as this is a 44 calibre Magnum, the most powerful handgun in the world, and would blow your head clean off, you've got to ask yourself one question: Do I feel lucky? Well, do ya, punk?' I mean, the man's a genius!"

Helene laughed out loud.

"This makes it all worthwhile," she said smiling. "I think you should have the Dirty Harry Dinner in honour of the occasion."

Charlie leaned over and kissed her cheek and Helene laughed again.

She ordered herself the seared tuna with pineapple ginger and coconut wasabi, then watched while Charlie chewed his way through sirloin, wild mushrooms, horseradish and roasted garlic mashed potatoes. She wondered if they sold Benecol in America.

Much to Charlie's great disappointment, Dirty Harry seemed to have the afternoon off. After hanging around longer than necessary, Charlie reluctantly agreed it was time to leave. Instead they walked back to the car and re-set the SatNav to take them to Dolly Wolford's place, a few miles out of town. Helene promised that they'd try for Dirty Harry again if they had the chance. It was a bit like promising Barbara Manfred that they'd try to come back and see her – one of those empty promises that are made so easily and mean nothing.

Even with electronic guidance and satellite technology, it wasn't easy to find the right address for Dolly Wolford but eventually they drove past an unmade road with a battered looking mailbox hanging forlornly from a post.

"That's it," said Helene.

"Yep, looks like," agreed Charlie and reversed the car to re-take the turning.

"Do you think we should go in on foot?" said Helene.

"No," he said. "Probably best if she hears us coming. We don't want to scare her."

When they reached the end of the lane, 'shack' seemed too

grand a word for the building in front of them. A motley collection of tired wooden planks seemed to stand upright without any visible means of support. The broken windows had been stuffed with newspaper and mended, at least for now, with duct tape.

Helene was afraid to knock on the door in case it fell off its rusting hinges.

"Bloody hell," said Charlie. "Do you think anyone lives here? This place gives me the creeps: it's all a bit too much 'Duelling Banjos' for my taste."

Helene had to agree: there was something of the whiff of Appalachian hillbilly about it. If she'd been by herself there's no way she would have entered. The fact that she was prepared to go in reminded her how dependent she'd become on Charlie. She wasn't sure she liked the change.

Helene knocked tentatively and called out at the same time.

"Miss Wolford! Hello?"

"I'm right behind you," Charlie said. "But if a pack of cross-eyed in-breeds answers the door, let's get the hell out of here."

He probably wasn't joking.

Helene knocked again and after a long silence, they heard the sound of heavy footsteps.

"Whaddya want?" shouted a deep voice.

"Oh, hi!" said Helene, trying to sound chirpy, but not salesman chirpy. "My name's Helene and this is Charlie and we're looking for Howlin'... er... for Hank Wolford. You're the only 'Wolford' in the phone book and we wondered if you were related – and if you are, where we could we find him."

"Who sent ya?" growled the voice.

"Barbara Manfred," said Helene clearly.

There was a long pause.

"Yer a liar!" barked the voice, sounding nearer now, and very angry.

"No, really," said Helene desperately looking at Charlie for help. "We saw her less than 24 hours ago. She was in rather a bad way. We're trying to help her: her and her dad. 'Wolford' was the only name she could give us."

"Prove it!" the voice snarled.

"Um... does Matthew Hopkins and the '*Malleus Maleficarum*' mean anything to you?"

Helene felt ridiculous saying it but maybe it would work better than 'Abracadabra'.

Slowly the door opened, trembling unhappily on its ancient hinges, and the most enormous woman stared out at them. Helene took in the colourful house dress, laddered tights, huge fluffy slippers and fists the size of a leg of lamb. Miss Wolford was no slip of a girl. In fact...

"Er, excuse me for saying so," said Helene, "but you're Hank, aren't you?"

"Well, aren't you the clever one?" said Dolly/Hank. "Saw clean through my disguise."

"It was tough," said Helene shakily, "but I'm a journalist so I'm trained to be observant. Er... great slippers by the way."

Charlie had taken a step backwards and was staring at Dolly/Hank with undisguised astonishment.

"Bloody hell!" he said softly.

Which was twice in two minutes, from a man not much given to swearing.

"You'd better come in," said Dolly/Hank.

Helene chewed nervously on her lip as she followed the hulking creature into the stygian gloom. She would have given almost anything to have her head torch right now. It would be a bloody silly place to break an ankle by tripping over a dead squirrel or falling through the floorboards into some homemade oubliette.

Dolly/Hank fiddled around behind a torn, dusty curtain and opened a heavy-looking door. Helene wouldn't have been in the least surprised if the corpse of the creature's dead mother was rocking quietly in a chair. But she was so far wrong, it was almost laughable. Instead of a collection of homemade taxidermy featuring family members, a pool of light revealed a small, round, submarine-style hatch at her feet. She was reminded of Charlie's bolt hole in the Highlands. Fooled again. She'd been utterly wrong-footed.

Dolly/Hank descended first and Helene climbed down the

metal ladder after him. With a quick look around, Charlie followed, one hand inside his jacket. As she descended, Helene glanced up, hoping that he had a gun with him after all. They hadn't talked about such things – not since Hawaii.

"Welcome to my Command Centre," said Dolly/Hank in a noticeably ordinary voice, not the growling, snarling weird sister he had been upstairs.

Despite his bizarre get-up, he looked and sounded, well, nearly normal.

The pod was a wall-to-wall collection of high-tech computer equipment: most of them Helene didn't recognise or could even begin to guess what functions they performed. Lights flashed and disks whirled and acres of cabling hung from the curved ceiling like sinister bunting.

"This place is amazing!" she breathed.

"Thanks," said Dolly/Hank.

"Is this the headquarters for the Gene Genies?" asked Helene.

"Kinda, I guess," said Dolly/Hank, looking at her shrewdly. "I think we've got some talking to do."

"You can say that again," said Helene with a mixture of relief and optimism.

Charlie was silent.

"Er, what do you like to be called?" said Helene delicately.

"Dolly or Hank is fine," came the reply, "although looking at your friend I'm guessing he'd been more comfortable with Hank."

As Charlie currently had his hands crossed stiffly across his chest and didn't reply, Helene answered for them both: "Okay, Hank, it is."

She took a deep breath. "Well, where do I start? At the beginning I suppose. It started..."

But Hank interrupted her. "No, honey, I'd like to hear lover-boy tell it."

Helene looked at Charlie, whose face was carefully blank. She shrugged. Over to you, her body language told him.

Continuing to stand rigidly, Charlie gave the sit-rep as briefly and concisely as possible: explaining how they met, what they'd done, where they'd been, and why they'd landed on Hank's doorstep. He left out nothing that was relevant, except perhaps, the execution of Bill, which Helene felt was his prerogative.

Hank listened with rapt attention, his eyes not leaving Charlie's face. When Charlie finished there was silence.

Eventually Hank stood up. The movement was so sudden that Helene gasped and Charlie's hand dipped back into his jacket again.

"Tea, I think," said Hank blandly. There was no way he could have missed their twin reactions but he didn't refer to it. "Sasparilla okay?" he continued. "It's good for cleansing the blood."

"Oh, yes, lovely," said Helene faintly. "I've never tried it but I'm sure it's delicious."

Good God! she said to herself. *I sound like I'm talking to the vicar.*

Hank took his time making the tea while Helene watched him. Charlie was inspecting Hank's command centre: Helene guessed he was making a mental audit of the banks of expensive-looking equipment, assessing their potential usefulness.

When Hank had reseated himself and handed out the tea, Helene felt the tension inside her rise again.

"So, what do you want from me?" said Hank.

Which wasn't quite the conversation opener that Helene had expected.

"Do you know what Wally Manfred found out about the link between the 1929 Wall Street Crash and the US debt at the end of the First World War?" she asked.

Hank's eyebrows shot up and he shook his head.

"All I can tell you is that Wally said he was working on something big but I never knew what it was. Sorry, honey, I guess that must be a big disappointment to you after all you've been through."

Which was the understatement of the century.

Helene rubbed her temples.

"Do you know where they took Wally?" she said. "We know he's not in the Warm Creek Nursing Home..."

Hank shook his head again, his expression dark.

"Nope. Could be anywhere. The NSA has got places all over where they take people. There's a huge facility underneath Area 51 that the government denies is there: but we know."

"Who knows?" said Charlie.

"Hackers: people like me," said Hank proudly. "That's why we do what we do: to keep the government honest; to show up the lies they tell us which are designed to keep us all in our little boxes and paying our taxes. My family has been searching for the truth since Roswell. We're from New Mexico," he added by way of explanation. "There have been aliens visiting this planet for millennia, but will the government admit it? No, siree!"

Charlie glanced at Helene. They'd landed in the asylum.

"What do you think they're doing with him?" said Helene, trying to keep the conversation vaguely on track. "What do you think happened to Wally?"

Hank looked sad.

"It's my belief that they killed him," he said. "Probably dug a deep pit and threw him in it. I just hope he was dead first: I have nightmares about being buried alive. Of course, it don't help living in this hole."

Helene took a deep intake of breath. This was not what she'd wanted to hear. Since she'd first heard about Wally's disappearance she'd imagined herself finding some way to get him released, of saving him. This wasn't how she wanted his story to end.

"But why would they have killed him?" said Charlie. "He was your top hacker: the NSA can always use people like him."

"Well, yes and no," said Hank mysteriously, looking from Helene to Charlie and back again. "Have you ever wondered why the US government can't shut down people like me for good?"

Helene assumed it was a rhetorical question because Hank showed no signs of waiting for an answer.

"Because we're better than their best," said Hank. "And I'll tell you why: all the Feds get their trainees straight from college. And I mean straight: straight A students with not so much as a 'didn't inhale' on their records. So these kids are all trained to think in the same way: logical, clinical. And that's why folks like me will always have 'em licked. Because most hackers aren't college educated: we're the drop-outs, the freaks, the weirdos, the ones no-one bothered to talk to at school – and believe me I know what I'm talking about. But the thing is with guys like me, our brains are programmed different. We're mostly self-educated: we've taught ourselves so we don't follow the same path as the college guys. They go in straight lines – logical; we go in circles, in loops, in crazy paving patterns, in double-helix swirls and who can say where our ideas come from. We're creative, imaginative, off-the chart, freakin' geniuses!"

Helene found herself smiling at Hank's colourful, grandiose description of himself.

"And Wally?" pursued Charlie impatiently.

"Wally wasn't really one of us," said Hank. "You see, what you've got to know about Wally is that he wasn't that great of a hacker. He was good, but not that good."

"But I don't understand," said Helene. "I thought he was the founder of the Gene Genies: I thought he was the one who wrote the software that Wikileaks uses?"

Hank shook his head, a lopsided smile across his face.

"Nope. It just suited him that everyone thought that. To put it another way, ole Wally knew that by taking the credit, it would protect someone else... and make him a target instead of..."

"Oh!"

Helene let out a soft sigh as the penny dropped.

"You mean it was Barbara all along?" she said.

Hank smiled.

"Got it one, honey!"

"But how did she do it?" said Helene. "She really had us fooled."

It was hard to imagine that the broken young woman Helene and Charlie had seen was really a hacker mastermind.

"Well, that's the clever bit," said Hank. "The Feds never thought she was a threat cuz they didn't know about her – thanks to Wally – so they just gave her some second rate security: an ankle tag and trip laser in the garden. It took her about two minutes to get around *that*! She pretended to be a recluse but really she'd come and go as she pleased. She sent you to me which means she's probably gone like the wind by now."

Hank looked pleased.

"What do you mean?" said Helene, suddenly disconcerted. "What do you mean 'gone like the wind'? Where has she gone?"

"Honey," said Hank, "she's been planning this ever since they took her old man. She's done some jobs, saved up the pennies – not that she wasn't pretty freakin' rich before – and now she's decided it's time to start her new life. So she's gone."

"But why now?" she persisted.

"Aw, honey. Don't you get it? Because she'd found you!"

Helene was so discombobulated that she paid no attention to Hank's odd phrasing.

"But you can contact her?" she said Helene.

"No, honey. I always knew that when she was gone, that would be it."

"But she must have left you something!" croaked Helene.

Hank shook his head, still smiling.

Helene felt like ramming the smile down his face with the toe of her boot – or somewhere darker and less accessible.

"But you know what, honey," said Hank, "she left *you* something."

"What do you mean?" said Helene looking from Hank to Charlie and back again.

"She left you a trail of breadcrumbs," said Hank. "She told you where to look."

Helene tried to squeeze some sense from her battered brain. At last an idea popped in: preposterous, impossible – but maybe not for the Gene Genies.

CHAPTER NINETEEN

HANK INVITED THEM TO STAY THE NIGHT. HE SHOWED Charlie a place where their car could be hidden: parked in a thicket and covered by a piece of tarpaulin, camouflaged with branches and leaves. Perfect: unless they needed to leave in a hurry.

"This place is totally secure," said Hank when they were back inside, patting the curving side of the pod. "I've got stored enough food and bottled water for two years. I could survive nuclear fallout here. Of course, if the San Andreas Fault blows or Yellowstone decides to yawn, we're all history anyway."

Helene nodded feeling it was more politic to say nothing that might stoke Hank's wilder conspiracy/end-of-the-world theories. Although she no longer doubted that the most extraordinary conspiracies were turning out to be true. It did make one wonder about Roswell: weather balloon or alien car crash? On the other hand, everyone needed a hobby.

Although Hank's hobby turned out to be needlepoint, or to be more specific, petit point. He showed them into a small side room of the pod that seemed to have been decorated like an old fashioned parlour. He even had a set of matching antimacassars.

There was a pair of neat occasional tables, decorated with

lace cloths and matching brocade lampshades. A *chaise longue* was covered with examples of Hank's extraordinary handiwork, butterflies chasing a ray of sunshine. Quite beautiful. Totally unexpected. And at odds with the Gibson guitar, displayed on its own stand: an expression of the 'Howlin'' part of his multifaceted (or possibly split) personality.

An old fashioned Victorian bedstead stood in the corner. Helene had no idea how Hank had managed to get that enormous piece of furniture into the pod: piece by piece was her best guess; followed by a bit of spot-welding after the event.

An embroidered counterpane covered the bed and Hank proudly showed her a delicate *bargello* stitch in the traditional Florentine flame pattern. It really was exquisite work.

"You guys can sleep in here," said Hank. "I assume you're together..."

"No!" said Helene quickly. "We're not."

Charlie gave her an unidentifiable look as he leaned against the door frame, listening, watching.

"Oh really?" said Hank. "That's a pity: you make a cute couple. Well, I'm afraid you'll have to share anyway, space being what it is. And I wouldn't recommend camping in the shack: I just keep that to scare away door-to-door salesmen but I think some raccoons are nesting up there and being nocturnal, they like to mosey around at night."

Helene was feeling impatient. It was certainly true what Hank had said about his brain working in a random pattern: it was very hard to keep him focused.

She sat down in a diminutive armchair and looked up at the man-mountain in front of her.

"Hank, can we talk about the Gene Genies?" said Helene.

"Sure, honey, whaddya want to know?"

Hank squeezed his massive frame onto a frail looking rocking chair opposite her and hooked one giant thigh over the other.

"Well," said Helene. "Who are they, for a start?"

"I couldn't tell you, honey, although I could make some guesses. We've never met face to face because we're an online community. It's safer for all of us if we don't know who everyone else is. They could be school kids or truck drivers or... well, just about anyone, anywhere in the world. Plus, most of them use voice disguisers and some will only type messages. But even so you can get a pretty good idea of whether or not English is their mother tongue, or whether they're from Britain or Australia or India cuz their English is usually better."

"I see," said Helene. "But do you trust them?"

"Those boys and girls know more about me and more about each other than anyone else," said Hank. "Even though we don't use first names or nothing, I trust them all."

And now for the prize question, thought Helene.

"Will they help us?" she said.

"Depends on what you're planning on doing?" he replied.

Helene looked up to meet his gaze and shook her head wearily.

"I don't even know myself," she admitted. "But this whole thing comes down to money; Wally told us as much. Right?"

"It sure seems that way," said Hank cheerfully.

"And you said that Wally thought he was on to something. And I think that 'something' must have been a file that he hacked. From what you've said it would be pretty easy for any of the Gene Genies to hack the same file."

"Sure," said Hank, "if we knew what files he was talking about, but it could be anything."

"Well, we can narrow it down a bit," said Helene, "because from what I've read, the roots of the present money crisis in America go all the way back to the Liberty Acts of the First World War and..."

"Uh-uh, honey," said Hank, shaking his great shaggy head. "I think you can look a bit further back than that. Haven't you ever heard of the 1907 Bankers' Panic?"

Helene shook her head.

"That's where the whole preoccupation with a Federal Reserve comes from." Hank stared at her but it was all new territory to Helene and Charlie, still leaning against the door frame, looked equally blank.

"Well, it's like this," continued Hank. "Back in '07 there

was no US central bank. Nothing. Nada. When the New York stock market suddenly lost 50% of its value over night because of some unregulated side bets at bucket shops, *people lost confidence in the system.*"

Hank emphasised the words. Helene thought she was beginning to understand why...

"Yup, people lost confidence in the system and there was a run on the banks. Lots went bankrupt, businesses collapsed and people lost their entire life savings. It was after this that the government set up the Federal Reserve System. You get what I'm saying? It's all about people having confidence in the system – because it's all a racket. The system is just make-believe: it's just a wish and a prayer. Just the slightest breeze and the whole deck of cards comes a-tumblin' down."

Helene nodded slowly but Charlie still looked lost.

"I don't get it: how does this history lesson help us now?" he said.

"You go ahead, honey," said Hank. "Explain to lover-boy. I'll go fix us up a mess o' beans for supper."

Sometimes Hank really overdid the hillbilly act.

"The whole financial system across the world is based on confidence," said Helene. She spoke slowly, trying to marshal her thoughts into order at the same time. "We put our money in banks and get a small amount of interest; they lend the money out at a higher rate of interest in the confidence that they'll get paid back. If the banks lose confidence, they stop lending money: businesses don't have the injection of cash that they need and can fold because their cash flow is buggered. But what happens if people lose confidence in the system?"

Charlie shrugged.

"Well, that's where the gold standard comes in," she finished lamely. "Something you can rely on."

Hank's voice floated in from the kitchen, "Follow the trail of breadcrumbs."

A spark ignited in Helene's brain: it was extraordinary – so bloody simple when she'd been making it so bloody complicated. All the evidence was there – hiding in plain view.

"I need to think," she said, frowning at her fingernails. "Just let me check a few things: I feel like I'm starting to see..."

Charlie shrugged and wandered off to make some more detailed checks on Hank's equipment while Helene pulled out her laptop from the grab bag and settled herself comfortably on Hank's bed.

If she was right, this could be the break through they'd been waiting for. If she was right...

Helene felt that her brain activity must be off the scale: it certainly felt like it was going to explode. She started looking up websites and making notes, pages and pages of notes, her mind in a frenzy, thoughts whirling.

A chair scraped loudly across the floor of the pod and she realised, to her surprise, that she was cold, goose pimples standing out on her arms. Not only that, but she was stiff as a board and had trouble moving out of the cross-legged position when Charlie came back in to sit next to her.

Without asking he leaned in to her and started massaging her neck, his strong hands easing the stiffness. He leaned closer, his warm breath sending sparks of electricity up and down her spine.

"Okay, thanks, that's better," she muttered pulling away.

Charlie shrugged, his face guarded.

She called Hank in from his cooking duties. He raised an eyebrow when he saw Charlie sitting on the bed next to Helene but didn't comment.

"Listen!" she said in a rush, "I think I've got something."

Hank took one look at her bright, excited eyes.

"You really have, haven't you?" he said. "Tell us."

"Okay," said Helene, brushing her hair out of her eyes. "Another quick history lesson so bear with me. Hank's already told us about the history of the Federal Reserve Bank. From there we go forwards to the First World War. France and Britain are in danger of losing against Germany and the US decides to enter the war. But first they have to finance it because guns, uniforms, soldiers' pay – they all cost a lot of money. Well, the US government doesn't have that sort of ready dough so in 1917 they push through the Emergency Loan

Act which is a way to stump up $5 billion in cash from the general public. People are virtually bullied into buying these bonds to fund the war. A few months later the Second Liberty Bond Act goes through to raise even more cash, but this time there's a little clause that few people notice. The government gives itself extra power to borrow and also sets a ceiling to the amount of public debt the country should have."

She looked up and Hank nodded encouragingly. Charlie merely watched her face.

"Okay, I'm with you so far, honey," Hank said, "but not quite seeing the relevance between a hundred year old war and today."

"You will," she said. "You will. Look at it this way: until very recently US government bonds – Treasuries – were generally considered the safest financial asset in the world. But by the summer of 2011 the US government loses its Triple A financial rating as a country. They nearly end up defaulting on paying their debts and that means teachers, soldiers and a whole host of civil servants from park rangers to meter maids are in danger of not getting paid. At the last minute Obama works out a deal and raises the $14.3 trillion debt ceiling again."

"Hang on," said Charlie, "that's quite a jump you just made. Where does the Wall Street Crash come in?"

"I'm trying to explain," she said hastily, "It's just that my brain is still reeling... the possible implications... okay, okay. The Wall Street Crash happens in 1929. It's devastating, not just for the US but for the whole of the industrialised West and 12 years of Depression follow. It was said that anyone who bought stocks in mid-1929 and didn't get rid of them saw most of their adult life pass by before getting their investment back to square one. When the stock market crashes, investment dies, businesses die and government income takes a nosedive. How can a government pay what they owe on a reduced income from fewer taxes? Reparation money from Germany is slow coming in, so the government has no choice but to borrow – and raises the debt ceiling again."

"Yah, I'm seeing a pattern here," said Charlie.

Hank smiled.

"Right," said Helene. "A bloody great big pattern. But the question is: what is a US government bond? What is a Treasury?"

She waited.

"Sorry," said Charlie, "I thought it was a rhetorical question."

Helene frowned in concentration.

"Well, kind of: a Treasury is a promise to pay. That's all: it's a piece of paper that says the US government owes you money and that they'll pay you back with interest. Just like a five pound note: you know, the bit where it says, 'I promise to bay the bearer'..."

"So?" said Charlie, more than puzzled.

"So," said Helene, "what's their asset? If you borrow money on a mortgage, your asset is your house. So what is the US government's asset? What have they borrowed against?"

Understanding dawned on Charlie's face.

"I see what you're getting at," he muttered. "It's all a giant gamble: the US government has gambled that the economy will keep growing, so the debt becomes actually less valuable. But the asset: well, that's a vault full of gold bullion in Fort Knox, isn't it?"

Helene looked serious.

"It should be, shouldn't it? Some there, and some in the 12 regional Federal Reserve Banks. Convenient, isn't it, to spread the whole asset of the United States across 13 holding centres: there are no public audits so no-one knows who's got what – probably not even the individual banks themselves. Well, that's what the conspiracy theorists say..."

"And they're wrong?" said Charlie, casting a glance at Hank who continued to sit mutely.

"Hmm," said Helene. "Yes and no: audits are performed every year by authorised private accounting firms..."

"I hear a 'but'," said Charlie.

"You do indeed," said Helene. "There's one significant exemption from the audit."

"Thrill me," he said.

"I'll quote you instead," said Helene. "I found this on a public service website about the Federal Reserve audits: it says, 'transactions for or with a foreign central bank, government of a foreign country, or non-private international financing organisation are excluded from the audits'."

She paused.

"So?" said Charlie.

"What if the gold isn't in the reserve banks?" she said in an excited voice. "What if it isn't anywhere? What if it hasn't been in the US for a very long time, because it's already been sold to foreign countries? That wouldn't show up on the audit and no-one knows if and when gold has left the country."

"Meaning?" he pressed.

"Meaning," she went on, "what if the US government had to sell off their gold to fund the First World War. What if they just couldn't raise enough cash from bonds so they sold their entire gold reserves?"

Charlie breathed out in a low whistle and Hank leaned forward, his eyes never leaving her face.

"How much gold are we talking about?"

"Well," she said, "the US doesn't publish figures but they're 'widely thought' to hold 9,300 tonnes of gold. Gold is selling for $1,500 an ounce – I make that about $2.4 trillion dollars."

Charlie thought about it then shook his head.

"Then what difference does that make?" he said. "The US debt is over $14 trillion dollars. You said so yourself."

"True," said Helene. "But what if you were, let's say, the government of China. You hold maybe $1.5 trillion of US Treasury bonds. Wouldn't you be just the tiniest bit nervous if you knew that the US couldn't pay your debt if you called it in? I mean, what would that do to international trade if the US was known to be on the point of calling in the bailiffs. What are they going to do: sell Hawaii? Lease out California?"

"Oh shit," said Charlie.

"I still don't see why this is enough to get Wally disappeared," said Hank.

"Well, think about it this way," said Helene. "What would

happen if the world found out that the US couldn't pay its debts?"

He shrugged.

"The US government would have no choice: they'd have to reset the clock and revalue the dollar: $1,000 old dollars would equal $1 new dollar. That way they'd essentially wipe out their debts. Meantime, the world economy shudders to a halt, businesses are bankrupt all over the world, governments fall, countries go to war, millions die. Ultimate chaos: the fire sale of all time."

There was a shocked silence.

"You think this is what Wally Manfred worked out?" said Charlie. "I don't want to rain on your parade, Helene, but if you could work this out in a couple of hours, surely others could as well."

"Of course," said Helene crisply. "In fact you'll find this sort of thinking on any number of conspiracy websites. I wouldn't be surprised if some of the Gene Genies have had the same idea – which could explain how Wally stumbled on to it in the first place."

"So," said Charlie, "explain to me why this is the news that got Wally Manfred kidnapped – if it's already in the public domain."

"Because," said Helene, "I think Wally Manfred didn't just have all this as a theory: I think he had evidence – something so damning that not even the US government could get away with plausible denial..."

She hesitated for a second.

"Not only did Wally know the US government have sold all their gold," she said. "He could prove it."

CHAPTER TWENTY

Charlie spoke first.

"If you're right about all this – and I'm not saying that you are necessarily because it's just so far out there – then we have to get hold of any proof that Wally had – otherwise it's just speculation and we're just pissing in the wind. If you tried to publish with what you have now, you'll be ridiculed as Loony Number One."

Helene nodded slowly.

"I know."

She rubbed her eyes tiredly. They felt hot and scratchy, her mind fuzzy and unfocused after all the new data she'd been trying to make sense of.

Hank looked uncertain. Helene felt irritated with the pair of them. She knew, she just knew that she'd finally found the trail of breadcrumbs that Wally and Barbara had left for her.

"Okay, honey," said Hank gently. "I'm with you so far, but how do we prove it?"

"What we need to do," said Helene, "is to get our hands on those private audits that the US government commissions..."

"I thought you said they were worthless," said Charlie, "because of the exemptions of sales of gold to foreign governments."

Helene eased herself off the bed and started to pace up and down.

"Yes!" said Helene, excitedly. "Yes, but there's still a paper trail. Just because those gold sales aren't listed in the audit, doesn't mean that they don't exist. What we need the Gene Genies to do is to find out exactly how much gold the US has sold on the QT in the last 100 years."

"This could take months!" said Charlie. "The info you're looking for will have the highest level of security on it."

"Is that right?" said Helene to Hank. "Would it take the Gene Genies months?"

"Twenty-four hours," said Hank, challenging Charlie with a stare. "Give us 24 hours – maybe less and you'll have the information that you want. Actually it sounds like it's gonna be kinda fun."

Helene really had to question Hank's idea of 'fun' but as it was going to help them...

"That's marvellous, Hank!" she said.

Helene leaned over to give the man-mountain a hug and was almost swallowed among the swathes of material that smelled faintly of lily of the valley.

She looked at Charlie: if she didn't know better she would have said he was sulking.

That evening they sat down to a delicious stew prepared lovingly by Hank and much better than the threatened 'mess o' beans'. Helene guessed that he was enjoying the novelty of having company over and she had to admit that his apple pie was to die for.

"Mmm! This is wonderful! How do you get the pastry so light?" she said.

Hank beamed.

"It's all in the quality of the ingredients, sweetie. Good butter is important but the less handling of the pastry the better. Plus you gotta have cold hands: cold hands and a warm heart, as my ma used to say. And then there's my secret ingredient."

"Which is?" said Helene.

"A secret, sweetie," said Hank, raising his eyebrows.

Charlie looked bored although he'd made a good meal from Hank's efforts.

"When are we going to talk to the Gene Genies?" he said.

"You're not," said Hank severely. "You think they'd talk to you? These people are paranoid: better leave it to me. I've already scheduled a meeting."

"Whatever," Charlie muttered under his breath.

Helene thought she saw him mouthing the words, 'bunch of nutters', but she couldn't be sure.

After washing up the supper things as her contribution to the domestic chores, Helene joined the men in the main pod. A sense of anticipation filled the small space.

At precisely 8.27pm the computer screens around the room blinked into life. But instead of the faces of the hackers, each was represented by a different cartoon character. Helene wondered who Hank had chosen for his character: Penelope Pitstop, perhaps?

"Good evening, Genies," said Hank. "Your mission this evening, should you choose to accept it, is to hack into the files of the Fed Reserve banks and find out how much gold has been sold to foreign governments over the last 100 years. It's the secret audit files that we're after. We wanna know what they've sold and how much they *say* they've still got. This is the big one, folks, it's a task set by our leader – and we've got just 24 hours to complete the mission."

"Holy baloney, Hank!" came a voice from the computer screen that was represented by a giant Bugs Bunny. "We're really going to hit them?"

"Sure am, Bugs. Tonight we start the fight back. For Wally."

Twelve disembodied voices muttered, "For Wally," followed by half a minute's silence out of respect for the lamented, believed to be 'late', Wally Manfred.

"Okay, Genies, let's do it! Make it so!" ordered Hank.

There was a short pause.

"Er, who's doing what?" came a voice from the Buffy cartoon screen. "There are the National Archives, the State Archives, plus the 12 Fed Reserves and Fort Knox: I'd like to do Dallas. It's a cowboy thing."

Someone else insisted on having St Louis, and at least three people were arguing over Minneapolis. It reminded Helene of a visit to a school she'd made once as a favour to one of her bosses at the newspaper. What a bunch of juveniles.

There was a huge tussle over who got to do Cleveland with at least four Cleveland Brown fans in the room: eventually Hank got them sorted out and the 12 computer screens went blank.

Charlie frowned at Helene and the look that passed between them agreed: Good Lord! We're counting on these people? Charlie continued looking at Helene and mouthed the words slowly: "We are so fucked."

Helene shook her head, not because she thought he was wrong but because it was all just too ghastly for words. And when it came down to it she thought Charlie was probably right.

Even so, they all had their jobs to do. Hank was hacking Richmond because he said he'd visited there once and had been arrested. Helene didn't ask what for. Charlie had gone into town to get supplies and 'equipment', whatever that meant, despite Hank's protestations that a) he had everything they could possibly need, and b) it wasn't safe to be seen out.

Helene stayed out of the ensuing argument which ended when Charlie had stalked off. Instead Helene fired up her laptop again. It seemed to have wilted slightly, looking embarrassed to be compared to the gleaming technology surrounding it. Helene reminded herself it wasn't the packaging that was important, but the contents. As a woman in her late forties, she'd used that line a lot.

She had got her notes bang up to date and was listening for Charlie come back, when she sensed Hank leaning over her shoulder.

"It's gonna be alright, honey," he said kindly, a massive fist stroking her shoulder. "Aunty Hank has never let a friend down before and he's not gonna start now."

"Thanks," said Helene, tiredly, "but you don't even know me. Oh! Not that I'm not grateful because I am – obviously."

"I'm pretty good at reading people," said Hank softly. "I've had to be because of the way I look: I don't have to explain myself to you, I know. Anyway, I can tell you're one of the good 'uns." Hank looked over his shoulder towards Charlie who had just climbed back down into the main pod. "Him I'm not so sure about: you be careful, young lady, you hear me?"

Hank walked away before Helene had a chance to ask him what he meant, but when she looked round at Charlie, he was staring right at her, his expression cold. A chill rippled down her spine.

She stood up and stretched and paced around the pod trying to act naturally. Charlie ignored her and, eventually, with nothing better to do, Helene lay down on Hank's bed and covered herself with the counterpane. She fell asleep to the gentle clicking of fingernails on keyboards.

She woke up once in the night and saw the light from the main pod glowing brightly under the closed door. The bed beside her was empty. She sighed, turned onto her side and went back to sleep.

By morning the results of the mass illegal hack were already starting to trickle in. Helene took a quick shower and began to analyse the data while Hank her hair dried naturally. Hank whipped up a batch of pancakes with maple syrup and a pile of bacon. Helene groaned for her cholesterol levels, but it did smell good.

Charlie still wasn't speaking to her. The silence between them was beginning to get on her nerves.

The data, on the other hand, was puzzling. According to the figures, the US Treasury seemed to have its full complement of gold. The figures for Boston and Fort Knox were still to come in, but otherwise...

New York : 1,800 tonnes
Philadelphia : 900 tonnes
Cleveland : 755 tonnes

Richmond: 2,225 tonnes
Atlanta : 125 tonnes
Chicago : 1,310 tonnes
St Louis : 50 tonnes
Minneapolis : 750 tonnes
Kansas City : 154 tonnes
Dallas : 156 tonnes
San Francisco : 200 tonnes.

Hank spun the stats through some of his home-made programs, ran them against the private details of foreign bullion sales and sat scratching his head. Eventually he turned to Helene, a pitying look on his hairy face.

He shook his head. He didn't need to say more.

Helene took the print-outs from him and sat poring over them while Hank finished the food.

"I'm sorry, honey," said Hank, ladling pancakes onto her plate, "even if Boston and Knox turn up short, there doesn't seem to be any missing gold. At least nothing worth offing poor ole Wally for."

Helene shook her head. "Then what's wrong with this picture?"

The two men stared at her. She saw sympathy in Hank's eyes and what... a certain impatience in Charlie's. He was so hard to read and spending 24/7 with him for the last ten days hadn't helped much. My God, she thought, is that all it's been: just ten days. She felt like she'd aged a couple of decades at least.

"I... I need to get some air," she said. "It'll help me think."

"It's not safe out there, honey," said Hank, concern evident in his voice.

"I'll come with you," said Charlie. "I could do with getting out of here for a while, too."

He threw a tight, angry look at Hank.

Helene felt the weight of Hank's disapproval as she climbed out of the pod, but then again, she was used to feeling that around most men.

The forest looked very different in the morning light. The perfumed scent of cypress wood rose on the air. In the distance Helene could hear the sound of cars and beyond that, the familiar yet strange sound of surf crashing onto rocks. She had to remind herself that this was the Pacific Ocean not the Atlantic, and she was a long way from home.

Charlie was staring gravely through the trees up towards the sky. Being cooped in someone else's pod didn't suit him but Helene didn't have time to worry about his moods. She had to work out where she'd gone wrong: in what way had her thinking been faulty.

In silence, each locked in their own thoughts, they followed a trail through the forest. Helene couldn't tell whether it had been made by animals or people. The former, she hoped. She had no wish to bump into some hikers now, especially if awkward questions might ensue. On the other hand, she hadn't thought to ask Hank if bears were to be found in the forest. She really hoped Charlie had that gun.

After an hour's yomping, they sat down to rest. Or rather Helene sat down to rest, Charlie still had buckets of energy to use up. Helene wouldn't have been particularly surprised if he'd started swinging through the trees like some latter-day Tarzan, he was so wired.

"What next?" he said unexpectedly.

Helene shook her head.

"We're close to the truth: I can feel it, we've just missed the trail somehow. Any ideas?"

"The Gene Genies could be wrong," he said. "You could be wrong."

"It's possible," she admitted, "but somehow I don't think so. Let's look at the evidence again."

"I don't know if you've noticed," said Charlie bitterly, "but we're a bit thin on evidence right now."

Glumly, Helene had to agree. She leaned back against a tree and tried to let her mind drift: maybe if left to its own accord, it would stray back to the correct neural pathway.

Charlie slid down next to her and she was glad to feel him close to her again.

"If it's not about the gold," he said resting his head on his knees, "what else could it be?"

"I don't know: that's what I've been trying to figure out," she said wearily.

Suddenly they heard the sound of a twig cracking in the distance.

Immediately Charlie was alert. He rose silently and listened intently. Helene felt a sweat break out across her back.

"Time to go," said Charlie, bending down and breathing softly into her ear.

He pulled her up by the arm and they crept away through the forest. Helene was lost but Charlie was utterly sure-footed. Helene didn't remember crossing a stream – and she certainly didn't remember wading through one. In fact, Charlie made her cross and re-cross the stream several times.

"In case there's anyone out there looking for us and in case they've got dogs," he whispered.

Two hours later they were back at the shack. Helene was exhausted, wet and muddy. Also very, very pissed off. But at herself and her stupidity on insisting she went for a walk in the first place. Would she ever be able to recognise good advice when it was given to her? It seemed unlikely: learning had not taken place.

Hank was practically gnashing his teeth at their tardy return.

"Straight into a hot bath for you, missy," he growled, tossing a baleful look at Charlie whom he clearly blamed for leading Helene astray. The look bounced off Charlie's broad shoulders. In fact Helene recognised that he had perked up considerably after their close encounter. She guessed he was one of those soldiers who was brilliant to have around when on active service, when imminent danger was in the air; and a complete nightmare back at home barracks. A friend of hers had had a dog like that once: a Weimaraner who was so highly strung it needed constant distraction or it chewed the furniture.

She was soaking in the old fashioned sit-up-and-beg hip bath and wondering what Hank had cooked for lunch when the thought suddenly hit her. She sat up so suddenly that a small tidal wave of soapy water slopped over the tub's edge.

Cursing softly, she lurched out of the bath, and mopped up the mess as best she could, Hank being so house-proud. Then she dressed hastily and presented herself clean and alert in the kitchen.

"I've had another idea," she said.

At least neither of the men groaned, even if mentally they were rolling their eyes.

"I've been thinking about this business of the gold," she said, "and I still think I'm right: there's just more to it than I'd thought. At first I thought that the gold must be missing but unless the auditors are making up the figures, which is entirely possible, then there's something else going on."

"Granted," said Charlie, "but what?"

She didn't answer directly.

"When the economy goes really badly," she said, concentrating hard, "governments want to put their money into strong currencies – like the Swiss Franc. A totally over-rated currency for a piss-pot of a country the size of Wales, wouldn't you say?"

Charlie shrugged and Hank looked askance at her bad language before lunchtime.

"And if things go really, really badly," continued Helene, "governments don't want cash, they want something a bit more certain – they want gold."

"Yah, so what?" said Charlie, clearly bored.

"Time for another history lesson," said Helene, getting into her stride. If she saw Charlie rolling his eyes for real, she pretended not to.

"If people don't have confidence in the currency, the whole system is in danger of collapsing," explained Helene. "Going back five hundred years, dear old Henry VIII wasn't quite the bluff King Hal everyone thought he was: in reality he as a war-hungry, greedy bastard. His father had spent a lifetime making England into one of the most stable economies in Europe but it wasn't a case of like father like son: until Henry's reign, English currency was made of gold and silver so the face value was pretty much the same as their bullion value. But Henry had some expensive vanity wars to pay for so he mixed the silver in his coins with a base metal, copper. But he didn't stop there: it was such a good wheeze that he kept on doing it. Soon the so-called 'silver' coins were more copper than silver. That's how Henry got the nickname 'Old Coppernose' because where his portrait was stamped onto the coins, his nose was the highest part of the profile. When the coins got rubbed in people's pockets, the silver got rubbed off the nose first, it showed the copper underneath."

"Okay," said Charlie, "Enough of the history lesson."

It clearly hadn't been his favourite subject at school.

"No, it's important," said Helene, "because I think it explains what's happening now. Henry's coins were so debased in value that it caused rampant inflation: people wanted two 'silver' coins when before they would just have one. Foreigners wouldn't accept English money and the economy was shot to hell and back. Eventually the debased coins were withdrawn because *people had no confidence in them.*"

"Yeah, so?" said Charlie, looking even more bored.

"So what if the US government has been doing the same thing?" she said. "What if, when they moved the Bullion Depository to Fort Knox in 1937 some of it – or maybe all of it – was replaced with tungsten and just plated with gold?"

The men were silent, considering her crazy idea.

"What if the US has been selling fool's gold to foreign powers? I mean – who'd think to check? Like Old Coppernose: what if the gold has been debased for years – decades... and what if these countries eventually got a tiny bit curious about how the US was financing its debt and started checking up that the gold they'd bought from the US really was gold and not tungsten or lead or some other non-gold metal."

"I don't know," said Charlie softly, his eyes suddenly interested.

"I guess they'd be selling a lot of home chemistry sets," said Hank, finally joining in.

"Not half!" said Helene. "But imagine you were the Chinese government with your $1.4 trillion worth of US debt and then you found out that you weren't holding US gold, but some rubbish shipped out to your country when you were still in short trousers: you'd be pretty damn pissed off. Either you would demand real gold to replace what you'd been given, or..."

"Or?" Charlie and Hank said in unison.

"Or," continued Helene, "you'd demand preferential trade terms, ad infinitum, to keep quiet. Or you might demand other terms: that the US doesn't intervene in Chinese ambitions in Taiwan or Tibet, for example, or turn a blind eye when China buys up land in Africa and India. They might even want to be able to buy US aerospace companies – Stealth fighter technology, say. And I can't help thinking that the new Chinese J20 stealth fighter is an awful lot like the F117. The Chinese have put out a press statement that they reverse engineered it from a downed jet during the Kosovo war... but maybe they had a bit more help than that."

"Holy shit!" said Hank.

"This is almost unbelievable," said Charlie. "So the Chinese, or whoever, would have the US over a barrel."

"Yes, but it gets even worse," said Helene, thinking on her feet. "The stock market is so uncertain these days that investors regard gold as a hedge against devaluing currencies. Everyone wants gold. They said that Nixon scrapped the gold standard 40 years ago: but what if he was just trying to prepare the country against the day when the US government has to come clean and say, 'Sorry, folks, but we're broke'. Not many people can afford to consume the way Americans do: and neither can the US anymore. So they keep on borrowing – America is mortgaged up to the hilt but their only asset is a slowing economy and some falling real estate. All the government can do is just print more money – but the cupboard is bare, there's nothing left – just some fake gold."

She stopped, breathless.

"Maybe," said Charlie, frowning. "It all sounds pretty far-fetched."

Unlike Helene's other theories so far.

"Don't you see?" said Helene impatiently. "The only currency that has been consistent for the last 5,000 years is gold. But if the US government has been debasing their gold, the economy would be utterly buggered. And not just the US economy – the whole world would be affected. I think this is what Wally was working on: he was trying to figure out how much of the US gold reserve was real – and how much had been debased."

Charlie still looked unconvinced.

"Okay, suppose you're right," said Hank. "How could we prove it? And I assume there's no online way of doing it..."

"I've got an idea about that, too!" said Helene, her eyes shining dangerously like some born-again zealot. "There is an online way of doing it: we work out how much gold has been mined around the world in the last 100 years – or last fifty years if that's too hard to find out. But as near accurate as we can get it. And I don't just mean from the US: from every continent on the planet."

"This is ridiculous," said Charlie. "How the hell could we ever pull that amount of information?"

"Not easy, I grant you," she said, still grinning from ear to ear. "But have we or have we not got a direct line to the world's top team of hackers?"

Charlie shook his head impatiently as if trying to explain to a wayward toddler that eating six ice creams in a go was not a good idea.

"Even if we could find out the information," he said, "how can it possibly help us?"

"Ah, but it can!" said Helene, sounding like a magician who was about to produce a rabbit from her back pocket. "Because then we match the amount of gold mined around the world with what the US have sold off and what they say they still have. If the US share is too high, if it seems as if they're selling more than their share of what has been mined, then it means that some accountant is doing some fancy footwork. We'll be able to prove that their own audits are a complete work of fiction!"

Charlie shook his head.

"That won't work," he said.

Helene stared at him belligerently.

"For two reasons," he said. "Firstly, we already know how much gold is mined each year: it's about 2,500 tonnes, according to the World Gold Council – if you'd taken the trouble to even look at their website. About 2,000 tonnes goes towards making jewellery and the rest is bought up by investors."

Helene shook her head furiously. "We can't rely on their figures – they could just be a bluff. We need to find out for ourselves."

"And the second reason," continued Charlie without a change in his expression, "is that we'd need to know how much gold other governments had sold, too. Otherwise the stats are totally meaningless."

"Not necessarily," said Helene. "If the quantities of gold the US have sold are unusually high – and I'm betting that they are – then we know we're onto something because they can't sell huge quantities of gold and still have trillions of dollars of it without there being a balance – or obvious imbalance somewhere."

"This is crap!" said Charlie angrily. "Can you hear how desperate you sound? This isn't *evidence*; this is all just *speculation*. We can't use this – it doesn't help us! There must be something else: something else that Wally found and that we're missing. We need to think again. For God's sake, we need to think again!"

Helene scowled belligerently at him, which only infuriated him further. She was convinced that her reasoning was sound whatever arguments he scattered in her path. She'd found the trail of breadcrumbs – she was sure of it.

But by this time she didn't need Charlie's support because Hank was grinning at her and reluctantly acknowledging that it might not be a completely crazy idea.

"And who," said Helene finishing with a flourish, "loves an impossible challenge more than the Gene Genies?"

CHAPTER TWENTY-ONE

AT 6.59 PM THE GENE GENIES WERE ALL ONLINE AGAIN. IT really was a game to them, Helene realised. They thought they were rebels of the world united, but really, hacking top secret government files was just their idea of good, honest fun. On the other hand, Helene suspected that more than a couple of them would have enjoyed the idea – if not the reality – of worldwide chaos. Even hackers like hot showers and flushing toilets.

When Hank, stunningly attired in a purple taffeta gypsy smock with silver jewellery accessories, explained their new mission, there was a decided lack of enthusiasm. Where was the fun in doing pure research into dull gold mining stats when they could be hacking UFO sightings over Area 51?

"Well now, Genies," said Hank, "it's like this: once we've collated the data on gold mining versus sales of US gold, we should be able to work out if the gold in the Federal Reserve banks is bogus. Or not."

That was enough motivation for most of them although the Genie represented by the cartoon of the Roadrunner sent over a picture of Tweety-pie giving the bird.

"Oh well," sighed Hank, "you can't please all of the people all of the time."

Too true, thought Helene. Charlie was acting like a bear

with a beer hangover. Even though he was a pretty good hacker himself, as evinced by the first class tickets and unlimited hotel accommodation they'd been enjoying, he knew he was out of class around the Genies; even Hank was a better hacker than him – and it pissed him off.

He paced around the pod like a wild tiger in a snare, or rather one of those perpetual motion management toys that had been popular in the seventies. Helene hoped that Charlie never got sent to prison because he'd surely go stir crazy, although he'd probably exercise his considerable brain power by working out how to escape. On reflection, he'd have done well in Alcatraz.

At length Charlie stopped his pacing and looked at Helene, slumped over her laptop, trying to turn her notes into something Frank wouldn't toss straight in the wastepaper basket – if they ever got that far.

"You know this isn't going to work, don't you, Helene?" he said tightly.

She looked up at him: the same thought had been burning a hole through her dwindling resolve. Nevertheless...

"We're running out of options, Charlie," she sighed. "If you have a better idea, I'd love to hear it."

"Look, even if we find out that the mining quotas don't quite add up, it's not real evidence, is it?" he replied. "What we need is hard facts not just circumstantial shit – or we'll spend the rest of our lives in hiding. And I don't know about you, but I'm nearly up to my neck with lying low."

His vehemence surprised her. She'd supposed him immune to the discomforts of the job. Yep, he'd have done well in Colditz, too. No wonder that had appealed to him as a childhood game.

She shrugged tiredly. "Like I said – I'm open to suggestions."

He surprised her by sitting down next to her: he was so close she could easily have reached out and touched his face. The temptation was almost overpowering.

He stared into her eyes.

"We need to break into Fort Knox," he said.

"What?" she said, totally off balance. "What?!"

She wasn't sure she'd heard him properly. His blue eyes had made her dizzy, the proximity of his body had...

"We have to prove once and for all if the gold is there or not," he said seriously. "If it's not, that's evidence. If it is, we need to test it to find out if it's really gold. All we need is a drop of nitric acid: we take a random bar of gold and scratch it with something metal – a nail file or whatever. Then we put a drop of nitric acid on the scratch and watch to see if there's any reaction. If there's no reaction, it's gold; if it's bright green, it's base metal; if there's a bit of green it's gold leaf over base metal; and if it goes a milky colour, it's gold leaf over silver. It's a bit trickier to work out the carat because you have to..."

"Woah, woah, slow down!" said Helene, staring at him, breathless at this extraordinary solution to their problems. "How the hell are we going to break into Fort Knox and steal a bar of gold?"

"Not steal, Helene," he said patiently. "We're not going to steal it, just find out if it's really gold, that's all."

Helene felt like laughing hysterically – except that Charlie was serious.

"That's all! Oh well, that's alright then. We'll just knock on the door and ask nicely if we can please test their gold because we think it might be fake, but not to worry because we've got no intention of stealing it. Oh well, no problem!"

"Is that a note of sarcasm, Ms La Borde?" he said, smiling impishly.

"Oh, no. It's not a note of sarcasm, it's a whole damn symphony!" she said testily.

"Look, Helene," he said seriously. "I've thought about it over and over: I've thought about nothing else since *you* came up with the theory that the gold is fake. After all, it's the only thing that makes sense so far. But we have to prove it – and this is the only way."

"Charlie, you're crazy," she said. "There is *no way* we can break in to Fort Knox and test their gold. We'd be caught before we got ten paces. It's not possible to break into Fort Knox."

"Actually," he said, smiling, "we'd have to break into the 12 other Federal Reserve banks, too. We'd have to prove conclusively that there was fake gold in all 13 locations."

Helene sat staring at him, her mouth hanging open like a goldfish in a pasty-eating competition. If it weren't for the fact they'd hardly been outside in the last 48 hours, she'd have been certain he had sunstroke.

"Do you know how crazy you sound?" she gasped at last. "Do you realise how completely bonkers that idea is? It's so far past impossible that we're approaching Never Never Land. It's…"

Hank interrupted what was turning into a first class rant.

"I'm with lover-boy," he said.

"What?" shrieked Helene. "Are you both completely deranged?"

"Well, one doctor thought so," said Hank evenly, "but I have always disagreed with that diagnosis."

Helene was speechless.

Hank looked at Charlie, a slight smile on his face: partners in crime.

"Just listen to yourselves!" said Helene, her voice rising another half octave. "It's not possible. It. Can't. Be. Done."

"What's your plan?" Hank said to Charlie, ignoring Helene completely.

"Three plans, actually," said Charlie. "The first plan is to get into the vault. Now that's going to be really difficult because bullion vaults are always timed; only the most trusted staff are allowed in there and always in pairs. So, it'll be difficult, but not impossible: not with the help of the Gene Genies. They could get all the layouts, timings, codes and passwords that we'd need. It would help to have a man – or woman – on the inside, but we can manage without if we have to."

Hank nodded thoughtfully. "Hmm, like you say, difficult but not impossible."

By this time Helene was through the looking glass at the bottom of the rabbit hole. Either that or both Hank and Charlie were completely psychotic. Helene was favouring option two.

"What are the other plans?" said Hank.

"Well," said Charlie, "I reckon it would be much easier to test the gold while it was in transit. Assuming they move the fake gold around to keep up appearances, at some point it's got to be loaded into a security van."

"Marvellous," said Helene to herself, "after having successfully broken into Fort Knox and having escaped without a stain on our characters, we're going to hijack a bullion transfer. Why didn't I think of that?"

Charlie shot her an irritated look. "We don't hijack it: we hack the details of the security company they're going to use, find out where and when the transfer will take place, and make sure that our 'staff' are the ones that are available. It should be pretty easy to set up a fake company and siphon off the intel we need."

"Sounds good so far," said Hank, "and Plan Three?"

"Pretty similar to Plan Two," said Charlie, "except this time we check on the gold *before* it gets onto the security van. We clone a couple of high level staff passes at the bank, make duplicates, and then when the transfer is about to take place, make sure that we're in the staff corridor when they're moving the bullion on one of those steel trolleys that they use."

"How would you get the time to test the gold?" said Hank thoughtfully. "I'm not seeing how that would work."

"The schedule would be tight," agreed Charlie. "We'd have to time it perfectly so that two of us were in the lift with the gold when it was being sent up to the ground floor. One person starts chatting to the guards, the other drops the nitric acid."

Hank nodded. "And, of course," he said, "we film the whole thing, every last test."

Charlie smiled. "You took the words right out of my mouth."

They both looked at Helene.

The sound of blood rushing through her head was almost deafening. It was like looking up at six feet of overhead wave just before it broke over you, pounding you into sand on the seabed.

"If we get caught," she said slowly, "which we will – there

are one of two possible scenarios that could occur: one, we end our days in solitary confinement in some well-hidden containment facility that makes Guantanamo look like a holiday camp. That's the best case scenario. Or they just catch us then torture us to find out what we don't know and can't prove; then they shoot us and bury us in an unmarked grave – just like Wally."

Charlie looked at her. "Then we don't get caught."

Helene sighed. "Is there any way on God's green earth that I can talk either of you out of this apocalyptic madness?"

"Nope," said Hank.

"'Fraid not," said Charlie, his eyes bright with excitement. "Besides, I thought you liked a challenge."

Helene shook her head. "A challenge, yes, a suicidal mission for people with a death wish, no."

"If you're really not into this, Helene," he said quietly, "I can't force you. You've come up with some good ideas but it isn't hard evidence. I'm sorry, but it's not. I won't blame you if you're not up for this anymore: I'll help get you a new identity and you can live anywhere you like in the world. But you won't ever, *ever* be able to go home. But if that's what you want..."

She stared at his face, the planes of his cheekbones, the curve of his lips, memorised and as familiar to her as her own aging face in the mirror. Then she thought of Barbara, hiding like a thief for three years; the nameless man rotting away in the Warm Creek Nursing Home; the staff who had been fired from there for saying what they'd seen; Mrs Jenkin half terrified out of her well-starched skin; even Bill, food for maggots somewhere in Japan – all the people who were just collateral damage on the journey.

She felt sick with fear, a compression, a twist of the gut. But something in her said, No, I will not go quietly into the night; I won't be bullied by thugs in suits; I won't be hunted by a democracy in wolf's clothing.

She looked up and spoke, her voice steadier that she'd expected.

"Okay. If you can't beat 'em, join 'em. Let's see this thing through."

Hank bent down and hugged her. "I knew you wouldn't let us down, honey. It's just not in your DNA."

Charlie grinned at her.

"I have no idea how you just talked me into this," said Helene, a reluctant smile creeping across her face. "There's obviously a case of crazy on the loose and we're all infected."

"Crazy isn't such a bad place to be, honey," said Hank comfortingly. "I've been there for years."

Helene didn't doubt it.

"So, what do we do now?" she said.

Hank looked at Charlie as he spoke. "We get the Gene Genies on the case. Oh boy, they are gonna love this! What a ride!"

Hank was right. The Gene Genies, when congregated that evening, showed remarkably more enthusiasm for the new challenge than they had for the dull, unrewarding slog of unravelling decades of mining reports from across the globe. Despite that, they'd done a good job: an amazing job, in fact, considering the very little time they'd had to work on it. It was clear to Helene that none of them could possibly hold down a day job. She wondered how they earned a living then she shook herself: what an immensely stupid question. These people were so bright they could produce enough mental energy to run an entire power station. It was probably a good thing that she was giving them employment: who knows what mischief they could conjure up without the present focus. Yeah, right. Working out how to break into a Federal Reserve bank was such a useful life skill to acquire. Helene could hardly imagine how she'd lived without it for so long. On the other hand she wasn't sure it would help her to live much longer either.

But now the gloves were off and the Genies were working with a purpose that could have shown up a President's re-election campaign team. Even the Roadrunner was back on board now that he (or possibly she) had a hacking job worthy of attention.

While the men folk went about their plans, Helene trawled through the data the Genies had sent in on gold mining. It soon became clear that it was a pretty thankless task: records were sketchy from a number of countries, mostly those whose human rights records seemed to be the poorest. From what Helene knew of the way blood diamonds were mined, she had no doubt that the two things went often hand-in-hand.

Her head was spinning from the tables of figures, some in imperial tons, some in metric tonnes. Then there were the different grades of ore mined and, in a few cases, the weight of ore moved rather than the gold found. Helene suspected she detected signs of a bored Genie in that particular example: probably the one who had Batman for a personal logo. She promised herself she'd be having words with that young man (or woman) later.

Having spent the whole day at the figures, she came to two conclusions: one, it had been a bloody lousy idea of hers to attempt to analyse a hundred years of gold mining records; and two, the US figures just didn't stack up. Whichever way she twisted and turned, the US appeared to have sold huge quantities of gold – most of which they didn't appear to have either bought or mined in the first place. It was evidence, of a sort. Not enough – but not bad. It certainly added weight to her theory if not the sort of evidence that a court of law would willingly admit. But maybe enough to embarrass a worried government?

Suddenly a thought occurred to her.

"Hey, look at this," she said. "I think I might be onto something."

Charlie looked over at her. "What have you got?"

"I'm not sure... China has been buying a lot of US gold..."

"Which we knew already," Charlie reminded her.

"Sure, sure," said Helene, trying to get her thoughts in order, "but look who else is buying up US gold: not Russia – they can dig up their own, but several oil-rich countries in the Middle East..."

Charlie shrugged. "That's no surprise: they're planning against the day when their oil reserves dry up and they need to base their economy on something else. They're following the Swiss model of basing their currency on gold reserves. Woah! Is that Iran you've got there?"

"Yup," said Helene. "Now *that's* going to embarrass the US government just a tad but there's another country who's been buying even more..."

"I'm waiting for the finale," said Charlie.

Helene smiled briefly.

"Germany," she said.

Charlie looked surprised. "Okay, not what I was expecting you to say. Firstly, how can they afford it with the Euro at rock bottom and the costs of reunification and secondly, how does this affect your theory?"

"It's odd, isn't it," said Helene. "How they afforded it, well, their economy is one of the strongest in the Euro-zone and if they keep pushing, they could well be on their way to being head of the United States of Europe. But think about this: if they found that they'd got landed with a load of phoney US gold, how's that going to look?"

Charlie shook his head. "Not good."

"No, not at all," she agreed. "Well, they're not going to admit that they've shafted big time by the Yanks but it's going to make the NATO friendship mighty shaky if they can't trust the US. After all, the UK government is already looking towards Russia as the big cheese in the world market: our faith in the shoulder-to-shoulder with the US has been severely shaken by the way they've treated the UK as second-class citizens – which we are. But what if the UK isn't the only country that's looking eastwards? We could end up with an economic and political bloc from the Irish Sea to the Russian border with China – and the US would be totally out in the cold."

They were both silent.

"You know," she said, turning to look at Charlie who had been poring over blueprints of air conditioning ducts and electrical cables, "if we really can get the evidence of fake gold, we..."

Suddenly an alarm sounded inside the pod.

Hank lumbered into the bedroom, his face ashen.

"Intruders," he yelled. "We gotta go! Now!"

Helene hoisted her grab bag and pushed her coat inside

with her laptop. Charlie was already at the top rung of the stepladder, gun in hand.

Hank had his own version of a grab bag: a necklace of memory sticks and a diamond bracelet that looked genuine. Plus something that looked horribly like a grenade, cradled in one beefy mitt.

"Ready?" Charlie hissed.

Then the door of the pod was wrenched open.

Charlie fell backwards, crashing into Helene, who landed hard on her bad hip. A bolt of pain sliced through her and she cried out. Hank had been faster: when he'd seen her fall, he'd skipped out of the way and tossed the hand grenade up and out of the pod. The percussion of the explosion deafened her and smoke poured into the confined area.

Choking, Helene flung out her hand trying to find her grab bag. She could feel Charlie shouting her name through muffled eardrums. Then something was thrown down into the pod and she felt another, smaller explosion vibrate through the floor.

Tear gas! Her eyes immediately spilled over and her lungs started to burn. Abandoning attempts to find her grab bag she tried to crawl away from the fumes. She could hear Hank bellowing out some atavistic war cry and the ricochet of gunshots whined above her. She covered her head with her hands and tried to re-orient herself.

Another tear gas canister exploded behind her. Helene struggled to breathe. As she passed out she thought she heard the crackling of a fire fight echoing through the pod.

CHAPTER TWENTY-TWO

DARKNESS.

Helene knew she was awake but her body didn't respond to the commands of her brain. My God, I'm paralysed, was her first thought. But then she realised she had been secured with her hands cuffed painfully behind her back and that she was seated on a hard chair. Her feet were tied to the chair legs and her eyes were covered with a piece of material. When she tried to open them she was aware of a bright light behind the mask.

She experimented with moving her tongue and found that her throat was dry and her lips papery.

"Water," she said hoarsely. "Please, can I have some water?"

There was no reply. A wave of nausea and panic threatened to overwhelm her.

Instead, with her other senses immobilised, Helene concentrated on calming herself and listening. She was sure there was someone else in the room. She thought she could hear them breathing, but the longer she listened, the less certain she became.

She tried moving her chair, but somehow it had been fixed to the ground. Nevertheless, there was a faint echo from the scrape of her feet which made her think the room was concrete and quite large. She could feel a faint breeze of cooler air on her left cheek but she didn't know what that meant.

Years ago, as a journalist about to go into a war zone, she'd been sent by her employers on a survival training course, specifically designed for non-combat personnel. She forced her brain to recall those lessons. She knew she had to try to converse with her kidnappers: to try to make them think of her as a person rather than just a bankable asset. Whether or not that applied to being taken by secret US security services she couldn't say, but with other options scarce, it seemed worth a try.

She tried to speak again, although the dryness of her mouth made it feel like she was talking with cotton wool wadded up in her cheeks.

"My name is Helene La Borde," she rasped. "I'm a journalist. I'd really like some water. Could you give me a drink, please?"

There was no reply, just the hollow echo of her own voice mocking her efforts. Still, she had the unshakeable belief that there was someone else in the room. And somehow that was more disturbing than being alone: the idea that there was someone there, watching her, studying her in silence – an interesting scientific experiment.

Make human contact, her training insisted.

"I'm a British journalist," she said again. "My name is Helene La Borde. Can you tell me why I'm here?"

This time she heard the distinct sound of footsteps crossing the room, a whiff of perfume, or maybe aftershave: a door opened, then slammed shut again. This time Helene felt the room was empty, as if she herself had simply floated away and ceased to exist. Utterly empty: unless you counted dread as a companion.

A wave of something like vertigo overtook her and Helene felt as if she was on the edge of a precipice, the gaping maw of a cavern into hell just inches from her feet. If she tipped forward, she would fall forever: she'd be gone, lost.

Don't panic, she told herself. *Don't let the panic take you.*

Slowly she counted backwards from a hundred and forced herself to breathe deeply. She tried to remember everything that had happened before she'd woken up in this room.

There'd been gunfire and she'd heard Charlie shouting her name. In her memory he'd been calling her desperately. Hank had been roaring like Finn McCool, the mythical Irish warrior born to vengeance.

The click of the door opening set her heart racing again. But this time there was a voice.

"You are being held in a secure, sound-proof room. No-one will hear you if you scream."

"You'll hear me," said Helene, trying to sound calm. "Who are you?"

The voice belonged to a woman although it was hard to determine her age from her voice. The voice, Helene observed clinically, was often the last thing to show the signs of aging. This voice was as cool and as emotionless as water.

"Remove her blindfold. Let's make Miss La Borde a bit more comfortable."

Helene blinked as the blindfold was removed. It was an unexpected and worrying change of circumstance: it meant they didn't care if she saw them. Not good.

She massaged her wrists and ankles as the blood started to flow more easily. Then water was put on the table in front of her.

Helene drank deeply, wiping her mouth on the back of her hand.

"Why am I being held?" she said.

"There's someone who wants to speak to you," said the woman.

She was tall and thin, unremarkable externally, but Helene sensed power.

Then the door opened again and this time a deeply tanned man entered with a stook of iron-grey hair. Helene recognised him immediately, although it took her brain a second to catch up.

"Clive Jackson, Ms La Borde. Good to meet you, although the circumstances are... regrettable."

Smiling Clive Jackson: the Vice President. Jesus, the Vice President? This thing really did go all the way to the White House!

He held out a well-manicured hand for Helene to shake, which she did automatically, her fingers nerveless.

"Why am I being held here, Mr Jackson?" she said, trying to stop her voice from breaking.

"Well, now, Helene," he said smiling, "there's no need to be naïve is there? You're being held on terrorism charges, you must know that."

Helene's eyes widened with surprise. "Terrorism? I'm a journalist."

"Yes, you are... or rather you were. You used to be a pretty good journalist but the sources you're using these days... dubious, Ms La Borde, definitely dubious, and when you plan to start spreading malicious rumours... rumours that could damage our economy and international standing... well, I'd have to say that counts as terrorism in my book."

Helene shook her head. "I don't know what you mean, Mr Jackson."

"Don't fuck around with me, Ms La Borde," he said, still smiling. "You were caught in the headquarters of the so-called Gene Genies, one of the most anti-government, anti-capitalist commies we know. They're anarchists, Ms La Borde. That's why we've been watching them. When you visited Barbara Manfred, we were watching."

He paused to allow the effect of his words to sink in.

"These hackers, this bunch of twisted deadbeats, their raison d'être is to bring down the US government by any means possible. They're in touch with terrorist organisations all over the world... and they're in our own goddamn backyard. Well, we can't have that, can we, Ms La Borde? And I have to say, you'd be doing us a helluva favour if you could give us information leading to their whereabouts."

He paused expectantly.

Helene shook her head. "I don't know anything about affiliations to either extremists or foreign terrorists," she said. "And..."

"Well, I think we know a little bit more than you do about that," he said, still smiling, but with a steely edge to his voice, one that the electorate never got to hear. "All you need to tell us is where they are and how you contact them: we'll do the rest."

"I don't know," said Helene.

"Now, Ms La Borde..."

"It's true," she said. "Other than the hub that you found, I have no idea – that was the only contact point I'd been able to find."

"Yes, and we're rather curious about how you did find that," said Smiling Clive.

Helene was silent.

He shrugged: "We can come to that later. Right now we want names and locations. You can help us, Ms La Borde. You can be a good citizen."

"I'm sure I don't need to remind you that I'm British," said Helene bristling slightly.

"No, indeed, and I'm sure I don't need to remind you," said Smiling Clive, "of the special relationship our two countries enjoy and have enjoyed for a number of years; a special relationship that shouldn't be jeopardised. We have to stand firm, shoulder to shoulder against the enemies that mass against us even as we have this conversation."

"Is that what this is?" said Helene. "A conversation? Because I'd have said, in the circumstances, that it was an interrogation."

He waved a hand.

"Semantics, Ms La Borde. But you're right: words can be dangerous weapons. Now I need you to tell me everything you know about the Gene Genies."

"Then let me speak to the British Ambassador," said Helene.

"In good time," he said smoothly. "Tell me what you learned from those computer geeks," he said.

"Nothing useful," said Helene.

"We can decide what's useful," he said, the smile beginning to look rather strained.

"Really, nothing at all," said Helene.

It sounded lame even to her own ears.

"Don't treat me like a fucking moron," he said, the smile vanishing like mist.

"I'll tell you everything – what little there is," said Helene, shivering slightly, "once I've been released and have met with the British Ambassador."

"You know," said Smiling Clive, leaning back in his chair, "I've met women like you before. You hear a bit of rumour or gossip and suddenly you're trying to make it into something it's not. You goddam fucking journalists. But if you start peddling your gossip to the newspapers, Ms La Borde, then it's going to undermine our efforts to continue building the economy, to continue protecting ourselves against our enemies. You wouldn't want that, would you?"

Helene was silent.

Smiling Clive sighed, as if he were genuinely sorry the conversation hadn't gone better.

"Well, Ms La Borde, you can't say I didn't give you a chance. You see the problem is I really can't let you spread your lies in the tabloids. I really believed I'd find you a reasonable woman but I guess if you spend all your time in the gutter, sooner or later you start acting like the scum you find there. Good day, Ms La Borde."

He stood up, fastened one button on his jacket and strode from the room.

"I know what happens at Warm Creek!" she called after him.

He turned, looked at her briefly, muttered something to the tall woman, and left.

A tingle of apprehension ran down Helene's spine. Then the tall woman walked forward and forced the blindfold back over Helene's eyes. Her arms and legs were re-tied tightly. Too tightly. Helene began to lose sensation in her hands and feet.

"No-one will hear you if you scream," repeated the voice quietly. "A polygraph is being fitted to you – a lie detector: we will know if you try to deceive us. You will cooperate with us."

Soft, dry hands attached wires to Helene's upper chest. She recoiled at the touch but her body had nowhere to hide.

"I don't know anything," said Helene again.

To her own ears, her voice sounded shrill and agitated. How was anyone supposed to sound sincere with this machine strapped on to them? Just the thought of it made perspiration leak from her armpits and back, and her heart began to race painfully.

"We will start with two control questions: you will answer with 'yes' or 'no' answers. Is your name Helene La Borde?"

"Yes."

"Have you ever climbed Mount Everest?"

"No," said Helene. "I'm a British journalist and I have rights."

"You have no rights here," said the voice.

"What about my right to counsel?" Helene asked. "What about the Fifth bloody Amendment?"

More silence.

"Who were the two men in the bunker?" said the voice.

Helene was surprised. Was this a trick question or did they really not know?

"Look," she said. "I'm still dehydrated and my eyes are stinging from the tear gas you used. I need more water."

"Answer the question," said the voice.

Helene wasn't sure how to answer without implicating the Gene Genies, but then inspiration came to her.

"The tall, thin man was Charles Paget, a British citizen, like me; the other man was... Wally Manfred."

More silence as if the questioner was weighing the value of the answer: either that or waiting for instructions from someone else. Then the voice spoke:

"You're lying. Not a smart move, Ms La Borde."

"Please can I have some more water?" said Helene, her only reply.

"Tell us about Charles Paget," said the voice.

"Who's 'us'?" said Helene.

The blow when it came, whipped Helene's head to one side. The sharp crack echoed around the room along with her cry.

"Tell us about Charles Paget."

"Okay! I'll tell you." Helene's eyes were watering. At least it's washing out the residue of tear gas, she told herself. "He told me he was in the military. In Britain: either the regular army or the marines, I'm not sure. Maybe the SAS. He'd been freelance for at least three years – but you know that already."

The voice came closer.

"There is no record of anyone with that name in British Ministry of Defence records."

Helene was stunned.

"Of course there is: your records must be wrong!" she cried out. "I don't know which regiment – he never told me. But he's ex-military."

"There is no record of anyone with that name," said the voice. "You are lying."

"I'm not! Look at your damned machine! I'm not lying."

Helene was confused: was there really no trace of Charlie or were they trying to break her down, make her mistrust what she knew – or thought she knew? Anyway, how could they have not known Charlie's name if they'd been followed, as he'd intimated, since leaving the UK? She recognised the interrogation as one of the nine steps in the Reid interrogation technique that she'd learned about during her training: confrontation, theme development, stopping denials, overcoming objections... Christ! What were the others? The ninth step was confession.

"Tell us about the second man in the bunker," said the voice.

"His name is Wally Manfred," said Helene. "At least that was the name he used with me."

"You're lying," said the voice.

"I'm not. I mean, I don't know," said Helene. "He contacted me and told me he had information about your government, the US government. I was interested so I went to talk to him. And then you people arrived."

"How did he contact you?" said the voice.

"Via my website," said Helene.

The second blow made her left eyeball feel as if it were about to explode out of her cheek.

"How did he contact you?" said the voice.

"Via my website, I swear it! I erased the messages after I'd read them," said Helene desperately. "I thought that was safer. The website is the only way anyone can contact me at the moment. You must know that!"

"The man you met was not Wally Manfred. Who was he?" said the voice.

"I don't know! I don't know! That's the name he used. But I don't think he was really Wally Manfred because I came across a man with that name in the Warm Creek Nursing Home. He'd been there for two years: the nurse told me his daughter had visited there. So I don't know who the man I met in the bunker really was. He called himself 'Wally'."

"Don't lie to us!" said the voice, with a slight edge. "We can make this far more unpleasant for you. And if you lie again, I'd really like to have an excuse to do just that."

Helene swallowed, a lump of fear sticking like a pebble in her throat.

"I'm finding it really hard to believe, Ms La Borde," the voice continued, "that you're just an innocent bystander in all this."

"I didn't say I was a bystander," said Helene quickly, "I'm a journalist. You must have heard of the freedom of the press? The right to..."

" '...the right to freedom of opinion and expression; this right includes freedom to hold opinions without interference, and impart information and ideas through any media regardless of frontiers'. Don't you use your filthy mouth to speak about those things," spat the voice. "They weren't meant for sewer rats like you to hide behind."

"I... I don't know what you mean," said Helene, panting slightly.

The voice was close now: Helene could feel the breath on her neck, smell that the voice had been drinking strong coffee.

"People like you make me sick," said the voice neutrally. "A journalist hiding behind rights that were designed to protect patriots. You're one of those people who despises anyone who has more than them, aren't you? You're not even a very successful journalist, are you? Fifty-two and down to your last nickel." The voice began to rise again. "You're pathetic. If it weren't for us your little piss-ant country would have sunk without trace by now. We tolerate your liberal whining because it suits us to do so, but you're pathetic. And you try to tell us how to run our country."

"At least we don't kidnap innocent people and send them to concentration camps," snapped Helene.

The voice laughed.

"Don't be naïve. Your government does exactly that when it suits them. You live in this fantasy world that your government is a democratic one. Bullshit! At best it's a benign dictatorship but you'd rather believe in fairytales. Well, I'm going to use my magic wand, Ms La Borde, and you'll tell me everything you know."

Suddenly the most appalling pain sliced through the wires attached to her and Helene screamed. She thought she was having a heart attack as a band of pain wrapped itself around her chest. The lie-detector, unmasked, clearly had another, darker purpose.

"We really need to talk about trust, Ms La Borde," continued the voice almost conversationally. "We need to be able to trust your answers and right now, I have to say you're making that difficult."

Helene was still gasping with pain.

"'The only function of economic forecasting is to make astrology look respectable'," said the voice. "Another fucking liberal, just like you, said those words. But this country stays stable because of economics: because of trust in the machinery of government. You've been trying to play in a game where you don't understand the rules. Well, the rules are going to be explained to you very carefully but for now you're going to tell me everything you know – and everything you think you know, aren't you?"

The pain shot through her again and Helene's scream burst out. Something inside her broke and all her defiance fell away, fell into the chasm she had sensed before her but could not see.

"Alright, I'll tell you! Please don't – I can't take it! I'll tell you everything," she cried.

"I know you will," said the voice.

Helene told the voice about Bill Bailey, about Kazuma and about Hassan Ali. She explained how she'd followed the thread of Wally Manfred to the bunker. But she didn't mention what she'd found out about Barbara Manfred or that she knew Hank's name – or what the Gene Genies had been planning.

"And that's everything, I swear it," she gasped. "If Charlie has another name, I don't know what it is: both Bill Bailey and Kazuma knew him as 'Charlie' so that's all I can tell you."

By now Helene was pleading.

"We'll see," said the voice, once more unemotional.

The pain came again, fast and hot.

Helene screamed again. Then she lost control of her bodily functions: she wept as the smell of urine soaking through her jeans filled the room.

"God!" said the voice in a tone of disgust. "Take this bitch away and clean her up."

Helene's legs crumbled as she was dragged from the room. Somewhere nearby she was laid down on a sloping table, something like a dentist's chair, but hard and cold. A piece of cloth was placed over her mouth and water cascaded down, icy cold, making her gag.

Water forced itself into her mouth and nose and lungs. Helene desperately tried to turn her head but she was held too firmly. She was coughing, choking, gasping for air.

You're drowning, her body said. Fight, you have to fight!

She tried to kick out, to swim free, but she was held down.

Unconsciousness took her brief seconds before her heart broke.

～

When she came to, she was sitting back in the hard chair: she couldn't tell if minutes had passed or hours. It was like some cruel game the gods had decided to play on her. Her jeans were still wet and her shirt was soaked through. Liquid was dribbling from her nose and mouth and she could feel wet hair hanging on her forehead. Her ribs ached and every breath reeked of pain.

The voice was still there.

"What else did the man in the bunker tell you?"

Helene tried to speak but spat out water instead. She shook her head weakly. The voice was relentless, a machine programmed to ask questions that she couldn't answer.

"What else did the man in the bunker tell you?"

"Nothing," whispered Helene. "He didn't have time."

"Don't lie," said the voice coldly. "You were in there for at least 24 hours. What did he tell you?"

"Nothing else. I've told you everything," I swear," said Helene humbly. "He had some crazy story about the US gold reserves. He was checking mining quotas against bullion sold by the US government. It didn't make much sense. I thought I was wasting my time."

Helene felt numb. It was hard to know what was real anymore: only this room, this voice.

"Do you know what will happen if your nasty little fiction comes out?" said the voice stiffly. "Well, I'll tell you: first of all the world markets will collapse; trade will come to a standstill; inflation will soar in every developed country and most of the developing ones; there'll be war; governments will fall; millions, maybe billions will die. Is that what you want, Ms La Borde? Are you one of those naive end-timers who think that the chaos of resetting the clock to zero will save the world?"

Helene shook her head, still too dazed to speak.

"Well, if that's your little anarchist's dream, you're even more naïve than you pretend, because it won't happen, Ms La Borde. And I'll tell you why: because no-one will believe you."

Helene's brain flickered with recognition.

"It was you: you sent me that message to my website. It was you, wasn't it?"

The voice ignored her.

"Women of your age are often prone to breakdowns, Ms La Borde, did you know that?" The voice was almost conversational again. "It's not just the hormones – or lack of them – it's the realisation that you're superfluous to society – that you have nothing left to offer. You're extinct as far as procreation is concerned and functionally you're a washed up has-been with a bitterness brought on by your lack of success in the world. It's not unusual, it's almost a stereotype. It's a shame: the breakdown of what was a fine mind but these days all sorts of medicines are available to help you. How long have you been bipolar, Ms La Borde?"

"I... I'm not!"

"Denial is a common symptom, of course. How long have you had voices in your head telling you to bring down the government?"

"W-what?"

"You must recognise that your thought processes are illogical? How long have you been feeling suicidal?"

Helene was silent.

"One of the most common ways for a woman your age to kill herself is an overdose of sleeping pills and anti-depressants," continued the voice. "Of course coming off Prozac so suddenly was bound to disrupt the balance of your mind."

"What do you want?" said Helene in a low voice.

"I want to be sure that you're not holding back information. Where had you arranged to meet your accomplices?"

At last the voice had made a mistake. And the mistake was to give Helene hope: Charlie and Hank hadn't been captured... unless, of course, the voice was trying to trip her up again.

"We hadn't arranged anything," said Helene. "We were taken by surprise – that's the truth."

"I don't think you have any conception of the truth," said the voice, much nearer to Helene now. "You're a lying bitch and I'm going to laugh my ass off when I see you sitting in the Warm Creek Nursing Home wallowing in piss and shit."

The loathing in the voice coupled with the delight in the punishment it planned was more terrifying than anything else Helene had ever heard.

"I can't tell you what I don't know," she said, trying and failing to suppress the tremble of fear.

The cell door opened again and Helene felt the voice move away. A mutter of several people talking reached her ears. The voices became louder, clearly disagreeing about something of importance.

"This is fucking ridiculous!" shouted the voice Helene feared the most. Footsteps returned and the voice swore at her once, then used the machine to send a jet of pain through her. Her heart exploded, the agony almost merciful as she blacked out.

No part of her was aware as her carcass was untied and dragged, inert, from the concrete cell.

CHAPTER TWENTY-THREE

THE GLARE WAS SO BRIGHT THAT IT HURT HER EYES, EVEN though they were still closed; two punctures of needle sharp light pressed their way into her brain. Was she lying in the sun, baking in the Californian desert? Or maybe she was back in Bahrain and the cormorants would start pecking out her eyes...

Helene's eyelids fluttered open a fraction then. She caught a glimpse of a white room which made her think of Heaven but nothing in the tales from childhood had ever described Heaven as being so damned painful. Every muscle, joint and bone in her body throbbed. From which Helene concluded that most of her was alive.

She opened her eyes again, blinking rapidly as they began to water, her pupils contracting to pinheads. She tried to speak but her throat had closed up. She licked her lips but her tongue was dry and the skin around her mouth cracked. She tried to clear her throat and, at last, a sound came out: inarticulate, inhuman even, but a sound, nevertheless.

"She's waking up," said a distant voice.

It wasn't *the* voice.

Thank God.

A ghostly face loomed over her: a man in a white coat. "Back in the land of the living?"

What a stupid, bloody question. Not even the doctors could tell if you were alive or dead it seemed.

Helene tried to get the word 'water' past her dried lips but failed. Instead she tried to mime picking up a glass of water but her own hand was too heavy to lift and she lay, blinking like a dying fish.

Then the first person who had spoken returned: a woman with an arid, rasping voice. She lifted up Helene's head and held a plastic child's beaker to her mouth.

"Drink this."

The beaker forced Helene to take small sips but at least most of the water went into her mouth, not dribbling out to form small pools on her chest.

Exhausted, Helene allowed her head to fall back on the pillow and the light began to spool away from her; further and further until darkness engulfed her.

She couldn't tell how many hours later it was when she awoke again. Maybe days. This time her memory had been reconnected and woken up with her; she began to recall details from before: the cell, *the* voice, the interrogation, the pain binding her chest.

The room was silent. Helene lay quietly trying to put all the pieces into place, sorting events in her mind. She wondered what had happened to Charlie, to Hank. She hoped they'd escaped. She thought they might have. Didn't the voice say they had? She hoped that they weren't in a hospital ward with needles stuck in their arms.

Thinking of Charlie was painful, too. She closed her eyes against the memory but it flickered like an old cine film in her brain: the way his eyes sparkled when he was amused; the graceful way he moved; how terrifying he'd been when she thought he'd murder Bill.

She wondered what was going to happen next but whatever it was couldn't be worse than the room with the voice.

Helene's brain skittered away from such raw memories: it was too soon to think about that... but the fear of that room continued to gnaw at her. *The* voice in that room. The silence stretched intolerably and Helene's wild mind filled the vacuum with fear.

Beyond the hospital ward was silence: no voices, no footsteps, no nurses looking harassed, no doctors on their rounds.

Finally, Helene tried to sit up but the effort was beyond her. She could see a fresh beaker of water just out of reach. It was only inches from her outstretched fingers but it may as well have been on the moon.

She let her body relax but her mind was now wide awake. What if no-one came? What if she was left here to die? What if nobody noticed? What if she wasn't missed? How long would Mr Jenkin mow her lawn, tend her roses, collect her post? Would any of her friends notice the absence of her usual, hasty Christmas missives? Then she thought of Frank: he damn well would notice because he'd want his damn money back. My God, she thought, Frank might be the one person who ends up saving me!

The thought was absurd: fat Frank squeezing himself into chainmail and charging in on an old nag to demand her release.

Helene began to laugh: a hollow, breathless cackle.

Footsteps. A door opened and Helene heard someone enter.

"Awake again?" said the rasping voice.

The woman came nearer, lifted Helene's head and helped her to water once more.

"Where am I?" Helene struggled to get out the words.

"Prison ward," replied the woman.

"Where?" repeated Helene, confused.

"Chowchilla, honey... Valley State Prison."

"Never... never heard of it," said Helene, feeling more and more confused. "A prison hospital?"

The woman looked at Helene curiously. "Hey! Where are you from? That's one daisy of an accent you got yourself."

"I'm English," said Helene weakly. "From England."

"Wow!" said the woman excitedly. "Did ja ever meet the Queen? She's one helluva dame."

"No," said Helene, trying to smile, despite the pain encircling her ribs.

She forced herself upright and the woman's brawny arms lifted her like a child, plumping up her pillows comfortably behind her.

Helene looked around her: there were a dozen empty beds and windows high above her, barred. She tried to move her arms but found that the left one was handcuffed to the bed and the right one attached to a drip. She had been immobilised.

The woman in front of her looked as tough as cowhide, her hair a harsh shade of yellow; long creases down her cheeks told of an equally harsh life. Her eyes were grey like tiny pebbles but she didn't look cruel.

"My mother was invited to a tea party at Buckingham Palace once," murmured Helene, "for services to the community."

It was the longest sentence she'd spoken in...what... days?

"Wow!" said the woman again. "You wait till I tell the other gals in here: we're all big fans of Queen Kate. She's awesome."

Helene tried to focus on what she needed to know. "I need to speak to someone in charge," she said. "I'm being held against my will."

"Honey," said the woman sympathetically, "we're all being held against our will. No-one signs up for stir: well, maybe a few crazies, but I ain't one o' them."

Helene closed her eyes. The throb between her eyes made it hard to think clearly.

"How'd you get here anyway?" said the woman thoughtfully. "I ain't never heard of no British broad being in here."

"I... I don't know," said Helene. "I was being questioned. They had a machine and... and"

Helene's voice faltered.

"That's okay, honey," said the woman, almost kindly. "I..."

At that moment the man in the white coat came back.

"That's enough chit-chat, Chavez," barked the man. "Get back to your rounds."

The woman left without another word. The man in a white coat took her place. A doctor.

"What's happened to me?" said Helene. "I remember some..."

"Just take lie back," said the doctor briefly and without sentiment. "You've had a myocardial infarction: a heart attack. You've lost about 15% of your heart muscle function. Permanently. Not too much to worry about – most people don't use it all anyway except maybe a few top athletes. You should make a good recovery: you're not in bad shape for your age, considering."

He paused.

"We couldn't find any medical records for you: where were you before Chowchilla? There must have been some mix up – it happens. At the moment we've been treating you as a Jane Doe until your notes arrive..."

Helene stared at him. "Am I in prison? That woman said it was a prison ward..."

The doctor shifted uneasily. "Temporary memory loss isn't unusual after an infarction. How long have you been on Beta Blockers?"

Helene shook her head dully.

"I've never been on Beta Blockers. It was that bloody machine that gave me a heart attack: they kept shocking me – electric shocks."

The doctor sat down next to her and spoke quietly, almost kindly, but maybe there was a warning in his voice, too.

"I don't know what you're talking about but you'd better be careful who you tell that story to," he said softly. "Look, tell me your name and I'll try to get the paperwork sorted out."

"My name is Helene La Borde," she whispered. "I'm a journalist. I was in Carmel investigating a... fraud when I was taken and questioned. I think it was the NSA. They tortured me. They..."

The doctor laid his hand on her shoulder to calm her growing agitation.

"You know, there are some drugs that can give patients

vivid nightmares: dreams that are so awful but seem completely real. It's not unusual for patients to believe that care givers have tortured them. I don't have your notes here but if you were treated with some blood pressure pills that could..."

Helene tried to shake her head but the effort was exhausting.

"I've never been on blood pressure pills. Never. My name is Helene La Borde," she said again, more insistently. "I'm a journalist. Just Google my name and photo – you'll find me..."

The ward door clanged open.

"We'll take it from here, doctor," said an authoritative voice. "I specifically ordered that I be informed the moment this patient regained consciousness."

"What's going on?" said the doctor, standing up. "Who are you people?"

One of the men in suits flashed a badge. It was impossible to tell what it said or which agency it represented.

"Who do you work for?" said the doctor, crossing his arms.

"None of your damn business," snarled a woman's voice.

Helene blanched: it was *the* voice.

"All you need to know if that we're taking this prisoner to another location. Get her ready for transfer."

"I can't do that!" said the doctor, starting to raise his voice. "This is my *patient*, I am her *physician* and I'm telling you she's not fit to be moved. She's recovering from..."

"I don't give a rat's ass what she's recovering from," hissed the voice. "Get her ready to be moved, or you'll find your licence to practice has expired and you'll be collecting welfare cheques."

The doctor's voice quavered but he tried once more. "I need to know where she's being taken – for my records."

The tall woman in a dark suit loomed over Helene. "She's being taken to a nursing home," said the woman – the woman from the cell – *the* voice.

Helene gasped: from shock, from recognition, from fear.

"Not Warm Creek," she cried. "Don't send me there!"

The tall woman frowned in irritation. "Someone shut this bitch up."

The doctor looked horrified – and scared, too.

"But Warm Creek is a home for dementia sufferers," he said. "It's not a secure facility and this patient shows no signs of dementia... This is most irregular..."

"Don't let them take me!" begged Helene, grabbing hold of his sleeve.

Her voice was shrill, the panic etched on her face.

The doctor stared down at her, the horrified expression frozen on his face, his eyes dark with concern.

The woman stepped forward and slapped her hard; Helene fell back onto the pillow. The doctor called out, trying to fold himself over Helene to protect her. He was restrained by two of the suits and escorted from the ward, still shouting, appalled and powerless.

"We can't take her to Warm Creek now," said one of the men.

The tall woman shook her head impatiently.

"Just get her there for now then we'll arrange to transfer her to our facility on the East Coast."

The man ducked away, throwing one final look towards the ugly scene as the tall woman seated herself comfortably on Helene's bed.

"Our last chance for a little chat," she said, staring into Helene's petrified eyes. "You know what we can do – what we *will* do unless you cooperate."

"I... I've told you everything I know," whispered Helene. "For God's sake! Don't do this!"

"Where were you going to meet your accomplices? What were they planning to do?"

Helene shook her head dumbly.

"You know," said the woman conversationally as she stood up, smoothing down her suit jacket, "I don't normally take much interest in vermin like you once I've passed you on to another facility, but in *your* case..." She pushed her face into Helene's "...in *your* case, I think I'll come visit just to watch you drool and shit your shorts."

A frightened looking nurse entered the ward, a syringe in her hand. The suit woman pushed past her and left.

"I'm so sorry..." whispered the nurse.

She injected something into the drip and seconds later Helene was out cold.

CHAPTER TWENTY-FOUR

BRIGHT COLOURS SWIRLED AROUND HELENE'S HEAD. SHE squeezed her eyes shut but the colours kept colliding behind the lids and a terrible roaring in her ears was deafening.

She was an orange, a huge, juicy orange and the hands were trying to squeeze the juice out of her. They kept squeezing and squeezing and the pressure was all over her. Squeezing and squeezing, now trying to squeeze the pips out of her. The noise in her head increased with the pressure: she tried to put her hands over her ears to block out the noise but she couldn't move her hands. It was as if her hands had lead bars attached to them; she couldn't lift them, couldn't move any part of herself. There were spiders in her hair, trapped, scrabbling around. Spiders in her ears, in her nose, scuttling over her eyelids.

She tried to cry out, but only a low moan escaped. A dribble of saliva glistened from one corner of her mouth. Tears stung her eyes. She almost knew what was happening to her.

～

"Nurse Gillan?" called a voice.

Patience groaned softly. She'd been looking forward to a quiet evening with her soaps. She didn't like watching the news: the misery was far too humdrum and familiar, but on the soaps, sorrow was presented in day-glow colours – much easier to digest, especially given her present job.

She didn't mind working at the Warm Creek Nursing Home: she treated the residents with a benign practicality that bordered on thoughtfulness. She prided herself on her attention to detail. She was the one who noticed if a resident had a toothache, or dry eyes because of their drug regime, or if they weren't eating, or eating too much.

Most of the residents didn't talk, and when they did communicate it rarely made sense, so someone like Patience was an asset for the true well-being of the people she helped. Not that it made any difference to her pay-check but it was almost enough that her pride made her do her work well.

Every fifth week Patience took her turn on the nightshift. Most of the carers and nurses didn't like working the graveyard shift because their sleeping patterns got all messed up, but Patience didn't mind: she didn't sleep much anyway so it was all much of a muchness to her.

Most nights would pass fairly peacefully: the residents were medicated early in the evening to help them sleep. After that, all most of them could manage were the shouts resulting from night terrors and some helpless twitching. Usually it was quiet.

Which was why Patience was surprised and annoyed to be disturbed that Wednesday night.

"Nurse Gillan?"

It was Miz Preston who was calling her. She was the night manager: a thin, chilly but efficient nurse. None of the staff liked her much, but she was respected.

So Patience responded just a fraction more quickly than she would have done if it had been Mr Buzzerd who called her, the day manager.

"Yas, Miz Preston?" said Patience.

"We've got a new patient coming in tonight, Nurse Gillan."

A smile twitched at the corner of Patience's mouth. All the staff were required to call the inmates of Warm Creek 'residents' instead of 'patients' but Miz Preston had always ignored the directive. She wasn't one to pander to political correctness.

"A new patient?" echoed Patience. "We don't usually get them coming in so late."

"No, we don't," said Miz Preston. "And I'm not happy about it: they're sending us a patient with no paperwork. They say it'll come in the morning, but I'm not happy about it: not happy at all. Still, we must do what we can to prepare for her arrival. Could you make up room 113, please?"

Patience nodded. "I'll stop by the supplies cupboard and get the room fitted out until we know whether she's coming with her own furniture and linen."

Miz Preston was pleased that it was Patience who was on duty: she followed instructions but was also able to think for herself – something Miz Preston valued in a care assistant, and Nurse Gillan was first class helper.

Patience looked around 113. Until recently it had been the home of Biff Cooper: an old time rodeo rider who looked as if he belonged on the plains, even at 93. He'd been one of Patience's favourite patients: a sweet old man with hands like saddle leather and thick, white hair that grew in wayward clumps. He used to get Patience confused with his daughter Maude. An unflattering comparison for both women, as Maude was pushing 70, thin as a rake and white; whilst Patience was 50, built for comfort and black. Maude declared that her father was a much nicer man now he had dementia: as a father he had been neglectful, distant and with a volcanic temper. Dementia had softened his edges and made him loving and grateful. Any female who showed him kindness was called Maude. Patience never stopped being surprised at the different ways in which a damaged brain continued to work.

When Biff died, Patience had been sorry. Several Warm Creek staff had attended his funeral. Maude was there with her scrawny, underfed husband, but the star of the show had been another old boy in full Western regalia with a loaded six-shooter that he proceeded to fire over Biff's grave. It was a better send off than most folks got, that was for sure.

Now the room had been stripped of his memories: photos

of Biff's glory days, rodeo posters and an old, yellowing picture of Maude as a child with the same wild, clumpy hair, forced into awkward braids, scowling out at the camera. His rocking chair had been donated to the day room so now the room was emptied of character: only an unmade bed, empty dresser and old wardrobe remained. Patience didn't know what had happened to the pictures. She hoped Maude had wanted to keep them.

Patience wheeled a small, trolley table from the storeroom and found a roll of drawer liner that smelled faintly of roses. Carefully she lined the empty dresser drawers and left the wardrobe door ajar to let it air. Then she made up the bed with clean, white sheets; made sure the bed's restraint straps were functioning and correctly positioned. She checked the en-suite bathroom was stocked with shampoo, conditioner, soap and, because the new arrival was a woman, a pot of face cream. Patience believed that keeping things as close to normal as possible helped new arrivals to settle in more easily, thus making the carers' job easier, too.

When she'd finished, she went to report that she'd finished.

Miz Preston was standing outside in front of the main door. Patience joined her and together they stood in silence, watching the stars and waiting for the new patient.

The air was so still they heard the ambulance when it was some distance away. A wheelchair stood at one side of the reception area in case it was needed. Nobody had informed the Warm Creek staff whether or not the patient would be mobile, sedated or restrained. You had to be ready for either/or and Miz Preston prided herself on ensuring all events could be catered for promptly.

The ambulance swept softly up the tarmac drive and came to a halt by the large, double doors. Miz Preston stepped forward and Patience stood to one side, keeping out of the way until she was needed.

The driver muttered something to Miz Preston and shrugged his shoulders. Patience could tell by the irritated twitch of the shoulders that Miz Preston was annoyed about something: probably the absence of paperwork. After all, how were they supposed to know what drug regimen the patient needed? Plus, it was dangerous for a patient to suddenly come off their medication.

A flicker of concern, an unpleasant thought, made Patience stand a little straighter, trying to look into the ambulance's interior. Only once before had a patient arrived in the night with no paperwork. Patience hadn't been there on that occasion, but she'd heard about it.

A stretcher was pulled out of the ambulance. Patience tucked the wheelchair back into the foyer: it wouldn't be needed tonight.

The ambulance crew went to get back into the front cab: they had done their job, abandoning the wheeled stretcher on the drive. Miz Preston was furious but the crew ignored her ferocious demands and drove off into the night. That was odd: they weren't even waiting to get their stretcher back. Patience didn't mind doing a bit of portering so she walked to the front ready to push the stretcher into the foyer.

She looked down at the face of the patient, a slight form under a thin blanket. The shock of recognition made Patience cry out. It was the woman she'd seen the previous week visiting Wally Manfred. There was no doubt. But now the woman was gaunt-eyed, slack-mouthed and unwashed. If Patience hadn't seen her so recently, recognising her would have been out of the question.

"What's the matter, Nurse Gillan?" said Miz Preston, whose bat-like hearing had picked up Patience's low cry.

"I... she looked like someone I used to know," said Patience quickly. "It's not, but for a moment..."

"Hmm," said Miz Preston, wrinkling her brow. She didn't look entirely convinced: she wasn't the kind of woman who missed much.

Patience schooled her face to blankness and wheeled the patient inside.

Doctor Gibbon was waiting for her. Who'd called him? Patience had never seen him at the nursing home in the night before.

"This is the new resident?" he said.

"Yes, doctor," said Patience, trying to look as dim and unthinking as he generally believed all the carers to be.

"I'll be personally overseeing her medication," said the doctor curtly.

"That's highly unusual," said Miz Preston who had entered unheard. "The nursing staff normally administer all medication and we don't even have any papers for this woman yet."

The doctor scowled. "I have the paperwork, nurse. You may go – back to whatever it is you do."

Miz Preston wasn't giving up that easily.

"I'd like to see that paperwork, doctor," she said calmly. "The ambulance staff were unable to give me any details at all. It's odd that they've come through to you. At night."

The doctor's tone was hostile. "I wasn't aware that you were running this facility," he said sharply.

"Just the nursing staff, doctor," she replied briskly. "And I presume this patient will need nursing care."

The doctor was furious at what he saw as an attempted usurpation of his divine right as a physician, where knowledge was power.

"*I* will supervise this *resident's* medication," he hissed. "I'll leave the diaper-changing to *you*."

He jerked his head at Patience, indicating that she follow him with the stretcher. Silently Patience manoeuvred the wheeled bed into the lift and they travelled up to the next floor.

The doctor allowed Patience to assist him in transferring the patient from the stretcher to the bed. Then he bound the woman's hands and feet with the thick, leather restraints. She was starting to moan and trying to move, her eyes flicking restlessly between the doctor and Patience. The doctor frowned and took a hypodermic from his breast pocket. Patience guessed it contained some sort of sedative because the woman's pupils dilated and her body went limp.

The doctor nodded. "I'll be back in the morning," he said. "She won't give you any trouble now."

Patience felt cold all over and sick to her stomach. She knew for a fact that this woman had been perfectly within her right mind a week ago. Whilst a breakdown could happen overnight Patience knew, without a shadow of doubt, that this woman was being illegally detained and medicated to make it look like she was psychotic – or demented. Just like Wally Manfred. Just like him.

Dear God.

Patience didn't know what to do. For the rest of the shift her mind squirmed uncomfortably. She checked on the woman called simply 'Jane Doe' but each time her breathing was deep and even.

As dawn arrived with the pink promise of a warm day, Patience drove home. Her husband was hunched over the sports pages as he finished his breakfast. She wanted to tell him about her night, to hint to him what she suspected but he'd put down his paper, looked her in the eyes, closed his ears and simply told her it was none of her business and that unless she wanted to lose her job – which wouldn't be easy to replace at her age – then she should forget what she knew, or thought she knew, what she'd seen and what she thought she'd seen.

Then he'd picked up his tool bag and headed out the door.

Easy for him to say, thought Patience, as she made herself a sandwich. He wasn't the one who would have to see it every day. For two anxious nights Patience had watched the new patient – not too closely just in case her actions aroused suspicion, but closely enough to know that Doctor Gibbon was the only physician allowed to attend to the new patient or to see her notes. For two anxious nights Patience had hoped that the young man who had accompanied the new patient, now officially listed as Jane Doe, would come to retrieve her. When he didn't come she began to wonder if she'd misread him. And yet somehow she doubted that.

An air of unease hovered over the Warm Creek Nursing Home. None of the care staff – except Patience – wanted to have anything to do with the new patient. She was so much younger than most of the residents for one thing and for another her namelessness and lack of records worried them. The carers sensed something was rotten but were too disempowered to know what to do, other than to walk by on the other side.

Patience washed and dressed the inert body. Sometimes she sensed something behind the dilated pupils, a latent awareness, perhaps? Patience had worked with dementia sufferers long enough to be able to interpret most attempts at communication. Somewhere inside the drugged body was a mind, still alert. It was a distressing thought.

Patience wondered if a discrete call to SAMHSA, the mental health administration would help. She toyed with the idea for several days, weighing the potential risk to herself against the potential benefits to the patient. She even stopped by her church to ask God for guidance. But He gave the answer she didn't really want to hear.

So one evening, a week later, on her way home from the day shift, Patience pulled into a Wal-Mart she didn't usually patronise and found one of the few payphones that still worked. SAMHSA was closed for the day, of course, but she found the courage to leave a message on the office voicemail, telling them merely that a Jane Doe had been installed at Warm Creek and that staff were concerned about her care. She didn't leave her name, no siree. Carefully she wiped the phone with an antiseptic wipe: she'd seen *CSI*. Then she worried about the fingerprints she must have surely left on the quarter with which she'd paid for the phone call but there was nothing she could do about that now...

∽

When Patience came into work the next day, she found Warm Creek in uproar.

"What's going on, Loretta?" she said to one of the carers just going off shift.

"Oh, my!" said Loretta, "You was lucky you wasn't on night shift, Patience: one of the patients, I mean, one of the residents done gone missing!"

Patience felt slightly relieved that it was something so minor. That happened from time to time: a patient would wander off and be found a short time later, confused and hungry.

"Oh well, I expect they'll turn up," said Patience. "Who was it?"

"That new woman," said Loretta, "the Jane Doe that none of us is supposed to talk about. She's vanished!"

A feeling like icy water trickled through Patience.

"Jane Doe? They're saying she upped and walked off?"

"I know!" whispered Loretta, her eyes darting around her to make sure that no-one could overhear their conversation. "There was no way she was walking outa here. But that's what they're saying. And Miz Preston done been given her cards. Them fired her! And her desk has been cleared already!"

"Why'd they fire her?" said Patience, her eyes large.

"Well, they're blaming her for losing a p... a resident on her watch, but I heard her yelling at Doc Gibbon and saying something about her being taken away in an ambulance by men with guns!"

Patience felt her heart racing.

"And SAMHSA are on the way," said Loretta. "Apparently they got an anonymous call about that Jane Doe. Doc Gibbon reckons it was Miz Preston but she was denyin' it. They had to escort her offa the place yellin' and screamin'! You never saw nothin' like it! It's gonna be a fun day, Patience. You's better keep you head down, girl!"

Loretta was walking away when she remembered something else.

"Oh," she said, "I near forgot to tell you: Wally Manfred died last night. Doc Gibbon says he had a stroke or somethin'. Poor Wally."

CHAPTER TWENTY-FIVE

HELENE WAS VAGUELY AWARE OF THE SENSATION OF SWAYING: it reminded her of a hotel she'd stayed in once where she'd had use of her own personal hammock. It was very soothing.

But this was... somewhere else.

Her body woke up nerve by nerve, muscle by muscle: a toe twitched, her calf jerked, her thigh, her stomach, arm by arm and finally the muscles in her face gave her the resemblance of a sentient being. Her mind, however, was still blurred and fuzzy. She tried to understand where she was.

Eyes open but as yet unspeaking, her gaze wandered around: a small, metal capsule – with a demon guarding her. Helene screwed her eyes tightly shut: if she closed her eyes and pretended they weren't there – that she wasn't there – sometimes the demons went away. Sometimes.

When the pumping of her heart had slowed and the blood pounding through her veins had eased, she dared to open her eyes again. No, not a capsule: a vehicle. A van? No, she was in the back of an ambulance and the demon was a nurse of some description – or a guard.

Cautiously, her eyes on the uniformed man, she tested her arms again. No movement. She tried moving her legs: they, too, were leaden and uncooperative.

Slowly, her head began to clear a little but her limbs felt weak as if her muscles hadn't been used for a long time.

A pothole in the road jolted the guard fully awake. He studied her with wary eyes.

"Water," she croaked. "Water, please."

He continued to stare at her but didn't reply. Helene wondered if she'd actually managed to say the words out loud. She wasn't sure. It was hard to be sure of anything when your brain felt like glue. She tried again.

"Some water? Please," she mumbled.

"Cain't give you nuthin'," he muttered at last. "Cain't even talk to you."

"Why?" said Helene.

He looked surprised, as if he hadn't expected such a question.

"They tole me you wouldn't wake up," he said belligerently. "You're not supposed to wake up."

Helene was too disorientated to argue.

"Where am I?" she said tiredly. "Where are we going?"

"Cain't tell you that," said the man stubbornly. "Prisoners don't need to know."

He scowled at her. His face said: I should have guessed that talking with this ho wouldn't lead anywhere good.

He crossed his arms with finality.

Then without warning the man threw himself on top of her.

Or at least to Helene's confused senses that's what seemed to happen. In fact the ambulance suddenly lurched to one side, screeching metal against tarmac as it slid haphazardly down the highway. Only the ringing in Helene's ears and the pounding in her skull explained that there'd been a small explosion somewhere in front of, or underneath the vehicle, tipping it turtle-wise onto its side.

The guard seemed stunned and was moving groggily, his dead weight on Helene's bruised ribs making it hard to breathe.

There was shouting outside and the ambulance doors were wrenched open. Helene couldn't see anything but when the huge, shadowy figure of a man blocked the light from the doors, his shape seemed familiar.

"Don't worry, honey." Hank's voice came from a very long way away. "We're gonna get you outa here."

A set of bolt cutters held in one beefy hand were used to stun the guard into full unconsciousness. Then Hank snapped free the handcuffs and unbuckled the ankle restraints that held Helene onto the stretcher. The thick restraining belt around her waist took longer: the leather unyielding and the metal lock too close to Helene's flesh to make using the bolt cutters easy. Her weight pulled sideways on the belt making it taut.

Finally she was released and with gentle hands, Hank scooped her from the bed.

"Oh, honey," he said softly. "What have they done to you?"

He half carried, half dragged her from the stricken ambulance. Helene's muscles seemed incapable of independent movement.

He bundled her onto the back seat of a dark Sedan and the car roared away. Helene glimpsed the ambulance lying on its side, a section of the engine strewn across the road, and a flash of blue eyes staring at her from the rear view mirror.

The next time Helene woke, the world had stopped moving. She opened her eyes slowly. She felt limp, but for the first time in weeks, her mind was clear.

"She's waking up."

The voice drew Helene's eyes.

A woman was standing beside the bed. She was thin with light brown hair; young, but with deep lines creasing the side of her mouth.

"Barbara?"

Helene barely recognised her own voice, it was so cracked and dry; the merest whisper of words.

The woman smiled.

"Hello, Helene. It's good to meet you again."

A familiar, beefy shape filled the doorway.

"Oh, honey! You're awake!"

Hank limped into the room and threw himself onto a chair beside Helene's bed that groaned as his outsize frame crushed it. He covered Helene's skeletal hand with his own meaty paw and squeezed it gently.

His voice quavered as he spoke in a rush, his fingers gently stroking the back of her hand.

"You've been gone so long, honey, I didn't know if we'd be able to bring you back. Here, have some water. Don't try to speak."

He raised her head gently and helped her to sip some water.

Helene tried to sip but she choked instead and the tears in her eyes spilled over. The sobs wracked her thin body, huge shudders running through her. Barbara slipped away and Helene didn't see Charlie standing at the entrance, turning away as her tears continued to fall.

Hank cradled her in his arms and rocked her gently until she cried herself asleep.

It was several days before Helene was well enough to sit up in bed, let alone think and talk lucidly. It was painful to remember the flashes of consciousness from the previous weeks. She had to force her mind to revisit the scene of the crime... otherwise she'd never dare to close her eyes again... waiting for the demons to return.

"What happened to you, after... after..." she whispered.

"After the fire fight, me and Charlie-boy disappeared into the forest," said Hank. "We just couldn't reach you; there were too many of them. But I promised myself that we'd get you back. We just had to wait till they made their move."

Helene nodded slowly.

"Thank you. But how did you find me?"

Hank frowned.

"It was lover-boy who found you. He'd been listening in to various phone lines including Warm Creek. He had a hunch about it: I guess he was right. One of the care assistants made a call to the SAMHSA offices about the treatment of a Jane

Doe. We knew straightaway it must be you. At least one person in that place gave a damn."

Helene shuddered at the vague memories that haunted her.

"They were going to send me the same way as that poor man they called Wally," said Helene, her voice strained, trying to keep control. "We have to get him out somehow."

Hank looked down.

"I'm sorry, honey, but that poor son of a bitch died the night you were moved. Died or was put down, more like. Anyhow, he ain't suffering no more. And I think there'll be some changes at Warm Creek from now on."

Helene turned her head away and closed her eyes.

"They'll just move on to somewhere else," she said tiredly. "There'll always be some place, some doctor willing to help the NSA or the FBI or whoever those bastards were."

The truth hung between them, a ghost.

She raised her eyes to meet Hank's.

"What... what did they do to me?" she mumbled.

Hank shifted uncomfortably in the chair.

"You sure you want to talk about this now, honey?"

Helene closed her eyes and nodded.

"I need to know," she said at last.

Hank sighed.

"Well, when we picked you up, we had two independent doctors assess you. It was... well, evidence... you see."

He sounded embarrassed.

"They were pretty shocked and wanted to admit you to a hospital, but we paid for them to keep quiet..." he sighed. "Anyway, they found that you'd been subjected to some sort of crude electric shock treatment and... er... that's what caused the heart attack."

He paused, checking her face for signs that he should stop.

"And," he continued slowly, "they took blood to test for drugs so we'd know what you'd been given... and how to get you off safely..."

"What had they used? You have to tell me," she said softly.

"Well," he said heavily, "there were at least two different anti-psychotic drugs, opiates to keep you quiet and... traces of

LSD... enough to trigger psychotic episodes. I'm sorry, honey. We're dealing with some soulless bastards... anything goes. The doctors don't think there's been any permanent damage – except for your heart – but we're to watch you signs of PTSD: flashbacks, anxiety attacks..."

He glanced at her nervously: her eyes were squeezed shut.

"How did I end up here?" said Helene at last, changing the subject.

Hank smiled crookedly.

"Barbara wasn't quite as 'gone' as we thought. She was following our progress, so to speak, and when we found out where you were, she contacted us to offer you a safe house: welcome to Shiloh, Ohio."

"But why?" said Helene, sounding confused. "Why is she risking her new life by helping me? Helping us?"

Hank's smile faded.

"There are still good people in the world, honey. Among all this grime and hatred, there are still people who care. Don't forget that. And for all his pretty-boy looks, Charlie cares, too. I admit I had my doubts about him... I thought he was a pretty cool customer but he was like a man possessed till he found you. There's love there, I think..."

Helene wasn't so sure. Charlie had barely been near her since her release. He'd looked in once or twice as she'd been falling asleep, but he hadn't risked a conversation with her. And now the silence was becoming awkward.

"But I don't trust him either," said Hank thoughtfully. "His motives... he's never really been one of us. Not like you, honey."

Perhaps that was true.

"What happens next?" said Helene, dully. "I can't stay here forever: none of us can."

Hank nodded and a trace of humour suggested itself beneath his beard.

"Yep, we've been working on that," he said mysteriously. "That is, the Gene Genies haven't been idle. You'll be pretty impressed with what they've come up with. Righteousness never sleeps!"

Helene had to smile. Hank so wanted to be a superhero. In her mind, he already was.

The following evening Helene felt strong enough to get up and join the others in the kitchen. Her appetite was smaller than a sparrow's but she was beginning to gain strength. It was a slow job.

Charlie was quiet, closed in; but Hank was positively brimming with pep. Barbara sat calmly smoking a cigarette, observing the proceedings.

"So," said Helene. "Do we have a plan?"

"We sure do," said Hank. "Actually it's the same plan as before: the same three plans. We're gonna penetrate the security of every Fed Reserve bank; we're gonna find out the truth."

Helene glanced at Charlie: his face was in shadow – it was impossible to tell what he was thinking.

Hank continued.

"Of course, the plan has got a little more developed, more sophisticated since we last spoke..." He paused: they were all thinking of the reason why their planning had been interrupted... why it had been a while since they'd last discussed it...

"Well," he said awkwardly, "I've set up a security solutions company and with a bunch of phony recommendations, so I'm starting in business. I've got Gene Genies running the franchises and within a couple of months, maybe less, we'll have tested gold in each of the 13 locations – including Fort Knox."

Helene gaped. "How?"

Hank shrugged, but she could tell that his nonchalance hid considerable pride.

"It's not so difficult," he said somewhat disingenuously, "I just had to fake some existing contracts, produce some vetting records, hire personnel and vehicles, set up the website, file tax returns going back a dozen years..." He grinned. "Yeah, it was a ton of work, but by God! it feels good! I'll get those bastards back for what they did to you!"

He spoke the words with real feeling.

Helene looked down.

"Sorry, honey," he mumbled. "I don't mean to keep on reminding you..."

"It's okay," said Helene, softly. "Really. I can't thank you enough for what you've done – all of you."

She looked at Barbara and finally allowed her eyes to rest on Charlie. She thought she detected a slight smile, but it was hard to be sure.

"What happens to me?" said Helene. "How can I help?"

She was surprised that it was Charlie who answered.

"You do what you were always going to do: you tell the story."

Helene shook her head, looking doubtfully at Hank.

"There's no way anyone will dare to publish this story, even with the scant evidence I've got."

"The evidence isn't scant," said Hank. "You'll have A-grade evidence: facts, figures, photos, film footage. We've got it all... we'll get it all. And to start with we've got those two medical reports about what was done to you... It's what's gonna keep you safe, honey. You give this to the Press and the NSA won't dare touch you."

"Besides," said Barbara, speaking for the first time, "even if you're right and it doesn't get published the traditional way, the Gene Genies will leak bits and pieces of it. Someone will listen: someone always listens. It'll be enough for them – the government – to keep their sticky fingers off you. We've just got get you to New York so you can deliver the story in person."

"What about you?" asked Helene.

Barbara smiled. She was far from being the broken young woman that Helene had first met. In fact she radiated the calm assurance that comes from knowledge and power. Helene found her slightly unnerving.

"I'm going to be just fine," said Barbara. "Don't worry about me – I have ways of disappearing if I need to. But until then, I'm going to make the Gene Genies the most famous – or notorious – hackers in history. Dad would have liked that."

She paused then took a deep breath.

"And I've thought about how we can track the gold. We can't use anything radioactive because they're bound to do full spectrum sweeps every time they move the gold. But they won't be looking for something as simple as Smart Water."

Helene blinked. She'd got the bit about radioactivity but she had no idea what Smart Water was. From the looks on the others' faces, she was the only living in the State of Ignorance.

"Er... is someone going to explain that to me?" she said.

"Sure, honey," said Hank kindly. "SmartWater is an inert metal-based chemical compound; well, a colourless liquid that we can just dab onto the gold. It's permanent and it's been pretty much designed to withstand routine cleaning – not that anyone is likely to wash the gold – but ya never know."

"I've never heard of it," said Helene.

"It's been around a while," said Charlie, shrugging. "People have started to use it as an anti-theft device. You can use it to code all sorts of items such as jewellery, ornaments, even your car if you want. Each bottle contains a unique chemical code that's registered to one person, or company. No-one will find it unless they're looking for it. But it glows under ultraviolet light making so we'll mark the gold on the underside. Only Hank's people will know where to look for it."

"Lover-boy's right, honey," said Hank, earning himself an irritated glance from Charlie. "Each bottle is registered to a user so we'll just register it to my new security company. Easy as apple pie."

Barbara smiled at Helene's surprised expression.

"Every time Hank's company makes an intervention, his people will spray this on the gold..."

She showed Helene a small aerosol that looked like a breath freshener.

"How does it work?" said Helene, amazed at the technical aspects of Barbara's ingenuity.

"Well, it's pretty simple really: it's odourless and, like Hank said, colourless and it leaves no visual trace. Then we'll track the gold as and when it's moved and use the info to build up a database of every movement the government makes."

Her dark eyes glinted and Helene felt uncomfortable. She

was a tiny cog in a vast machine over which she no longer had any control – if she'd ever had any, which seemed increasingly unlikely.

The project Barbara had described could run for decades – indefinitely, even.

Helene turned to Charlie.

"What about you?" she said quietly.

His voice came from the shadows. "I'm going to get you to New York."

"And then?" she whispered.

He leaned forward and his blue eyes startled her with their intensity.

"You'll be safe," he said. "Nobody will be able to touch you. You'll be able to go home and – live your life."

"But what about you?"

He leaned back, his face hidden again.

"Oh, I'll be alright. Don't worry about me."

Helene bit her lip. It was the only answer he seemed prepared to give, at least for now. She hoped he'd be more communicative when they were alone. Although it was definitely more of a hope than a belief.

"Don't worry, honey pie," said Hank. "Me and lover-boy will get you to New York. You just gotta get yourself healthy first."

But Barbara interrupted him.

"I can't allow that, Hank," she said, a note of new authority ringing in her voie. "It's too risky for you: you're needed here to finish setting up the security. If you don't get this bit right, you'll be risking Helene's long term security."

Anguish was plain on Hank's face: the big man was torn wide open. Helene could see it.

They argued it backwards and forwards for a few more minutes but Barbara was firm and, even Helene, who felt desperate at the thought of saying goodbye to Hank agreed it was in everyone's best interests for him to stay behind. In the end he agreed to stay in Ohio. But he didn't like it.

"It's okay," said Helene, trying to smile. "Charlie can get me to New York. I'll be fine. You need to carry on with your... work... here, Hank."

~

For two weeks, Helene continued to rebuild her strength. She ate, exercised gently and rested.

Barbara put Charlie and Hank to work. Helene would find them poring over blueprints or eyes staring fixedly at reams of numbers flowing down banks of computer screens.

Barbara's bolt hole was a duplex, the second half of the building lying empty. Helene didn't know if that was lucky convenience or careful contrivance. Either way, there were no neighbours nearby.

The sparsely furnished building had at least benefitted from Hank's homely touch. The white interiors had been transformed by bright pairs of curtains with matching pelmets that Hank had run up on an old Singer sewing machine, purchased at a thrift store in Dayton.

When he wasn't umbilically attached to a computer, he sat on the porch with Helene doing his needle point, chatting about everything but what really mattered.

Every time he spoke to her it sounded like goodbye.

The weather was turning cooler and, outdoors, Helene wrapped a thick quilt around her. Barbara insisted that none of them go out in the garden without wearing a hat: too many opportunities for a spy in the sky or remote satellite to see them. Better to stay hidden, for now. But the porch was deemed an acceptable alternative.

Hank's quiet company was soothing. Helene was still troubled by nightmares, flashbacks and vivid re-experiencing that left her shaken and exhausted but the episodes were becoming less frequent.

But for Helene the best therapy was writing. Hank had happily delivered the files from her laptop via a memory stick. Helene had had no idea that anyone had been backing up her work so at first she was taken aback but then delighted that so many of her notes had been saved. Tentatively at first, then with increasing confidence, she worked on the story that she was going to deliver to Frank. With the agreement of Hank and Barbara, she left out the Gene Genies plans to track the gold. Instead her article posed the question: what if? She had a paper trail that showed the US government had traded an inexplicable quantity of gold over the last 20 years to a variety of international customers. Helene wrote up the findings in a way that would allow readers to draw their own conclusions.

Writing about her kidnapping and ordeal at Warm Creek was harder, not only because so much of it was still hazy, but because Helene would really rather not have thought about it. Instead she relied on the medical evidence – the facts – and wrote in a clinical style that used the third person. Only in the conclusion would she allow herself to become personal. That section she would write only when she got to New York and the story, or at least her part of the story, was finished.

There was a heated debate between Hank and Barbara about whether or not Helene should mention Smiling Clive Jackson's role. Hank had been all for it but Barbara had been more circumspect.

"There's no evidence," she said. "It's just Helene's word."

"That's good enough for me," yelled Hank, bristling like a grizzly bear.

"But there's no damn evidence," snarled Barbara. "If she tries to publish *anything* without evidence they'll have her labelled as a loony and the story will be killed stone dead."

Hank growled a bit more but they all knew Barbara was right.

"Don't worry about that s.o.b. Jackson," she told Helene. "We'll be watching him."

"And then we'll fix his wagon, but good!" bellowed Hank.

Helene wanted to hug him. It was so wonderful to have someone fighting on her side so vociferously.

Following Barbara's suggestion – or was it an order – Helene deleted all references to Smiling Clive. For now.

Barbara herself was at times detached and at times in the thick of the plotting: it was like she was two different people. Maybe the last three years had taken their toll in more than one way. Helene wasn't sure she understood either part of Barbara's personality and, for her part, Barbara treated Helene with the kind indifference you might give to an inherited pet who was a bit old and past it.

Helene couldn't help noticing that Charlie avoided being alone with her. At first she was hurt but then she became irritated.

Damn him! After everything they'd been through together! Why was he avoiding her? Why couldn't he look her in the face?

CHAPTER TWENTY-SIX

IT WAS TIME TO LEAVE.

Helene was appalled by how vulnerable she felt. As the front door swung open, it seemed to hover over a cavernous pit, a dangerous open space filled with faceless and un-named enemies.

Crossing the threshold to the drive, she started to perspire, her palms greasy with sweat, her legs trembling.

"It's ok, honey," said Hank worriedly, squeezing her hand, "you're bound to feel a bit shaky. You've been through a lot."

Then he gathered her to him in a huge bear hug, holding her tightly. Helene leaned her cheek against the familiar bushy beard, softly scented with lily of the valley. In her honour Hank was wearing a pretty rose-coloured tea-dress. Where he'd found such a thing to fit his vast frame in Shiloh, Helene couldn't imagine. Surely mail order would have been too risky? But then again being a super-hacker must come with some fringe benefits. Or frills.

Hank took her arm and helped her climb up into the beige SUV that had been acquired for the journey.

Charlie was already sitting in the driver's seat, sunglasses in place, eyes hidden, face without expression – a soldier on duty.

"You take care, honey," said Hank who was clearly trying not to cry.

"I'm going to miss you so much," whispered Helene, feeling a constriction in her throat as she stroked his beefy arm. "Goodbye, Hank."

"Aw, honey, don't say that," the big man pleaded. "Don't say 'goodbye', more like 'see ya' or '*au revoir*' as the Frenchies say. One day when you don't expect it I'll be there – I promise."

"I do hope so," said Helene trying to smile. "Thank you. Thank you for everything you've done."

"*Vaya con Dios*, honey!" he called as Charlie pulled out of the drive.

Helene twisted round to watch Hank waving frantically and the little house disappearing into the distance. Barbara had said her goodbyes indoors. Charlie, it seemed, had none to say.

Gloom seemed to settle over the car as they swept out onto Interstate 76.

"Just you and me again," said Helene at last, trying to break the tension

"Thank God!" said Charlie in something like his old tone. "I couldn't take another night of Hank's meatloaf with Country & Western on the side. That man has problems."

Helene smiled.

"Possibly, but he was a good friend to me – to us."

Charlie didn't reply.

After a short pause he said, "We've got a ten hour drive ahead of us: I suggest you get some rest. You're still not back to full strength."

It was true: Helene's once reliable stamina had been utterly drained and she tired easily. But there was a confession she had to make – and something that she'd long been wanting to ask him. Now she had a captive audience.

She phrased her question carefully.

"You know that when I was being questioned," she said softly, "I gave them your name: or rather confirmed what they already knew... I am sorry about that. Truly..." She paused, waiting for the anger to come, but he didn't comment.

"Well," she continued, slightly encouraged, "they said that

they couldn't find any trace of you on any MoD database: no-one with the name Charlie Paget existed."

He shrugged. "And it didn't occur to you that they said it to shake you up so that you wouldn't trust me?"

"Yes," she said softly. "It did occur to me, but still... I wondered..."

He grimaced.

"They said it so you'd be more likely to give me up. So that you'd be more likely to turn to them. Classic interrogation tactics, Helene. I would have thought you'd know that... and I would have thought that after everything that we... I would have thought that you'd trust me."

He sounded really angry now. Almost upset.

"I do trust you," she said, aware how feeble and insincere the words sounded. Somehow trust between them had been suspended. She didn't know how or when or why, just that it had someone happened. Maybe it had been his silence amongst the Gene Genies. Maybe...

"I do trust you, Charlie. But... you've been so... distant and... and quiet since... well, since..."

She trailed off, unsure how to continue.

He looked at her sideways.

"I prefer to pick my own team," he said.

Helene wasn't certain what he meant by that. Sure, they'd rather stumbled into a group encounter with the Gene Genies, but it had been enormously beneficial. Unless, unless he meant that he'd preferred it when it had just been the two of them. Helene felt irritated with herself.

But she still wasn't convinced by his answer but she knew she couldn't ask him again without causing a serious and maybe permanent rift. Besides, once she got back home, she could check the information herself.

Home. That still seemed an impossibly long way away.

"What will you do when all this is over?" she said, neutrally. "Will you go back to Suse?"

He smiled. "I rather think that boat has floated."

"Then what? Will you go back to... to work?"

"Let's get you to New York first," he said.

Helene sighed. If he didn't want to talk, there was no way she could make him.

"Maybe I'll come and see you in Cornwall," he said, quietly. "After all, I know where you live."

Helene laughed out loud. It felt good to laugh. Charlie smiled quickly, glancing over at her, his eyes crinkling the way they did when he was happy.

"Yes, you certainly know that. I shall expect a knock on my door when I least expect it."

She turned her head and gazed out of the window, smiling to herself.

The traffic flowed by as they oozed onto the I-80 and Pennsylvania swept past in a haze of autumnal grey.

Helene fell asleep and only woke when she felt the car slowing down, several hours later.

Clearly there hadn't been a lot of choice for places to eat but Charlie had found a Buckhorn truck stop that looked clean if not fancy.

Helene climbed out of the car stiffly. The high foot plate gave her some trouble but she managed to get down without being helped. She treasured the hint of independence: it had been too long. Limping slightly, she followed Charlie into the diner.

"I hope you've got a bit more of an appetite, Helene," he said, "because all these meals look enormous."

Helene glanced at over at a well-padded family who were giving serious attention to a bucket-sized dish of barbeque ribs. Just the sight of it made Helene feel queasy.

"I think I'll stick to the soup and salad," she said, running her eyes and up down the grease-spotted menu.

"You sure that's enough," he asked, raising an eyebrow. "Hank gave me quite a long lecture on making sure you eat properly. I'd hate to have a man like that come after me."

The words weren't entirely ironic. But despite Charlie's admonishment, she decided to stick with the light meal. The waitress, however, had other ideas.

"The pancakes are real good," she said, "if you don't want fries. And I can do bacon on the side."

Letting Helene squirm for a while, Charlie finally came to her rescue and ordered bacon, waffles and eggs, sunnyside-up for himself. The waitress also pressed him to have the fried green tomatoes and southern-style grits. He agreed, accommodatingly.

"I have no idea what a 'grit' is," he admitted to Helene, "but I could never say 'no' to a woman."

"Even one old enough to be your mother?" queried Helene.

He leaned back smiling and Helene shook her head in amusement.

When the food arrived it was well cooked and hearty. Even Helene's salad was surprisingly tasty and fresh, although rather too drenched in blue-cheese dressing. She scraped off what she could and enjoyed the thick, crusty bread and spicy soup.

She waved away the offer of a jug of coffee and sipped a glass of tap water instead. Her body was still on the mend and the thought of a stimulant, even a mild one such as caffeine, was a bit too scary at present.

When they got back on the road, Helene felt sleepy but something about Charlie's demeanour had changed. Tension was in the air again.

"What's up?" she said.

"Mmm, not sure," he said, his voice wary. "There's a car behind us that was at the truck stop."

Helene felt a lurch in her stomach that made her regret the spicy soup. She sat up straighter and cautiously looked over her shoulder.

"Is it following us?"

Charlie shrugged. "Not sure yet. I'll try changing lanes a few times; see if they do the same."

Several more miles fell behind them and it still wasn't clear if they grey station-wagon was tailing them.

Helene felt increasingly anxious and Charlie remained alert, his eyes flicking to the rear view mirror more frequently than usual.

As they began to see signs for New York City, Helene almost dared to feel hopeful.

But when they merged onto the Newark Turnpike, they

began to hit heavy traffic. The grey station-wagon was still two cars behind them but that didn't necessarily mean they were being followed. After all, it was a safe bet that New York City was the destination for most of the vehicles on the road.

Charlie didn't say any more but Helene noticed that his lips were pressed tightly together.

The traffic began to slow perceptibly, despite a small proportion being siphoned off into the Jersey City suburbs. The majority began the stately crawl down from the toll plaza to the Holland Tunnel, the twin concrete tubes that ran under the Hudson River.

Charlie was noticeably tense now.

"Helene: be ready to move if I say so," he said, quietly.

"What? Are you serious?" she stammered nervously. "Surely we're not going to bail out in the middle of the tunnel?"

"Hopefully not. But that car is definitely following us. If they're going to try and hit us before we get to the newspaper offices, they'll have to do it soon."

"How do you know?" she said queasily, hoping against hope that he was wrong. "I mean, how do you know they'll try to stop us getting to Frank now?"

"Because that's what I'd do," he said shortly. He glanced over at her. "Take only what you need: leave your bag. Get ready to run."

Helene's heart began to gallop and she thought she was going to pass out. But his instruction gave her something to focus on. She emptied her shoulder bag and took out the memory stick with all her work on it and her mobile phone. She also had two fresh passports that somehow Charlie had managed to secure: one in her own name, and the other in the name of Ellen Fitzgerald, citizen of Ireland. How, she had no idea. Well, some idea: the Gene Genies were in their element at that sort of thing. So was Charlie.

Cars around them were putting on their lights, ready for the dim lighting of the tunnel. Suddenly there was a full-beam flash of lights in the rear view mirror.

"This is it," he said calmly, his eyes bright with anticipation. "They're coming."

Without further warming, Charlie slammed on the brakes and wrenched the hand-brake, forcing the car to spin 270 degrees in a slow turn. The car following hit them side on, pinning the driver's door tightly. The front and back were hit simultaneously by cars in the other lanes.

Helene had braced herself tightly against her seat, avoiding some of the whiplash. But the second and third strikes stunned her.

Shaking her head like a dog coming out of water, she ripped open her door.

"Get to the side of the tunnel," shouted Charlie. "Run! I'll be right behind you!"

Helene threw herself from the car and half ran, half crawled to the narrow sidewalk that edged along the tunnel. She hunched down, covering her head with hands and sprinted awkwardly in a half crouch. Bewildered drivers were starting to exit their mashed cars when the first bullet whined over her head. Someone screamed and a thunder of shots echoed through the tunnel. She kept running, heart hammering, adrenaline spurring her on.

In the distance she saw the telltale pin prick of daylight that indicated she was nearing the exit.

A squeal of tyres made her dodge into a small recess in the wall and every second she expected to feel the punch of bullets smashing into her. Then she recognised the mop of short, blond curls.

"Get on!" yelled Charlie.

A squat, heavy-looking motorbike was clamped between his knees, the original owner probably crudely dismounted somewhere in the tunnel beyond.

Without a word, Helene staggered to the bike and wrapped her arms tightly around him, pressing her face into the soft suede of his non-descript jacket.

She ducked lower as she heard more gunshots. Charlie twisted the accelerator and the bike leapt forwards, jerking Helene roughly.

They sped out of the tunnel and roared onto the Lincoln Highway. Squad cars coming towards them flashed their lights, but Charlie wove between them as easily as the chicane at Silverstone.

He swung left and roared along the centre of the road, scattering pedestrians at one crossing like so much confetti. Whistles blew and police sirens sang in Helene's ears but Charlie didn't stop. He swerved right, leaving a tell-tale trail of burning rubber as smoke poured from the overheated tyres.

Canal Street was at a standstill. Charlie jumped the motorcycle onto the pavement, strewing coffee drinkers left and right. He braked hard to avoid a gaggle of children.

"Why aren't you at school?" screamed Helene as the children toppled like ninepins.

The bike skidded and Helene felt herself falling. She landed rolling, the soft palms of her hands torn by the tarmac. Fifty yards away, he wrenched the handlebars hard round and the back tyre span out. Helene heard him grunt with pain as the bike's full weight landed on his leg.

Charlie abandoned the wounded motorbike and ran back towards Helene. He grabbed her arm, dragging her behind him. Together they staggered across the busy street, dodging the surprised crowds as he towed her down an alleyway. The police sirens sounded nearer now but in the confusion, they seemed to have escaped.

Helene stumbled and Charlie helped her keep her balance by wrenching her arm upwards.

"Got to stop!" she gasped.

"No! Come on!" he urged her in a low voice.

Helene answered by being violently sick. All the soup and salad and crusty bread found its way back onto the alley. She spat futilely while Charlie held her gently.

"S..sorry!" she whispered, trying not to gag.

He didn't reply, just pulled her up, more gently this time, and half carried her to the end of the alley.

"Can you walk?" he said, looking rapidly about him.

Helene nodded and, trying to look as normal as possible, walked as quickly as she could manage down a narrow street past the incurious eyes of customers at Lombardi's pizza restaurant.

She felt sick and dizzy and the sound of her blood pounding was loud in her ears. She stumbled onwards, trusting Charlie to lead her. Trusting him to protect her.

They hurried past the old cathedral, and the red brick and grey blocks of the Mulberry Library rose from the pavement. Frank's agency was next door.

Helene was at the end of strength. Her legs were trembling and her each breath was gulped down, a drowning woman in a sea of city people.

"We're here," he said, huskily. "You'll be okay now."

"You... I..." but Helene was too exhausted to speak.

Suddenly Charlie pulled her close to him and the heat of his body seared her. He swept her backwards, her arms clinging to his neck and kissed her hard. She responded with her whole body burning, bolts of electricity making her shiver. Her lips pressed to his, breathing his breath, flesh on flesh.

"Now go!" he whispered, pulling her back to her feet. "Tell the story. Tell *your* story."

She staggered slightly and when she'd caught her balance, he was gone and she was alone again. As alone as you can be, in a city surrounded by a ring of astonished spectators.

Helene pushed open the street door to the agency offices and half fell into the marble clad atrium of the smart building. Her face was red and sweaty, her hair a matted nest, clothes torn and stained. The horrified receptionist's expression said it all. But this was New York: the receptionist recovered fast.

"May I help you?"

The woman sounded extremely doubtful and Helene herself thought it was likely that she looked beyond help.

"Frank Milson, please," she gasped. "Tell him it's Helene La Borde: he's expecting me. Sort of."

Helene's face felt frozen in shock.

The receptionist hesitated just long enough to show that she thought an appointment with Mr Milson extremely unlikely. But the insolent glance bounced off Helene's slight shoulders. It was liberating not to care. Especially when she knew she looked like Hell and that her hands were dripping blood onto the polished parquet floor.

She barely listened to the receptionist's brief conversation and increasingly bemused high-pitched voice.

Eventually, in a tone that suggested God himself was descending in the elevator, she informed Helene that Frank was on his way down.

Helene collapsed into a new-looking Mies van der Rohe chair and kept an eye on the street door in case her followers hadn't had enough of shooting up lower Manhattan.

The lift doors opened and Frank appeared in a haze of cigar smoke, ignoring the ban that every other office building was obliged to abide by.

"Jesus wept! It *is* you! You look like shit, Helene!" he grunted.

A deep, deep laugh was building inside her.

"Stop the press, Frank," she said, smiling thinly. "Have I got a story for you!"

CHAPTER TWENTY-SEVEN

IT WAS STRANGE TO BE HOME AGAIN. ALTHOUGH THIS HOME-coming had been very different from the last time Helene was in Cornwall.

For one thing, the story of her abduction and torture had been on the front page of every broadsheet and tabloid newspaper across the Western world. Her questions about fake gold and the dollar debt had been more quietly recorded but the White House press office had been in full denial, despite the damning evidence provided by the doctors' reports and the circumstantial evidence elsewhere.

Smiling Clive Jackson had found himself in the middle of his own scandal when photographs of him with an underage boy had been published on the internet. His denials had sounded hollow and Helene had the satisfaction of seeing him fall on his sword, nanoseconds before he was pushed. She knew the Gene Genies were exacting revenge – or more specifically she recognised the light touch of Hank's work – whether or not the accusation were true.

Every TV channel, radio programme and web media site wanted to interview her. Helene had told her story so many times that it began to feel unreal.

Frank had been delighted with the scoop and made a small fortune handling the story rights. Helene let him manage access to her, as well. It helped to have him bulldoze reporters and organise media bodyguards and his office also gave her someone to manage her phone and email.

Now she was weary. Tired to the bone.

After a fortnight of the media circus in London, Helene headed back to Cornwall. She was immediately swamped by local reporters who normally only got to report on fun runs, fishing rights and car boot sales. Helene fielded their questions thoughtfully and became a nine-day wonder in her village.

The Jenkins were stalwart in helping her: Mrs Jenkin became a celebrity in her own right, recalling the day she had driven off intruders, probably armed, from Helene's cottage. Helene was more than glad to hand the limelight over to her neighbours and had the deferred pleasure of seeing Mrs Jenkin bask in the unfamiliar glow of stardom, whilst Mr Jenkin hovered in the background, growling at any reporter who came too close to his own Celtic Boudicca. Even their dog, Alfie, had become a minor celebrity, and had somehow become a canine hero of mythic proportions, nipping at the heels of the CIA or NSA or whoever. No-one seemed to care much about that detail. The small, round dog, took fame in his stumpy stride.

As promised, £100,000 plus a small sum in per diems was deposited into Helene's account by Frank's agency. It was enough for her to take early retirement on if she was careful, despite the fact that Helene was now more in demand as a celebrity reporter and interviewee than she'd ever been in 25 plus years on the job.

She was considering several potentially lucrative contracts as a columnist. Even one of these would give her a steady income before her newly bright star began to wane, as it inevitably would.

But for one thing, Helene would have been content: she'd heard nothing from Charlie.

Each day she'd checked her private email as well as the Helene of Troy website which had remained secret.

Each day she was sure that this would be the day when he

would contact her, or, better still, knock on her door as he had almost promised.

The memory of that kiss was burned into her brain. But he didn't come and even Hank, contacting her in code, reported that he had no word of him, let alone from him.

There was no-one else she could talk to about him. She was tempted to write down what she was feeling but that would make it seem more dream-like and unreal. And she very much wanted it to be real.

Worse still, her contacts at the MoD had come up with nothing: no trace of a Charles Paget existed in any of the armed services; not even the police could find anything of him.

So who was he? Who was the man she had followed, who had followed her, who had saved her over and over again? Nobody seemed to know, and each day that passed with no news, he became more and more shadowy.

Helene had to force herself to face the fact that she had no idea who Charlie was – and would probably never know. He had disappeared from her life as completely as if he had never existed. Only the fact that she was still alive proved that she hadn't imagined him.

As the weeks passed, Helene's world began to return to something like normal.

But one day in early autumn, on a mild October evening, she was wandering restlessly through her garden when she saw Mr Jenkin standing at her gate.

"Evenin', Miss La Borde," he said.

She smiled.

"I really wish you'd call me 'Helene', especially after everything that's happened... after everything that you've done for me."

The old man blushed and stammered. He could no sooner call her by her Christian name than fly to the moon. It didn't matter: first name terms weren't a prerequisite of intimacy and understanding. Not for a man like Mr Jenkin.

"Be the last day of our Indian Summer," he said thoughtfully.

"Mmm, it has been unseasonably mild," she agreed.

"Aagh, the south westerlys will be picking up," he said. "I'll come and dead-head those roses for you. Garden could do with a little bit of nurturing." He looked up at her kindly. "And I think maybe for you, too. Maybe have a bit of a holiday? Have a rest?"

Helene shook her head.

"No time for that," she said. "Anyway, I've been away for long enough. It's much better to, you know, get on with things."

As she said the words she realised that she meant them. There was nowhere else she wanted to be except in that small, pretty cottage in the furthest corner of Cornwall. Of course, it would be wonderful to share it... with the right person... the right man...

The old man nodded his head thoughtfully. He looked the picture of wisdom, possibly Methuselah himself.

"This came for you," he said, interrupting her whimsy. "What with all the helter and skelter, the postie put it in the wrong box."

He held out a postcard.

"Thank you," she said softly.

Mr Jenkin touched his cap and disappeared back into his own kitchen, where he stood watching her from the window.

When Helene looked at the frail piece of cardboard she held in her hands, she almost dropped it from shock. The picture showed a photograph of the shrine at Kompira-*san*. She would have recognised it anywhere.

With trembling hands she turned over the postcard. Apart from her address, there were just four words written on it:

'Wish you were here.'

Nothing else. Unreasonable joy pulsed through her.

She turned on her heel and by the time she ducked through her kitchen door, her heart rate had trebled and she thought she was going to faint. It was a sign! At last! A message. A message only she would understand. It meant he was safe and that he was back in Japan.

No, she was wrong. Helene looked at the postcard and read the words again – more carefully this time.

Wish you were her

The sudden joy was swiftly dissolved by a disconcerting chill as if someone had just walked over her grave. A cold feeling seeped through her.

Oh, God. Japan. Did that mean he was back with Mayumi? Back with the *Yakuza*?

'*Wish you were her*'

Helene had a bad, bad feeling.

She turned the card over and over in her hands, looking for some other clue. *Wish you were her*, not 'wish you were *here*'. But could she be certain it wasn't a typo?

Helene turned on her computer, impatient with the twenty seconds it took to fire up. First she checked her email. Nothing. Then she checked the Helene of Troy website: still nothing. Seething with frustration, she paced up and down the kitchen pointlessly.

Then a thought occurred to her. An appalling, distressing, unshakeable thought. She put up the website for her bank account and logged in.

The shock hit her in a wave of nausea. One hundred thousand pounds had been removed from her account.

And she knew who had done it.

The bastard! After everything they'd been through together! He'd been playing her. Waiting for the moment when her money would be paid in.

Fury raged through her and then another thought occurred to her. One hundred thousand pounds had gone, but the per diem money and her meagre savings had been left untouched. He could have taken everything and left her penniless. Maybe there was a reason for his behaviour – and explanation?

Hadn't they escaped the clutches of the *Yakuza* rather too easily? After all, they had knowledge of Bill's murder and they had simply been allowed to walk away. Maybe he had promised the money to save them – to save her: after all, the turnaround of events in Kotohira had been rapid and unexpected. Had he given the *Yakuza* that money to pay off a debt? Was he still paying it off by working for them?

Helene longed to know the truth: what had it all meant? To her? To him?

Over the next two days she had numerous and interminable conversations with the bank manager, the police and the Serious Fraud Squad, which seemed cruelly ironic. But the money had undoubtedly vanished and the bank staff were adamant that Helene herself had removed it. How else could anyone have got through all their substantial security?

The police were suspicious: they suggested that Helene was using the event to drum up further publicity for herself. She was furious but knowing what she knew – or suspected she knew – ill equipped to fight back and prove her innocence. If indeed she was innocent.

Helene lurched from fury to lethargy and back. Sometimes she felt like screaming and sometimes she accepted that it was a fee payable to Charlie for a job well done. And, in the end, had it truly been her money? She had extracted the promise of it from Frank with a lie. Who, in fact, had committed the fraud in the first place? In her darker hours she wondered how deep had become Charlie's relationship with the Matsumotos.

She was grateful that her per diems and money earned from interviews had remained untouched. It was a gesture that seemed thoughtful. But it still wasn't quite the nest-egg that she had anticipated. Early retirement was now an impossibility. And there had been no further communication from Charlie – the man she wasn't sure she could think of as Charlie any more.

Nor could she tell the world the full story of the Gene Genies or of Smiling Clive Jackson or of the secrets that lurked within the Federal Reserve banks. Neither could she write about Kazuma, Hassan, the Matsumotos, or even Bill Bailey with impunity. The list of events and people that she could never mention grew unfeasibly longer.

But Helene did have one weapon: she was a writer after all. And if she couldn't write the facts, there was no-one stopping her from writing fiction – at least, she didn't think so.

So one day, when the first frost of a hard winter had sprinkled icing onto her rose bushes, Helene sat down at her computer. Her hands hovered over the keyboard, and then she began to write...

Have you ever listened to a stranger's conversation at an airport, or on the bus, or on a train? I did. And it changed my life...

THE END

REVIEWS

Reviews are love! Honestly, they are! But it also helps other people to make an informed decision before buying my book.

So I'd really appreciate if you took a few seconds to do that.

Thank you!

ABOUT JHB

If you've read one of my romance books, you might be a little surprised at suddenly finding that *Exposure* is a thriller, but I do enjoy writing these twists and turns, too. So, is Charlie a good guy? Hmm, the jury is out on that one.

I do love reviews! Other readers do, too, because it helps them decide whether or not a book will suit them. So please leave a review on—it would be really appreciated. Thank you!

MORE BOOKS BY JHB

Series Titles

The Education Series
An epic love story spanning the years, through war zones and more...
*The Education of Sebastian (Education series #1)
*The Education of Caroline (Education series #2)
*The Education of Sebastian & Caroline (combined edition, books 1 & 2)
Semper Fi: The Education of Caroline (Education series #3)

The Traveling Series
All the fun of the fair ... and two worlds collide
*The Traveling Man (Traveling series #1)
*The Traveling Woman (Traveling series #2)
*Roustabout (Traveling series #3)
*Carnival (Traveling series #4)
*Gypsy (Traveling series #5)

The Justin Trainer Series
The bodyguard and the billionaire
Guarding the Billionaire (Justin Trainer series #1)
Saving the Billionaire (Justin Trainer series #2)

The EOD Series
Blood, bombs and heartbreak
*Tick Tock (EOD series #1)
* Bombshell (EOD series #2)

The Rhythm Series
Blood, sweat, tears and dance
*Slave to the Rhythm (Rhythm series #1)
*Luka (Rhythm series #2)

Standalone Titles
Contemporary Romance
The Lilac Cadillac
Battle Scars
One Careful Owner
*Lifers
At Your Beck & Call
The New Samurai
Exposure

New Adult
*Dangerous to Know & Love
Dazzled
Summer of Seventeen

Paranormal
*The Dark Detective: Venator (Book #1)
*The Dark Detective: Paukúnnum (Book #2)

Novellas
Playing in the Rain
*Behind the Walls

Anthologies of Short Stories
*The Year Book Volume 1
*The Year Book Volume 2
*The Year Book Volume 3

Audio Books
One Careful Owner
(*narrated by Seth Clayton*)

On the Stage
Later, After: Playscript
Trailer

With Alana Albertson
Father Figure

* These titles are published in languages other than English. Please check Jane's website for details—and receive **a free short story every month** when you sign up for her newsletter :)

QR code for Jane's website

ROMANCE WITH STUART REARDON

Books written with my lovely co-author

Two book series - contemporary romance
*Undefeated
*Model Boyfriend

Three book series - romcom
*Gym Or Chocolate?
*The World According to Vince
*The Baby Game

Standalone
Survivor Love Island *(romcom)*
*Touch My Soul *(novella)*

WRITING AS BERRICK FORD

Police Thrillers, UK

Dead Water
Dead Man's Dive
Dead Reckoning
Dead Shore

www.berrickford.com